BROTHERS

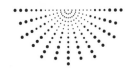

ANGELA HUNT

Hunt Haven

Which of us has known his brother?
Which of us has looked into his father's heart?
Which of us has not remained forever prison-pent?
Which of us is not forever a stranger and alone?

—Thomas Wolfe, *Look Homeward, Angel!*

PROLOGUE

THEBES, EGYPT

ZAPHENATH-PANEAH, Father to Pharaoh and acting ruler of all Egypt, caught his breath as Queen Tuya lifted his hand and pressed it to her cheek. The hot, dry wind of the famine's second year blew over the palace garden as the lovely woman struggled to frame an answer to his proposal of marriage.

"Asenath is a lovely woman, and you have two fine sons," she finally whispered, her eyes glinting with warmth. "You will not be happy loving one wife and offering kindness to the other."

A wave of relief flooded his soul. She was wise, his Tuya, but she had always been perceptive beyond her years. More than once in Potiphar's house she had guided him away from foolish mistakes, helping him remember that he was no longer Yosef, the pampered son of Yaakov, but *Paneah*, a slave to an Egyptian. And even though he now ruled all Egypt at the young Pharaoh's side, Tuya's insight and love still sought the best for all.

Curving his hand around her cheek, he pressed his lips together, not allowing himself to protest. The queen lowered her thick, black lashes and from the corner of his eye, Yosef saw a servant enter the garden. He dropped his hand and turned, composing his face into dignified lines as the dark-haired slave hurried past the reflecting pools where lotus blossoms bloomed in abundance.

The attendant fell at Yosef's feet. "Life, health, and prosperity to you, most noble and excellent vizier!"

"Yes?"

The man lifted his head a few inches from the pathway. "The steward of your house begs your indulgence and your pardon for this interruption. He waits outside Pharaoh's gate to give you a message."

"A message?" Yosef asked, aware that Tuya had moved away. "What is of such importance that I must be interrupted when I am with the queen?"

"Ten men from Canaan wait at your house to buy food," the servant said, a note of apology in his voice. "Your steward says you would want to be told of them at once."

Yosef took a quick, sharp breath. "Ten Canaanites?"

"From Hebron, my lord."

A thrill of frightened anticipation touched Yosef's spine. "You were right to disturb me. Tell my steward I will join him in a moment."

As the servant leapt up and retreated, Yosef turned to say farewell to Tuya. But like the early part of his life, she had vanished amid the breathless beauty of a royal Egyptian garden.

CHAPTER ONE

"You two! Come away from there!"

Mandisa snapped her fingers at the two giggling slave girls who lingered in the doorway of the north loggia. With fewer manners than ignorant children, they had partially hidden themselves behind a pair of painted columns to gape at the dusty travelers milling about in the vestibule. At Mandisa's rebuke, the two young ones bowed their heads in shame.

Mandisa stepped forward to herd the girls away from the open doorway. "Ani will be far less gentle than I if he finds you away from the kitchen."

"But my lady," the first girl said, a glint of wonder in her eyes, "they are so strange a group! So much hair covers their faces!"

"We were wondering—" the second slave lifted her fingers to her lips to suppress another giggle—"if they are as hairy all over. Look! Hair sprouts even from the throats of their garments!"

Despite her best intentions, Mandisa cast a quick glance through the doorway. She was accustomed to seeing foreign dignitaries in the vizier's vestibule, for since the advent of the famine representatives from all the world's kingdoms had come to buy Egypt's grain. But the men who now stood in the house wore neither the richly patterned garments of the

3

Assyrians nor the carefully pointed beards of the Mitannis. They were clothed in the common woven garments and animal skins of herdsmen. Compared to the shaven Egyptians, they were as hairy as apes, with hair to their shoulders and long, full beards.

What madness had possessed Tarik when he allowed this rabble through the gates of the vizier's villa?

She dismissed the question; the steward undoubtedly had his reasons. "Not everyone lives as the Egyptians do," she said, turning back to the ill-mannered slaves. She placed a firm hand on each girl's shoulder. "Now away with you, get back to your work in the kitchen. If the vizier has agreed to meet these men, he may want to feed them, and you may be sure that hairy men are hungry men. So hurry back to your grinding, lest Ani or Tarik finds you out here."

The two girls scurried away at the mention of the steward and the captain of the vizier's guard. Mandisa smiled, grateful that her words carried weight with *someone* in the house. Lately her son Adom had balked both at her requests and her suggestions, reminding her again how stubborn twelve-year-olds could be . . .

She folded her hands, ready to seek her mistress, but paused outside the vestibule, curiosity overcoming her finely-tuned instincts. The men beyond were like thousands of others who had come to Egypt in this second year of famine, so why had this particular group of Canaanites been invited to meet Egypt's royal vizier?

The strangers did not appear wealthy or highborn. Theirs were the faces of sunburned herders; they gripped their staves with broad and callused hands. Generous strands of gray ran through several of their heavy beards; only one or two possessed unlined faces. They stirred, their hands and eyes shifting as if at any moment they might have to reach for a knife or spear to defend themselves. With one look, anyone could see these unruly shepherds had run as wild as the wind since infancy.

Mandisa bit her lip. She had seen men like these before. Her father and brothers were herdsmen. Like dogs, they marked their boundaries and charged any lion, bear, or stranger who dared violate their territory. They, too, had habitually worn an uneasy look.

Memories came crowding back like unwelcome guests and Mandisa closed her eyes, refusing to entertain them. Whoever these men were, they had nothing to do with her past or present. They would probably not be allowed to waste more than five minutes of the vizier's valuable time.

A snatch of their conversation caught her ear and Mandisa tensed, recognizing the Canaanite tongue. The sound stirred up other memories of a time before Idogbe the Egyptian carried her away from her clan. She reached for one of the pillars, steadying herself against the tide of strong emotions she could not stanch, then realized that the men in the room beyond had grown silent.

"This Egyptian prince has pretty slaves, I will not deny that." A sharp voice cut the silence as she opened her eyes. The man who spoke stood apart from the others, his hands on his hips, a confident smile upon his face. An air of command exuded from him, and at the sound of his voice the entire group turned toward Mandisa.

She ducked behind the column, her cheeks burning. She had not meant to be seen! They must think her as ill-mannered as the two slave girls. And she was not a slave, but a free woman and the personal maid to Lady Asenath.

"Ah, you startled her," another man said, a thread of reproach in his voice. "You should not be so brash, Shim'on. She will tell her master that we are brutes and then we shall never obtain what we have come for."

"We will, Levi, never fear," the commanding man answered. "We will get our grain and leave Egypt as soon as we can. But what is the harm in admiring a pretty face while we are here?"

Mandisa flew out of the hallway and flattened herself against the wall separating the vestibule from the north loggia. How foolish she had been, allowing these rough men to gawk at her. If they had not been ignorant foreigners, they would have known by her dress that she was no slave.

She shuddered in humiliation. The powerful one who had spoken had appraised her like a stockyard animal, then allowed his gaze to cling to her face as she burned in embarrassment.

By all that was holy, she hoped these herders were guilty of robbery or treason. She'd love to see them squirm before her master. Especially the bold one who had propelled her into such an undignified and hasty retreat.

Wrapping the rags of her fragile dignity about her, Mandisa peeled herself from the wall and went in search of her mistress.

CHAPTER TWO

SHIM'ON GROWLED UNDER HIS BREATH WHEN ANOTHER PAIR OF STONE-faced Egyptian guards entered the great hall into which he and his brothers had been escorted. Did they think the sons of Yisrael planned to steal the vizier's treasures in broad daylight? They had come to buy grain, nothing more, and yet they had been yanked from the line outside the royal granary as if they were ten of the kingdom's worst criminals. But criminals, he reflected, would not have been ushered into a villa fit for a king.

A king, it seemed, was determined to have an audience with them. The ruling Pharaoh, twelve-year-old Amenhotep III, had not yet attained maturity, and everyone who entered the Black Land known to Canaanites as *Mizraim* learned that the acting regent was one called Zaphenath-paneah, a man so wise and gifted that the common people believed him to be a gift from the gods. Apparently this Zaphenath-paneah had either an extreme liking or distrust for men from Hebron, for as soon as the brothers told the royal scribe their father's name and their place of origin they were accosted by guards and herded to the vizier's palace.

"Why do they stare at us?" Shim'on muttered, fastening his gaze to the cool faces of the smooth-skinned guards. "Do they think we are beasts?"

"Who can tell what they are thinking?" Levi answered, his fists flexing behind his back. "They don't speak our language, and they hide their feelings behind those painted eyes." He whirled to face Re'uven, the eldest. "I tell you, Re'uven, we should not have gone to the granary together. We attracted too much attention, arriving in a large group."

"Be silent, Shim'on and Levi, and wait," Re'uven said, planted like an oak on the tile floor.

"How can you be so accommodating?" Shim'on lifted a fist. "We have done these people no harm. We have never even entered this cursed country before, and yet we were plucked from the mob and dragged away to face their almighty vizier. Why?"

"Perhaps God is testing us," Yehuda said, turning to face the others. He had been walking around the room, studying a detailed mural on the wall. The painting made no sense to Shim'on, for it depicted seven fat, healthy cows on the banks of the Nile. Shim'on hadn't seen a fat cow in two years.

Yehuda stopped before Re'uven and offered a smile. "You forget, brother. Though *we* have never made the journey to Mizraim, our great-grandfather Avraham once brought extreme sorrow upon Pharaoh's head. I have often heard Father tell the story."

"But this vizier would know nothing of our forefathers!" Levi protested, joining the circle. "And we cannot be held accountable for some sin Avraham committed years ago."

"Yet God knows all." Yehuda nodded toward Levi. "As He knows the hearts of all men. If the people are right and the spirit of God lies upon this vizier, perhaps he knows more than we think. Perhaps he even knows what happened . . .at Dotan."

A palpable chill moved through the group. Shim'on felt it, and resisted. "We did nothing wrong at Dotan," he said, his mood veering from irritation to anger.

"Have you forgotten that we sold our brother to a caravan bound for the Black Land?" Yehuda went on, his voice hardening. "To *Egypt*, my brothers. Our brother, if God wills that he still lives, is a slave in this land. Perhaps in this very house."

"Our *brother*," Levi spat the word, "is certainly dead. Yosef was too proud to survive as a slave. Can one who imagines that the moon and stars must bow to him survive long under the whip? You cannot seriously believe that a man as great as this vizier—" he waved at the ornate columns covered with ornamental inscriptions--"would endure the insolence of our favored brother."

"Levi is right," Shim'on snapped. His voice, like his nerves, was in tatters. The unendurable frustration of waiting had destroyed what little satisfaction he felt when they finally reached their destination. "Yosef is gone. Instead of worrying about the past, we should discuss how we shall answer this vizier." Sarcasm laced his voice as he turned to Yehuda. "And I would not worry, Brother, about the power of the vizier's god. The spirit of God Almighty is far from this heathen land. Did you see their temples, their stone idols?"

"The Almighty does not dwell in houses made with human hands," Yehuda looked at Shim'on with a wry but indulgent glint in his eyes, "but in the hearts of men. How do you know that this vizier does not hear God's voice?"

"Because El Shaddai chose *us!*" Levi thumped his chest. "We are the people of the Almighty. We, the sons of Yisrael, are the chosen ones. Shim'on is right, we have nothing to fear from this Egyptian. He has no supernatural power."

"His natural power concerns me most." Re'uven nodded for emphasis. "He commands Pharaoh's army; at this moment a host of guards wait outside to answer his bidding. He has the power to put all of us in prison, and without the grain he controls, our little ones will starve. Think, brothers, before you speak rashly in his presence."

Dan stepped forward and held up his hands in a gesture of peace. "Let us answer whatever questions he might ask. If we please him, we will soon be on our way from these loathsome, painted people."

"We will answer all his questions truthfully." Yehuda folded his arms as his gaze crossed Shim'on's. "Look at the wealth of this place, of this man. See the guards at the doors, and remember the strong company of men who brought us here. Strength and power are on the side of this vizier, and we will not risk his anger."

9

"I've looked around," Shim'on snapped. "I've seen, I've heard, and it should all be cursed. The people here clothe themselves like their forefather Ham, who spied upon his father's nakedness without remorse. They wear garments as thin as a spider's web, covering their bodies without hiding them. Their women are clothed indecently, yet they walk with their heads held high as if they are proud of their shame. One merchant offered to sell me a kilt and bragged that it was as light as woven air."

"Their habits are not our concern," Levi inserted. "Let us satisfy this man and be gone."

Shim'on opened his mouth to argue, but stopped when a trumpet blast ripped through the hall like the alarm of war. A dozen hulking lance bearers, each clothed in a snowy white linen kilt and a leopard skin belt, marched in double columns toward the front of the room. Only when they had parted and stepped aside could Shim'on see the trim, imposing figure who marched in the midst of them: the Egyptian, the vizier of the Two Kingdoms, the Father to Pharaoh and acting ruler of the Black Land.

The one called Zaphenath-paneah.

A WHIRLWIND of emotions ripped through Yosef's soul as he stared into the faces of the Canaanites. His network of spies had been alerted to watch for men from Hebron, and this time they had actually snagged his brothers. Ani reported there were ten—who was missing? Binyamin, without a doubt. The others had either thrust him out, killed him, or left him at home with Yaakov. Why? Did they still hate the sons of Rahel, the true and beloved wife? Or had their hate been reserved for him alone?

Ceaseless questions hammered at him, but he could not speak. He stared at his brothers, his eyes narrowing. *Joy, be still! Dread, contain yourself! Laughter, tears, be gone! This is not the time to voice emotion; it is a time to be wary and carefully take the measure of men capable and guilty of murder, malice, and monumental jealousy.*

Twenty-two years had passed since he had last seen these who were his own flesh and blood, more than half his lifetime, yet the memory of their treachery rose before him as fresh as the morning breeze off the Nile. He would never forget a single detail of that day and night at Dotan: the pit, the pain of his broken arm, his brothers' taunting jests, and their expressions, which ranged from indifference to smirks of delight. His gaze darted to Levi's hand, which had clutched his many-colored robe, then shifted to Shim'on's fist, which had gripped a hungry dagger. As the images focused in his memory, the old anguish of knowing that his father mourned seared Yosef's heart again.

Though his mind burned with memories, he fixed his face into stern lines, determined that they should not see beyond the painted shadows of his eyes or the thick texture of his wig. Thinking of the multi-colored garment they had torn from his back, he fingered the pleated linen of his spotless vizier's robe. A flicker of irrational fear licked at his heart, then resolve overrode all emotions.

What could they do to him now, these sons of Yisrael? They had stared at him for a full five minutes, and not one had recognized him as their long-lost half-brother. Apprehension glimmered on their faces; drops of sweat glistened above Re'uven's lined lip. Yehuda kept his eyes to the ground as if shame held him on a leash; Yissakhar, Zevulun, and Dan leaned heavily upon their staves, their eyes hooded. Shim'on and Levi stood with defiant fists clenched; Gad, Asher, and Naftali cowered like children about to be punished.

Almighty God, how am I supposed to address them?

A dim ripple ran across his mind; a long-forgotten dream materialized and focused. He and his brothers had been binding sheaves of wheat in the field, and their sheaves had animated themselves and bowed down to his.

Yosef uttered an abrupt order to the captain of his guard: "Tell them to bow."

TARIK HEARD the undercurrent of emotion in his master's voice and barked out the command: "Bow before the royal majesty of Zaphenath-paneah, Father to the divine Pharaoh, Sustainer of Breath, the Bread of Life!"

He was not certain how much the Canaanites understood, but they could not mistake the tone of his voice. They fell to their knees on the tiled floor, one or two moving more slowly than the others. Tarik thought he spied an expression of resentment upon the face of the largest, most muscular man, but it vanished when one of the guards lifted his lance and stepped forward.

"We will need a skilled interpreter," the vizier said, keeping his voice so low only Tarik could hear. "These men speak the Canaanite tongue. Though you have managed well thus far, Tarik, I would not miss a single shade of meaning in their words."

"The woman who serves your wife speaks Canaanite," Tarik volunteered.

"Good. Send someone to fetch Mandisa." As Tarik gave the order and jerked his head toward one of the guards at the door, his master completed his appraisal of the men before him with a cool look, then turned with regal grace toward the gilded chair in the center of the room.

The guard fled with the speed of a gazelle and returned a moment later with Lady Asenath's handmaid. Tarik noticed that Mandisa flushed as she entered the room, her gaze darting from her master to the prostrate men on the floor.

At a careful distance from the Canaanites, Mandisa bowed before the vizier. "May I serve you, my lord?"

"Stand, Mandisa, and interpret whatever these men say." Zaphenath-paneah sank into his chair as his dark eyes moved over the group. "Do not spare a word for their sakes, but speak truthfully and honestly."

"Yes, my lord."

Mandisa stood and turned so she faced both the Canaanites and her master. After a moment's hesitation, the vizier spoke in a deep tone Tarik had never heard. "From where have you come?" he demanded in the Egyptian tongue. Mandisa interpreted and waited for a response.

For a moment no one answered, then a gray-haired man in the midst of the men lifted his head. He did not speak as rapidly as

12

Mandisa, and Tarik had no trouble understanding the Canaanite's halting words. "Tell your master that we are from Hebron, in the land of Canaan. Like so many others presently in your city, we have come to buy grain."

After hearing the interpretation, Zaphenath-paneah shifted his weight as if to establish perspective, then folded his arms and shook his head. "No. You are spies; you have come to look at the undefended parts of our land."

"No!" another man cried after hearing Mandisa's reply. He lifted his shaggy head, but remained on the floor, cringing like a scolded puppy. "Assure him, we have come only to buy food. We are not spies. We are honest brothers, all the sons of one man."

Mandisa repeated their assurances. The master's eyes flashed with some indefinable feeling, then he wrapped his hands around the arms of his gilded chair. "Tell them," he said, his body tensing, "that I am certain they have come to spy out the nakedness of the land. We are in the midst of famine, they want to take advantage of our weakness."

Tarik put his hand to his sword as Mandisa spoke the interpretation.

"This is crazy!" The muscled man with angry eyes lifted his head and shoulders as if he would rise to challenge the master. Tarik was about to step forward and answer with a blow, but another brother silenced the loud one with a reproachful glance.

"Tell your master," the more reasonable man continued, "that we are his servants. We are twelve brothers in all, the sons of one man who lives in Hebron."

The captain caught his breath. Already they had lied.

"You are ten!" he shouted, stepping forward.

"Tell your master," the careful man went on, bowing his head, "that we are not twelve today because our youngest brother is with his wife and children, at home with our father in Hebron. And our other brother . . . is no more."

Mandisa began to interpret the man's words, but something in Zaphenath-paneah's expression worried Tarik. A suspicious line had etched itself into the corners of the master's mouth, and the vizier's eyes

13

gleamed strangely—were they wet, or was the sunlight from the high windows playing tricks upon Tarik's eyes?

"They are not twelve today," Mandisa said, as Tarik observed an unusual ripple of passion beneath the polished exterior of the master's handsome countenance, "because their younger brother is home with their father—"

"You say your father lives, but you are old men," the vizier interrupted in a harsh, raw voice. "How can I know you speak the truth?"

After Mandisa interpreted, the silver-haired one lifted his head. "As I live, my father was alive when we left him. I am Re'uven, my lord, the first born. If I am lying, you may take my life."

"I will hear no more," Zaphenath-paneah said, interrupting the translation. As the Canaanite men lay with their foreheads pressed to the ground, the vizier closed his eyes, his jaw clenching.

Something tightened in Tarik's chest. There was more to this encounter than he knew, something awesome and mysterious and hidden. A warning voice whispered in the captain's head as Zaphenath-paneah's chiseled face distorted with anger.

"No!" he shouted, his voice ringing in the great hall as he leapt to his feet. "It is as I said, you are spies, and by your own speech you will be tested. As Pharaoh lives, you shall not leave this place unless your youngest brother comes here to prove your words!"

Zaphenath-paneah slapped his hands together in an explosive sound; the unexpected gesture startled an aproned page who waved an ostrich-feathered fan at the vizier's side. "I will release one of you that he may bring your brother to me, but the rest of you shall remain confined," the vizier pronounced, an artery throbbing in his neck as he surveyed the men before him. "We will see whether there is truth in you. If you are lying, even in this, then by the life of Pharaoh you are spies."

The vizier did not wait for the interpretation, but swept out of the reception hall. Tarik hesitated, then hurried after his master. Behind him, he could hear Mandisa quavering through the translation of the master's last words.

14

Zaphenath-paneah stopped in the hallway. "Tarik?" he asked, not turning.

"My lord, I am here."

The vizier squared his shoulders as if an invisible enemy stood before him. "Take them to Pharaoh's prison in the house of the captain of the royal guard. They shall spend this night in the prison pits."

"Yes, my lord."

Tarik nodded in a quick bow, then hurried back to the hall. Upon entering, he motioned for the lance-bearers to ready their spears.

"By the command of the Lord Zaphenath-paneah, Vizier of the Double Kingdoms," he called, his voice crisp and clear in the Canaanite language, "you shall be confined in Pharaoh's prison." To reinforce his meaning, he pulled his sword from its sheath.

"Confined?" One of the brothers rose to his knees, his face clouding with fear. "For how long must we remain? Our families are starving, our father will worry."

A half-smile tugged at Tarik's lips. "You will remain in Pharaoh's prison until Zaphenath-paneah is inclined to show mercy."

CHAPTER THREE

"Tell me, Mandisa," Asenath urged, her lovely eyes filled with dark trepidation, "what is it about these Canaanites that disturbs my husband so? He came into my chamber after seeing them, and his countenance was much troubled."

Mandisa turned away to lift her mistress's full wig from its stand, hoping the younger woman wouldn't see the anxiety in her own eyes. The afternoon had been totally unnerving. First she had embarrassed herself by spying on the visiting herdsmen; then the master had asked her to interpret their words. Standing before them, feeling their eyes upon her, she had relived her humiliation all over again.

"I'm not certain why these men are troublesome, but they are," Mandisa answered, taking pains to keep her voice steady. "Perhaps the master has heard rumors of Canaanites who plan to attack Egypt. But these are things we need not concern ourselves with, my lady."

"My husband has dealt with rumors of war before," Asenath answered, studying her reflection in a bronze looking-brass as Mandisa pulled the wig over her lady's close-cropped hair. "And he has never held such worries close to his heart. Something happened today, Mandisa, that shook my dear one to the core. Though he pretended nothing was amiss, his hands trembled when he came to see me, and his eyes were as remote as the stars." She pressed her lips together as she lowered the looking brass. "Tarik would know what troubles my beloved."

"I daresay the captain of the guard does not know more of my lord's heart than you," Mandisa replied. "My master shares with Tarik all things concerning the governance of Pharaoh's house, city, and country, but matters of the heart he reserves for you alone."

Asenath turned and lifted a questioning brow. "Were these men so unusual? Were they disfigured or sick? Did they display some sorcery that upset my husband?"

"They were ordinary herdsmen, my lady." Mandisa lowered her hand to her mistress's soft shoulder. "When I lived in Canaan, I saw hundreds of men like them, rough as the wind and as steady as the sun. No, there was nothing in their appearance or manner to disturb the master."

At the sound of leather slapping against tile, Mandisa pulled away, prostrating herself on the floor as Zaphenath-paneah entered the room. Asenath bowed her head, but when Mandisa looked up, she saw her mistress peeking through the fringe of her bangs, keeping a wary gaze on her pacing husband.

"I said I would keep nine and send one back to Canaan," the master muttered, thrusting his hands behind his back. He spoke in the Canaanite tongue, amazing Mandisa with his fluency. If he spoke it so well, why had he needed her to interpret? And whom was he addressing now? His wife did not understand the language of Canaan.

"Something in me demands that they suffer the darkness of the prison pits for as long as I did," he went on, speaking to the air. "I wonder if they are tasting the fear that filled my mouth, even my heart, when they turned their backs on me. But they are grown men, and I was only a boy—"

"My husband?" Asenath interrupted, her voice a mere squeak in the room.

The vizier stopped pacing and looked at the women as if seeing them for the first time. "I am sorry, my dear," he said, speaking in careful Egyptian. "And Mandisa, you may rise. I forgot to thank you for your help this morning."

17

"It is an honor to serve you, my lord," Mandisa said, standing. Her heart yearned to ask for an explanation, but though the vizier ran a remarkably easy-going household, a well-trained servant did not inquire after her master's business.

Asenath rose from the low stool and crossed to her husband's side. "My lord, your skin is cold," she said, pulling his hands into hers. "And you are trembling! Shall you not tell me what has upset you?"

He looked at her. For a moment Mandisa thought he would speak, but he only gave her a slow, sad smile. "You are so young," he whispered, brushing the back of his hand across her curved cheek. "Why should I burden you with sorrows of the past? Bring my boys to me, Asenath, let me play an hour with Efrayim and Menashe. They always lighten my heart . . . they help me forget."

Asenath pulled away to fetch her sons from their schoolroom. Mandisa was about to follow when the master stopped her with a question: "Mandisa, know you of El Shaddai?"

A terrible tenseness seized her. The master was speaking again in the Canaanite language, and he spoke the name of a God she had never expected to hear in this black land.

"My lord?" she stammered, her tongue thick and unwilling.

"I know you were not born in Mizraim," Zaphenath-paneah answered, using the Canaanite word for *Egypt*. He lowered himself to his wife's stool. "But, like me, you have adopted this land as your own."

"My husband was Egyptian," she said. "And my son is thus an Egyptian, so I never thought to go anywhere else."

"There will come a time," the master went on, still speaking the foreign tongue, "when my sons will not think of themselves as Egyptian, for I am not of this place. Like you, I was brought into this country as a stranger. I was born Yosef, the son of Yaakov, the son of Yitzhak. When last I saw my father, he had settled in Hebron."

Mandisa's breath caught in her lungs. "I have heard of this Yaakov; he was a prince in the land of Canaan. My father said Yaakov was rich in possessions, servants, cattle and flocks. The elders of my village called him a wise man filled with the knowledge of God."

The beginning of a smile tipped the corners of the vizier's mouth. "So you knew Yaakov as a prince?"

"And as a distant kinsman, my lord. My father's uncle was Uz of Aram, and his father Laban, the father of Lea and Rahel."

"My father's wives." To her surprise, the vizier showed little reaction to her announcement that they shared a common heritage. Though he smiled, the weight of apprehension did not lift from his strong face. "And so the Almighty works again in ways I cannot fathom. But you have not yet answered my question, Mandisa. What do you know of El Shaddai, the God worshipped by Yaakov of Canaan?"

She shook her head. "My family knew of him, my lord, but my father and my father's father worshipped other gods." She lowered her gaze. "I often heard stories of how Yaakov's God increased his flocks and brought his wives to bear many sons, but my family did not make sacrifices to El Shaddai."

The vizier tipped his face to a stream of sunlight pouring through one of the high windows. "I have not ceased to pray to God Shaddai since I came to the Black Land," he said, a spark of some indefinable feeling in his eyes. "He lifted me out of prison and slavery and made me sit at Pharaoh's right hand. More than that, He saved Egypt, perhaps even the entire world, from this famine that shall continue for another five years. Until today I thought God's plans for me had been fulfilled. But an hour ago I looked out upon the faces of Yaakov's sons—my treacherous brothers."

His *brothers?* Mandisa stared, speechless.

"I wanted to run forward and embrace them," he continued, his voice dropping in volume, "but on at least one face I saw anger and hatred as strong as it was the day they cast me into a pit." He stiffened as if ashamed. "I was almost afraid."

"You are not a coward, my lord."

The vizier smiled and studied his hands. "I no longer fear for myself, but for my father and my other brother. I fear they may hate Binyamin and hurt him, and so bring my father to his grave with sorrowing."

"And so you cast them into prison." Mandisa uttered the words in a neutral tone, not knowing whether he hoped for approval or condemnation.

"Binyamin is the only other son of my mother," he said, lifting his gaze to meet hers. "How can I know the sons of Lea do not hate him as they hated me? How can I be certain they will not do him harm?"

"They said he is alive and well with your father." Mandisa lowered her eyes, uncomfortable with the frankness of the conversation.

"My father, if they speak truly, has lived one hundred twenty-nine years," he went on in a hushed whisper. "Binyamin is a grown man, probably with children of his own. For his sake and the sake of his family, I must test the hearts of the other ten."

Mandisa bowed her head. "I will do anything I can to help, my lord."

The laughter of children danced into the room, and the vizier's mouth curved into an unconscious smile as he recognized the sounds of his sons. But before they entered, he turned again to Mandisa: "Do not speak of this to anyone, not even your mistress. Do not reveal my past or my link to the men in Pharaoh's prison. I must seek the face of Almighty God before I know how to proceed."

She bowed again as the boys spilled into the room. "I will do my best to serve you."

CHAPTER FOUR

As his brothers snored around him, Shim'on lay upon his back and studied the dark circle of sky above the prison pit. Glorious Thebes had held them in awe as they entered the city, but no signs of its marble-washed opulence existed in this place. No colorful or ornate pictures adorned the mud-walled pit into which they had been thrust after leaving the vizier's villa; the primitive structure did not even allow the luxury of a view. With scorched black earth around them and an ebony sky above, Shim'on felt as if they had fallen into the abyss. How could they have plummeted so far in such a short time?

They had observed no signs of trouble afoot when they approached the royal capital. Though drought had scorched the fields outside the walls, reports from passing travelers indicated the city's granaries and storage houses overflowed with barley and emmer-wheat, onions and leeks, lettuce, pomegranates, apples, olives, figs, and the smooth wine of Ka-en-keme, better and sweeter than honey. Thebes was a luxury-loving lioness that rejoiced to feed her young, passersby told the brothers. Because of her generous bounty, the river at her breast teemed with boats large and small, for joy inhabited her gates.

Thebes lay like a glittering jewel in the merciless Egyptian sun, her crowded streets laid out in straight lines that crossed at neat angles. Even in the grip of famine, fishes glittered in her ponds and nesting birds squawked beside her pools.

The Egyptians in the merchant stalls seemed simple, cheerful, and likable. Slighter than the robust men of Canaan and better adapted to the weather, the simple people wore their brown hair short or shaved their heads. The dry, intense heat dictated the uniform of the day: men wore eggshell-colored kilts of pleated linen; occasionally a wealthy man appeared in a voluminous cloak edged with colored weavings and embroideries.

Naked children scampered among the crowd at the riverside market-place; regal young women in gossamer gowns kept a careful eye on them as they bartered for household goods and exotic trophies from foreign lands. The women of Egypt dressed themselves in long shirt-like garments exquisitely sewn and tied at the neck with delicate tassels. They seemed industrious, happy creatures, but Shim'on found it difficult to consider anything but their revealing attire.

After inquiring among several merchants for direction, the brothers followed a sea of visitors to the royal granaries. An official explained that all first-time foreign visitors had to register directly with the vizier's representative. After this initial contact they would be spared the journey upriver and would be permitted to buy grain from one of the more remote outposts.

The brothers waited for hours in the hot sun and finally reached the head of the line, where an Egyptian official sat on the ground, a papyrus reed in his hand, his lips pursed with boredom.

Shim'on closed his eyes, struggling to remember every detail of the morning. Surely they had said something or committed some small act that aroused suspicion. He could think of nothing he had done, but any one of his brothers could have lost custody of his words or actions for a moment. Perhaps Levi had frowned at one of the naked slaves, or Yehuda had unconsciously snubbed one of the bald priests.

"What is your name, and from where do you come?" the scribe had asked in a bored tone, not even looking up. Re'uven, as eldest, stood at the head of the line, with Shim'on immediately behind him.

"I am Re'uven, son of Yaakov of Hebron," he answered, folding his hands. "We have brought silver to buy a ration of grain from Pharaoh. There are ten of us, and each man will need four hundred-weight of grain, emmer, and barley—"

Even from where he stood Shim'on saw the sudden tremor that shook the scribe's hand. "Re'uven, son of Yaakov?" he interrupted, looking into Re'uven's face. "From Hebron of Canaan?"

"Yes." Re'uven strengthened his voice and lifted a hand to indicate the others. "These are my brothers."

The scribe's face drained of color. "Hold your place, but you must excuse me," the man muttered. Without hesitation, he rose and ran doubled-over into a brick building near the domed granaries.

"What did you say to him, Re'uven?" Gad called, joking. "Or perhaps I should ask what you have eaten of late. Did your breath make him ill?"

"No more than yours would," Re'uven answered, but Shim'on could see a lightning bolt of worry in his eyes.

They waited thirty eternal minutes. The cursing and sweating foreigners behind them lost all patience. First they called upon their gods to deliver them from the heat that covered the city like a blanket, then they demanded that their gods curse the man responsible for the delay.

Finally another official appeared and addressed Re'uven: "By the order of the Lord High Vizier, Father to Pharaoh, Acting Ruler and Commander of Pharaoh's Royal Army, you and your company are to come with me."

Re'uven's heavy brows shot up in surprise. "Where are we going?"

"Are we not allowed to buy grain?" Shim'on stepped forward. "Are we and our families to starve?"

From out of nowhere, three dozen armed men appeared, instantly silencing the noisy rabble behind the brothers. Lance bearers, the sharp blades of their spears gleaming like razor-sharp talons, surrounded Yaakov's sons.

"You will come with me," the Egyptian commander repeated, eyeing the brothers with a critical squint.

23

"We will come without argument if we may know where we are going," Yehuda said, moving toward Re'uven.

But the commander had not answered, and in the face of such armed force, the brothers did not protest. In a frightened, bewildered huddle they stumbled to the gates of the largest villa Shim'on had ever seen, then they were escorted into the front hall of the house itself.

And for what? Though he had struggled with questions all night, Shim'on still had no idea why they had been culled from the thousands in line at the royal granaries. Had they offended one of the Egyptians' stone gods? Or one of the naval commanders at the river? Had their father or grandfather conducted some secret dealings with the Egyptians that now bode ill for his descendants?

Shim'on could find no answers in the night sky. Groaning, he turned onto his side and closed his eyes against the depressing darkness. For a shepherd accustomed to sleeping with the unfettered breath of the open land on his brow, the pit was cramped, claustrophobic, and cruel. He did not know who deserved the blame for thrusting them into this prison, but when he discovered the truth, that one would be made to pay.

CHAPTER FIVE

Three days after the Canaanites had been taken to Pharaoh's prison, Mandisa received a summons from her master. She hurried to Lady Asenath's chamber where Zaphenath-paneah was breakfasting with his family.

"My master and mistress, may you live long and happy," she murmured, prostrating herself on the floor.

Zaphenath-paneah wiped his hands on a small square of linen on his breakfast tray. "Mandisa, would you ask your son to take my boys into the garden to play? But please, return here after you have spoken to him."

Mandisa rose and held out her hands to Efrayim and Menashe, the vizier's young sons. "Come, boys," she said, smiling. "Adom is in the courtyard with Tarik, learning how to throw a lance. Would you like to join him?"

The two boys, ages five and seven, offered their trusting hands and let her lead them from the room. She found her own son, Adom, on the front portico, his gaze wistfully trained on the courtyard where the captain inspected his guards.

"I thought Tarik was going to teach you this morning," she murmured, slipping up behind the slender boy.

Adom cast her a quick glance over his shoulder, then returned his gaze to the men in the courtyard. "I don't think he has time," he replied, his voice heavy. "He has to do the inspections, then the vizier wants him to bring some captives from Pharaoh's house."

"There will be another time, then," Mandisa said, giving what she hoped was the proper dose of encouragement. Stepping to his side, she lifted the smaller boys' hands. "But I've brought you something to do. The vizier has asked if you would take his sons to the garden."

Adom's gloomy expression brightened. "Of course," he said, grinning at Efrayim and Menashe. "I don't mind."

"You're a good son."

Adom shrugged off the compliment, but took the younger boys' hands and led them toward the garden. Mandisa paused to watch the trio depart. Efrayim and Menashe were blessed to have a loving father and myriad caretakers to teach them all a boy ought to know. Adom was less fortunate, for he had her alone, and a single woman could do only so much with a son . . .

She tucked her thoughts away and urged her feet back toward her mistress's chamber.

SLAVES WERE REMOVING the breakfast trays when Mandisa returned. Zaphenath-paneah listened to his wife's pleasant chatter while the room was cleared, but when the slaves had gone, he folded his arms and regarded Asenath with a grave expression.

"What?" A flicker of a smile rose at the edge of her mouth, then died out. "Have I done something to displease you, my husband?"

"No, beloved." The vizier's eyes flickered toward Mandisa, then he motioned to an empty stool near his wife. "You may sit, Mandisa. I want you both to hear what I am about to say."

Without speaking, Mandisa slid into her place.

"My love," the vizier of all Egypt began, his eyes melting into his wife's, "days ago you asked why the arrival of a group of men from Hebron upset me. I could not tell you then, being unsure in my own mind what I should do, but I have prayed to the Almighty God and today I have an answer for you."

"Go on, my husband," Asenath said, her hands fidgeting in her lap.

The vizier gave her a strained smile. "I have told you, wife, of my past and the treachery that brought me to Egypt. Now I must tell you that the men in Pharaoh's prison are my brothers, the sons of the maids and the sons of Lea."

Mandisa heard her mistress's quick intake of breath, but Asenath said nothing. She sat motionless at her husband's side, blank, amazed, and pale.

The vizier's gaze shifted from his wife to her handmaid. "I have decided to remove the men of Canaan from prison today, and will need an interpreter when I speak with them."

"But if they are your brothers—" Asenath began.

"I must know the intentions of their hearts before I reveal myself. I had thought to keep nine of them in Egypt and return the one who wields the most influence with my father, but in these hungry times it is too dangerous for one man to attempt the desert journey alone. I had also thought to punish them," his voice softened, "but God has shown me that revenge is not the answer."

Mandisa nodded. Her master had obviously thought much about what to do with his recalcitrant guests. "So you will allow them all to leave?"

"No." Zaphenath-paneah gave her a slow smile. "I will keep the one most likely to cause trouble among the others. There are five years of famine yet to come, so they must eventually return to Egypt for more food-rations. As long as I am holding one brother, they will return to Thebes. My father is an honorable man; he will demand that they redeem whomever is left behind."

Asenath's hand flew out to rest upon his muscled arm. "My husband, what if they never come back? Won't you regret sending them away without telling them the truth?"

The vizier leaned forward, his elbows on his knees. "Mandisa, you are a Canaanite, you know their ways. Tell your mistress—if these men were of your clan, would they return to secure your freedom?"

27

Mandisa felt her heart shrivel at his words. Her father had married her to Idogbe, a man she did not love, and allowed him to carry her to Egypt against her will. In thirteen years no one from her family had visited or sent word. If not for the goodness of Zaphenath-paneah and Lady Asenath, both she and her son would be enslaved or dead, for none of her father's people cared that Idogbe had vanished and left her pregnant and alone. But if she had been born a son instead of a daughter, the situation would have been different.

"Yes, my lord," she whispered in a strangled voice, denying her own bitter reality. "If I were a man, they would be honor-bound to come for me."

He sat back, reassured. "God knows what is in my brothers' hearts, but he intends that I discern their hearts myself. Mandisa, be ready to face them within the hour. I am sending Tarik to Pharaoh's prison to fetch them."

"My husband?" Asenath spoke in a ragged voice. "Should I be with you . . . when you face them?"

"Not now, beloved," the vizier answered, taking her hands in his. "If God is willing, you shall be at my side on a far happier day."

FEELING IRRITATED, gritty, and uncomfortable, Shim'on shifted beneath his robe as he followed his brothers into the vizier's great reception hall. In the vestibule slaves had removed their sandals and washed the black dirt of Egypt from their feet, and as the brothers entered the spotless and elaborate hall, another army of servants lined the walls, each waving an ostrich-feathered fan to circulate the incense wafting from ornately-carved stands along the sides of the room. From some place out of sight, a harpist's gentle hands played soothing music.

Shim'on steeled himself for whatever was to come. Whoever had ordered these gestures of sweet softness meant to emphasize the difference between the vizier's luxurious presence and the brothers' barren prison. Why?

After a few moments of nervous silence, a pair of trumpets sounded. The double columns of lance bearers marched into the room and the elegant vizier ascended his gilded throne. His linen garment, falling like chiseled marble from his throat to the floor, did little to disguise the strength of his frame. A heavy chain of gold hung about his neck; the finest leather adorned his feet. His heavy wig had been shaped and oiled to frame his aristocratic face.

For a long moment no one spoke. As much as Shim'on wanted to look away, he found himself staring at the king's regent. Zaphenath-paneah's handsome features nudged some distant experience in Shim'on's memory, but he pushed the feeling aside. The vizier *should* look familiar, for his likeness had been painted on half the statues and frescoed buildings in Thebes. Though Shim'on guessed the man was less than forty years old, his sharp profile spoke of power and ageless strength. Yet his mouth wore an expression of familiar softness, the way Yaakov looked just before he smiled.

From lowered lids, Shim'on shot a hostile look at the man. Was he gloating over his harsh treatment of the brothers? Did he think they would confess to spying because they spent two days and nights in his pitiful pit? Or was he enjoying the thought of what he would do to them if they did not confess to spying in this encounter?

"Grace and peace to you, most high vizier." Re'uven sank to his knees. The other brothers followed Re'uven's cue and lowered themselves until every man lay prostrate on the gleaming floor. From another entrance to the room, the female servant who had previously acted as interpreter came forward and interpreted for Re'uven again.

"You may kneel before me," Zaphenath-paneah responded, holding out a golden rod. "I have consulted my God, and have brought you out of prison to speak what is on my heart."

Re'uven rose to a kneeling position. "My brothers and I are listening."

The vizier waited for the interpretation, then seemed to fix his gaze on Shim'on, who had lifted his head as high as he dared.

"I have asked my God for wisdom," the vizier said, derision and sympathy mingled in his expression, "and He has provided an answer. If you do what I will tell you, you shall live, for I fear God."

Shim'on shifted his gaze to the woman as she interpreted, and lost all custody of his eyes as the vizier's words flowed from her tongue. He had noticed her on their arrival, for what man would not? But today her loveliness seemed to fill the room with light.

Slender and poised, the woman stood in the slanting sunbeams from the high windows. The dark curls of her wig twisted and crinkled above glowing eyes that pierced the shadows of the room. A leather belt defined the smallness of her waist, and the apricot tones of her skin blended into the sheer material of a gown that did little to disguise the womanly curves beneath. She paused, her gaze flitting around the room before it locked with Shim'on's. He caught his breath, but she dropped her eyes before his steady stare.

"What shall we do, my lord?" Re'uven's voice jerked Shim'on back to reality.

The vizier's voice rose in a commanding tone. "If you are honest men, let one of your brothers be confined in prison. But as for the rest of you, go, carry grain for the famine of your households. And when your food-rations are depleted, bring your youngest brother to me, so your words may be verified. If you are willing to do this, and you have not lied, you shall live."

"Bring Binyamin?" Zevulun gasped. "It is impossible, our father will never agree to let his youngest son go."

The vizier listened to the translation, then managed a short laugh and a reply.

"Zaphenath-paneah says your brother is a grown man and married; he is no longer a child," the woman interpreted. "You must bring your younger brother before the vizier of all Egypt."

A flicker of apprehension coursed through Shim'on at the words *your younger brother.* Once the sons of Yisrael had known two younger brothers, but though Yosef still haunted Shim'on's dreams, he was forever gone. Only Binyamin remained.

Re'uven responded to the interpreter's words: "My lord, let me speak to my brothers."

His request needed no interpretation. Apparently understanding, the stony-faced vizier nodded in assent.

Re'uven stood. Turning his back to the vizier, he looked at the others. "We must do as he says," he murmured. "We have no choice."

Yehuda's brow creased with worry. "Father will never allow it. He would die himself before he would let us take Binyamin from Hebron."

"Would you rather our father lose ten sons?" Levi snapped. "If we agree to this, we will have time to prepare Father for what must be done to appease this Egyptian."

"Levi is right," Dan added. "And the man has made a reasonable request. If we do not consent, we are practically admitting we have lied. The vizier will be convinced we are spies, and he may kill us all—now." He lowered his gaze. "Perhaps we deserve death. After what happened at Dotan—"

"Dotan was more than twenty years ago," Shim'on snapped, stiffening as though Dan had struck him. Though their absent brother's name singed every conscience, if they did not speak of him, they would not have to remember. "Our father has put the past behind him."

"Our father has not ceased to mourn for Yosef," Re'uven interrupted. His voice, cold and exact, echoed in the cavernous hall. "You know I speak the truth. Answer me truly, Shim'on. Did I not warn you that we should not sin against the boy? But you would not listen, and now we will pay for what we have done."

A sudden choking sound disturbed the silence, and Shim'on turned in time to see the vizier, his hands over his face, rise from his chair and flee the room. The captain of the guard followed his master like a pursuing shadow.

"Now we will be meat for the vizier's dogs," Levi said, his mouth grim as he turned to the others. "Whatever the Egyptian ate for breakfast does not agree with him, and we shall pay the penalty for his sore stomach. We must agree to his plan, and we must agree quickly."

"But which one?" Asher looked around the circle. "Which of us will remain here in prison while his family suffers alone?"

No one spoke until Re'uven lifted his chin. "We all have children," he said, giving Shim'on a compassionate and troubled look. "But we do not all have wives. You, Shim'on, have no wife waiting at home. You should volunteer to remain behind."

Shim'on glared at his brother. "I may not have a wife, but I am the only one of you who remembers to provide for our sister. With no husband to look after her, Dina has only me for support."

"I'll look after Dina," Yehuda volunteered.

"And my sons?" Shim'on frowned. "Who will see to them? I would sooner die tomorrow than remain here one day longer than necessary."

"But we have wives!"

"I have six sons!" Shim'on answered, seething with mounting rage. "You, Re'uven, are the eldest, why don't you volunteer for prison? You're always quick to speak up when it is to your advantage. Or Yehuda! With all your talk of God and holiness, why doesn't you offer to stay?"

"Father listens to Yehuda," Dan said, "while you howl like the desert winds and our father pays no mind. You bring nothing but trouble."

"Enough!" Yehuda lifted his hands and stepped into the center of the circle, turning until the bickering stopped.

When the brothers stood silent, Yehuda ran his fingers through his hair in a distracted motion, then looked up to the ceiling as if the answer would be found there. "El Shaddai will make the choice," he said, his shoulders drooping. "We will listen and accept his will."

CHAPTER SIX

MANDISA TRIED TO FOLLOW THE RISING BABBLE OF THE BROTHERS' conversation until she felt the light touch of a hand upon her arm. "The master seeks you," Tarik whispering, lingering behind a column as the prisoners bickered in the center of the chamber.

Mandisa turned and followed Tarik into a small room off the great hall. The noble Zaphenath-paneah sat motionless on a bed as if his mind and body were benumbed. His eyes were red with weeping, and dark stains of kohl streaked his cheeks.

"Please, Mandisa, freshen my toilette," he said, offering her a fragile smile. "I must not appear weak before them."

He offered no reason for his behavior, and from Tarik's mystified expression Mandisa intuited that the master had not explained his connection to the troublesome men in the hall. She reached into a cosmetics box she carried for such emergencies and reapplied the master's face paint in swift, sure strokes. Within a moment he had assumed his former regal appearance, but his voice was unsteady when he thanked her.

"Here," she pulled a scrap of linen from a basket on the floor. "Let them think, if necessary, that the desert winds have elicited a cough."

He took the square of linen and crumpled it in his hand, then leaned forward as if to stand up. "What are they arguing about?" he asked. "Were you able to hear?"

"They are quarreling over who should remain behind," she said, folding her hands. "The spokesman, Re'uven, says the one called Shim'on should remain in Egypt, for he has no wife waiting in Canaan. But this Shim'on—" she felt her cheeks color as she said the bold one's name—"says he has a sister and six sons who need him."

"Six sons." A wistful note echoed in Zaphenath-paneah's voice, and Mandisa felt her heart contract in sympathy. The single sorrow that lay over the vizier's household resulted from the fact that the royal physicians had warned Lady Asenath that another child would certainly hasten her death. She had borne two healthy sons during the days of plenty, then had suffered three miscarriages, the most recent of which had occurred during the time of the Nile's last flooding. That unborn child nearly dragged Lady Asenath with it into the Otherworld.

Now the mistress's womb lay as barren and shallow as the starving Nile. Zaphenath-paneah had consoled his wife with tenderness and compassion, assuring her he loved her even though he would no longer visit her chambers when she might conceive a child. He was content with her and two sons, he often told her, especially since his responsibilities to the kingdom and Pharaoh often drained him of strength.

"But you renew me," Mandisa had heard him whisper to his whimpering wife one afternoon, "you and Efrayim and Menashe. I am blessed beyond measure, for your smile alone is enough to strengthen my heart, soul, and body."

The master looked as though he needed one of his wife's smiles now. He remained absolutely motionless for a long moment, then stood and moved toward the hall with long, purposeful strides.

Drawn by curiosity and duty, Mandisa and Tarik followed.

WITH THE FULL intensity of his brothers' eyes upon him, Yosef mounted the dais and turned toward them. "Tarik will take the one I chose to prison," he said, speaking in Egyptian. As Mandisa translated in a breathless voice, Yosef lifted his hand and pointed squarely at Shim'on.

The man was a thorn. Twenty years ago, he had been one of the first to call for Yosef's death after they dropped him into the pit. Before that, at every family gathering, Shim'on had managed to find a reason to needle the others. As strong as an iron chain and as unyielding as a rock, his opinions inevitably divided the brothers. In Yosef's day, even the women had learned to avoid him.

Without Shim'on, the others would have a more peaceful journey home, seventeen or eighteen days of relative calm. Yaakov would not have to hear Shim'on's negative version of their encounter with the Egyptian vizier, and Binyamin would not have to make the long journey to Egypt in the company of a murderous madman. For an instant Yosef wished he'd had enough forethought to order Levi's detention, too, for he and Shim'on usually united to cause trouble. But of the two hotheads, Shim'on was the most likely to erupt.

At Tarik's command, a column of guards moved into the knot of Canaanites and separated Shim'on from the others. As a pair of guards advanced to bind the captive's wrists, the burly shepherd lunged, grabbing and neatly breaking one guard's arm over his knee.

Two guards grabbed for Shim'on's right hand and were then launched across the room; another had the misfortune of connecting face-first with Shim'on's fist. Yosef heard the snap as Shim'on's punch broke the man's jawbone. A shoulder throw sent another pair of guards crashing to the floor. One foolish fan-bearer, who thought to enter the fray with only the pole of his fan for a weapon, found himself lying at Shim'on's feet, the breath snuffed out of him like a winking candle.

A melee' broke out; the dignity of the chamber vanishing as full-throated shrieks echoed from the high ceiling and bounced among the pillars. Most of the cries came from Shim'on and the injured guard, for the other brothers cowered against the wall, their expressions ranging from embarrassment to sheer horror. Mandisa, Yosef noticed, covered her eyes, rather than watch the spectacle.

As the wounded retreated, the lance-bearers tightened their circle.

Though the captive still crouched in a position of menace, his allies had fled; the fight was over. Tarik waded through the injured guards to catch and bind Shim'on's flailing fists; another Egyptian shackled and hobbled the shepherd's feet with a length of rope. He could still run, but he would not get far.

Yosef smothered a grim smile. He should have warned Tarik. A man did not grow up with twelve brothers without learning how to fight. And it was not on mere whim that the others had named Shim'on "the Destroyer."

With Shim'on bound, Yosef looked out at the brothers with a dispassionate stare. "The rest of you may go. But if you return, you will not see this one again unless you bring your younger brother and thus prove your own words. Then you may come and trade for food in peace." He paused, concern and contempt warring in his soul, as Mandisa translated in a trembling voice.

"I give you one warning—use the grain of Egypt for bread, not for seed. Nothing will grow for five more years. Now go," he rushed on, aware of a disturbing quake in his self-control, "and may all be well with you and your father."

The trumpets blared as he stood. Amid a blizzard of mingled shouts from the brothers, the guards led Shim'on out of the room. Ignoring their farewells, Yosef left the hall through another exit.

Safe from prying eyes in the small adjoining chamber, he turned to Tarik, who had followed. "Listen carefully," he said, keeping his voice low. "Do not return the man to Pharaoh's prison, but prepare a secure room in my house. Do not withhold from him any luxury save that of his freedom."

Tarik blinked. "Is this a wise course, noble vizier? He is an unruly sort."

"I do not believe he will hurt anyone here. He is a shepherd; he obeys the law of fight or flee. I should have warned you."

"My men should have been better prepared," Tarik answered, his face flooding with color. "Their shameful performance—"

"They did well." Yosef rested a hand on his hip. "Shim'on is strong. And he has always been dangerous."

If Tarik was relieved by Yosef's assurances, he didn't show it. "And what of the others, my lord?"

"Allow them to purchase grain-rations from my own granaries, but have the scribes return each man's silver to the mouth of his sack." He clapped a hand on the captain's bronzed shoulder. "I can't take silver from my own brothers."

When surprise blossomed on the guard's handsome face, Yosef held up a warning finger. "Not a word to anyone. My wife knows the truth, and Mandisa. But no one else."

"Should Ani be told?"

Yosef gave Tarik a conspiratorial wink. "Ani is a wise man, but his wisdom is forever flowing from his tongue. He will not be harmed by not knowing."

Tarik bowed. "Is that all, my lord?"

Yosef paused. "They will need fresh donkeys and provisions for their journey. Have Ani make preparation for these things, then send the brothers away as soon as possible." He grimaced. "The sooner they are home, the sooner they will return and take their troublesome brother with them."

Tarik's usually stern mouth spread in a toothy grin. "It shall be done as you say, my master."

SHIM'ON STARED around the room in wonder. After his outburst, he had expected to be thrust into another prison pit, one even more barbaric than the first, but instead he had been marched through the villa's courtyard and given a private room within the walls of the vizier's palace. Why?

Skins, cushions, and fresh linens covered the low bed of polished wood and the neckrest had been padded with the softest down. A pitcher and basin stood on a stand near a high window that brought in fresh light and air. Next to the bed, a half dozen lotus blossoms floated in a bowl of water and scented the chamber with a sweet aroma.

Shim'on sank onto the seat of an elaborately carved chair and fingered his beard. He could imagine several explanations for this unusual treatment, but the most obvious answer was that Egypt's vizier was a lunatic. Alternately hostile and forgiving, this ruler had already demonstrated capricious whims of fancy. Shim'on had heard that the Egyptians were a cheerful and superstitious lot; this Zaphenath-paneah probably hoped to pacify some god by allowing Shim'on to enjoy a few days of luxury before relegating him to some dungeon of torture.

But though the chamber was pleasant and probably better furnished than the half the houses of Thebes, Shim'on was no city dweller. He wanted the open spaces of the earth around him, the spiraling stars above. Not for him the sweet scents of lotus blossoms and delicate taste of dainty shat cakes, he longed for the earthy perfumes of goat and cattle dung, the robust flavors of desert-toughened meat, and rough breads sweetened with wild honey.

Yes, Shim'on reflected, lifting his eyes to the rectangular window higher than his reach, for a man of the wilderness, in time even a king's palace could become a prison. Perhaps Zaphenath-paneah was not insane after all.

⚡

TARIK SUMMONED MANDISA AND ANI, the steward, to the foyer off the vizier's bedchamber. "Our master is with Pharaoh for the rest of the day," the captain said, lifting his head in unconscious pride, "and he has instructed me to tell you what we shall do with this captive in our house. We three shall deal with him. None of the others shall have access to the prisoner."

And two of us, Mandisa thought, watching Tarik with an observant eye, *know who and what he is. But though he is the vizier's own brother, he is dangerous, too powerful to be held here . . .*

The steward bowed his bald head as a sign of respect, an unnecessary gesture because Ani was at least as important as Tarik in the villa's social system. An Egyptian steward ran the house, overseeing and orchestrating every action from simple housekeeping and meal preparation to the fields, granaries, and livestock. And though Ani looked like a little wet bird, behind his self-deprecating facade lay a dynamic mind, a force born of wisdom and certainty. Of no steward in Thebes was more expected, and none of the others came close to duplicating the elegance and prosperity of Zaphenath-paneah's estate.

"I was curious about the man," Ani admitted, his lined mouth cracking in a smile. "I found the circumstances of this morning quite . . . *unusual.*"

"We are not to talk of this man with the children or the other servants," Tarik went on. "His needs are to be met daily."

The captain's eyes turned toward Mandisa. "If you are willing, lady, the master asks if you will consent to take the prisoner his food and tarry if he feels the need for conversation. There are few here who speak the Canaanite tongue as fluently as you do."

Mandisa paused. She knew her master well enough to know he would not command her to obey his wish, for she carried a full work load attending to the vizier's wife and sons as well as Adom. She had every right to decline the job of caring for a captive with the temperament of an underfed lion, especially when the smoldering flame in his eyes frightened her.

But no one else spoke his language. And she knew the pain of not understanding or being understood.

"Do not worry, I will get one of my guards to tend to him," the captain said, waving his hand.

"There is no need, I'll do it," she said, avoiding Tarik's eyes.

"So be it." The captain tilted his head as if he weighed her motives. "If at any time you wish to surrender this responsibility, you may."

"I understand."

"I see." Tarik pressed his lips together. "The master will periodically ask you for news of this captive. You are to speak freely with Zaphenath-paneah, apprising him of anything that happens with the prisoner while he is with us. Such information may be useful in the future."

"Of course." Mandisa lifted a brow and turned toward Ani. "I am not accustomed to working in the kitchens. Halima is a kitchen slave; may I have her help to prepare the captive's meals?" She looked back to the captain of the guard, "And is it permissible for me to take Halima with me when I visit this herdsman? I would fear for my safety if I ventured into his room alone."

Tarik and Ani studied each other, then Ani folded his arms. "If it is to fulfill the master's wish, you may use any slaves you please."

"I see no harm taking the girl with you," Tarik added. "But no one else is to visit him. Only we three, and the slave Halima if you need her. Of course, if you feel threatened at any time, you may call one of the guards to stand outside the door."

Mandisa nodded. "Thank you."

"Is there anything else?" Ani asked.

"No." Tarik thrust his hands into his sword belt. "Let us hope the uncouth beast remains silent and does not disturb the household. I will beg the gods of Egypt to swiftly return his brothers so we may be rid of him."

CHAPTER SEVEN

YOSEF DISMISSED HIS GUARDS AT THE GATE OF HIS VILLA AND WALKED
alone up the winding pathway through his courtyard. He felt hollow, lifeless, totally spent by the affairs of the day. The meeting with his brothers
had drained him completely and his afternoon with the young Pharaoh
left him feeling like a man twice his age. His back ached between his
shoulder blades; he knew his face looked pale and pinched. More than
once Amenhotep had asked what troubled his most trusted friend and
counselor. Yosef only smiled and said that Pharaoh would understand
once he had established a family of his own.

The hot night was so quiet that Yosef thought he could hear the
lapping of wavelets on the shore of the Nile outside the walls of his estate.
The sun had dropped behind the western Theban cliffs, joining the dead
in the Valley of the Kings. Torches burned along the pathway, pushing at
the gloom, and the noise of laughter echoed from the slaves' chambers,
warming the courtyard with sounds of life.

Yosef's heart lifted. His brothers had come and gone, expanding and
emptying his heart in the space of twenty-four hours, but Shim'on
remained behind, breathing the same darkness, hearing the same heart-
warming sounds. What was he thinking, the one they called the
Destroyer?

Yosef followed a branch of the courtyard path to the small temple of his estate. Like the temples of other Theban villas, the elegant structure had been designed to hold images of the household's gods, but his temple stood empty, without idols or trays of burning incense. Yosef had only allowed Ani to install two torches that burned through the night in case a visitor wanted to enter the temple and pray.

Yosef knew his servants thought it odd that their devout master did not worship a visible god, for everyone knew that Egypt grew gods as abundantly as the black, fertile land grew grain. When Tuthmosis IV elevated Yosef from prison to the palace, however, that Pharaoh proclaimed that the spirit of God rested upon the man who would henceforth be known as Zaphenath-paneah. After his divine proclamation, no one in Thebes, or all of Egypt, would dare doubt the significance of the vizier's beliefs. Those who knew him understood that he worshipped the invisible and almighty God known in the Canaanite tongue as El Shaddai. The Egyptians had another name for this most ancient deity: *Neter*, the almighty God who was One.

The torches cast a dim light in the small temple, and Yosef leaned against the doorpost and studied the small chamber. In deference to the master's chosen God, Ani had painted the wall above the empty altar with the picture sign for Neter, an ax-head fastened to a long wooden handle by thongs of leather.

A smile ruffled Yosef's mouth as he studied the drawing. "The mightiest man in ancient days was he who had the best weapon and could wield it with the greatest effect," he murmured, crossing his arms. "If your power, El Shaddai, were an ax, how well did I display it today?"

The still, small voice he had heard a dozen times before did not answer, and Yosef lowered his eyes. "I do not know if they will come again. And I do not know what I shall do with Shim'on if they do not."

Wait.

A thrill shivered through his senses. His heart recognized the Voice, more a certainty than an audible sound, and Yosef closed his eyes. God had brought him to this place; God would keep him. And obviously God had not yet finished His work.

Humming , he turned and walked toward the house.

"MY HUSBAND?"

Yosef stirred on his bed, struggling to find wakefulness through the embracing folds of sleep.

"My husband, Ani is here with his morning report. Shall I send him away?"

"No," Yosef said, forcing his eyes to open. He sat up, throwing off the linen sheet that covered him, and ran his hand through his close-cropped hair. Age had not lessened his strength, but it had increased his requirement for rest and recovery. But the pressing needs of a Pharaoh, a kingdom, and an estate could not wait.

"Tell Ani to come in," he said, focusing on Asenath for the first time. She hung shyly about the doorway, a vision of loveliness even at this hour of the morning. Youth and freshness still radiated from her oval face; she had grown from an attractive girl to a beautiful woman. When she smiled at him, he held out a hand, beckoning her closer. "Why do you linger in the doorway like a child?" he said, his voice gruff with sleep. "Come and kiss me, wife."

She flew to him like a bird, wrapping her arms about his neck and covering his face with happy kisses. "I've missed you, beloved," she said, the scent of her perfume warming his senses. "You were busy from sunrise to sundown yesterday. Your sons and I sorely missed you."

"And I have missed you," Yosef murmured. He smiled against her mouth and drew her into his arms, returning her kiss.

"My lord and master, live forever." Ani's voice, brimming with suppressed humor, interrupted their embrace.

Yosef lifted his lips from Asenath's long enough to command the steward away. "For the space of a few moments, at least," Yosef called, nuzzling his wife's neck. "I would like to spend some time with the lady of the house."

The old man chuckled and moved into the hall. "As you wish, my lord."

"A few moments?" Asenath asked, a teasing note in her voice. She buried her face against his throat. "Why not longer?"

Yosef laughed as he stroked her cheek. "Because Pharaoh will demand to see me this morning. And before I go to him I must check on the captive in our house."

"Pharaoh does not sneeze without asking your advice first," Asenath answered, tweaking his ear. "And the prisoner is in Tarik's custody. He will not escape or do harm."

She kissed him with her eyes, and he met her lips with his own, tempted by the idea of a sweet rendezvous with his beloved wife. When a nagging thought intruded, however, he pulled his face away and regarded her with gentle reproach.

"How long has it been since your red moon flowed?"

Her lips shaped into a pretty pout. "I don't know, husband. Mandisa keeps account of these things."

"Asenath—tell me. Don't be coy."

Her lower lip edged forward. "I'm certain it's all right, beloved."

"How many days?"

She closed her eyes in a gesture of defeat. "One week. Ten days."

He sighed, amazed at her careless attitude. Though the physicians had warned her that another pregnancy might cost her life, Asenath seemed not to care.

He brushed a gentle kiss across her forehead. "Not today, my love, it is too dangerous. I would not risk losing you for a hour of pleasure."

Her hands tightened around his neck. Even now, her painted eyes teased and caressed him. If he could not escape the tumultuous feelings she aroused . . .

"Ani!" he called over her shoulder, pulling her hands from his neck. "I am ready to hear from you."

Asenath stood and brushed wrinkles from her gown, unspoken pain glowing in her eyes.

"I'm sorry, my love. When the time of conception is past—"

44

"Of course," she said, moving away. She threw a falsely bright smile toward him as she moved through the doorway. "Your steward is here, my lord."

"Send him in."

Yosef lowered his feet to the floor and buried his face in his hands, grateful that Ani would demand nothing of him so early in the morning.

ASENATH KEPT her composure until she reentered her chamber, then she sank to her bed and covered her face as the salty tears of despair splashed her fingertips. Life was not fair! Of all the women in Thebes, she should have been the most blessed, for everything Zaphenath-paneah touched thrived and blossomed under his care. His God had blessed him with beauty, wealth, power, wisdom, and the adoration of the Egyptian nation, yet wagging tongues throughout the royal court were proclaiming that the vizier's wife could no longer bear him children.

She loved Efrayim and Menashe dearly, but their lives had been won without a struggle; they fell from her womb as easily as she had learned to love her husband. A powerful man needed many sons, and Zaphenath-paneah should have had more than a dozen. Yet she could offer only two. Three times she had conceived children and failed to bring them into the world, and now, at twenty-three, the bloom of her youth was fading. Once she had asked her husband if he would be willing to sleep with Mandisa in order to gain more sons, but he shook his head and smiled at her in tender refusal. He kept insisting he was happy, and he took pains that she should not conceive again, yet Asenath did not believe that a man in his position could be satisfied with only two sons.

Rumors from the palace did not help her anxious state of mind. Tattling tongues and jealous palace rivals had often gossiped that Asenath's beloved cherished a secret love for Queen Tuya, Pharaoh's royal mother. Within the last week, Asenath heard that Zaphenath-paneah had once asked Queen Tuya to marry him. And only a few months ago, a rival to the throne had accused the vizier of fathering Pharaoh Amenhotep.

Her beloved was cleared of the charge and his accusers sent into exile, but a shadow of doubt lingered in Asenath's mind. Queen Tuya was breathtakingly lovely, even for a mature woman, and she and Zaphenath-paneah shared a past of which Asenath could never be a part . . .

Her husband loved her, she knew he did. But they were fifteen years apart in age, and she often suspected that he thought of her as someone to please and pet, a child to spoil. She had been a mere girl when Pharaoh Tuthmosis IV presented her to the newly proclaimed vizier as a prize, and Zaphenath-paneah had guided her to womanhood and thrilled her with the power of his unseen and almighty God. She *had* been a child, easily impressed, devoutly in love with her husband's beauty and character, overwhelmed by his integrity and kindness.

During the years of plenty she had loved him with the ardent hero-worship of an adolescent. Now that she had reached maturity she yearned to love him as an equal, a *partner*. But what could she do to foster such love? He did not need her to manage the estate. Ani ably handled the house, the fields, and the government of the vizier's villa. The steward made certain that Efrayim and Menashe received instruction from the most capable tutors in the kingdom. Tarik controlled the guards and the force of men necessary to safeguard the vizier's family. Mandisa saw to every personal need Asenath or her sons might have ever anticipated.

If she were to become more than her husband's child-bride, she would have to prove herself worthy of him. She would have to provide something no one else could: sons.

She wiped her tears from her eyes, gathering her courage. Until now she had been willing to wait and hope that her husband's desire for more children would override his insistence that she was not strong enough to endure another pregnancy. But her patient waiting had come to an end. She had stolen a look at his ten brothers; she had inwardly trembled after seeing his reaction to their reunion. Though he had tried to hide his feelings, his meeting with them had left him sorely shaken. His eyes had glinted with hope and fear and something else . . . a sense of *completeness*, an overriding joy at being reunited with his family.

She herself had been overwhelmed by the realization that a single man could have twelve powerful sons, any one of whom would stand out in a crowd. And her husband, the brightest of them all, had only two.

She clenched her jaw to kill the sob in her throat. She would have to do something. If Zaphenath-paneah would not sleep with her handmaid or take another wife, Asenath would bear him sons herself. And since her husband's invisible God had been unable to give life to the children within her womb, she would return to the gods of her childhood.

Her father served as a high priest at On, known more familiarly as Heliopolis. Tomorrow she would arrange for a caravan; she would go home and consult her father about her situation. And while she sojourned at Heliopolis, the primeval birthplace of the earth, she would beg her father's gods for another son.

Zaphenath-paneah would not like the idea of her journeying so far to worship another god . . . but what her husband did not know could not disturb him.

CHAPTER EIGHT

SHIM'ON STIRRED ON HIS BED AS SOUNDS OF ACTIVITY REACHED HIS EAR.
Cattle lowed in the stockyard; outside his chamber Egyptian slaves
laughed and chattered as they went about their morning chores. Occasionally he heard the squeak of saddles and the shudder of horses, the
magnificent animals he had only glimpsed from a distance. On this
morning the scents of hot dry earth mingled with the lusty odors of dust
and livestock, and the mouth-watering aroma of baking bread wafted into
his room from the kitchens.

How clever was this vizier, how fiendishly evil! While pretending to
attend to Shim'on's comfort, this maniac of ferocious genius had instead
arranged for even sounds and smells to torture his captive. Of what
comfort was a spacious, well-furnished room when the man inside
yearned to be outdoors in the discipline of the sun? To hear horses and
not examine them was agony; to smell baking bread and not taste it was
an exquisite torture. He had been given a soft bed; he was used to sleeping
in the sand with his head pillowed upon a rock. Four stout walls isolated
him from the activity of the household; Shim'on was accustomed to the
constant company of his brothers, his sons, and his servants. Someone
had left a breakfast of fruit and milk on a tray inside the door, he wanted
goat meat and honey over rough brown bread.

How long could he endure such bedevilment? He could have borne the claustrophobia of the prison pit better than the soft succor of this brightly painted room.

Frustrated beyond endurance, he closed his eyes and screamed in fury.

CHAPTER NINE

"Use the green eye color today, Mandisa," Asenath said the next morning, peering into her looking brass with a perturbed expression. "We are going to visit my father at Heliopolis. He mustn't think that I look tired or aged."

Mandisa managed a diplomatic laugh as she picked up the delicate alabaster kohl pot containing her mistress's favorite color. "You are five years younger than me, my lady. If you are aged, then I am as old as Pharaoh's beard."

Asenath stared into the mirror, then burst out laughing. Though only twelve and unable to grow a beard himself, Amenhotep wore the royal beard of state on all official occasions. The long, narrow braided hairpiece, attached to the king's chin by straps which hung over his ears, had been worn by a succession of pharaohs, including Hatshepsut, a woman who ruled in her young son's place for twenty-one years.

Mandisa smiled at the light of joy in her mistress's eyes. After the death of her last baby, Asenath had been troubled and depressed for many months. She had done nothing but lie on her bed and moan that she had nothing to offer her husband. But on this morning, at least, Asenath seemed happy to put the past behind her.

"What will you wear, my lady?" Mandisa asked. She pulled the polished stone applicator from the narrow tube and gently stirred the iridescent mixture that would sparkle like the waters of the sunlit Nile on her mistress's eyelids.

"I think," Asenath answered, closing her eyes while Mandisa applied her cosmetics, "I shall wear the new beaded gown wrought for me last week. And the fringed wig with many layers. My father has an appreciative eye for the new fashions."

"A good choice, my lady." Mandisa lowered the alabaster container and picked up the black kohl pot to outline her lady's eyes. As she stirred the applicator in the narrow tube, she wondered if she dared ask what had brought on this desire to visit the priest of Heliopolis. Mandisa could not remember Asenath ever venturing out to visit her father. The venerable priest had come to Thebes only three times: once to pay his respects upon Pharaoh's coronation, and twice to congratulate his daughter after the birth of her sons.

"I know what you are thinking." Asenath looked at Mandisa with a faint gleam of reproach in her eyes. "You may as well ask. You'll worm the answers out of me sooner or later."

Mandisa felt an unwelcome blush creep into her cheeks. "It does not matter why you want to visit your father, my lady. My only wish is to serve you."

An easy smile played at the corners of her mistress's mouth. "Then serve me well in this: whatever I may do in Heliopolis, you need not mention it to my husband."

Mandisa bowed her head. "As you wish. But if you have need of anything, I am certain my lord the vizier would move heaven and earth to procure it for you."

"What I need the vizier cannot procure for me," Asenath said, picking up the looking brass again. "And I have tried to move heaven, but my prayers to the invisible God have availed nothing. I will speak to my father and sacrifice in his sacred temple. Then we shall see if my petitions are successful."

51

MANDISA HURRIED through the hall of the villa toward the spacious kitchen. She had less than a quarter of an hour to say farewell to Adom, take the vizier's captive his daily ration, and meet her mistress in the courtyard to join the caravan to Heliopolis. For an instant she regretted her decision to serve the rugged Canaanite—she was a ladies' maid, after all, and unaccustomed to the ways of brutish goat herders, even if they were the vizier's half-brothers. But Zaphenath-paneah had asked. And since the day he had found her abandoned, impoverished, and desperate enough to sell herself and her son into slavery, she had not been able to refuse her gracious master anything.

She found Halima in the kitchen, her round face flushed by the heat from the fiery ovens. "Hurry, help me prepare the tray and let us be on our way," Mandisa said, wiping a trickle of perspiration from her forehead. Her braided wig seemed unusually hot and heavy, and she found herself wishing she could go bareheaded like Halima.

Halima pressed her hands to her ample chest and cast Mandisa a frightened glance. "Must I go with you again into *that* room?"

"Yes."

"But he is so loud! You did not hear him, for his room lies far away from the family quarters, but yesterday he screamed for more than an hour. Though I couldn't understand a word of what he said, I'm sure he cursed us, our master, and even Pharaoh himself."

"Then he shall answer to us, our master, and even Pharaoh," Mandisa said, placing a tray in Halima's outstretched hands. Rummaging through baskets, bowls, and jars, she selected foods she thought the man might like—a hearty helping of ox meat basted with sweet-scented honey, a bowl of brown beans and chick peas mixed with lotus seeds and flavored with marjoram, coriander, and dill. She grabbed a slice of bread that had already been softened with water, and a jug of beer flavored with pomegranates and figs.

"This platter is fit for Pharaoh's table," Halima said, eyeing the food with a covetous glance, "but the loathsome toad to whom it is going will not appreciate one bite."

"He's not a loathsome toad," Mandisa said, moving through the doorway ahead of Halima. "A loud one, perhaps, but not loathsome."

SHIM'ON STIFFENED as he heard the wooden bolt slide away from the door. The treble murmur of voices informed him that the two women stood outside; the pretty one who spoke his language and the hefty one with eyes as wide and nervous as a rabbit's.

He bit back an oath, annoyed that they did not send someone more daunting to deal with him. Did no one know or care that a son of Yaakov was imprisoned in this heathen's house? Yaakov was Yisrael, the keeper of God Almighty's covenant promise to bless the entire world! Yaakov was a leader among the people of Canaan, a wealthy man and a respected one. And Shim'on was his second-born son!

The door opened, the timid woman held it while the pretty one walked in and placed the tray on a stand near the bed. She had courage, he had to admit, especially since he had recently decided to do whatever he could to make the Egyptian vizier regret his decision to imprison a son of Yisrael.

The woman swallowed hard, lifted her chin, and boldly met his gaze. "Have you need of anything today?" she asked, speaking his language. "Have you any news for my master the vizier?"

"I want proper food." He made a face as he poked a finger into the mushy bread. "Real meat cooked over charcoal, not boiled to mush in a pot."

She turned away, ignoring him. How dare she! His mouth tightening with mutiny, he scooped up the hunk of meat and flung it across the room. True to his aim, the congealed glop missed her head by inches and struck the wall. Like a living creature, it clung to the painted plaster, then slid downward, marking the wall with a sticky brown trail.

The timorous woman squeaked and covered her mouth with her hands, but the slender one wheeled toward him, her hands on her hips. "If you continue to waste your food in such a way," she said in the tight tone she might have used to scold a child, "you will starve. The vizier's cooks do not feed men who do not appreciate their efforts."

"I would rather starve with my brothers than eat this rot."

"Your brothers," she said, tossing the words at him like stones, "are neither starving nor complaining. The vizier sent them away with bags of Egypt's best grain and their treasure as well. They have their silver, their bellies are full, and, because you are gone, they are enjoying peaceful quiet, probably for the first time in their lives!"

"Careful, woman." Rancor sharpened his voice. "She who uses a sharp tongue will cut her own throat."

"You'd do well to heed your own advice," she answered, picking up the tray. Without another word, she turned to leave.

"Wait," he called, putting out a hand to stop her. She jerked away at his touch, revulsion on her face.

"What sort of game is your master playing?" he asked, choosing to overlook her expression. "Why does he accuse my brothers of spying and then fulfill their request to buy grain? And why would he return their silver?" He lowered his voice. "Is he truly mad?"

She paused, a flutter of apprehension shadowing her face. "I do not question my master," she answered, moving toward the door. "And you should not. His way is not always my way, but he holds my life in his hands—as he holds yours."

"He holds nothing of mine," Shim'on retorted. He lay back and crossed his hands under his head. "And yes, I have a message for your master. Tell him I defy him. Tell him I intend to make his life miserable; indeed, I will make you all miserable until he releases me. Or let him kill me, I care not. But if my brothers return and learn that I am no longer here, your master will have to deal with Yaakov of Hebron."

The slender woman handed the tray to the fearful slave, then turned and faced Shim'on, every curve of her body speaking defiance. "You will not order me around," she answered, lifting her chin. "I am not a slave, but a free woman and handmaid to Lady Asenath. I am here because my master cares whether or not you are comfortable. If I were you, I would try to show a bit of gratitude."

"Your master may rot in Sheol!" Shim'on retorted, rolling to his feet. He clenched a fist, ready to strike something, but she saw the gesture and hurried through the doorway.

"If anger is your meat, you may have it for dinner," she said, throwing him a bright smile. "We will take ourselves out of your way."

He picked up a vase and flung it toward her, but the woman slammed the door. Amid the shattering of pottery, Shim'on heard the bolt slide into place.

CHAPTER TEN

LIKE A CAGED ANIMAL, SHIM'ON PACED BACK AND FORTH IN HIS DARKNESS of his chamber. The sun had not yet risen; soft gray shadows still decorated the bed, the chair, and the chest against the wall. He hated the gilded luxury; the room was nothing but a pleasure palace for simple, soft Egyptians. But the endless solitary confinement, without the company of his brothers or any who could even speak his language, tortured Shim'on worse than physical pain.

He had considered and abandoned every means of escape within his first two hours of confinement. Only one door led into the room, and his captors kept it barred and bolted. He would not be able to dig through the polished marble floor with his bare hands, and he had no tools. Even if he could chisel a passage through the thick walls, they only led to other hallways in the villa. Two high windows brought in air and light from the outside, but though they were as wide as Shim'on was tall, they were no more than a hand's length in height. A child might have been able to shimmy through the opening and drop to ground below, but Shim'on could never manage it.

He had never been so alone in his forty-five years, and Shim'on was horrified to realize that solitude terrified him. With no human companionship to distract him, ghosts rose in his memory, and he spent his daylight hours pacing as if he could outrun them. In moments of unendurable frustration he pounded the walls, cracking the shiny plaster, then fell upon his bed, slumped in morose musings. When tides of weariness and despair completely engulfed his body, merciful darkness and sleep finally pressed down upon him.

But he could not find rest even in sleep. Often he dreamed that he stood in the center of a burning lake, unable to escape a dry heat that split his lips and parched his tongue. Other nights he would awaken in a cold sweat, convinced that whole sections of his body had been torn away. Shivering in the dark, Shim'on tasted thoughts as bitter as gall until the night finally grayed into dawn. Instead of relief, however, the sun brought a new resolve to thwart his captors and a fresh hatred for Zaphenath-paneah and all things Egyptian.

At his moments of greatest loneliness he yearned to see the dark-eyed interpreter, reasoning that hostile discourse with an acid-tongued wench was better than no conversation at all. But she had not appeared since the day she warned him that anger would be his dinner. Now only the pale, plump servant brought his food, and she was always accompanied by the small, tightly muscled man in charge of the vizier's guard.

Their morning routine did not vary: the guard would slide the bolt and open the door, a strong light of disapproval in his eyes as he stared at Shim'on. As quick as a rat down a rope, the female slave would rush in, leave the tray on its stand, empty the sand-filled drawer under the wooden toilet seat into a refuse container, and hurry out of the room. The guard never spoke, but watched Shim'on with speculative eyes until the slave girl had safely departed. Then the door would close, and the bolt rumble into place.

Shim'on stopped his pacing and slammed his fist against the wall, his breath burning in his throat. Oh, if only Levi were with him! Levi was cunning and clever, he'd think of some way to get the guard into the chamber. While one of them held the sloe-eyed Egyptian in a rear hug-hold, the other would grab the guard's sword and cut the tendon at the man's ankle. After a front snap-kick to the Egyptian's groin, they'd leave him gasping on the floor while they stole horses from the courtyard. The

Egyptians would try to catch them, but Shim'on and Levi would be halfway to Hebron before the vizier and his men gathered their wits and launched a pursuit.

But he was alone, without Levi, without Re'uven, without even the younger ones like Yissakhar and Zevulun. They were home with their wives and children, and they might not even think of him . . .

Did they think of him? Had any of his brothers made plans for his rescue? If Re'uven or Levi had been taken prisoner, Shim'on would have rallied the others to storm this vizier's house. Yisrael possessed great wealth, and though the Egyptian vizier was undeniably clever, he was obviously not well-informed. If Zaphenath-paneah had known who Yaakov of Hebron was, he would have asked for compensation and arranged for Shim'on's return. Yaakov's second-born son was certainly worth his weight in silver, unless. . .

Would his father care enough to send a ransom for the Destroyer? His father did not like him for many reasons, but chiefly because he sprang from Lea, not the lovely Rahel. Binyamin was the only fruit remaining from that beloved wife.

Shim'on slid into a crouch and hugged his knees to his chest. With every passing morning he wondered if his father might not be more willing to let Shim'on languish in prison and the rest of the family starve than to send Binyamin, his nearest and best-beloved son, to Egypt.

Shim'on bit his lip until it throbbed in time with his pulse. He had never thought he could miss the babble of his brothers' bickering or the sound of women complaining. Even the laughter of the children, which had always grated on Shim'on's nerves, would be welcome in this heathen's house. Except for a busy hour in the morning and mealtime at noon, this Egyptian palace was altogether too quiet. Though he occasionally heard the lowing of cattle and the distant thunder of drumming horses' hooves, the sounds of running water from the garden muted the rich sounds of community.

Simon let his head fall back to the wall. A faint glow low from the opposite window told him that the sun had crossed her threshold. He tilted his head and listened for the sound of approaching footsteps. Today he would insult the guard again. He might even threaten the slave girl. He'd do anything he could to rouse the man to anger, for if the captain lost his temper, perhaps he would drag Shim'on before the vaunted vizier. He would yet show the great Zaphenath-paneah how fierce a son of Yisrael could be.

His heart thumped against his rib cage at the soft sound of voices and the patter of sandaled feet. The woman and captain stood outside, doubtless eager to get this despised chore out of the way before they began their day. He heard a whisper at the door, then the dull grumble of the beam as it slid from its place.

The door opened, the guard's blank eyes met his. Shim'on stood, eager to face his jailers.

"Speak to me, you whose breath is fouler than a lizard's," he growled, moving forward, but the stalwart Egyptian did not respond. The woman paused and glanced at the guard; he nodded and placed his hand upon his sword. The unspoken message was clear: *move and I will strike.*

Shim'on tensed, debating his options. Every fiber of his being screamed for action. The Egyptian captain came only to Shim'on's shoulder, he was not a great threat, but he was quick. He would draw his blade if Shim'on lunged, and the woman would panic and might be hurt in the struggle . . .

Shim'on could not, would not be responsible for hurting a woman. Not after what had happened to Dina.

Reluctantly, he stepped back.

Taking a deep, unsteady breath, the woman advanced into the room, lowered the tray to its stand, and scurried to clean the toilet area. Shim'on crossed his arms and would have moved to the bed, but a muscle flicked at the guard's jaw, and Shim'on understood the unspoken warning. The mighty vizier had probably told the guards that this Canaanite was no great prize and would not be missed if his death proved unavoidable.

As the woman went about her work, the guard stood motionless in the doorway, his painted eyes narrowing into a thoughtful expression. What was the man thinking? Did the idolatrous dog dare mock a son of Yaakov? In a silent fury, Shim'on slammed his arm onto the fragile table next to him, shattering the delicate wood. The slave screamed, nearly dropping the burden in her arms, but the guard only lifted a brow.

"You will not jeer at me, you demon-eyed jackal," Shim'on roared, fury nearly choking him. "You think I am your captive, but I am only waiting until my brothers return. Then, you devil, you shall know the full fury of Yaakov's wrath, you shall see the power of Yisrael's God unleashed upon this land!"

Though the outburst left Shim'on seething, the captain only motioned for the slave girl to hurry about her duties. As she finished her work, the guard folded his arms and stared at Shim'on. His brows flickered as he spoke in the Canaanite language: "My master commands me to wish you peace." After making that simple declaration, he stepped back and motioned for the slave girl to leave.

Shim'on watched in wordless amazement as the woman hurried past. Like a child who gazes at an animal in mingled wonder and fear, she lifted her eyes and stole a terrified glance at his face.

Shim'on sank onto his bed as his eyes clouded with visions of the past. His bride had worn just such an expression when he had carried her to his tent . . .

CHAPTER ELEVEN

HIS FIRST WIFE HAD LIVED IN THE CITY OF SHEKHEM, THE PROSPEROUS walled town situated in the green valley between Mount Ebal and Mount Gerizim. As the children of Yisrael prepared to move their flocks and tents into the region, Yaakov, who had been strong and confident in those days, reminded his sons that when Avraham set out from Ur of the Chaldeans, he and his people passed through the country as far as Shekhem. "There the Lord appeared to my father's father and said, 'To your descendants I will give this land,'" Yaakov announced one night at dinner, his hand falling upon young Yosef's shoulder as he spoke. "And so to you and your descendants, my sons, this land will one day belong."

Shim'on had not fully understood why Yaakov chose to reenter Canaan after so long an absence. He had been only twenty-two at the time, and ignorant of the situation that led to the dispute between his father and his uncle, Esav. He only knew that one morning Yaakov woke up determined to lead his people and possessions from the region of Haran to the land God had promised.

Shim'on left his youth and idealism behind forever on the day Esav marched with four hundred men to meet his brother, Yaakov. There, in a visible display for the entire world to see, Yaakov defined the depths and limits of his love, and Shim'on saw his uncle for the first time.

Yaakov had ordered that gifts for Esav be sent to the front of the procession: she-goats, two hundred, and kids, twenty; ewes, two hundred, and rams, twenty; nursing camels and their young, thirty; cows, forty, and bulls, ten; she-asses, twenty, and colts, ten.

After the generous gifts, Yaakov's own herds of cattle, sheep, and goats followed.

Finally, Yaakov advanced his family. The two female slaves, handmaids to Yaakov's wives, mounted donkeys. With their four sons, they fell into line behind the flocks and herds. Shim'on remembered the gritty taste of desert sand between his teeth as he stood beside his mother, waiting for his father to lead them to meet the brother he feared. But Yaakov had not even glanced their way. "Lea, you and your children will proceed next," he called over his shoulder, his dark eyes squinting toward the distant horizon.

"My lord?" Lea cried, stunned to the point of tears. But Yaakov had been too engrossed in what might happen to hear her.

"Go now, and your sons with you," he said, gesturing toward them as if they were stray cattle. "Have the older boys take care of Dina. Do not fear, for I will go ahead of all of you. But take care that Rahel and Yosef remain at the back of the procession, in case trouble lies ahead."

In that instant, with fearful clarity Shim'on understood a lifetime of his mother's tears, his aunt's victorious smile, and his father's haggard expression. His father did not love his mother. He loved Rahel, Yosef's mother, the beautiful wife who now struggled with the nausea of another pregnancy.

It stood in front of the morning, that truth, killing all joy. In that moment, the larger-than-life enthusiasm with which Shim'on had always confronted the world compressed into a shrinking space between the weight of his mother's despair and his own welling anger. How could his father treat his first wife with such blatant indifference?

Reluctantly, his movements stiff and awkward, Shim'on followed his mother and brothers in the procession. The harder he tried to deny the truth, the more it persisted. He had always accepted his father's aloofness as a natural part of the world, yet Yaakov had now cut through the veil of assumption and revealed his true feelings. If Esav comes with an approaching army to kill us all, Yaakov's actions proclaimed, let him kill me, the maids and their children, Lea and her sons, but Rahel and Yosef must remain alive to inherit God's blessing.

The bitterness of gall rose in Shim'on's throat as the desert wind slashed and shoved against him and his brothers. Beside him, his mother's pale face, red-rimmed eyes, and quivering chin revealed her unspoken hurt.

For the first time, Shim'on understood the reason for her pain.

ESAV HAD NOT COME to kill, but to forgive. With joy and praise, Yaakov, now known as Yisrael, reentered the land of his father. After some weeks, he came to the town of Shekhem and bought a piece of land from Hamor. There he erected an altar and called it El-Elohe-Yisrael, *God, the God of Yisrael*. Shim'on watched his father worship the almighty God called El Shaddai, but his heart, filled with bitterness for his mother's pitiable plight, was not stirred by his father's fervent reverence.

In the camp, Shim'on now watched the usual comings and goings of his family with enlightened, wary eyes. Rahel, her maid, and her children lived in one spacious, well-appointed tent; Lea dwelt with her handmaid and her younger children in another tent not nearly as large or luxurious.

Yaakov's older sons, Re'uven, Shim'on, Levi, Yehuda, Dan, and Naftali, had long since left the women's tents to sleep under the stars with the flocks they guarded. Re'uven and Levi had already begun to talk about taking wives for themselves, but Shim'on could not bring himself to discuss marriage, especially not in his mother's presence. Couldn't the others see the pain in her pale eyes? Were they going to abandon her, too?

Of all Lea's children, Shim'on supposed that Dina might have special empathy for their mother's sorrow. After all, Dina was a woman, too, albeit a young one. But he soon discovered that his fourteen year-old sister's sympathy turned in only one direction: inward.

One afternoon not long after their arrival at Shekhem, he found Dina sitting outside Lea's tent, her lanky form bent into an ungraceful crouch, her face covered by her hands.

Shim'on knelt beside her. "What ails you, Sister?" His voice sounded more abrupt than he'd intended, so he made an effort to soften his tone. "This wind is biting, you should go inside."

"Not with her," Dina whispered. She lifted tear-filled eyes to his face. "I'll not stay inside with Mother one more minute. Rahel isn't feeling well and Mother is upset. She has taken to her bed with a headache, and she blames me for everything."

"What could you have done to upset her?" Shim'on pushed a tangle of curls away from her wide forehead. "Rahel carries a baby, she can't help her sickness. And you ought to be more help to Mother. She does not have an easy time of it here."

"*She* does not have an easy time?" Dina shrieked, an edge of desperation in her voice. "She is a wife of Yaakov, the wealthiest and most respected man in Canaan. She has a maid, servants, and the costliest clothing a woman could want. Her husband is respected in the city yonder; by her our father has eight sons."

"But has she his love?" Shim'on's gaze drifted toward Rahel's tent. Even above the dull roar of the constant wind he could hear Yosef's carefree laughter spilling from that habitation. "Think, Dina, of the pain our mother endures. Think of what she must face every night when Father finishes his dinner and then goes to—" he inclined his head—"the *other* tent."

"I don't care!" Dina screwed up her face like a petulant child. "Mother doesn't have to live with twelve brothers! Mother isn't the only girl; she has a sister! She has never known what is like to be the only daughter."

Shim'on was tempted to slap sense into the overgrown girl's head, but he only grunted in disapproval. "You talk like a spoiled brat."

"No." Her voice grew still, and through the dark arch made by her falling hair he saw a tear run down her cheek. "Look at me, Shim'on," she whispered, her tone light and bitter. "I am a woman. I am old enough to take a husband, but my father and my mother care more for their sons' plans than for their only daughter's. They have not given one thought toward finding me a husband. There has been more discussion about finding wives for you and Re'uven and Levi."

"I do not want a wife," Shim'on said, bored with the conversation. He slapped sand from his legs and stood. "And if you are wise, little sister, you will go about your business and rejoice that you are a daughter of Yisrael. Even if you never marry, your life will still be richer and fuller than any Canaanite girl's."

He reached out to pat her head, but Dina ducked, retreating from his reach. She closed her eyes and shook her head, signaling that he had transgressed the bounds of human understanding.

"You are a fool, Shim'on." She stared past him as the wind blew the mane of tangled curls across her oval face. "You will never understand."

"You are the one who does not understand," he said, listening to the sound of his mother's weeping from inside her tent.

DINA WANDERED AWAY, alone, from the family compound that day, and the next, and the next after that, but Shim'on paid her no mind. She was probably sulking in the desert, he imagined, or trying to incite them to worry about her. She would hide if he went out to search for her, so he would not give her the satisfaction of knowing that he missed her. But because the Canaanites considered unmarried women legitimate prey, Shim'on slipped away from his flocks each night and hiked back to the family tents long enough to make certain Dina slept in her usual place beside Lea.

One afternoon he found his sister where he least expected to see her. He and his brothers had been moving the herds from one field to another, and at the well he saw a group of gaily-painted girls. The Canaanite women were godless idolaters, Yaakov had warned his sons, and the sons of Yisrael were not to speak to them. But forbidden fruit casts a sweet spell, and Shim'on found his gaze drifting toward the chattering group of women as he and his brothers approached.

The painted courtesans said nothing, but coyly continued their giggling conversation until the sons of Yisrael were nearly upon them. Without warning, one of the unveiled girls shrieked and sprinted toward the wide gate of the walled city. "Shim'on!" Re'uven cried, disbelief echoing in his voice, "That was our sister!"

Shim'on started to object, but glanced toward the girls again. The remaining circle of women had stopped their chattering to stare at the sons of Yaakov with stone-cold eyes. Why would they do such a thing unless Dina had poisoned them with lies?

"Dina!" Shim'on gripped his shepherd's staff and ran toward the city, his sandaled feet skimming the sandy ground. "Dina, daughter of Yaakov, come out! I must take you home!"

The gray stone of the city's protecting wall loomed in his vision and he halted before the gate. A knot of men had gathered there, and they blocked his path, staring at him in undisguised curiosity. The people of Yisrael had not had many dealings with the men of Shekhem, and Shim'on instinctively knew he would not be welcomed in the city.

Craning his neck, he peered past the men. Beyond the gate, the city hummed with busy women and romping children, people going about their daily affairs. But nowhere could he see any sign of Dina.

Faltering before the sharp eyes of the men, Shim'on stepped back. "Excuse me," he said, bobbing in a quick show of respect. "I thought I saw my sister enter here. But I must have been mistaken."

One of the men snickered and whispered to his companion, and Shim'on felt heat scald the back of his neck. He, one of the chosen people, had no obligation to deal with uncircumcised barbarians. Before any one of them could speak to him, he whirled and left the men standing in the city gate.

DISTRAUGHT AND CONFUSED, he and his brothers returned to the fields. A few hours later a messenger arrived from Lea. "Your sister Dina arrived home a short while ago, her face watered with tears," the servant said.

"Your mother asks you to come home at once. Hamor the Hivite is at the compound, asking for permission to speak to your father."

"Hamor the Hivite?" Re'uven asked, a frown settling on his brow.

"I have heard of him," Shim'on answered. "He lives in the city of Shekhem." He glared at the messenger. "What was our mother's mood when she bade you summon us?"

The servant's face went grim. "She has not ceased to water her couch with tears. Yaakov entertains his guests in a gracious manner, but your mother will not come out of her tent. She remains inside with Dina, and both women do nothing but weep."

"Why do they weep?" Shim'on snapped.

"It is said," the servant whispered, his expression hard and resentful, "that Shekhem, young son of the prince Hamor, has defiled your sister. By force he has humbled her."

"I knew it!" Shim'on slammed his fist upon his palm. "Nothing but evil could come of Dina's sporting with the women of that heathen city. I warned her to remain at home!"

"This is not good," Levi said, his fist tightening around his staff. "But we will not cast blame until we have heard the tale." He nodded toward the messenger. "We will come at once."

They hurried home, borne on wings of indignation and curiosity. When they arrived at Yisrael's camp, they found Hamor the Hivite, a tall, slender man with a carefully shaped beard, seated beside Yaakov's fire. Hamor rose in a measure of respect as Yaakov acknowledged his sons; then the Hivite extended his hand to introduce a younger man who sat beside him.

"This is my son, Shekhem," he said, nodding. He drew his richly-colored robe closer about his shoulders. "He is a fine youth who stands to inherit all I possess." Respectfully, the older man turned his attention back to Yaakov. "The soul of my son longs for your daughter, Dina. Please give her to him in marriage. Then, as I have told you, our communities shall be joined. You shall dwell with us, your daughters will marry our sons; your sons may take wives from among our daughters. The land will be open before you, live and travel in it, acquire property in it. The land is rich, my friend Yisrael, and we can prosper in this place together."

Shim'on felt his anger begin to boil at the older man's words. Hamor offered riches and prosperity as if the land was his to give, but he was an ignorant fool! Why should they share Canaan with this man when God had already promised all of it to Yisrael and his descendants?

Not to be outdone by his father, the younger man stood. "May I only find favor in your sight," he said, his dark-eyed gaze passing from Yaakov to his sons, "However much you say to me, I will give in payment. To whatever extreme you multiply the bride-price and the marriage-gift, I will give it. Only please, I beg you, give me the girl to be my wife!"

"Hasn't he already taken her?" Re'uven growled in Shim'on's ear.

"This man has done a disgraceful thing," Dan murmured, his voice pitched for his brothers' ears alone. "Such a thing ought not to be done."

"Careful, brothers," Levi whispered, a forced smile on his face. "We will not arouse the anger of these people. Hamor is a prince in the land; he commands many warriors within the city. Would you have them come and take Dina by force? We must stall them, we must think of some way to gain some time."

Shim'on looked to his father—Yaakov was watching them, his expression an unreadable mask. Why didn't he rise to Dina's defense? Why didn't he say *anything*?

As if he had read Shim'on's thoughts, Yaakov turned to the Hivite. "My sons," he said to Hamor, tilting his head toward the brothers, "confer among themselves, my esteemed friends. "They are close to their sister, closer even than I am. Since what you propose concerns their future, let them decide what we shall do. I will abide by their wishes."

Hamor frowned slightly at Yaakov's words, but Shim'on turned to his brothers with a new sense of purpose. He shouldn't have been surprised that Father wished to cast Dina off; he had practically washed his hands of all Lea's children since the day of their births. Now Yaakov sat dumb by the fire, without remorse for his daughter's defilement, without regrets, without concern for any of them. Very well. Since he didn't care what happened to Dina, he shouldn't care if his sons chose to avenge their sister. If Yaakov would not defend Lea's children, Lea's children would defend each other.

Shim'on looked up at Re'uven. "What shall we do?"

When Re'uven faltered, Dan spoke: "We should give her to this youth. He is a comely lad and he seems to genuinely care for her. I have heard nothing but good spoken of Hamor's son since we have come to this place."

"We can't give her to uncircumcised idol-worshippers!" Yehuda said, aghast. "And what Hamor suggests is impossible. We should remain a separate and distinct people, we are not to intermarry with those who serve strange gods."

"Hamor would never accept our refusal," Re'uven spoke up at last. "He would see it as a sign of hostility. He and his men would come for her when we least expect it. Can we leave our mother and father unprotected while we are away with the flocks? Are we prepared to fight off Hamor's men if they should begin to harass us in the wilderness? We will die if we refuse this man. I am certain of it."

"Then we shall not refuse him," Levi said, a slow smile spreading across his face. "We will give him what he wants, for now. Then we will defeat him before he can strike at us. We will redeem our sister and bring her back."

Shim'on couldn't believe he'd heard correctly. "We will give Dina to them?"

"Yes," Levi answered, his strong hand gripping the back of Shim'on's neck. His eyes smoldered. "We will tell this Hamor and his son that we would be pleased to intermarry with them. But, we will say, we cannot give our sister to one who is uncircumcised, for that would be a disgrace to us. Only if every man in the city becomes circumcised can we give our daughters to them. We will tell them that if they agree, we will settle among them and become a single people."

"He will never agree." Yehuda shook his head. "It is too much to ask of a man."

"Did you not see the light of love burning in the young man's eyes?" Levi asked, gesturing toward Hamor's handsome son. "He will agree, I would take an oath on it. And when they have fulfilled their part of the bargain, we will take our sister and make young Shekhem pay for his lustful folly."

As much as he wanted to believe Levi, Shim'on was surprised when Hamor and Shekhem agreed to the proposal. And when Zilpa, Lea's maid, brought Dina forth from her mother's tent, Shim'on gaped as his sister walked forward with a tremulous smile on her face. He had expected to see pain, humiliation, and shame, but love shone from her gray eyes, lighting her narrow face with beauty he had never seen in her before.

"I will not delay to do the thing you have requested," Shekhem said as he took Dina's hand. Though he spoke to Yaakov and the brothers, his eyes never left his bride's face. "And I accept your daughter as my wife. I will live with her nobly, and bring her nothing but honor all the days of her life."

"I will speak to the men of our city tomorrow," Hamor promised, turning to Yaakov. "When the men meet at the gate of the city, I will tell them that this union will benefit both of us. We shall live as one, your children and mine, and together we shall become a great nation."

Shim'on heard Hamor's words as if from a great distance, so amazed was he by the aura of loveliness emanating from his sister. Her slim young figure, now enveloped in a gauzy cloak of iridescent colors, moved with the sure grace of a dancer. Loose tendrils of shining dark hair softened her face; her eyes shone bright in the pale light of the transforming moon. She stepped toward Shekhem and reached for his hand, then laced his fingers with her own.

Could she truly love this son of a goatish barbarian?

He shook his head, denying the thought, and stood with his brothers as the wedding couple left the camp and walked toward the dull glow on the horizon that marked the torchlit city of Shekhem.

THREE DAYS LATER, well before sunrise, Levi and Shim'on slipped away from the herds and hurried toward the walled city. They had sharpened their daggers, and each brother sprinted with a deadly lance in his right hand. On the previous night, a spying servant had confirmed their hopes: Hamor, prince of the city, had spoken to the other men at the gate. The greedy fools, eager to share Yaakov's wealth, had consented to circumcision. And today, twenty-four hours day after the mass ritual, every man in the city was bound to be incapacitated.

As the first tints of the rising sun touched the city walls, Shim'on and Levi attacked. The brothers dispatched the guards at the gate and then they separated, each going his own murderous way. Revenge was easy, for most of the city's men lay deep within drug-induced sleep. In each house Shim'on slew every male without remorse while one thought echoed in his brain: "For Dina. For Lea. For those Yaakov has cast aside."

The screams of waking women and crying children alerted the settlement's remaining inhabitants, but Shim'on and Levi rolled through the city like a stormy sea, overcoming anyone who rose up against them. Shim'on felt his pulse quicken when he entered a large house and recognized Hamor in his bed; he struck before the old man could draw breath to protest. When a stumbling noise from an adjacent room led Shim'on to a slow-moving Shekhem, Shim'on paused a moment, his dagger in one hand, his lance in the other. His brother-in-law stared at him with eyes like clear black glass, impossible to read.

"No!"

As Dina screamed and threw herself in front of her husband, Shim'on dropped his lance and used his free hand to pull her away from the young man crouching beside the marriage bed. "Get dressed and rejoice that you are going home."

"Shim'on!" She screamed his name in a shriek he would never forget. "What are you doing?"

"I am taking revenge upon the stranger who defiled you. He is not a fit husband for a daughter of Yisrael."

"But you promised! You and the others, you gave your word!"

"A word spoken to a liar is not a lie."

He crouched and shifted his position, never taking his eyes from the man beside the bed. Shekhem's eyes seemed to dim, then leaked little strings of tears as he shifted his gaze from Shim'on to Dina.

Shim'on saw his chance and lunged forward, but Dina grabbed his hand, pulling the dagger from his grasp. Shekhem sprang forward, his weight toppling Shim'on. The younger, lighter man gasped as he kicked and threw an effective punch, but Shim'on brought his knee up in a forceful thrust, centering on his adversary's vulnerability.

With an agonized cry, Shekhem reeled away and coiled into the shadows of the room, releasing a tiny whine of mounting dread. Regaining his balance, Shim'on glanced around for his weapons, but saw only a stone in the doorway, a solid doorstop. Using both hands to lift the rock overhead, Shim'on brought the stone down and silenced Shekhem's cries.

"My husband!" Dina sank to the floor and keened the dreadful ululation of mourning. "Why? Why have you done this?"

Shim'on rocked back on his heels, then brought the palm of his hand across his mouth, wiping a trail of blood from his face. He spotted his dagger and lance on the floor, and bent to retrieve them. "Find your robe, Dina. And hurry."

"I loved him! You killed him! I shall hate you forever!"

She was on him before he could respond, scratching at his arm, struggling for his blade. A scream clawed in her throat as she grappled for the weapon, and for an instant Shim'on could do nothing but stare at her. Then he saw blood from her hands upon the silver of his dagger and realized that she intended to harm herself and die with the idolaters.

"May God forgive you!" Without thinking, he drew back his hand and slapped her. Sobbing, she fell at his feet and pressed her hand to the red mark on her face.

"You don't know what you are doing," Shim'on said, anger and pity twisting his heart as he stared at her. "You are a child, you know nothing of love. And I am taking you from this cursed place, so put on your robe and your shoes."

She did not answer, but reached for a pair of delicate sandals, turning away as she tied the laces. "You are the one who knows nothing of love," she whispered in a broken voice. "Perhaps you never shall."

Ignoring her comment, he pulled her from the floor and led her from Hamor's house. They had just stepped outside when a babble of familiar voices greeted them. "Ho, Shim'on!" Re'uven hailed him, his sword in hand and a smile on his face. "We have come to join you!"

"You are all but too late," Levi answered, grinning as he walked up. He reached for Dina's limp hand and lifted it like a trophy. "We have our sister again! And every man in the city is dead!"

"It seems the city is ours," Yehuda said, looking around. "Rejoice, brothers, for whatever you see belongs to you. We have conquered this place today in the name of our sister, daughter of Yisrael!"

His statement brought fresh weeping from Dina. Sighing, Shim'on caught Asher's eye and told the younger brother to take his sister home.

Asher's gaze swept over the rich settlement as he took Dina's hand. "Are you really taking everything?"

"Whatever we can carry or drive out," Levi answered. "Flocks and herds, donkeys, women, children, and whatever wealth we find in the houses. The spoils of war, little brother, may be hard won, but they are ours!"

While Asher led Dina away, Shim'on moved through the buildings, helping his brothers herd weeping women and wailing children into the streets and alleys. One dismal-looking structure stood in an isolated corner of the city. Unable to recall if he'd visited this house on his killing spree, Shim'on carefully approached the sprained door.

Shadows wreathed the single room inside. A small table near the door bore a handful of treasures, as if the owners of the place had been about to gather their belongings and flee. Shim'on lifted his shepherd's sling from his shoulder and tossed the golden idols, earrings, and silver trinkets inside. A richly- embroidered garment hung from a peg in the wall, and he took that, too, tossing it over his shoulder. When he felt confident the house had nothing else to offer, he lifted his sling and turned toward the door, but froze when a soft gasp broke the stillness.

A warning spasm of alarm erupted within him. Had one of the men escaped?

His hand darted to the dagger in his belt. Silently he pulled it free, then turned in a quick move and knelt. His fear and anxiety tumbled out in a flood of curses when he saw a young woman crouching beneath the table, bright copper ringlets curled on her forehead and the nape of her neck. Her frail knees trembled beneath the hem of her tunic, and her dirty bare feet were delicate, completely unlike Dina's.

Something about her fragile innocence sapped the killing strength of his arm. "Come out," he commanded, his hand dropping to his side. He gentled his voice and gestured to her. "Come out or die, for we will burn what is left of this city."

She crawled out then, a girl of about Dina's age with tangled curls, fragile wrists, and eyes as wild as a spooked horse's. And when Shim'on lay with her under the stars that night and claimed her as his wife, he told himself the wrongs committed at Shekhem had finally been put right.

IN ONE MORNING Yaakov had gone from being one of the wealthiest men in the land to *the* wealthiest from horizon to horizon, but his face purpled in fury when his sons strode into camp, herding the flocks, women, and children of Shekhem before them. Without a word he took Yosef's hand and stalked to Rahel's tent, steadfastly refusing to look upon his other sons.

Shim'on watched him go, feeling the distance between them more acutely than ever. What had he expected, congratulations? A display of fatherly pride?

Yaakov confronted them when they gathered to eat. "How could you do this?" he cried, his features contorted with shock and anger. "Without thinking you have rushed in lunatic flight toward destruction, both ours and Shekhem's!"

Shim'on looked down at his hands. Dried blood still darkened the crescents of his nails; deep smears covered his arms and legs. Levi and the others looked equally as gruesome.

"You are all a shame to me!" Yaakov cried, pathos in his voice. "Adorned in jewels, and yet dripping with blood!"

"We had to do something, Father," Re'uven spoke up. "Shim'on and Levi were right to take vengeance for our sister's cause. And you gave us permission—you told Hamor we would decide our sister's fate."

"So we did." Levi thrust his jaw forward. "And you should be proud. We have avenged our sister. We have brought you slaves and great riches."

"What did it matter if Dina married Shekhem?" Yaakov lifted his hands in despair. "The girl was happy. And I would not have allowed you to take women from that city! I wanted you to journey to your eastern kinsmen for brides, just as I traveled to Haran to find my Rahel."

Shim'on's rebellious emotions erupted. "And your Lea," he said, a thin chill on the edge of his words. His eyes glared into his father's.

Yaakov stared at him answering. "Yes, and Lea," he answered. "But now you have taken the women of Shekhem by force, a worse crime than Shekhem committed, for Dina has confessed that she encouraged the young man's attentions. You have brought trouble on me; you have made me odious among the inhabitants of the land. In fear for their cities, the Canaanites and the Perizzites will attack us, but we are few in number, and they are strong. Prepare yourselves, my foolish sons, for they will gather against us. If God Shaddai does not protect us, we will be destroyed."

Re'uven stepped forward. "Should he have treated our sister like a harlot?"

But Yaakov waved him away and turned toward the tent where Rahel and his beloved Yosef waited.

THE NEXT DAY, Yaakov commanded the entire household to gather up the tents, animals, tools, and shelters. "God has told me to go to Bethel," he told his sons. "I am to construct a slaughter-site there to God-El, who appeared to me when I fled from my brother Esav."

A new and unexpected vigor radiated from his body, and an odd vitality rang in his voice. His gaze seemed to probe his sons' souls as he looked at them. "You must put away the foreign gods you took from the houses of Shekhem. You must bathe and purify yourselves, and change out of the colored garments you took from the men of that city. Take the rings from your fingers and ears, and bring all the spoil from that place to me."

Spurred by their father's command and their own guilty consciences, Shim'on and his brothers gathered all the goods they had taken. They released the slaves and piled the pilfered goods into baskets. The girl Shim'on had claimed, however, refused to leave. "Nothing remains for me in that cursed place," she said, her eyes as clear as the wide sky above. "You called me your wife, and so you shall be my husband from this day forward."

After all the goods had been collected, Yaakov led the train of treasure-laden donkeys to the majestic oak that grew outside Shekhem. There he and his sons buried the spoils. Shortly after returning to camp, the entire company set out for Bethel.

The journey was tedious, the weather hot and dry. Whirlwinds spun and danced across the plains; the distant cliffs shimmered in the rising heat mirage. Dina and Lea rode in woven baskets that hung on opposite sides of a single camel's hump and Shim'on noticed that Dina spent much of the time with her head hanging out of the swaying basket, her face as pale as death. On a camel in the rear, the very-pregnant Rahel curled into a similar basket opposite eight-year-old Yosef, who was too spoiled to dirty his feet on the trek.

After reaching Bethel, where Yaakov built an altar and spoke with his God, the company moved on. They were nearing Ephrath, or Bethlehem, when a shrill cry halted the caravan. Yaakov's face paled when Zilpa announced that Rahel's travail had begun. The uncomfortable journey and the heat had apparently sapped her fragile strength, for shortly after giving life to a boy, Rahel died.

Shim'on, his brothers, and the servants sat in silence outside the hastily constructed tent, their ears tuned to the mingled wailing of a newborn infant and his grief-stricken father. After three hours of weeping in protracted grief, a strangely quiet Yaakov stepped out of Rahel's tent and held the baby aloft for all to see.

"His name is Binyamin, son of my right hand," he said, his ragged voice breaking. "And she who bore him is lost."

Yaakov's face had the withered look of a thirsty blossom. He sat in the shade of the tent, holding the baby on his knees, as tears rolled down his craggy face. One by one, mumbling excuses about tending the herds or erecting shelters, Yaakov's older sons slipped away. As an act of mercy, Yehuda pulled Yosef from the tent where Lea and the maids prepared Rahel's body for burial.

Shim'on remained near his father, wondering if he should feel guilty for the relief flooding his soul. He had liked Rahel and was sorry for her death, but for his mother's sake he could not mourn. So he sat across from his father and silently rejoiced that after years of suffering, Lea would finally enjoy her husband's undivided attention.

He breathed in the thick, oppressive air and watched the play of desert light and shadows on his father's lined face. The baby mewed softly, seeking a life-giving breast, but Yaakov did not call for a wet nurse. He lifted the child in his hands and regarded the boy, an expression of mingled fascination and revulsion on his face. Then the baby cried in earnest, flailing its tiny fist. Yaakov pressed his lips to the child's wrinkled forehead.

Shim'on sighed, grateful for one small breach in the tent of grimness enclosing his father. Yaakov's soul was heavy with grief, but in time he would come to cherish the child.

"He is a handsome baby," Shim'on offered.

"Shim'on," his father spoke without lifting his eyes from the baby in his arms, "I want you to know something."

"Yes, Father?"

Yaakov looked at him, his face a stone effigy of contempt. "If you and Levi had not attacked the city of Shekhem, we would not be camped in this wilderness. And Rahel, who could not withstand the journey, would not be dead."

He said no more, but his meaning and intention were unmistakable: he held Shim'on and Levi responsible for Rahel's death, and he would not soon forgive them.

Shim'on said nothing as he stood and walked away. But he felt ice spreading through his stomach, frigid fingers seeping into every pore of his skin. The coldness, like fire, twisted and turned inside him, upending every belief, every dream, every hope, until Shim'on knew he would never be the same again.

CHAPTER TWELVE

A PAIR OF OBELISKS, CALLED *TEKHENU* BY THE EGYPTIANS, ROSE UP FROM the sacred city of Heliopolis at the site where the annual inundation of the Nile first began to recede. The city's soil, fertilized by rich layers of silt and nurtured by the life-giving sun, received a full measure of all the gods had to offer. To the Egyptians the hallowed ground represented rebirth and creation, and Mandisa knew her mistress hoped the holy city would bless her womb and enable her to bring forth another son for Zaphenath-paneah.

They had enjoyed a week's visit with her lady's parents, but now Asenath wanted Mandisa to rise before dawn each morning and accompany her to the sacred temple of Khnum. Her mistress wished to greet the god as he awoke in hopes of impressing him with the earnestness of her desire.

"Perhaps," she whispered one morning as Mandisa applied kohl to her lady's sleep-heavy eyelids, "the god will think I have remained in his temple all night, attending to him without even stopping to sleep."

Mandisa lifted a brow, but did not answer. If a god could be so easily fooled, how could he be a god? For many months she had watched Zaphenath-paneah, and she had to admit that his great and invisible God seemed more powerful and logical than any Egypt had to offer. His God was all-seeing and all-knowing, she had heard the master tell his sons, so nothing a man did could trick or sway the Almighty One. God Shaddai knew every individual's name; He even knew the secrets of a man's heart.

Apparently Asenath had never placed much faith in her husband's lessons. "Khnum is the divine potter. He fashioned the other gods, the divine kings, and all mortals on his potter's plate," she murmured as Mandisa completed her toilette. "He will not fail me."

Mandisa answered out of simple politeness. "Why is this god special, my lady?"

Asenath let her bare head drop forward onto her folded arms. "He knows the secrets of creation. His priests taught the ancient pharaohs how to mix water and clay to create the living stone of the pyramids. His breath turned a handful of reddish-brown clay into the first mortal man."

"And you think this god of clay can create new life in you?" Mandisa slipped her mistress's wig from its stand and waited until Asenath opened one eye and lifted her head.

"He will," the young woman answered, "for I have my father's prayers to support me. He has dedicated himself anew to the worship of Khnum, and he is a powerful priest. Today we are to join him and beg the god to think favorably of us."

Mandisa slipped the wig over her mistress's shorn head, then jerked it downward for a tight fit. For Asenath's sake, she hoped some good would be accomplished. She missed her son, she missed Thebes, she missed Halima. *May the gods help me,* she thought, patting Asenath's shoulders. *Though I was happy to leave the responsibility of his care behind, I might even miss the noise of the obnoxious captive in my lord's house.*

POTIPHERA, high priest of On, clapped in approval when his daughter stepped out of her litter at the temple. As shriveled as an old fig, he wore the white kilt of the priesthood and had shaved his entire body, including his eyebrows, lashes, and whatever sparse hairs might have grown on his chest. A paunch bulged over the waistband of his kilt, advertising his prosperity and his secure place in Pharaoh's favor.

Mandisa lowered her gaze as she followed her mistress out of the litter. The sight of Potiphera, glowing and bald in the torchlight, lifted the curtain on memories she had tried to forget. Idogbe had fancied himself a priest of Sebek, the crocodile god who represented the destructive power of the sun, and had shaved his massive body in a similar way. Once he had tried to become a lay priest at the temple in Thebes, but because he kept insisting that Sebek desired human sacrifices, the chief priests dismissed him.

Mandisa shook her head as if she could dislodge the disturbing memories. Once, long after she had been safely installed in Zaphenath-paneah's house, she had asked Ani about the Egyptians' sacrificial rites. He told her that women slaves were often sacrificed at the graves of their dead masters during the first dynasty, but no one now would consider such a barbaric practice. In the enlightened eighteenth dynasty, a few temples called for animal sacrifice on special occasions. But only the cult of Osiris, of whom Pharaoh was the principal figure, incorporated human sacrifice into worship. "The only human life worthy of sacrifice," Ani had said, "is the divine king's. Because he is god and man, he alone has the power to bridge the gap between the gods and mankind."

Asenath tugged on Mandisa's cloak, jerking her back to reality. Potiphera was leading them into the rectangular enclosure surrounding the innermost temple, so Mandisa lengthened her stride to keep up. When they had entered the gate, the old priest pressed his hand to his daughter's cheek and took his leave of them. But Asenath knew what to do. Pressing her hands together in front of her bosom, she walked toward the god's habitation, her eyes wide with expectation.

From the outer courtyard they moved into Per-Hair, the House of Rejoicing. In the stillness of this columned hall, Mandisa could hear the ghostly sounds of ritual chanting. From Idogbe's tales she knew that the priests rose in the darkness each morning to chant and purify themselves in the sacred pool before entering the temple.

Catching her breath, Asenath stopped. Mandisa stepped forward to see what had distracted her mistress. Like a procession of spirits in the morning gloom, the line of shaven, white-robed priests snaked out of a subterranean chamber. Their hairless chests gleamed with the sacred water; the white of their kilts dazzled even in the dim light of dawn.

"Look at my father," Asenath whispered, a note of pride in her voice, and Mandisa noticed that the venerable old priest led the others, walking in the place of highest honor. "He will personally speak to the god for me," her mistress murmured, her voice no more than a breath in the reverent stillness. "And the god will supply what I am seeking."

While the priests ministered to Khnum, Mandisa waited with her mistress and recalled what Idogbe had told her about a temple's morning ritual. At dawn's first ray, the clay seals to the god's inner sanctuary would be broken, and the doors opened to disclose the idol that represented the divinity. The highest priest would enter and lie prostrate before the image, then, upon rising, he would utter prayers while other priests perfumed the air with incense. The god's nightclothes would be removed; then the figure would be bathed, anointed, and clothed in fresh apparel. Food and drink would be offered. After the god's spirit had sufficient opportunity to feed itself, the priest would open the doors to any and all supplicants who wished to address the divinity.

Finally a priest beckoned and Asenath moved through a pair of heavy double doors into the innermost sanctuary.

In the holy place, Mandisa lost all custody of her eyes. She stared upward and outward, blinking in unexpected brightness. Gold covered every conceivable surface, sparkling in the gilded paints on the muraled walls, in the serving pieces, in vases and bowls that stood on trays before the stone statue. Rush torches in their brackets threw wavering lights that made the bas-relief carvings dance on the walls.

The god sat upon a platform behind a flower-strewn altar. The statue of Khnum rose over fifteen feet into the air; Mandisa felt like a mere sparrow before it. The image had a slender, well-formed man's body, but a ram's snout and face. Two horns snaked to the right and left through his braided wig, upon which he wore the traditional crown of reeds and ostrich feathers.

No amount of gold or decoration could disguise the idol's ugliness.

Mandisa stepped back in stunned revulsion, but Asenath fell to her knees and bent to touch her head to the floor three times. Though she had not visited a temple since her marriage to Zaphenath-paneah, apparently she intended to atone for her past indifference.

"Speak, child, of your petition to our mighty Khnum," a voice called. Mandisa lifted her head. The voice belonged to Potiphera, but she barely recognized it in the thickened air.

"Divine Khnum, creator of all that lives and breathes and exists," Asenath said, not lifting her eyes from the floor, "your daughter has a boon to ask of you."

"And what is it you seek?" the priest prodded.

"A child, most divine god, a child only you can provide. You have given me two sons, but a man as great and favored as my husband should have more."

Potiphera turned to face the gruesome god standing in the torchlight. The ebony eyes staring out from the ram's head seemed to fix upon Asenath.

"Beautiful is your shining forth on the horizon, O living Khnum, beginning of life!" Potiphera called.

"You who bring children into being in women, and make fluid and clay into mankind,

Who nourishes the son in the womb of his mother,

Who soothes him so that he weeps not, O nurse in the womb!

Who gives breath in order to keep alive all that he has made;

When he comes forth from the womb on the day of his birth,

You open his mouth in speech, and give all that he needs.

You have created the earth according to your desire, while you were alone.

You are in my heart, and there is no one who knows you but Potiphera, your son.

Hear me now, O Lord of the Sacred Land, and grant this woman's request.

For you, O Divine Potter, Lord of the Kingdom, have molded men upon your potter's wheel, and given them strength to walk upon the earth . . . "

On and on the priest droned, his voice rising and falling as he flattered, cajoled, and finally threatened the god into hearing and granting Asenath's request. After a while, the sense of awe that had surrounded Mandisa faded. She clenched her jaw to stifle a yawn.

Why did her lady want another son so desperately? She had two fine boys, as handsome as they were bright, and Zaphenath-paneah adored them. As far as Mandisa knew, the master had never expressed a desire for more children, yet Asenath seemed willing to risk even her life for the simple pleasure of placing another child in Zaphenath-paneah's arms.

Could she not see how much the vizier loved her? Why couldn't she rest in his love?

Mandisa felt the corner of her mouth twist in a wry smile. She would never be blessed with a love like that, and one son had managed to fill her life. Adom was a fine boy, but how he tied her hands! He was too full of himself at times, grown up in some ways, but such a child in others. She would have to teach him, for while the master's sons would be tutored in the scribe's schools, Adom, son of a servant, would not be welcome there. A father could lead him; a man could explain the things a woman was not permitted to know. Soon Adom would have questions she could not answer, and even now he yearned for a man's attention. Tarik and Ani were friendly to the boy, but they had so many responsibilities and so little time . . .

Her son needed a father. Mandisa did not necessarily want a husband, for she'd been married once and had no wish to repeat the experience. But Adom needed a man to guide, teach, and train him. Because she was too gentle, he would have a difficult time outside the protective walls of the vizier's villa because he had never learned how to defend himself. And soon he would want to know about a man's way with a woman, and how could she explain what she did not completely understand herself?

Adom needed a father, but how was she supposed to provide one? For a brief moment she considered joining her mistress in prayer, but she could not offer her deepest secrets to a ram-headed idol that stared at food without eating and listened to hour-long prayers without hearing.

Yet Zaphenath-paneah's invisible God was present everywhere, or so the vizier had said. If her master spoke the truth, this El Shaddai would hear her prayer even if it sprang from Khnum's temple. And perhaps, if she found favor in his sight, he would answer. In any case, it would not hurt to attempt one small petition . . .

While Asenath pressed her forehead to the floor and her father doled out more flattery for the granite god, Mandisa closed her eyes and asked El Shaddai to send someone from whom her son might learn to be a man.

CHAPTER THIRTEEN

THE NEW TABLE, DELICATE IN DESIGN AND INLAID WITH GOLD, CRASHED against the door. "You stinking Egyptians will learn this about me!" the prisoner roared, his words punctuated by the shattering of pottery. "I once killed a thousand men in a single morning! If God is willing, I will do it again!"

Outside the captive's chamber, Tarik smiled at Halima. "My grasp of the Canaanite tongue is improving," he said, consoling the trembling slave girl. "I understood every word of that threat. The man thinks he will kill us all."

"Sometimes I think he will," Halima answered, the breakfast tray in her hand shaking so violently that the bowls clattered against each other. "I have nightmares about him. In the dark sometimes I feel a demon sitting on my chest and I open my eyes, expecting to see him."

"Never fear, sweet Halima," Tarik said, glancing around. Because they stood alone in the hallway, he took the tray from the poor girl's hands. It wouldn't do for the captain of the vizier's guard to be seen helping a kitchen slave, but this young woman had shown uncommon courage in facing the Canaanite devil.

He smiled again when her eyes came up to study his face. "A runner has come from Heliopolis. The lady Asenath returns within a few days. Soon you will not have to deal with this sour Canaanite."

"I do not mind . . . so much." Her round face softened in a wistful expression. "But I would not attempt it without you, Tarik."

He shrugged off the implied compliment. "I would not have persevered if not for our master's command. A prisoner belongs in prison, not in a house." He stepped away from the captive's door as another object collided against it. A chair, from the sound of the crash. "But Zaphenath-paneah says the man is not to be harmed, nor shall he be allowed to harm himself. Yesterday I discovered that he had shredded his garment into long strips, doubtless attempting to fashion a trap of some sort. So I had the strips removed, as well as what remained of his garment. Today he wears nothing but an Egyptian kilt. If he attempts to shred it, he shall have only his inflated dignity to clothe him."

Halima laughed as color rose to her cheeks. "Tarik, you are shameful!"

"I am only obeying our master's orders. And though I would rather throw this Shim'on to the dogs than keep him here, I will obey the vizier. In the nine years I've known the master, I've never seen him made an unwise decision."

"What about the Canaanite's food?" Halima rested her fingers on the tray in his grasp. "I have prepared a delicious choice of breads, and we ought not to waste it."

"It will not be wasted." Tarik knelt, lowering the tray to the floor. "Let the ants eat the meal; at least they know how to behave. If the prisoner insists on raging like a wild animal, we will let him starve like the lions of the plains. Keep his water jug filled, but do not feed him until he grows more appreciative."

"Very well." Halima paused. "I suppose I should return to my work."

"Yes," Tarik answered, standing. Halima took a few slow steps toward the kitchen, then quickened her pace in a resolute stride. Tarik watched her go and wondered why she had hesitated to leave him.

BORED AND FRUSTRATED, Adom wandered through the villa's wide halls. In his hand he clutched a spinning top of carved quartz and a length of papyrus twine, but Efrayim and Menashe were involved with their tutor and too busy to let him entertain them.

Adom stuffed the twine and top into a pocket of his kilt and tried to think of something else to do. He missed his mother. She had been gone nearly three weeks, and once Adom heard Menashe remark that his mother had gone to live with her father in a place called Heliopolis. Wherever Menashe's mother went, Adom's mother followed, and for several nights he'd been terrified to think that the two women might not return to the villa. But then he caught Zaphenath-paneah in the hall, and his heart had warmed when the noble vizier looked him in the eye and smiled with gentle understanding. "Of course your mother is coming back," the vizier had said, his hand warming the boy's head. "Very soon, in fact."

Soon wasn't soon enough. Adom had spent the morning wandering through the stables, but the master's groomsmen chased him away. "Get out of here!" one of the slaves yelled. "One kick from the masters' spirited horses will crack that soft head of yours like a melon!"

From the stableyard Adom wandered into the area where the granaries held the villa's stores of grain and wheat, but his mother's warning voice echoed in his brain. Countless children and drunken fools, she often told him, had climbed the stairs to peer into the open tops of the hive-shaped cones and fallen in, suffocating as they struggled to climb out.

A line of donkeys and their attendants stood before the granaries where Zaphenath-paneah's servants measured grain for an official who had not planned for the famine. Overwhelmed by the sight of so many serious faces, Adom sprinted across the yard, through the front courtyard, and into the main hall of the house. Several visitors waited outside the central reception hall for an audience with the vizier, and Adom got as far as the vestibule before a guard caught his arm.

The guard bent to look him in the eye. "Where are you going, Adom?"

"I am looking for my mother."

"She and the Lady Asenath are still away."

Adom felt himself fidgeting. "Then perhaps I can ask the master when she will return."

The guard chuckled. "No, my young friend, you cannot. The master is busy. The Double of the King, the Good Shepherd of the People is meeting with four kings of Megiddo, two princes of Shahuren, and one king from Ascalon."

"I will wait for him, then. I will be quiet."

"No, Adom. The Nourisher of Egypt, the Prince of Mediation dines today with shepherds from Syria and Lebanon, Bedouins from Edom, and the host of kings who visit with him now. They have come a long way to seek your master's face, and they have been waiting longer than you. Run along now, and play with your friends."

"They are having their lessons."

"Then find them, and listen to Ani as he teaches. Even the son of a servant should know the truth of the world."

When the guard straightened, Adom knew he was no longer welcome in the house. Head down, he walked through the front portico and followed the path that led to the garden.

Efrayim and Menashe sat on papyrus mats before Ani, steward of the estate and tutor of Zaphenath-paneah's children. Though Ani seemed a thin, shrunken man when he stood next to the vizier, now his extraordinary eyes blazed and glowed. Efrayim and Menashe looked like two dolls seated before a giant, so imposing was the old man's manner as he swayed and spun a tale.

Aware than Ani had seen him approach, Adom knelt on the stone pathway. The two boys, intent upon their teacher's story, did not stir from their mats.

"In the beginning—" Ani drew an imaginary line in the air— "nothing existed but one God, the invisible God who cannot be configured in stone."

"Neter?" Menashe interrupted.

Ani frowned. "You are not to interrupt, young master. A wise student questions only after his teacher is done with explanations."

When Menashe's shoulders drooped, Ani placed his freckled hand upon the boy's shaved head. "Do not be discouraged, little prince. You may discern the answer to your question before I am finished."

Menashe looked up again and Ani continued. "This invisible God is not to be found in shrines; no habitation can contain Him, and you cannot conceive His form in your heart. This God is One and alone, and no others exist with Him. He is the One Who made all things. God is from the beginning, and He has existed of old when nothing else had being. He is the father of Beginnings, the eternal One, the infinite One who endures forever and ever. He shall endure to all eternity. He is hidden from gods and men, and He is a mystery to His creatures. No man knows how to know Him; His true name is a mystery even to His children. Though some call Him Neter, his names are innumerable, they are manifold and no one knows their number."

"If no one knows his name, then why do my father and Mandisa call him El Shaddai?" Menashe interrupted again.

From a safe distance, Adom grinned. Menashe was always asking questions. No mere warning would silence him.

Ani sighed. "Listen, Menashe, and you will understand. 'El Shaddai' is a Canaanite term for 'almighty god,' a name which describes one of his attributes. God is almighty, just as He is truth. He lives by truth, He feeds on truth. He is the King of truth, He rests upon truth, He fashions truth, and He executes Truth throughout the world. God is life, and through Him alone man lives. He gives life to man, He breathes the breath of life into his nostrils.

"God is father and mother, the father of fathers, the mother of mothers. He begets, but was never begotten; He produces, but was never produced. He creates, but was never created; He is the maker of His own form, the fashioner of His own body. He is the Creator of the heavens, the earth, the deep, the waters, the mountains. When He spoke His word it came to pass, and His word shall endure for ever."

"If there is only one God," Menashe said, his face twisting into a frown, "then why are there so many temples in Thebes?"

Ani held up a finger. "The invisible God is the father of the gods. He formed mankind along with the primeval potter Khnum who turned men and gods out of His hands, forming them upon a potter's table."

Adom ran his finger over a flagstone. He could never keep the names of the gods in his head. There were too many to remember.

"You see, my students," Ani sank to a papyrus mat, "once neither heaven nor earth existed, nothing but the boundless primeval water shrouded with thick darkness. The water contained within it the seeds of things, and at length the spirit of the water felt the desire to create the world. The spirit of the water uttered a word, and the world sprang into being, just as the spirit of the water had decided it should. The next act of creation was the formation of an egg, from which sprang Ra, the sun-god, in whose shining form we see the mighty power of the divine spirit."

"That's not what my mother says," Adom announced.

Three pairs of eyes turned to him. "Adom," the tutor said, his voice heavy, "why aren't you helping someone in the house?"

Adom looked down at his hands. "There's no one to help. And . . . I wanted to listen."

"Then remember what I just told Menashe. A wise student listens. He does not disagree with his teachers."

"But my mother says God created the world and then destroyed it with a flood. And Egypt came out of the flood, just like the rest of the world, and God never made other gods, only people. And not only she calls him El Shaddai, but so does the master, for I've heard Zaphenath-paneah talk about Him—"

"Enough!" Ani closed his eyes and held up a warning hand. "I think tomorrow we will talk of something else. We are finished today, boys. Run, go play, for I have work to do."

CHAPTER FOURTEEN

FROM HIS VANTAGE POINT ON THE RIDGE OF A HILL AT HEBRON, YAAKOV stared into the distance toward Mizraim, the Black Land. In the distance a traveling party crawled northward into the teeth of the gusty breeze that blew up small whirlwinds of desert dust and grit, but he could not discern Shim'on's broad shape among the men.

He sighed. So much for vain hopes and dreams. He had prayed Shim'on would find the courage and strength to escape the vizier who held him, but God had not seen fit to answer those prayers any more than He had answered Yaakov's desperate pleas when Yosef disappeared.

"Do I ask too much?" He lifted his tired eyes to the sky. "Why, Almighty God, do you allow your chosen ones to suffer so? Famine grips our land; the cattle are thin and hungry. My sons' wives are as withered and worn as the stones of these mountains, and yet you do not offer respite or rain. You have taken Rahel, Yosef, and Shim'on, and this foreigner of Mizraim demands my Binyamin, too. This I cannot do, Lord God. I cannot lose the son of my right hand."

In spite of his resolve never to revisit the past, his mind returned to the day when Binyamin had come in the world and Rahel had gone out of it. "He shall be called Ben-oni, son of my sorrow," she had gasped, knowing she would die.

"No." Yaakov rested his hand on her wet brow. "He is the son of my darling, my right hand. He shall be Binyamin, as dear to my heart as you are."

That parting remark was the first and only lie he ever told her. For though he did love Binyamin more than life, Yaakov could never look upon his youngest son without seeing the instrument God had used to take Rahel from him. And so, in the years after her death, Yosef received the fullest measure of Yaakov's devotion and attention—brilliant, handsome, charming Yosef, Rahel's long-awaited firstborn, the delight of her heart.

And then El Shaddai demonstrated His jealousy. To teach Yaakov that He deserved and demanded first place in a man's heart, El Shaddai removed Yosef, just as He nearly took Yitzhak from Avraham. Yaakov knew enough about his God to know that the Almighty would not tolerate an idol, be it a graven image or a flesh-and-blood creature. Anything given more love, more time, or more devotion than God could not be allowed to usurp God Shaddai's rightful place.

"You allowed Avraham to keep his beloved son," he whispered, aware that he had reawakened the memory of Yosef and the dull ache in his soul, "and yet You took mine. Was my sin so much worse than my forefather's?"

The sky glared hot and blue; the Almighty did not answer. But Re'uven was climbing the hill. Yaakov closed his eyes, guarding his secrets.

"Greetings, Father," Re'uven called, his voice unnaturally bright and careful. "I have just finished talking with the others."

Yaakov shifted on his stiff hips and opened his eyes to study the horizon again. "And?"

"The famine is still heavy upon us, Father. The seed we planted has not sprouted, for there has been no rain. We have grain for now, but soon, when there is nothing to harvest, we will starve."

When Re'uven paused, Yaakov braced himself for what he knew would come next.

"Father, we can go back to Egypt if you'll only allow Binyamin to go with us. The Egyptian will give us grain, enough to see us through the coming year."

"No." Yaakov ground the word out between his teeth. "No, no, a thousand times no! You shall not take Binyamin with you. I will not allow him to leave me."

"Father." Re'uven dropped the conciliatory tone. "Binyamin is a grown man, with children of his own. Your continual insistence that he remain in your camp embarrasses him. He wants to go with us, he is more than willing."

"No!" Yaakov felt himself shaking with impotent rage and fear. "I let Yosef go, and he never returned! You, the sons of the others, came back, with only his ornamented coat—" He gestured toward the ground as if the blood-stained garment still lay at his feet-- "and I knew I was wrong."

For loving him too much. For loving him more than God Shaddai.

"Father, listen to me." Re'uven's dark eyes narrowed and hardened. "Yosef left us a long time ago. Would you have all of us starve because of one accident?"

"As long as there is breath in my body, I will guard Rahel's remaining son with my life. Binyamin will not go with you." Turning on his heel, Yaakov flung the edge of his cloak over his shoulder and stumped toward his tent.

CHAPTER FIFTEEN

Docile and patient, the litter bearers waited under a blistering sun. Asenath paused on the marble steps of her father's villa, then reached out to embrace him one final time. "I shall miss you, Father." She placed her cheek next to his. "But please, continue to offer sacrifices and prayers to Khnum for me. I cannot tell you how earnestly I desire another son."

"Daughter." Potiphera pulled her from his embrace and held her at arms' length. "Do you love your husband?"

"Love him?" Asenath laughed, amazed that her father would question her devotion to Zaphenath-paneah, the flower of all Egypt. "How could I not love him? He is truly the wisest man in the land, except for you, of course, and Pharaoh could do nothing without my husband's guidance. He is kind, and gentle, and would do almost anything to please me."

"If you love him, Asenath, you should want to obey him. If he does not want another child, you are foolish to think you can make him happy this way."

"But he does not know what he wants! Father, he loves Efrayim and Menashe so much, I know he would adore another son, even a daughter! And so, no matter how much he protests on my account, I will pursue this." She lowered her voice, aware that Mandisa, who waited in the litter, did not completely approve of her plan. "And since my husband's god has not been strong enough to prevail in this, I beg you to seek help for me from Khnum."

"But the vizier's god is strong. His hand alone has preserved Egypt since Hapi's waters have failed to flood the land."

Fighting hard against tears of frustration she refused to let fall, she gave him a blazing smile. "Trust me, Father, I will win this time. My husband will come to me, the seed will be planted and bear fruit, and I shall be delivered of another son, perhaps even two. And when the famine is done, as my love says it will be, your grandsons shall grow strong and capable in Pharaoh's house."

Her subtle appeal to her father's ambition seemed to allay his fears, for he nodded and released his grip on her arms. "Be careful, daughter," he said, his eyes drinking her up as if he might never see her again. "Do not trifle with divinity, for a sleeping god may wake and take offense at your games. He may draw you out to a place where you can never return."

"Do not worry, Father. I have you to protect me." She gave him another quick kiss on the cheek, then turned and skipped down the steps to her litter. Mandisa pulled the sheer curtain aside, and Asenath sat and pulled her legs out of the swirling dust.

Her father had not moved, but lingered with a worried expression on his face. Foolish man, he was always worrying about something. Giving him a final wave, Asenath let the curtain fall and settled back among the pillows in the conveyance. "Tell the litter bears to proceed," she said, giving Mandisa a weary smile. "Tell them to run. I would like to be home as soon as possible."

CHAPTER SIXTEEN

"Life and health to you, Lady Asenath! We are so glad you have returned!" After delivering a formal greeting and bow to his mistress, Tarik gave Mandisa an exaggerated wink as she climbed from the litter. The perspiring litter-bearers, who had jogged in the merciless heat with only occasional breaks, looked as though they would expire on the spot. Lady Asenath did not even glance back at them as she hurried up the stairs of the villa's portico.

Mandisa turned to the commander of the guards who had escorted them from Heliopolis. "Refresh your men and these slaves in the garden," she murmured. "Take care not to disturb the family. I will sent food from the kitchens and fresh water from the well."

The commander gave her a stiff salute, appreciation gleaming in his eyes. Mandisa walked toward the house, then looked sideways, surprised that Tarik had fallen into step beside her. "Is there something I can do for you, captain?" She halted, her heart jumping in her chest. "Has something happened to Adom?"

"No." Tarik offered her a quick, reassuring smile. He gestured toward the path that led to the kitchens and led her away from the villa. "Shall we walk together? Your son is fine, except he continues to thoroughly bedevil Ani during the young masters' lessons. Apparently Ani's

97

recounting of the primeval creation does not agree with what you have told your son."

Mandisa smiled. "I don't know what is to be done about that. I have taught Adom what my father taught me, and I believe it is the truth. But Ani is a stubborn old man, he will not change his ideas."

"That is not why I sought you out."

"What, then?"

Stopping in the path, Tarik thrust his hands behind his back. "In your absence, the duty of looking after our lord's Canaanite prisoner has fallen to me and Halima."

She laughed at his somber expression. "And that chore has not been pleasant?"

"He grows more unruly and dangerous with each passing day. He has not eaten in nearly a week, for we cannot go near the door to bring him food. He throws things." The captain's brows drew downward in a frown. "If he were any other captive, I would have whipped him long ago, he would learn that such behavior will not be tolerated! But the vizier will not let us harm him. We are to leave him alone and let him rage."

"Is there nothing you can do?"

The guard's tight expression relaxed into a wry smile. "I have tried other ways to calm him. To thwart his devious plans, I removed all his clothing but a kilt, and we have not replaced the furniture, the vases, or bowls. As long as he rages, we do not even enter to clean his er, uh . . . private area. He sits in a loathsome, stinking shambles, and he still roars."

"A starving animal will bellow until it is nearly dead, Tarik," Mandisa said, moving along the path again. "And this beast is a particularly proud one, I daresay. He may not stop howling until he is too weak to be saved."

Tarik flashed a killer smile. "That is why the gods have returned you."

Oh no. She'd seen smiles like that before; they were bait for hungry fish. Well, this minnow would not bite.

"You think I can reason with him?" She grinned. "Ah, Tarik, you have been praying in vain. All the gods in Egypt couldn't force me into that room."

"But the vizier asked you to help."

"And I did. For several days. And the man hated me as much as he hates you."

"But he was not as violent when you visited him. And you are the only one fluent in his language. Surely you can reason with him."

Mandisa was about to argue, but movement caught her eye. Halima stepped out of the kitchen and offered a shy wave of greeting. Her singularly sweet smile faded, though, when she saw Tarik, and Mandisa did not need to be told why the girl's cheeks flooded with color.

Mandisa had long suspected that the slave girl was hopelessly in love with the vizier's captain. How could the foolish man not notice?

Smiling in the calm strength of knowledge, Mandisa returned Halima's wave, then looked back at the desperate guard. "I don't know how I can help, but if Halima will help me and if you stand guard when we go in, perhaps the three of us can manage the brute."

Tarik looked over his shoulder, saw Halima, and nodded in greeting. Mandisa watched, amused. Did he have any idea that love had bloomed in the poor girl's heart? Apparently not, for he only turned back to Mandisa and demanded to know if they could go immediately to face the Canaanite captive. "His room stinks. It is an affront to heaven itself, and if the vizier happens to wander in that part of the house—"

"I will go soon," Mandisa interrupted, moving past him to have a private word with Halima. "When I have refreshed myself. I am yet covered with dust from the journey."

AFTER TENDING to her mistress and unpacking the baskets of belongings brought from Heliopolis, Mandisa went in search of her son. She found him in the garden with Efrayim and Menashe. "Adom!" she called, her heart singing with delight at the sight of him.

"Mother!" He left his young playmates and threw his arms around her shoulders in a light embrace. "I am glad you are home!"

"I am happy, too." She breathed in his sweet scent. "But I hear you have been interrupting Ani's lessons."

"He tells the story wrong." Adom lifted his chin in a stubborn gesture as he pulled out of her arms. "He said that God Almighty created other gods."

"You should not contradict a teacher, especially an elder." She pressed her hand on the smooth skin of his shaved head and playfully tugged on the single long lock of hair growing from his temple. Soon he would have to surrender this childish coiffure and grow his hair out to a more manly length. Efrayim and Menashe still wore the long forelocks of children, but Adom was nearly grown. At some point in the near future he would have to find an occupation, something to fill his days, a way to earn a wage and make a life for himself.

"Adom," she said, drawing him near in a sudden rush of emotion, "I have prayed that El Shaddai would send someone to us. Someone who can teach you."

"Ani has taught me many things. I can read, and even write a little."

"Other things, my son."

"Will I have a tutor?"

She cringed inwardly at his assumption. He was a servant's son, and yet he too often assumed he was like the vizier's children, born to the aristocracy. Had she made a mistake in allowing him to spend so much time among people born above his place in life?

"Not exactly a tutor," she said, sinking to a garden bench. She pulled him to her side and ran her hand over the olive skin of his bare back. "I have asked God to send someone who can teach you things I cannot—how to work in the fields, perhaps, or how to mind the animals."

He nodded. "I like the horses. I wouldn't mind working with them."

She wrinkled her nose. The stables would not have been her first choice, but as long as the boy had *something* to do . . . "I suppose you could be of use to the stablemen. But I'm not certain who will come, or what he will teach you. But when this teacher comes, Adom, you must treat him with respect, listen to him, and learn from him. Do you understand?"

He regarded her with a wide, speculative gaze. "Is it the man in the locked room?"

Mandisa felt her mouth drop open. "The prisoner? By heaven, child, why would you think such a thing? Do you think God would send us someone as brutish as that?"

Adom shrugged. "I heard the slaves say he was from Canaan, the same place you were born."

"Well," Mandisa answered, annoyed with the gossiping slaves, "just because we come from the same region doesn't mean we are connected in any way. No, son, I am praying that God would send us a *good* man, an honorable teacher." She brightened her smile. "And I don't think the captive is particularly good or honorable, do you?"

Adom's mouth twitched with amusement. "No, Mother. I've heard him curse. He doesn't know I can understand him, but he yells the same words I've heard the sheep herders use."

"Don't listen to him or the herders." Mandisa gave him a playful nudge. "Now find the little ones and enjoy the time you have with them. But do not contradict Ani again."

Adom loped away. Mandisa took a moment to adjust the edges of her heavy wig, then turned toward the slave quarters. She had barely had time to bathe and reapply her makeup, but she had been determined to do so before facing the roaring lion of Canaan.

She frowned, remembering Adom's question. The prisoner as a suitable teacher—how had Adom come by such an outlandish idea? The captive was a feral monster, his hate a living, visible thing. Mandisa had seen bitter men like him before.

But she had agreed to help him. Girding herself with resolve, she walked with stiff, brittle dignity toward the captive's chamber.

NOT WILLING TO DEAL WITH the heightened emotions of Halima or Tarik for this first meeting with the Canaanite, she pulled one of the gate guards from his post. "Remain in the hallway and do not let the prisoner see you," she told him in a low voice. "I am going into the chamber alone."

The young man's brow furrowed. "But he is violent, and Tarik says—"

"Tarik has asked me to see to him," she said, cutting him off. "But I do not want him to escape and harm anyone in the household. So watch from behind the wall, out of sight, and if he leaves the room without me, summon help immediately. But if my suspicions are correct, there will be no need for a general alarm."

The guard shot her a half-frightened look. "The captain will not approve of this, lady. We are under orders that no one approaches that chamber without Tarik, and absolutely no one removes the bolt unless another guard stands near to offer assistance."

Mandisa waved aside his protests. "The stain of disobedience will be on my head, then, not yours."

SHIM'ON TENSED as he heard the slow rumble of the bolt. Had the guard come back? With that pale-faced wench who squeaked like a weasel every time he looked at her?

His stomach growled in anticipation of food; his anger strangled the sound. He glanced around the room, but he could find nothing else to throw. Broken shards of pottery and timber littered the floor; no furnishings remained but a down-filled mattress. Every costly piece of furniture and bric a brac had been shattered or ground to dust, a just penalty for the guard's foolish decision to take Shim'on's clothes from him. A decent man did not walk around half-dressed, not even in sweltering Egypt!

Crouched with his back against the wall, his hands gripped the sturdy linen of the kilt wrapped around his waist. If the guard came in, he'd lunge forward and kill the man with his own bare hands! Weak from hunger and numb from the monotony of confinement, Shim'on's strength and patience had completely evaporated. He would not bear another day of this torture.

The bolt fell to the floor outside with a hollow, thumping sound; the latch clicked. Shim'on frowned. The approach was different, the intruder's movements too carefree and confident. Could it be that the great vizier himself stood behind the door? If so, a hundred guards probably waited outside as well, each eager to aim a javelin at Shim'on's throat.

He slid upward along the wall, not even feeling the rough plaster as it scraped his skin. Cold sweat ran from his pores, beaded under his arms and on his upper lip. *God above, if this is the moment I must die . . .*

"Grace and peace be unto you." The words were Canaanite, the voice a woman's. Shim'on slumped back to the floor, his knees weak as the adrenaline left his body. His head swam as the door swung open. Then his eyes met the invader's, and he recognized her. The interpreter. The traitor.

"Grace and peace?" he snarled, wishing he had the energy and inclination to send her away. "What would you know of grace or peace? Only someone born in Canaan would speak as fluently as you do, so you have sold your heart and soul to these idolatrous people."

"I have sold nothing and am not for sale," she remarked, calmly stepping into the room. She actually turned her back on him as she lowered a water jug from her hip and closed the door.

Surprise siphoned the blood from Shim'on's head and dragged the power of speech from his tongue. He could think of nothing to say as she entered and pulled a fresh loaf of bread from a bag slung over her shoulder.

She kicked a few pieces of broken pottery out of the way, then knelt before him and extended the bread. "My family sold me to a passing Egyptian who thought to have me as his wife," she said, her paint-lengthened eyes intent upon his. "He brought me here and disappeared a year later. I am certain he is dead. He left me with a mountain of debts and a son."

Only half-listening, Shim'on focused on the door and the hallway beyond. He could not hear movement of any kind outside the door, so this was not a trick . . . unless it was a clever one. This foolish woman had apparently come to him unescorted, and though his strength had been depleted by hunger, he knew he could overpower her if he needed to. In this room, at least, he held the upper hand.

But he did not have to strike her now. Carefully, he reached out and took the bread. He sniffed it; the aroma was strong and hearty, without a trace of suspicious odors. And the loaf was crusty, not soft and mushy like that the other woman brought.

"So tell me," he said, breaking the loaf. "How did you come to live in the house of the mighty vizier?"

The beads in her braided hair clacked softly as she tilted her head. "I was sixteen when my husband disappeared. For three years I did whatever jobs a woman alone could find, but even in the time of plenty my son and I nearly starved. The man who owned the house where I lived threatened to throw my son and I into the streets because we owed him so much, and he finally brought his case before Zaphenath-paneah. Standing before the vizier, I had to admit I had no silver. And Zaphenath-paneah ruled that the landlord was right to collect what I owed him."

Her delicate features softened as she smiled. "I thought we would be sold into slavery and I would never see my son again, so I begged for mercy. And the one they call the King's Shadow Dispenser brought shade into my life. He paid my debts and restored my freedom, then he asked if I possessed any skills. When I replied that I would learn any decent trade in order to serve him, he said his wife, Lady Asenath, needed a handmaid. So Adom and I came to this house. We have been here nine years."

Shim'on ate silently, absorbing her words as his stomach rumbled in appreciation of the bread. She spoke with complete transparency and without hesitation, so she either spoke the truth or was an accomplished liar. But why would she lie? And why was she here? She had probably been ordered to feed him, and she had, but still she remained. What sort of plot was this?

"How many are outside the door?" he growled. "And why do I not hear them? They make me nervous, these plotting, prowling Egyptians . . ."

"No one is outside the door." She folded her hands. "One guard watches from down the hallway, but he is neither prowling nor plotting. I have been away with my mistress for many days, and thought you might like to talk with someone who speaks your language. Ani tells me that speech is civilization itself, so if we are to keep you civilized, you must be engaged in conversation."

Converse? With a woman? Is *that* why she lingered? Shim'on grinned and looked away, biting back the urge to laugh in her face. He might have missed the company of his brothers, his family, even his sons, but never in his life had he missed the conversation of women!

"Did I say something funny?"

Unable to stop himself, Shim'on threw back his head and let out a great peal of laughter. "By all the gods of this black land, yes! Why would I want to talk to a woman? Especially a painted harlot with an adder's tongue, a creature who serves the demented madman who holds me captive!"

She stood in a regal, powerful gesture. A crimson flood colored her face and belied her calm exterior.

"Ani also says isolation leads a man to depression, paranoia, and self-destruction," she said, moving toward the door. "But if it is only food you want, food is all you shall have." She paused and crinkled her nose as she looked around. "I had hoped we might clean this room."

"I am a herdsman, I like living like an animal," he snapped. Then, as he exploded in bitter laughter, she slipped from the room and slid the bolt back into place.

SHIM'ON KNEW she would not return that day, and something within him wondered if she would ever come again. By his harsh words he had probably sentenced himself to weeks of visitation from the captain and the squeaky slave girl, neither of whom cared enough to offer Shim'on a decent or interesting word. For the first time in his life, Shim'on began to regret something he'd done.

No one came the next morning, and Shim'on spent an hour tossing broken pottery chips at the door, certain that the Egyptians had decided to starve him. After a week had passed, perhaps longer, they would haul his emaciated corpse from this ruined chamber and disembowel it in one of their bizarre mummification rituals. Then, when his brothers returned with Binyamin to prove the vizier had imprisoned an innocent man, the deranged Zaphenath-paneah would summon servants who would bring in Shim'on's desiccated mortal shell. "Take *this* back to your father the old man," the vizier would shout. Yehuda would grow pale, unsophisticated Binyamin would faint, and Levi would throw himself at the guards, only to be killed by the steely-eyed captain . . .

Yes, Shim'on decided, sitting on the dusty floor with his hand over his ever-growling belly, he had definitely misspent his last chance for survival. He had almost been enjoying his conversation with the woman, until in one moment he insulted her beauty, her master, even her morality . . .

And women didn't forgive easily. He had only to remember his mother to understand *that* truth. After Rahel's death, his father had continued to spend his nights in Rahel's tent with Yosef and Binyamin, for he found little comfort in Lea's cold shoulder.

Yet at sunset, when Shim'on had almost given up hope, the woman returned. The bolt slid away as before, the door opened and she stood before him, her slender neck rising above a silken gown like silvery tissue. But this time she kept her eyes averted from his. Though she came into the room as bravely as she had the previous day, the bold and cheeky attitude had disappeared.

"If you are hungry, here is bread." Her sharp tone stabbed the air. She did not move to extend her hand.

"I am hungry," he admitted, rising to his knees.

She pulled the loaf and a bit of cheese from the pouch at her waist. Cautiously, she extended both, and as he stood to take them, her eyes lifted to meet his.

Ah, the pain there was like Lea's, dark and brooding. For a brief instant her eyes shimmered like pools of appeal, then she lowered her gaze and turned toward the door.

"Don't go." The words slipped from his mouth before he had even willed himself to say them.

"Why should I stay?" Her back was to him, yet she lifted her head.

"You are hungry, I brought you food. Surely there is nothing else you need. You *like* living like an animal, remember?"

"I was wrong." His voice grated in his own ears. "You were right, I would like—I need to talk to someone." *Levi would faint if he could hear me now.* "I would like to apologize. Please forgive me."

She turned, and the heavy lashes that had shadowed her cheeks flew up. "*Forgive* you?"

By the sun and moon, would she make him repeat himself? But these were conditions of war, and a man was allowed to do anything necessary to remain alive. "Yes. I must beg your forgiveness."

She tilted her head like a queen granting favors, and he thought he saw a faint look of amusement on her face. "I accept your apology."

He sank back onto the floor, attempting to put her more at ease, and unwrapped the square of cheese she'd given him. Cautiously, she knelt in a small cleared space by the door. "I suppose we could start with introductions," she said, tucking her legs under her. She folded her hands in her lap. "I am Mandisa, handmaid to Lady Asenath."

Shim'on nodded and swallowed a mouthful of cheese. "I am Shim'on, second-born son of Yaakov." His realized his tone was as dry as his mouth. "And I suppose you remember why I am here."

"Of course."

A long silence followed, and Shim'on cast quickly about for a topic of conversation. He was unused to the social company of women. He had married two, buried two, slept with them, eaten their food and disciplined their children, but he couldn't ever recalling *conversing* with a woman. Except Dina.

"How old are you?" he asked.

Caught off guard, she laughed, the most delightful sound he'd heard in weeks. "Why do you ask?" she said, her hand creeping to her brightening cheek. "Do you think me a horse, that you could buy me? Would you like to count my teeth?"

His mouth trembled with the need to laugh with her. "No." He looked at the bread in his hand, again at a loss for words. "Yesterday you said you were not for sale. I believe you."

They sat in silence, then Shim'on bit off a huge hunk of bread. As long as he chewed she wouldn't expect him to talk. And as long as he behaved, she wouldn't leave.

He didn't know why it was so important that she stay. She was unlike any other woman he'd ever met. She'd walked boldly into his room when he was at his worst, not flinching at his stench, his words, or his threatening aspect. And while most women chattered among themselves like a mob of sparrows, this woman weighed her words. Perhaps it came from working for a high-born lady, or perhaps her quiet spirit was innate, like his own quick temper . . .

She leaned forward. "Tell me about your family."

And so he did. As he ate he told her of his mother, Lea, and his father, Yaakov. He laughed, describing the comical exploits of his children, and sobered as he spoke of Re'uven and Levi, Yehuda and Dan. And as he talked, he found that revisiting his memories somehow brought his loved ones near, kept them close.

He might have talked for an hour or more; he only knew he was disappointed when she stood to leave. "Must you go?" he asked, glad the gathering darkness hid the blush upon his neck.

"My lady will need me to see her to bed," Mandisa answered, moving toward the door. She paused for a last look at his room before leaving. "I will send a maid to clean this pigsty if you promise not to throw things at her."

Shim'on flushed. "I will not . . . throw anything."

She smiled. "I will return tomorrow, and you can tell me more. Until then, sleep well."

CHAPTER SEVENTEEN

ANI WATCHED THE GROWING FRIENDSHIP BETWEEN MANDISA AND THE Canaanite captive with growing approval. The entire household had benefited from the relationship. Mandisa endured what she called her "daily trial" with good grace. The prisoner himself threw fewer tantrums and his rages of temper were generally less violent than before. Tarik, visibly relieved that he wouldn't be forced to kill Zaphenath-paneah's pampered prisoner, never ceased to praise Mandisa's gentle work with the captive, and Halima sang in simple gladness because she no longer had to venture near the room where the caged animal roared.

The proper duty of a steward was to act as the eyes and ears of the house, so Ani habitually crept along the hallways, listening at windows and eavesdropping with an ear to the walls. Zaphenath-paneah seemed strangely distant these days, and Ani assumed the vizier was preoccupied with the famine and the distribution of grain to the far-flung cities of the kingdom. But though the vizier rarely followed up on a prisoner after a sentence had been rendered, Zaphenath-paneah made a point of being in his wife's chamber every night as Mandisa readied her mistress for bed. During his nocturnal rounds Ani discovered that the master never failed to question Mandisa about the Canaanite captive.

One night Ani pressed his ear against the outer wall of his mistress's chamber and strained to hear the low murmur of Mandisa's voice. "I was wondering, my lord, whether or not it might be good for my son Adom to spend time with this Canaanite," he heard her ask. "Adom is half Canaanite, and I have asked your Almighty God to bring a strong man into his life. The captive is not as gruff as he would have us believe. I believe that under his rough exterior beats a vulnerable heart."

Ani clung to the wall in a paralysis of astonishment. Mandisa would trust her son to the caged beast?

Zaphenath-paneah must have read Ani's thoughts. "You trust him?" he asked. "I know he has calmed considerably, but he is unpredictable—"

"It if please you, my lord, I have heard him speak tenderly of his sister and his children," Mandisa answered. "I do not believe he would hurt Adom. But of course, I will be nearby."

"If you trust Shim'on, far be it from me to interfere," the vizier answered, a trace of humor in his voice. "But proceed carefully, Mandisa. The man has a vicious temper."

"By the horns of Khnum, don't we all know it," Ani murmured, leaning away from the wall. He rubbed his chin with his wrist and stared at the empty hall ahead. Zaphenath-paneah would never have agreed to allow Adom, of whom he was genuinely fond, to spend time with a spy. So if the vizier believed this Shim'on was innocent of the charges against him, why did he still hold him?

Ani walked away, carefully lifting his feet so his papyrus sandals made no sound across the marble floor. Something unusual bubbled beneath the surface of life in the vizier's house, but Ani had never stumbled over a mystery he had not been able to eventually unearth.

CHAPTER EIGHTEEN

MANDISA LICKED THE TIP OF HER FINGER AND DABBED AT A SMUDGE ON her son's cheek.

"Mother!" Adom complained, ducking.

"There. At least you look presentable." She turned back to the table in her small chamber and idly fingered her comb, wondering why Shim'on's opinion of the boy should matter. Adom was her son and she loved him; Shim'on was a prisoner who would soon leave the vizier's house and return to his home in Canaan. But in recent days she had entertained the niggling idea that God Shaddai might intend the Canaanite prisoner to teach her son. She had spoken to the vizier; she had prepared Adom. But she hadn't dared to ask Shim'on if he'd be willing to spend time with the boy.

Better to urge him gently, to let him volunteer. In her short time of marriage, she had learned that men responded better to diplomatic hints than forthright suggestions.

"Do you understand that you must not make him angry?" Mandisa asked, turning to her son.

"You've asked me that ten times already."

"Well, if you are to visit the captive with me, you must be on your best behavior."

"I understand, Mother," Adom answered, self-consciously tugging on his kilt. With a flash of understanding, she realized he was nervous. And why wouldn't he be? He had heard the screams and curses from Shim'on's chamber during those early weeks.

"Adom," she said, running her fingers over the silken lock of his hair, "you need not fear Shim'on. He has a sharp tongue, but the best way to take the wind out of an angry man's sails is to stay calm."

"I know." Adom squirmed under her touch. "Can we go? Efrayim and Menashe want me to tell them what he looks like and how he talks. Menashe has heard that the captive growls even in his sleep."

Her smile faded a little. "Surely you don't believe that?"

"No," Adom admitted. "I told them my mother wouldn't go near a man who growled."

"You're right, I wouldn't." Mandisa gave his cheek a playful pinch. "But our friend Shim'on is tired of being confined. He likes open spaces, and he misses his freedom."

"Then why doesn't the vizier let him out?"

Mandisa tilted her head. "I don't know, Son. If Shim'on can be trusted to control himself, perhaps Tarik will allow him to walk in the gardens or the courtyard. We shall have to ask our master."

Adom reached out and tugged on her hand so hard he nearly pulled her off balance. "All right, let's go!"

"I'm coming," she said, following him. "But first we find Halima and prepare his tray, then we visit the prisoner. Shim'on will be hungry."

As Adom raced ahead of her toward the kitchen, her thoughts filtered back to recent conversations in which Shim'on had spoken of his own children. He had six sons by two different wives, he told her, unaware that her smile dimmed when he spoke of other women. His oldest son was twenty-one, the youngest, fifteen, and they blended seamlessly into the family compound, no more Shim'on's children than Levi's, no less Shim'on's sons than Re'uven's. "Since my wives died and they have had no mothers to spoil them," he said, his eyes darkening with some emotion she couldn't interpret, "they have made themselves at home wherever they could. Yehuda's wife is good to the younger two, and Re'uven's wife is partial to the older ones—I think. In any case, I have never worried about them. They are in the good care of their uncles."

Mandisa couldn't understand why he would be willing to allow his sons to remain apart from him, for he seemed a natural and patient teacher. Once he put aside his resentment toward the vizier and his captivity, his tongue loosened and he talked to her of many things, mostly of his brothers, the land of Canaan, and the simple beauty of agrarian existence. Lately she had found herself recalling the life she had known before coming to Thebes, but she hastily closed the door on those memories. Nothing remained for her in Canaan, so there was no use thinking about the past.

Shim'on seemed to fill her thoughts a great deal. It was only natural, she told herself, that she should think of him when she spent at least two hours a day doing what Ani called "keeping the beast at bay." Without someone to talk to, the restless prisoner was apt to storm about his chamber and disrupt the household.

Even with her attention, he was often irritable and gloomy, but she learned how to lift his spirits by asking for his advice. On one occasion she brought him news of a sickness affecting the vizier's cattle, and he had prescribed powdered root bark of the *avionah*, or caper bush, the perfect poultice to draw out the infection. Another time she told him about a goat that no longer gave milk, and Shim'on prescribed a mash of falcon's eye, or chick-peas. The concoction spurred the nanny goat's milk to flow within two days.

He flushed in pleasure when she reported the success of his efforts, but his good nature could change as swiftly as a chameleon changes colors. Extremely stubborn, he refused to alter a position or opinion even if she pointed out its falseness, yet he was unfailingly loyal to the few people he held in affection: namely, his sister and his brothers. He could be caring and even gentle—once she was several hours late bringing his meal, and instead of the rage she feared, he greeted her with tenderness, concerned that some illness had befallen her.

Halima warned Mandisa that Shim'on might be using her. "He is a savage," she announced one afternoon as she helped prepare his dinner tray. "He will take advantage of your kind sympathy. When you least expect it, he will strike you and flee from this place. He hates us all. I've even heard him call down curses upon our master's god."

Mandisa did not believe Shim'on's newfound stillness rested upon ulterior motives, but she wondered if he could be trusted. Though he hated his confinement, he behaved as though it hadn't occurred to him that she might ask the master for permission for him to wander around the house and grounds. Yet he had to know such permission lay within her grasp. A few of her words in the master's ear would certainly win approval, and yet Shim'on did not suggest or even hint that she press for his liberty.

So what was she to him—an ally, a necessary evil, a benevolent captor? She did not know, but hoped he was friend enough to agree to spend time with Adom. Shim'on was rugged, rough, and wise in the ways of men, everything she was not, and Adom would need those qualities if he were to survive in the world beyond Zaphenath-paneah's house.

El Shaddai, she reasoned, worked in unexpected ways, but she could not doubt that He was working.

SHIM'ON LIFTED his head in anticipation when he heard Mandisa's familiar rap. An idea had occurred to him in the night, and he had many things to ask her. He wanted to know more about the Egyptian festivals, for if the vizier celebrated a feast day, perhaps he would be inclined to release his captives for at least a few hours of liberty . . .

The bolt thumped onto the floor outside and the door opened, but instead of the woman he expected, a slender, bright-eyed boy stepped into the room.

"What variety of desert dung are you?" Shim'on snapped. The boy stepped back, his mouth agape, and Mandisa swept in behind him, anger lighting her eyes. "In the name of decency, Shim'on, can't you bridle your tongue? This is my son, Adom."

Her reprimand tore away the few remaining shreds of his good humor. "Am I a monkey in a cage, that the children of this cursed house come to gape at me?" Shim'on's jaw clenched. "It is bad enough that I must talk to you or go insane. I never said I would perform for your son."

"Adom, wait in the hall for me," Mandisa answered, her eyes darkening as she held Shim'on's gaze. When the boy had left the room and closed the door, she advanced toward Shim'on with the fury of a tigress. "You have six sons and you ought to miss them," she said, her lower lip trembling as she glared up at him. "I thought it might do you good to spend time with a boy who needs a father."

"A father?" He nearly choked on the word. "By heaven, woman, what makes you think I want to be around children? I don't spend time with my own boys, I certainly don't want to entertain yours."

She stepped back, her eyes sparkling with tears, and Shim'on gritted his teeth, irritated beyond all reason. "I don't know what you want from me," he said, scrubbing his hair with his knuckles. "A father brings children into the world. That's what I've done. That's all I know how to do."

"A father—" Mandisa crossed her arms across her chest— "loves his children. He teaches them what they need to know in order to survive in the world."

"Well," Shim'on drawled, "perhaps that is what *your* father did, but my father did nothing for us. Yaakov, son of Yitzhak, beget twelve sons and divided his love among two. The rest of us were left to tend to our mothers and learn from each other."

She flinched and did not answer, but some of the fire went out of her eyes. Shim'on put his hand on his hip and looked down at the floor, disappointed at the unexpected turn of events. He had hoped to pass the afternoon with this woman, but now she was upset. And, like a woman, she wouldn't be able to walk away and forget this conversation. She'd want to talk about it, but Shim'on would not waste his energy talking about Yaakov.

"I'm sorry your father did not give you what you needed," she finally said, her voice fragile and shaking. She would not look at him. "But you must understand—I fear for my son, who has no father at all."

His mind rumbled with sour thoughts. "Perhaps he is better off."

"I think not." She looked at him then, and her eyes narrowed in pain. "Shim'on, my son needs someone to teach him, to talk to him. Efrayim and Menashe are too young. Tarik and Ani and Zaphenath-paneah are too busy."

"And I have nothing to do, is that it?"

She uncrossed her arms and lowered her head. "I have begged God Almighty to send someone to me. In the last few weeks I have realized that the someone God sends might be you."

Incredulous laughter floated up from his throat. "You think God put me in prison for *your* sake?"

She shook her head, but he could see the beginnings of a shy smile on her face. "I think God Almighty can transform ill into good. And you are from Canaan, as am I, and Adom speaks the Canaanite language. My son would be honored, he would be *blessed* to learn from a man of Canaan."

Shim'on stiffened, making an effort to conquer his involuntary reactions to that gentle look. No one had ever looked at him . . . as if he might be *admirable.* His anger evaporated, leaving only confusion.

A mocking voice inside insisted that she was not to be trusted, that she spied for the cursed vizier.

Shim'on stepped forward until he stood only inches away from her. "Tell me, Mandisa," he said, his tone commanding her to look up at him, "why would you trust your son to a man you consider dangerous? I am hated and feared in this house. I hear the servants whisper as they run by my door."

"You may be feared," she whispered, her eyes growing large as they lifted to meet his, "but it is your strength that frightens them. You have a temper, Shim'on, no doubt, but you have great courage and tenacity. There is much good in you."

He looked away, unable to think under her steady scrutiny. What if she was using him and trying to coerce a confession of some sort? Did the vizier hope to disarm and dupe his captive through the charms of a lovely woman? If so, he would fail.

Shim'on stood in the hush until he had an answer. If the vizier was using Mandisa, then Shim'on could use her, too. "I will talk with your son," he said, aware that the scent of lilies rose from her skin, "if you speak to the vizier about allowing me out of this chamber." He managed a ragged smile. "I have been a model prisoner of late; the guards will support your request. I want to be released for half a day every day."

"An hour or two only, and Tarik will not want you to leave the villa," Mandisa answered, looking away.

Shim'on smiled. Her reply had come too easily; she had anticipated his request. Either the captain or the vizier had coached her.

"Perhaps your son and I can walk around the villa together," he said, breathing in the scent of her light, warm femininity. "But you must take my request to your master before I will allow your boy to come into my sight again."

She did not look up, but nodded and moved toward the door.

"And Mandisa," he lowered his voice, "I don't know what good I will be for Adom. I don't know how to be a father. I'm not sure I knew how to be a son."

Her gaze filled with a tenderness he'd never seen in them before. "Thank-you, Shim'on," she said, her voice a velvet murmur in the room. "Thank you very much."

HE WAS NOT surprised when Mandisa rapped early the next day. The captain of the vizier's guard stood outside when she opened the door, and Adom stepped around the corner, his young face bright with eagerness. A quick glance left and right assured Shim'on that the captain had taken no chances. Guards stood in the hallways, blocking all possible means of escape.

"The garden," Mandisa said simply, pointing the way.

Ignoring the boy, Shim'on walked through the hall. A columned, roofed portico bridged the gap between the house and the garden's open expanse, and Shim'on strode through it, eager to feel the sun on his face. Once inside the walled garden, he closed his eyes in simple relief. Sunlight burnished the late morning air; he could almost feel his skin toasting under the warm rays. He breathed in the sweet-smelling wind as the air vibrated to a long drop of birdsong from the nearby Nile.

Opening his eyes, he knew he had never seen so spectacular a garden. A fishpond dotted with blue lotus blossoms dominated the large rectangular area, and the fertile black mud on its banks had been planted with a border of red poppies, blue cornflowers, and yellow-fruited mandrakes. Several varieties of flowering and fruit-bearing trees, each sitting in its own well of water, surrounded the fishpond— *carica* figs and sycamore figs; date-palms and *dom*-palms, carob trees, willows, tamarisk, myrtles, and brightly-petaled acacias. A host of gardeners, each working with a shaduf, poured water from the pond into runnels that criss-crossed through the garden plots. Standing amid the flowering beauty of the vizier's garden, Shim'on found it hard to believe that famine and drought raged just outside the villa's pink-washed walls.

"Come, boy," he said, after a moment. "Come sit beside me and I'll teach you how to get water from the desert grass."

"Truly?" The boy's countenance lifted as the long-legged youth approached Shim'on.

"It will be difficult, seeing that this is not the desert," Shim'on said, shrugging as he moved toward a stone bench beside the pathway, "but once you know a thing that can save your life, you don't forget it."

"I can learn," the boy answered, his eyes shining with enthusiasm. "Teach me something Efrayim and Menashe do not know."

Shim'on sank to the bench. "And who are Efrayim and Menashe?" He propped his elbows on his knees and glanced around. Mandisa and Tarik had retreated to the portico beside the house, giving him at least the illusion of freedom.

"Efrayim and Menashe are the master's sons," Adom answered. Shim'on lifted a brow. The names were remarkably similar to words he knew, but surely the Lord High Vizier of all Egypt would not give his sons Canaanite names.

Shim'on bent to the boy's level. "The most important thing to remember in the desert is *all trails lead to water*. And death comes quickly, my boy, to a man or an animal without water."

"All trails?" Adom asked, a skeptical look on his face. "Is a trail like a path?"

"By heaven above, woman," Shim'on called, looking over at Mandisa. "Has the boy never been out of this house?"

"Of course," Mandisa answered, indignation on her face. "But he does not roam about in the wilderness as you seem to expect he should."

Shim'on would have answered that the wilderness brought up better boys than the sissified atmosphere of an Egyptian villa, but he held his tongue. He had to be careful; he had worked too hard to earn this woman's trust. In her, he knew, lay the keys to greater freedom. If he had to play nursemaid to her son for a few hours of escape, he would do it. But nurturing did not come naturally, for the sons of Yisrael had never tolerated softness. Of all his brothers, only Yosef had ever played nursemaid to a younger sibling. From the first, Yosef had delighted in baby Binyamin, coddling him as if he could make up for the baby's missing mother . . .

Yosef again. Abruptly, Shim'on returned his thoughts to the matter at hand. "All trails—yes, paths—lead to water, and if you are thirsty, you should follow the direction in which all trails converge. Trails will be marked by signs of camps—campfire ashes, animal droppings, trampled terrain. Also, birds tend to circle over water. Most flocks fly to watering places at dawn and sunset. Just as the earth points to the Creator God, so birds will point you to water."

"Which Creator god do you speak of?" Adom asked, a strangely adult gleam in his eye. "Neter or El Shaddai?"

Shim'on lifted a brow. "Neter? Is this some Egyptian idol?"

"Neter is the unseen God of the Egyptians," Mandisa answered, apparently unable to resist meddling. She stepped forward. "But most people in Thebes pay Neter no attention. They prefer the gods who live in temples, gods they can see and placate."

Shim'on looked back to the boy, approving of the intelligence he saw in the lad's face. "Each man worships his own god, boy. You will have to make your own choice."

"Which god do you worship, Shim'on?" Adom asked.

Shim'on cast a quick look at Mandisa. "None, at the moment, for I am not at *liberty* to worship any. But my father worships God Almighty and clings to the belief that he and his people are part of a chosen race. He says the Almighty made a covenant with our grandfather Avraham."

Adom's eyes burned with eager curiosity. "What covenant is this?"

Shim'on stared into the memory of his past. "God Shaddai called Avraham out of his country and promised to make him a great nation, to amplify his name. In return for Avraham's obedience, God promised to bless those who blessed Avraham and his seed, and to curse those who offered curses instead of blessing. He promised to give us the land of Canaan as an eternal dwelling place, and to bless all families of the earth through our family lineage."

"A great honor," Mandisa whispered.

"A great fantasy," Shim'on answered, meeting her gaze. "The land of Canaan is not ours and has never been, we own only a small burial plot there. And our family has not been blessed, but cursed. One of my brothers died at seventeen, two nephews were struck down in their youth, my sister has been forever disgraced. That bloody business at Shekhem upset our father, then Re'uven slept with one of my father's concubines and angered the old man beyond belief—"

He stopped and bit his lip when Mandisa jerked Adom to his feet. "Your lesson is done," she said, pushing her son toward the house. "Go and find Ani, and ask where you might be of help."

Shim'on waited until the boy had left the garden, then he stroked his beard in what he hoped was a reproachful posture. "I'm sorry, but I warned you. I don't know how to behave around children. "

"You might learn to speak of more pleasant things," she said, wrapping her arms about herself as if to defend her honor from the wickedness he had described.

"My family is not pleasant," he responded, abandoning all pretense. "Murder, rape, incest, disloyalty, betrayal—all these I have known within my own kin. If my clan is not unsullied enough for your tastes—"

"Mine is no better," she answered, meeting his gaze straight on. "But I do not discuss such things around children. And I would not dare call the promises of Almighty God a mere fantasy."

"Your faith is stronger than mine, then." Shim'on stretched out one leg and crossed his arms. "Don't tell me you would chose the invisible El Shaddai over the Egyptian gods. I hear the idols take cruises up and down the Nile, they visit harems of beautiful women and bestow gifts to the crowds who follow them."

"I prefer a god who does not make me yawn with familiarity," she answered, moving toward the portico. She turned and cast her parting words over her shoulder. "A god who fills me with awe . . .a god I cannot control, but who can control me."

"Good luck on your search, then." Shim'on smiled at her naiveté. "When you find this awe-inspiring God, be sure to let me know. I may want to worship Him, too."

CHAPTER NINETEEN

MANDISA HAD NOT WALKED MORE THAN TEN PACES FROM THE GARDEN when she sensed that something was amiss. The ordinary, usual noises of the house had abruptly ceased and waves of silence seemed to reverberate through the hallways.

"Adom!" she gasped, fearing the worst. He could have run from the garden and dashed under the hooves of a chariot horse, or run in front of Tarik's archers as they practiced their marksmanship . . .

The hard fist of fear tightened in her stomach when she saw a crowd gathered on the portico at the front courtyard. The house slaves and servants had clustered in a knot on the front steps; herdsmen, stableboys, and guards ringed the periphery. Every eye was intent upon something in the distance, every mouth remained silent as the members of Zaphenath-paneah's household strained to hear whatever was happening near the gate keeper's lodge.

"What is it?" Mandisa cried, struggling to push her way through the crowd. "Is anyone hurt?"

One of the women on the portico turned, and Mandisa nearly melted in relief when she recognized Halima. "Halima, what has happened?" Her hand flew to her throat as a new thought struck her. "Have the brothers from Canaan returned?"

"We could not be so fortunate." The slave girl shook her head. "I don't know why the men are behaving like such fools. The master buys new slaves at least once a month."

"New slaves?" Mandisa's mind whirled. "All of this—the guards have gathered—just to look at new slaves?"

"One slave," Halima corrected, envy twisting her voice. "They've come pouring out of the woodwork to look at *her*."

Mandisa stared in confusion, and Halima pointed over the heads of the men in front of her. "Ani and Zaphenath-paneah visited the slave market this morning. I've already heard the story from one of the guards who accompanied them. It seems *she* was up for auction, and creating quite a disturbance, when one of the onlookers challenged Ani to buy her. He refused, knowing full well that such a woman only causes trouble."

"Trouble?"

"In fact," Halima lowered her voice as she pulled Mandisa from the crowd, "one of the bodyguards told me the master had already turned to go, but then, without explanation, the master ordered Ani to buy the woman and bring her here."

A shadow of distress crossed Halima's face. "I was thanking the gods because the Canaanite had calmed. But now our master has brought us another troublemaker—and this one will create a different kind of difficulty."

Halima stalked away, still muttering under her breath. Driven by curiosity, Mandisa wormed her way through the group of onlookers until she could see the gatekeeper's lodge. A woman in a gauzy garment stood there, her wrists and ankles shackled. Ani stood behind her, urging the gatekeeper to hurry and remove the woman's bonds.

Mandisa would have known the newcomer as a harlot even without the earrings, the nose ring, the bracelets and bangles. The woman's curled hair flowed down onto her shoulders in a soft dark tide that shone in the sunlight. Her bearing was about as subtle as a parade, her shape as sensuous as her ripe mouth. She stared out at her audience like a black panther, darkly beautiful and deadly. For some inexplicable reason, Mandisa felt her stomach contract in an odd little spasm.

"Who is she?" she murmured, not expecting an answer.

"Her name is Tizara," a guard next to her replied, his eyes as fixed as a stone idol's. "She is our master's new slave."

Amid a scattering of nervous laughter, one of the kitchen slaves joked: "I don't think the mistress will be letting the master anywhere near her."

Obviously uncomfortable, Ani lifted his eyes to the congregated slaves and clapped his hands in disapproval. As the slaves, guards, and servants reluctantly returned to their duties, a guard took Tizara's arm and escorted her to the slave quarters.

Mandisa had nearly reached her own small chamber when Ani appeared at her side. "You must help me," he said, shifting his weight from foot to foot. "I don't know what I'm to do with the creature, but I could not dissuade the master. I tried to convince him she'd be a problem, but he insisted I bring her here."

"Why did he buy her?" Mandisa asked. "Can't he see what she is?"

"He said something about no soul being beyond redemption, and how could I argue with that? You know he has a softness in his heart, he is continually buying slaves in order to free them."

"But what does she know how to do?" Mandisa interrupted. "I mean, of what *practical* use is she?"

"I don't know." Ani wrung his hands. "But if I put her in the kitchens, the men will fight over the opportunity to grind corn next to her. And if I send her to the fields—oh, by the gods, I could never do that. Nothing would ever get done, and she'd be too far away, I couldn't watch her. I could never assign her to the master or mistress, and *I* have no use for her."

Mandisa shook her head. "I still can't see why he bought her. He is not the type to be moved by a woman like that."

"Our master did not even look at her," Ani answered, color rising in his cheeks. "He had walked away, but the auctioneer called the woman's name and said she was from Shekhem."

Shekhem. That bloody business at Shekhem. . .

"She is a Canaanite," Mandisa said, not daring to look Ani in the eye.

He would not understand, but she grasped at least a little of the reason for the master's compassion. This woman was from his country, from Mandisa's and Shim'on's.

"So? What am I supposed to do with her?"

"Why don't you assign her to the children?" Mandisa suggested, giving the steward a small smile. "She can keep an eye on Efrayim and Menashe when they are not having lessons. Since the Canaanite captive has come, I do not have as much time for them as I used to. The slaves who have been watching the boys would rather be back to their former work."

A cry of relief broke from the older man's lips. "Ah, Mandisa, you are a jewel! For now, at least, you have solved the problem. And since this is your idea, you must help me. You must make certain that the girl never goes into the Lady Asenath's presence, that would never do. And since you are a lady of noble bearing, perhaps you can teach her how to be modest and carry herself like a proper lady."

Mandisa put up her hands. "Wait, Ani, I don't want to care for your little scarlet bird. The master told *you* to buy her."

"But what can I do with her?" The old man clapped his hand to his balding head. "You, my dear Mandisa, are the one to oversee her. Promise me you will."

"I won't."

"But it is your master's wish."

"He has said nothing to *me* about it."

"But he will. All I have to do is put a word in his ear."

Mandisa paused, knowing Ani spoke the truth. The same compassion that had inspired Zaphenath-paneah to ask if Mandisa would be willing to comfort Shim'on would soon ask her to guide this offensive harlot. Because she loved her master and his wife, she could refuse them nothing . . . and it would be more gracious to volunteer before being asked.

She lifted her hands in resignation. "All right, I'll look after her. Send her to me in the morning after our mistress is dressed, and I'll take her on a tour of the villa and tell her how to care for the children."

"Mandisa, I could kiss you," Ani said, clapping his hands together.

And then, while she gasped, he pulled her forehead to his lips and did just that.

𓅂

Two weeks later, as Thebes celebrated the arrival of a new year, Tarik was less concerned about the boisterous drunks in the streets than keeping peace within the walls of Zaphenath-paneah's villa. Standing by the gatekeeper's lodge, he stiffened as the new woman sashayed across the courtyard, two mystified boys in her wake. A man would have to be made of stone not to notice her, even *burn* for her, as she passed by. Her slow and swaying walk summoned lustful thoughts from their hiding places, and when her eyes turned toward a man, his face and blood grew hot . . .

"Tarik." A soft voice wrested his attention. Halima stood next to him, undisguised hurt in her eyes.

"What is it?"

"There is trouble in the kitchen. The baker says he is to serve Tizara and the children at the mid-day meal; the vintner insists it is his duty. An hour ago they came to blows. Though they have ceased striving for the moment, I am afraid one will kill the other."

"They are fools," Tarik muttered under his breath, willing himself not to take one last look toward the vixen in the courtyard. Placing his hand upon the knife in his belt, he strode toward the kitchen, dimly aware that Halima followed.

𓅂

"Will you little monkeys be quiet?" Tizara forced the words with studied calmness, afraid that one more boyish outburst would force her to scream.

Efrayim, the most naturally quiet of the pair, looked up. He lay under his brother in the sand of the courtyard, the loser in a lop-sided wrestling match.

"Tizara?"

"What?"

"Can we splash in the garden pool? If we promise not to make much noise?"

She sighed. If they got wet, she'd have to march them past a hundred scorn-filled, disapproving sets of eyes and into their chambers for fresh kilts and a hair-washing. But at least they'd be entertained for a while.

"Yes, but walk, don't run, to the garden. I will join you in a bit."

The boys took off like jackrabbits as Tizara bent to gather their tops, toys, and sandals. What was she doing here? Try as she might, she could not put all the pieces together.

She had not been surprised when she brought a high price at the slave auction, nor was she shocked to learn that she had been purchased by the Grand Vizier of Egypt, regent to the young Pharaoh. Her special skills were in great demand; she felt her power every time she walked before a crowd and adopted the role the men seemed to expect of her. The act was second nature to her now—a certain way of walking, a manner of half-closing the eyes, a bold smile that promised a moment of immortality, a sensuous purr . . .

But a nursemaid needed none of those skills. So why had the vizier paid a top price for her and assigned her to his children?

She had gaped in disbelief when the steward told her of the vizier's wishes. "Children?" she asked, stammering in confusion. "The vizier does not want me—for himself?"

"The vizier contents himself with the charms of his wife," the steward answered, his expression taut and derisive.

"Then perhaps he intends to give me to Pharaoh." She smiled and studied her manicured, henna-tinted fingertips. "Perhaps you should double-check with the vizier before you send me to care for children."

"Believe me, young woman, if given my choice, I'd send you into the street," Ani answered, his eyes narrowing. "But the vizier expressly asked me to find you a job, and I'm assigning you to his children. It is my wish; therefore it is your command."

Throughout her twenty-two years men had vied for her and lied for her. She had seen them make fools of themselves in order to spend a week, even a night with her. She had been used and abused, petted and praised, bartered and sold. She thought she had seen everything and nothing would surprise her again.

But Zaphenath-paneah had. She caught a glimpse of the handsome vizier in the slave market and sighed in relief when she learned he would be her master. Most of the men she encountered had been hardened by desire and uglied by determination. Whether they were soldiers, priests, husbands, fathers, farmers, or kings, they all wore the same twisted, lecherous look when they came into her tent. At the slave market she suspected that Zaphenath-paneah might be unusual, but she had no idea how different he would prove to be.

AS THE WEEKS PASSED, Mandisa rejoiced that at least one male in the household remained free of Tizara's influence. Since Shim'on's last visit with Adom had not gone as she expected, he had remained confined to his chamber and so had neither seen nor heard of Tizara. Mandisa was determined that he would not. The man was difficult to manage even in his calmer, resigned state of mind, so his boiling blood did not need to be stirred by the sight of a harlot from his own country.

Grudgingly keeping her promise to Ani, Mandisa met with Tizara each morning to outline the slave's duties with the children. After watching a blush run like a shadow over Adom's cheeks the first time he met Tizara, Mandisa decided that he did not need a nursemaid. Efrayim and Menashe, on the other hand, needed constant supervision. And though they were old enough to realize Tizara was pretty, they were young enough not to care.

Each morning Mandisa listened to Tizara's complaints with a vague sense of unreality. Though the slave understood well her effect upon men, she could not understand why the women of the vizier's household seemed to regard her with disdain. "Women just don't like me," she told

Mandisa one morning, lifting a slender bare shoulder in a gesture that captivated the guards twenty paces away. "I have no idea why."

Mandisa wanted to scream that perhaps it was because Tizara was shallow, flighty, egotistical, and lazy, but she had promised to help, not hinder. So she bit her tongue and walked toward the garden, reluctantly resigned to the fact that Tizara would follow.

Mandisa was willing to admit that Tizara provoked them all to jealousy, but her willowy beauty, while exceptional, sprang more from attitude than physical perfection. What was it that made her seem more sensuous than other women? Tizara's eyes were wide, her nose straight, and her lips full. But occasionally Mandisa caught the slave in an unguarded moment of deep thought, and the hard, bitter look on Tizara's narrow face was anything but beautiful.

The slave had but one duty—to watch over and attend to the master's sons—but while the boys studied with Ani, Tizara flitted around Mandisa like an annoying mosquito. The former harlot had both a low tolerance for routine and a wild imagination, and Mandisa found it difficult to keep her temper when the girl buzzed around with complaints and wild stories.

Through a stream of constant babble Mandisa learned the slave's history. Tizara had been raised in Shekhem, sold into slavery at a young age, and trained in the "art of pleasing" before she reached maturity. A group of camel traders had owned her first, carting her from settlement to settlement, offering her services for silver. She had known both pleasant and brutal masters, she told Mandisa, but never thought to enter as boring an existence as the one she had come to know in the vizier's house.

"I am caring for children!" she exclaimed, following Mandisa into the garden. "I don't know why. I will never have them and I don't really know what to do with them."

"You'll never have them?" Mandisa interrupted, stopping. Despite her irritation at the woman's ceaseless and shallow chatter, she was curious. "Surely it is a possibility for any woman."

"Not me. One of my masters paid an eastern physician to do something to me." For a moment, Tizara's eyes went as empty as a blind man's, then she shrugged. "But I never wanted children. What are they, but helpless little people?"

"Some would say they are the most precious treasures on earth," Mandisa answered, bending to snip a few lotus blossoms for Lady Asenath's afternoon bouquet. "Our master and mistress adore their boys. And your duties are not difficult. Some would say you are fortunate to care for children."

Tizara shook her head at the word. "I'll admit that life here is pleasant. There is enough food, and the steward does not beat his slaves. But I am not happy, I yearn for something . . . more."

Mandisa placed the flowers in her basket and shot Tizara a penetrating look as she straightened. "You live in the finest house in Thebes, only the king's palace is greater. You have a kind master. You care for two charming and delightful little boys—"

"Have you never wanted more, Mandisa?"

The question caught Mandisa off guard, and she felt herself stammering. "Of course not. I am happy to serve my master and mistress. I have a wonderful son. What more could I want?"

"Perhaps you have everything then," Tizara answered, "but I don't. I want to do something that matters. I want to know someone who cares. I want to *feel* again."

A dim flush raced like a fever across her pale and beautiful face, and for a brief moment her countenance seemed to open. Behind the mask Mandisa saw bewilderment, fear, and pain, then Tizara drew back inside herself.

She arranged her lips in a pout when she saw Mandisa watching her. "Don't take me so seriously, woman, no one else does. And tell me again why I shouldn't take the boys to the temple of Min. She is a fertility goddess, and her priests and priestesses perform the best dances."

"Our master's sons must learn to read and write, not dance." Mandisa sighed as she moved away from the lotus plants in the garden pool. "Please, Tizara, just make sure they practice their lessons. That is all you have to do."

LATER THAT AFTERNOON, exhausted from debating with Tizara, Mandisa picked up Shim'on's tray from the kitchen and took it to his room. She found him in a more sullen mood than usual.

"What, no greeting?" She set the tray on a stand. "No, 'Thank you, Mandisa, and how are things in the world today?'"

"Why should I care?" he growled. He was sitting on the floor in a darkened corner of the room, ignoring the fine furnishings Ani had supplied to replace the broken objects. Mandisa had assured Ani that the prisoner would not break anything else, but now, seeing the gleam of fire in his eye, she wondered if she had been too hasty in her promise.

"What's wrong?" She folded her arms and leaned against the wall in a pose of weary dignity. She would have to speak to Zaphenath-paneah. Because of her master's good nature and compassion, she did nothing these days but endure stubborn Canaanites.

"What month is it?" he snapped, not looking at her. "The house rings with the noise of celebration, and I've picked up enough of the Egyptian language to know that the people look forward to the coming of a new year."

"Of course," Mandisa answered, her voice heavy with sarcasm. "Are you upset because Pharaoh did not invite you to the palace? Or perhaps the star of the new year should not have risen without your permission."

"What month is it?" he repeated, giving her a black look. "How long have I been here? It has not been a full year."

"The vizier's house, as much as you would like to disbelieve me, does not revolve around your coming and going. Our year begins with the rising of the star Sirius, and the inundation of the river in the season of Akhet. You and your brothers came here during the season of Shemu, the drought. So you have been here five months."

"If the river is rising now, the flood will come and the famine will end," Shim'on remarked with a helpless wave of his hands. "My brothers will not come for me."

"Of course they will. Your father will send them."

"No, he cares more for the son at home than for me. Rahel bore Binyamin, you see; my mother was Lea. My father bears little love for anyone not born of Rahel."

Mandisa regarded him with somber curiosity, not knowing how to answer. She had sensed Shim'on's deep feelings of animosity toward his father, but she had never heard the state of affairs so baldly stated. Was this the unhappiness that fueled Shim'on's deep-seated anger?

"I am certain your father cares for you," she said finally. "All fathers love their sons. You need only to ask him, Shim'on. Confront him with your feelings, so he can tell you how much he loves you."

Shim'on's eyelids slipped down over his eyes. "It doesn't matter, I stopped caring long ago."

"Of course you care," she whispered, moving toward him. Her senses reached into his loneliness, struggling to understand the forces that had hardened his heart. In a sudden flash of insight, she wondered if God Shaddai might have placed her beside Shim'on not to serve Zaphenath-paneah or win a father's influence for her son, but to bring light to a tormented and dark soul.

She knelt to look into his face. "Your brothers *will* come for you. God has told Zaphenath-paneah that the river will not flood this year, nor the next, not until five more years of famine have passed."

Her words seemed to amuse him. "You are an intelligent woman, Mandisa. Yet you would believe the prophet of an Egyptian god."

Lowering her voice, Mandisa pressed her hand upon the fist he clenched at his knees. "Zaphenath-paneah listens to the Almighty God, El Shaddai. You will find no idols in his temple, no other god in his heart."

For an instant his eyes held hers, seeming to clutch at the hope her words offered like a drowning man reaches for the shore. But then the light in his eyes dimmed and he drew his lips into a tight smile. "El Shaddai is the God of Avraham, Yitzhak, and Yaakov, not of the Egyptians," he said, his voice flat and final. "The Almighty would not speak to your vizier. Your master has tricked you, Mandisa."

She closed her eyes, resisting the impulse to tell Shim'on that Zaphenath-paneah was his own long-lost brother. Surely then he would understand and have faith in the future! But the master had charged her to keep his secret, and she would not disobey, not even for this desperate and lonely man.

"You must believe me." She moved her hand to his forearm. "Your brothers will return, and you will be freed."

"They must; I cannot live long like this." His hand caught hers as his voice quavered with honest, long-suppressed emotion. "I feel like a bear in a pit, sometimes I think my heart will burst."

"This time of waiting will be over soon," she said, calming him. Gently, she reached out and nudged an unruly lock of dark hair from his forehead. Underneath his angry bluster he was as much a boy as Adom, and Mandisa had always known how to soothe her son.

But Shim'on was not her son. Abruptly, he dropped her hand and pulled his head away from her ministering fingertips. "If they do not come, I will escape this room and flee, even if it costs me my life." He crossed his arms and nodded at her. "If you hear that I have escaped, lock yourself in your chamber, for I will kill anyone who crosses my path or tries to stop me."

"Surely you don't mean a word you're saying." She reached for him, trying to recapture the tender emotion they had shared a moment before, but he leapt to his feet and retreated from her touch. Standing against the wall, tall, rawboned, and bearded, he looked like a giant, and she knew his strength of will matched the power of his arms and back. He meant every word of his warning. Did he also intend for her to pass his threat on to the vizier?

He could threaten all day and she could carry a million messages to the vizier, but not one of them would affect his situation. Shim'on might think the vizier controlled his destiny, but Mandisa knew Zaphenath-paneah waited upon God Shaddai.

How could Shim'on have grown up in the vizier's family, under the same father, without coming to know and serve the same God?

"I wonder," she said, rising, "do your strong arms never tire of resisting the Almighty God of your fathers? How blind are your eyes, Shim'on, that you cannot see Him?"

Stiffening in response, he closed his eyes, clenched his fists. And as she slipped from the room, she heard him bellow in despair.

CHAPTER TWENTY

SHIM'ON'S HEAD ACHED WHEN HE AWOKE THE NEXT MORNING AND SAT UP in bed. He'd passed a nearly sleepless night, bothered by dreams and images of people long dead and not quite forgotten. His wives, young Yosef, and the thousand men of Shekhem had all filed past his bed, pointing at him with glowing fingertips while blame and accusation burned in their eyes. "You, Shim'on, stole our lives while we were young and entitled to many more days," they all whispered, their hoarse voices mocking his fear. "For as long as you live we will steal your nights."

Clapping his hand to his head, he groaned and wished for Mandisa. But she would not come until later, especially after the scene last night. She had been an angel, kneeling at his feet as if to comfort him, but no one could comfort away the hurts of forty-five years.

How like a child she was, how naïve! She talked as if she had endured much in her past, but what could she have experienced in twenty-odd years of life? She lived in a magnificent estate, worked for a woman who adored and trusted her, and had been blessed with an intelligent, beautiful son.

Shim'on could even admit that she was charming. In a way she was more desirable than the vizier's coolly beautiful wife, whom Shim'on had glimpsed when he and his brothers first entered the vizier's palace. Like the esteemed Lady Asenath, Mandisa was small of form and features, but unlike the vizier's wife, she moved with the air of a woman who is at home in many worlds. He could imagine her drawing water from the wells outside his father's tents, and he had already seen that she was even at home in the throne room of a king's regent.

He had to stop this; why was he torturing himself? Mandisa had already made her home in a prince's villa. She had established a wholesome and prosperous life in Thebes. She no longer belonged to Canaan; he could not imagine her agreeing to return to a world of sandstorms and camels, of dung-fires, tents, and work-worn women.

Grunting, he turned and rested his elbow on the ridiculous padded support the Egyptians used to pillow their heads. A stentorian voice rumbled through the hall—the voice of the esteemed Zaphenath-paneah— and a slight chill passed over Shim'on as he listened.

How hauntingly familiar the vizier's voice was! Even though Shim'on understood only a few of the words, the man's tone rankled something in Shim'on's memory, jarred some fragment of recollection from its proper lodging place. But everyone in this house, from Ani the steward to the lowliest kitchen maid, revered and respected the great vizier. Unconsciously they copied his manners and morals, their voices imitated his. It was not surprising that the vizier's voice now seemed as familiar as the sun and moon.

Shim'on lifted his head, wondering if the great and mighty vizier would open the door to this room. *Come on*, he thought, not moving on his bed. *I won't stand up for you, I won't adjust my kilt, I won't even push the hair out of my eyes. You will take me as you find me, great vizier, and I won't care if you don't like what you see.*

But the door did not open. Strangely disappointed, Shim'on lowered his head and listened to the soft tramping of passing footsteps, undoubtedly the vizier's entourage of guards, scribes, and servants.

He turned onto his back and wearily considered the ceiling. Time, which he had once thought precious and fleeting, stretched before him like an endless and barren plateau more desolate than the deserts surrounding Egypt. The day would offer nothing new. Mandisa would come at some point to bring his meal and clean his room. Perhaps, if Shim'on was lucky, that little preening captain of the guard would enter, scowl, and exchange a threat or two.

In the mean time, he had nothing to do but plot his escape. Despite what Mandisa had said, Shim'on knew his brothers would not come back. Yaakov would sooner die than allow Binyamin to leave the family compound with the brothers who had "lost" Yosef. And if the famine ended, there would be no need for any of Yisrael's clan to journey to the Black Land. And the famine would end soon, no matter what the vizier had told Mandisa. Never had the earth known famine for seven years. The world could not survive such a disaster.

Zaphenath-paneah listens to the Almighty God, El Shaddai. You will find no idols in his temple, no other god in his heart. The memory of Mandisa's words brought a twisted smile to Shim'on's face. The woman was indeed gullible. How had the vizier convinced her that El Shaddai spoke to him? Mandisa was from Canaan, so the name of Yaakov's God was probably familiar to her. She had undoubtedly heard Zaphenath-paneah speak of the invisible Egyptian god and assumed that he spoke of El Shaddai. Or perhaps the vizier had the brazen boldness to claim that he spoke for the God of Yisrael! But Yaakov's God wouldn't— *couldn't* —speak to an Egyptian. He had adopted the children of Yisrael for His own; He had no use for the other peoples of the earth. The Almighty certainly would have no reason to speak to the cursed Egyptian who had imprisoned Yaakov's second-born son.

"When I escape," Shim'on murmured, locking his hands together behind his head, "I will find Zaphenath-paneah and kill him for his bold effrontery. Then no one will say that this vizier speaks for the God of Yisrael."

"MANDISA?" The Shim'on who greeted her at midday seemed relaxed and amiable, and she found it difficult not to return his disarming smile.

She lifted a brow as she entered with his meal tray, pleased that the prisoner seemed to be on his best behavior. He sat on the floor, his back supported by the frame of his bed, his bare legs stretched out across the cool marble.

"I am ready to venture out again, and willing to teach your son. But first, in fairness, there are things I should tell you. Can you talk today?"

Mandisa thought of Tizara, who'd soon be lingering in the hallways, waiting to hector her. "I have the time this afternoon," she answered, grateful for Shim'on's conversational mood. "My mistress has gone to the palace with Zaphenath-paneah, and there is nothing for me to do." She lowered his tray to a stand. "What did you want to talk about?"

His lips twisted into a cynical smile and the mask of good humor fell away. "I suppose I could begin by asking a question: what is the worst thing you have ever done?"

He spoke in his casual, jesting way, and she assumed he was teasing.

"I don't know." She moved toward the chair against the wall. "Once I ate one of the cook's shat cakes when he wasn't looking. Halima was about to be blamed for it, so I confessed."

His laughter held a sharp edge. "Is that all?"

She sank into the chair and settled back to search his face. "Why do you ask?"

His dark eyes narrowed. "You have asked me to spend time with your son. I want to do it, I want a few hours of liberty, but I'm not sure you know what sort of man I truly am. I have done many things, Mandisa, of which you would not approve."

"I think I know what sort of man you are, Shim'on, son of Yaakov," she answered, pretending to pick an imaginary piece of lint from her gown as she fought to control her swirling emotions. "You are strong and loyal. You have often been misunderstood."

"Would you like to know the worst thing I have ever done?"

"Not really."

"I once killed nearly a thousand men." She raised her eyes to find him watching her. Lines of concentration had deepened along his brows and under his eyes. "Of course, my brother Levi helped me. We did it to avenge our sister, Dina, who was taken by force and treated like a harlot."

Icy fear twisted around her heart. "You don't have to tell me this."

"That wasn't the worst, Mandisa. My sister Dina gave birth to a child. My father would have nothing to do the baby, for when the child came he was mourning Rahel's death. My brothers knew Dina would never be married if she kept another man's child, and so—"

"Stop." She cut him off, her heart in her throat.

"At the time I didn't think it was so terribly evil to rid ourselves of the infant. Many of the other clans in the area would not have hesitated. So, while my sister slept, I took the child away and left it in the wilderness."

"Exposure." Mandisa shuddered as the word slipped from her lips.

A cold, congested expression settled on his face. "I have nightmares; the men I have killed march by my bed and promise to terror my sleep for the rest of my life. They do not frighten me with their threats, but if I hear a baby's cry in the night—" His face darkened with unreadable emotions.

As Mandisa studied him, a cold lump grew in her stomach, spreading tendrils of uneasiness through her limbs. She was sitting alone with a murderer, and even worse—a baby killer. But she had known from the first that he was capable of such things, for Zaphenath-paneah had warned her. And the past was lost in the well of yesterday, and should not be dredged up again.

"Would you do it now?" she asked, dismayed to hear a faint thread of hysteria in her voice.

His mouth dipped into an even deeper frown. "What?"

"If Dina had a baby tomorrow, would you kill it?"

He stared at her for a long moment. "I don't know," he said finally, tenting his fingers in front of his face. "I don't think I would. But I don't know, Mandisa."

Pressing her lips together, she rose from her chair. "Your anger has led you to commit grievous acts in the past, Shim'on," she said. "And just as a reasonable man is seldom angry, an angry man is seldom reasonable. But I think you are becoming a reasonable man."

MANDISA'S HANDS trembled as she slid the bolt across Shim'on's door; the conversation had shaken her more than she cared to admit. Did the loneliness of his solitary confinement lead him to such introspection? She knew dark deeds and even darker thoughts lay in every man's heart, but she was not accustomed to being invited to hear such secret confessions, especially from a man she had come to admire.

She had changed the subject as rapidly as she dared, hastening to assure Shim'on that the river had not risen to its normal level, therefore the famine would continue and his brothers would be forced to return to Egypt. But he hadn't responded to her forced good cheer; he had only asked whether she would still allow Adom to visit, and if such a visit might be arranged for the afternoon.

She looked at him with surprise, remembering his initial hostility toward the idea and his reluctant confession. "I don't know, I suppose so," she said, nearly dropping his dinner tray in her anxious confusion. "I will find him and ask whether he wants to talk with you again."

She forced a smile to her lips and lightened her tone. "He actually enjoyed learning from you last time, Shim'on. He has begun to watch the birds fly home at sunset, knowing that they are flying to water holes."

"Call out your guards, then," he murmured satirically, reminding her of the other half of their bargain. "I will want to walk in the garden. And I promise your son will be safe with me."

She had nodded and promised to return before long with Adom. And now Shim'on was waiting behind the door, listening for her footsteps, wondering if she still trusted him enough to fetch her son.

She did. But she would feel better knowing there were guards around. She turned, and drew up in surprise when she nearly bumped into Tizara in the hall outside Shim'on's room.

"Are you all right, Mandisa?" the slave girl asked, a coy smile on her face. "You are flushed." She peered past Mandisa toward the bolted door. "And what, may I ask, is kept in that room? No one will tell me."

"Nothing," Mandisa answered, instantly on guard. She fixed her features in a stern expression and took two quick steps toward the kitchens. "Nothing that concerns you, Tizara."

"Since the door is bolted on the outside," the slave answered, moving forward and placing her hand upon the door's rough wood as if she would caress whatever lay inside, "you are trying to keep someone in." She quirked her brow. "Does Zaphenath-paneah have an idiot son who must be shielded from the light of day?"

"Our master has only two sons, those in your care," Mandisa answered, fighting the impulse to physically yank the girl from the doorway. "And if you must know, a captive resides in that room. Tarik supervises him."

"Tarik . . . and you."

"I do not supervise. I am needed because I speak Canaanite, and so does the captive."

"I speak Canaanite." Tizara leaned against the door, closing her eyes. "Is he a wild man, Mandisa? I've yet to meet a man I cannot tame. I've reduced many to sniveling idiocy. If our master needs this Canaanite brought to submission—"

"The master needs nothing," Mandisa answered, her voice hoarse with frustration. She gritted her teeth, irritated with this girl and herself. Ani expected her to *help* this harlot? A leopard could not change its spots.

"Wherever the children are, I'm sure they need you," Mandisa said, firmly taking Tizara's arm and pulling her away from Shim'on's door. "Find them, or I shall have to tell Ani you need more work to fill your hours. Perhaps kitchen duty would suit you."

"Perhaps it wouldn't," Tizara answered, laughing softly. She walked away, her glance cutting from Shim'on's door to Mandisa with a look that said she understood completely.

When the girl had disappeared, Mandisa knotted her hands into fists and blinked back tears of frustration. Why had El Shaddai brought that woman to this place?

CHAPTER TWENTY-ONE

ASENATH FELT HER SMILE FADE AS THE LAST OF HER GUESTS LEFT HER private sitting room. She had entertained twenty ladies of the royal court, young Pharaoh's cousins, concubines, and a host of other relatives. Though the extravagant party had been a rousing success by Theban standards, it left Asenath feeling dull and drained.

Four months had passed since her visit to her father's temple, and she had not seen a single sign that Khnum intended to answer her prayers. Zaphenath-paneah was loving and dutiful, pleasant and considerate as always, and he often took her into his arms to express his love in the intimate mystery reserved for husbands and wives. But never did he enter her chamber during the week when Asenath knew she might conceive. Even though the pressures of Pharaoh's kingdom, a host of duties, and the crisis of famine bore down upon him, her husband remembered to count the days on the calendar, to abstain from marital pleasures during the ten-day week when a chance visit to his wife's bed might result in a child.

And Khnum had made no difference. Over the past weeks she had written almost daily letters to her father, begging him to offer whatever Khnum required, be it incense, fruit, or even blood offerings. And just as regularly her father replied that the god did things in his own time, that she should be careful and not rash, that she should not unduly pester a cautious god.

"My lady."

Mandisa's gentle voice broke the stillness of the empty chamber, and Asenath tapped her fingers over her lips in a dainty yawn. "Come in. I was just thinking how relieved I am that they are all gone."

"Another letter has arrived, my lady. From Heliopolis."

More useless words of wisdom; more patronizing drivel. With an air of unutterable boredom, Asenath accepted the papyrus scroll in Mandisa's hand and studied the seal imprinted on the wax. The unusual design was not her father's mark.

She dismissed her maid with a wave of her hand. Mandisa did not leave the room, but moved toward the pottery lamps burning on low stands, snuffing the flames and trimming the wicks for their next use.

Intrigued, Asenath broke open the seal and began to read:

The priest Pe-uhem informs the Lady Asenath:

In life, prosperity, health, and in favor of Amenhotep III, King of the gods,

And Zaphenath-paneah, Nourisher of the King's Soul!

This is to let my lady know I have heard of your frequent discourse with your father. He has sent me to offer gifts to Khnum in your name. But if you will forgive my boldness, I have a more direct piece of advice for you, my lady.

If the gods do not bend themselves to our wills, sometimes it is because we pray to the wrong gods. If fertility and children are what you desire, why do you send gifts to Khnum, the divine potter? Offer your gifts instead to Min, the rain goddess who brings life to the barren earth and strengthens fields of wheat. Just as Min strengthens the weak limbs of men, my lady, she will bestow her powers of life and fertility upon you if you are willing to offer yourself. And I would be honored to be your ally in this your fervent desire.

Send word to me on the day of your choosing, when Min will most richly bless you. Together we will meet in the temple at Thebes and offer ourselves to the goddess who ripens the fertile plains of our land, who waters the earth with life-giving water. Do not let my brash desire to serve offend your gentle ears, but know that I am, in truth, wholly devoted in service to you, Zaphenath-paneah, and Pharaoh, may he live forever!

A BLUSH BURNED Asenath's cheek as she lowered the letter. Part of her soul recoiled from what was nothing less than a brazen attempt at seduction, but her brief embarrassment quickly faded to humiliation when she realized that someone else knew her most intimate secrets. What had her father told the other priests? How many wagging tongues knew of the vizier's unwillingness to bear a child with his wife?

Smarting in fresh resentment, she rolled the parchment and gripped it while her thoughts scampered. As she weighed the structure and probability of events, she gradually relaxed. If anyone of the royal court knew of Asenath's distress, some well-meaning tattler would have already alerted her. Some secrets were too delicious to be contained. Since she had heard nothing, it was likely her father had confided only in this young assistant.

Pe-uhem. His name echoed in the black stillness of her mind. She thought she remembered meeting him at her father's villa in Heliopolis. If she was associating the right face with the name, he seemed a pleasing sort, younger than her husband, but with a commanding manner and polished veneer.

But—to commit adultery! For that is how Zaphenath-paneah would see it. He would be wounded, perhaps angry, he would have every right to cast her away and put another woman in her place.

But perhaps the goddess Min would not see the act as adultery, and who but the gods could judge what was right and wrong? Asenath would surrender herself once, in an act of worship intended only to honor her husband. If by some remote chance the priest later attempted to accuse her of untoward conduct, she could simply deny the charge, for everyone in Thebes knew her as a faithful wife. No one would believe such an outlandish accusation, even if it came from a priest.

"Can I bring you anything, my lady?" Mandisa's gentle question startled her; Asenath had forgotten her maid lingered in the room.

"No, go now." She clenched the scroll tighter in her hands. "I shall not need you again tonight."

When Mandisa had gone, Asenath padded to the table where she kept a sheaf of papyrus parchments, a reed stylus, and a bottle of ink. Thanks be to the gods who urged her father to teach his daughter the sacred hieroglyphics! With a trembling hand she penned a reply:

The Lady Asenath inquires after the success of her father's friend, Peuhem.

In life, prosperity, health, and in favor of my husband Zaphenath-paneah and Amenhotep III, King of the gods! I say to Khnum and to Min every day: may you be in health.

Furthermore: your words contained wisdom I have not found elsewhere. I will send word to you at the temple of Min in Thebes, when the time is right to petition the goddess according to my heart's request. If there is any offering I should bring, I pray you to send word of it before the appointed occasion.

Have no anxiety about me. I am committed to my desire.

TWO WEEKS LATER, as the winter moon lit the high walls of the vizier's villa with a cold white radiance, Ani wandered in the black shadows of the courtyard below. Two sleepless nights were bearing down on him with an irresistible weight, but he would not allow himself to sleep. Some nameless trouble stirred in the house of Zaphenath-paneah, some impending disaster not even the master had sensed. But Ani, whose duty required him to foresee these things, remained ever alert, waiting for the bough to break.

Trials enough moved openly through the household. The simple presence of the harlot Tizara had sown discord among the men of the house, soldiers and servants alike. And Mandisa, who had promised to help him manage the girl, had proved to be no practical help at all. Whenever Ani asked her to teach Tizara a more ladylike way to conduct her affairs, Mandisa always found an excuse, an errand to run, or some reason why she couldn't be bothered. Most of the time her excuses centered on the prisoner, Shim'on.

And Shim'on—that Canaanite had lately proved himself altogether too adaptable. Something ailed a lion that did not roar, and Ani wasn't sure if the prisoner was sick, bewitched, or saving his strength for his next attack. But if he was stockpiling his rage to vent it later, the house might not be able to contain his next outburst.

Even Lady Asenath, that most gracious and predictable kitten, had been short, irritable, and bothered of late. Last week she had offhandedly mentioned that she would soon require a litter to visit a temple of Thebes during the Feast of Opet, but she had specifically remarked that Mandisa would not be accompanying her.

"The master will be with you then," Ani answered, bowing.

"No, the master will be with Pharaoh," Asenath replied, dropping her gaze. "I will take the litter alone."

"But it is not fitting! You must have a guard with you, at least. A lady of your position should not go about in the streets during a festival! The men will be drunk and the women senseless, there are apt to be sights unfit for your eyes."

"You may send a guard, but he must remain outside the temple with the litter bearers," Asenath answered, running her fingers over the alabaster tray holding the remains of her breakfast. "I am a priest's daughter, I can worship alone. How can I commune with the gods if I am watched like a hawk?"

For that he had no answer. But his dear lady's voice had been flat, absolutely emotionless, and the sound of it chilled him worse than the night breeze that now blew off the river and over the villa.

"Oh Thoth," he babbled, turning his chattering teeth into the wind, "god of learning and wisdom who has blessed me with insight and power, show me what to do! For I am at a loss. My senses and insight tell me that doom hangs over us like a black cloud, and I am powerless to banish it!"

ASENATH WAITED until the first full week after her red moon had flowed, then she summoned Ani and told him she would visit the temple of Min that night.

"Min!" The name slipped from the steward's tongue like a curse.

She knew his bird-like brain bulged with questions about why she wanted to visit the goddess of fertility, but he had no right to interrogate her.

"This parched land is in need of rain, which Min can provide," she said, avoiding his bright, speculative eyes. "I will need Mandisa to help me prepare, but only one guard to run beside the litter bearers."

"Tonight the moon will be full, and bright," Ani said, folding his hands in a form of entreaty. "Bright enough to embolden any robbers or strangers. Please, my lady, put this journey off until my lord your husband can accompany you."

"My husband has no use for the temples of Thebes, nor for Min," Asenath answered, the steward's unusual persistence gnawing at her confidence. "And I will not brook another word of opposition, Ani, so leave me!"

A warning cloud settled on his features, but he bowed and turned to leave. A small voice inside Asenath's head wondered why she had been so short with him. Ani was a capable steward and a harmless busybody; she and her husband owed much of their well-being to the careful way he regulated the household. Well, tomorrow she'd make it up to him. And when the vizier held a new son in his arms, Ani would be as thrilled and happy as the drunken fools who would celebrate a noble birth in the streets of Thebes.

In one fluid motion she rose and made her way to her innermost chamber. Without waiting for Mandisa, she dressed in a simple, elegant linen sheath that fell from her armpits to her ankles without wrinkle or ornamentation. Thin straps held the garment over her bare shoulders. After dressing, she oiled her skin, perfumed her neck, and carefully outlined her dark eyes—black kohl underneath, green malachite on the lids.

Her eyes, without a doubt, were her best feature. Zaphenath-paneah had often told her they shone like "stars of twilight fair." Well, tonight he would be with Pharaoh and her eyes would be shining elsewhere. The thought tore at her heart, but she drew a deep breath and forbade herself to tremble. If Zaphenath-paneah wanted to please her, he would give her what she desired. If he truly loved her, she wouldn't have to do this.

Mandisa came into the room, breathless, and blushed when she saw that Asenath had already dressed. "I'm sorry, I had no idea you wanted to go out," the servant said, wiping her hands on her skirt. "But Adom was with Shim'on, and I had to oversee them—"

"Help me with my cloak," Asenath interrupted, replacing her looking brass on the tray top. She had seen her reflection and was satisfied. Her wig was heavy and lush; her makeup all but disguised her features. Anyone who saw her in the concealing cloak and wig would never guess her identity.

"Going to one of the festivals, my lady?" Mandisa asked, slipping the full cloak over Asenath's shoulders.

"One of them," the lady answered. Before Mandisa could ask anything else, Asenath moved confidently out of the chamber.

CHAPTER TWENTY-TWO

"I must wear this?"

Tarik nodded, imposing an iron control on himself as he slipped a wrist cuff onto the Canaanite captive. Zaphenath-paneah had told Mandisa that the prisoner might be allowed to walk freely about the courtyard, not just in the walled garden, and Tarik knew he had no right to question his master's judgment. Still, such a move seemed ill-advised, particularly with a prisoner as ill-tempered as a wasp in a bottle.

The shackles were Tarik's idea. "While in the courtyard, you must remain tethered to Mandisa at all times," he said, slipping the other iron bracelet around the woman's fragile wrist. "That way, at least I know you will not get far if you decide to run out the gate."

"Why would I want to run with this woman?" Shim'on growled. "No man in his right mind would take a nagging tongue with him."

Tarik looked up, expecting to see hurt in Mandisa's eyes, but one corner of her mouth twisted in a wry smile. Apparently she had grown used to the Canaanite's surly manners.

"As you can see, Tarik, the emptier the pot, the quicker the boil," she quipped, lifting a delicate brow. "I suggest, Shim'on, that you calm yourself and try to be pleasant. If the servants hear your continual carping, they are likely to bribe me to keep you out of sight. If you want a change of scenery as much as you say you do, you should adopt a more peaceable demeanor."

Tarik smothered a smile as he turned to open the chamber door. The savage man may have been a brute when he arrived in Thebes, but already Mandisa had gained the upper hand. How long would it take the captive to realize he had been tamed?

Tarik stepped aside as Mandisa led Shim'on out like a puppy on a rope. Tarik knew every fiber of the man's body rebelled at the thought of being pulled about by a woman, but when he stepped from the hallway into the open air of the courtyard, his posture changed dramatically.

Even from a distance Tarik could see the man relax. His broad shoulders flexed as he stopped to inhale a deep breath. Ignoring the hustle and bustle of the courtyard, he placed his hands on his hips and lifted his shaggy head to the sun.

Mandisa stood by his side, silent and approving. With a gasp of astonishment, Tarik realized that love radiated from her dark eyes.

Well, why not? He rubbed his jaw. He should have known she would not spend hours with the captive unless she loved him, for she could have fed him and cleaned his chamber in the space of five minutes or had one of the kitchen slaves tend to the odious barbarian. But she had invested her time, herself, even her son. Perhaps unwittingly, Tarik thought, she had invested her heart.

Can a servant find love in the vizier's house? Tarik leaned against the wall and watched the twosome in the distance. His only thought, his highest aim, was to please his master. He had been born the youngest son of a simple farmer, probably the lowest position in the Egyptian social system, and yet he had systematically risen through the ranks of society by striving hard and doing his best in every undertaking. Though the others around him seemed consumed by the desire to eat, drink, and make merry, Tarik realized at an early age that success did not lie in the overwhelmingly approved national philosophy.

No, the way to achievement lay in planning one's work, placating the gods of prosperity, and pleasing one's master. His chosen god was Wepwawet, the jackal-headed god known as the opener of the Ways.

Wepwawet, who piloted the sun boat as it traveled through the chambers of the night, had guided Tarik toward success. And as long as he persisted in ardent worship and sacrifice, Tarik was certain Wepwawet would continue to lead him. For of what use was a god who allowed his petitioners to suffer pain? A man's god should lead him to prosperity, not failure.

And so Tarik had joined the local militia and accepted a promotion to Pharaoh's cavalry. In time he earned a place guarding the villa of a governor. There he caught Zaphenath-paneah's eye. Sometimes Tarik toyed with the idea of lifting his sights to serve in Pharaoh's palace, but as long as the king was under the age of majority, the real power lay in *this* house. As captain of the vizier's guard, Tarik held one of the loftiest positions in the land, and yet sometimes . . .

His eyes fell again upon Mandisa and her beloved captive.

. . . sometimes he wondered if life could offer more than success.

CHAPTER TWENTY-THREE

"*THIS* IS WHAT YOU'VE BEEN HIDING? NOW I UNDERSTAND YOUR REASONS for secrecy, Mandisa."

The voice was soft, sensual, and faintly mocking, and Shim'on jerked his head toward the source of the sound. From out of the courtyard dust, it seemed, a woman had materialized. She stood before him in the sheerest Egyptian gown he had ever seen, revealing a slender but voluptuous body. She did not wear an Egyptian wig, but allowed her wild hair to creep down her back in raveled hanks. Her dark eyes shimmered with dazzling light, and her appearance was so unearthly, so unexpected, that Shim'on took a hasty half-step back, struck speechless.

He must have worn his surprise on his face, for the woman laughed and put out a delicate finger to touch his bare chest. "You are pale, friend," she whispered in his own beloved tongue. "You should have made these devil Egyptians bring you outside sooner."

Her words implied that he could make his captors do anything, and his chest heaved in exultation at the reassuring sight and sound of her. Something about her reminded him of the wind-blown wilderness, and for a moment he forgot the chain about his wrist. His awareness of Mandisa vanished like a desert mirage.

"My name is Tizara," she whispered in a voice as intoxicating as the musk of her finest perfume. "I will see you later."

She turned and walked toward the gardens, emphasizing the sway of her hips because she knew he watched. Shim'on felt his blood rush to her fingerprint on his skin, and his heart thumped as a quiver surged through his veins.

"I think this heat has been too much for you," Mandisa said, yanking at the chain. Her voice was clipped. "Your face is crimson, Shim'on. You should not have stayed so long in the sun."

He scarcely felt her fragile strength upon the chain that held his wrist, but after a moment he followed her back into the cool hallway that led to his room. She was right, his eyes did burn with the afterimage of a white-hot heavenly body. He had been blinded. But not by the sun.

FROM HIS OBSERVATION post on the vizier's balcony, Ani shook his head. Foolish Mandisa, why had she led her newly-tamed cub into the panther's den? He clicked his tongue in silent sympathy. She should have known better, but she was young and still inexperienced in many things.

After a few moments, Mandisa reentered the courtyard alone, her hand shading her eyes from the sun and prying glances. "Mandisa!" Ani called.

She looked up. "Yes?"

"Come up here at once. I would have a word with you."

Reluctantly, she turned toward the house. Ani paced along the walkway, debating his approach. Should he be honest and tell her that this Canaanite would soon leave and join his own family? That she had no business risking her heart when her loyalties belonged to the household of Zaphenath-paneah?

Women in love rarely wanted to hear truth.

"Yes, my lord Ani?"

She had been crying, the wetness of tears still clung to her lower lashes.

"Sit, my child," he said, indicating a stone bench carved into the railing. He paused, pressing his lips together. "I saw what happened in the courtyard."

Her pretense vanished; tears again welled within her eyes. "I don't understand him, Ani!" she said in an aching voice. "I have willingly cared for him these many months. I, a free woman, have cleaned up after him like the lowliest slave. I have borne his jests, his cruelty, and his anger. I have listened to his stories about his home and family; I know secrets the clan of Yaakov would kill to keep silent!" She paused as a hot tear rolled down her cheek. "I know he is a murderer and a hot-headed rogue, and yet my heart breaks just to look at him. I shared my precious son to help ease his loneliness. But for all my efforts, he forgot I existed when that harlot walked by!"

Ani clapped in satisfaction. "So he is unredeemable. You now hate him. This is good."

"But there is such strength in him! When he is not thinking about the past, he is loyal, devoted, and concerned about people. And he is wonderfully wise about the desert and all sorts of animals. He has taught Adom so many truths I would never understand. And he knows many stories about the invisible and almighty God. He is proud of being one of God Shaddai's chosen race, he respects his brothers and is quick to defend his mother's memory . . ."

"Our master knows the stories of the almighty God, too," Ani said, stiffening. "And yet he is quite a different man from this Shim'on."

"Our master," Mandisa said, making an obvious effort to choose her words with care, "worships the Almighty God. Zaphenath-paneah trusts in Him. But though Shim'on speaks of this God, I do not think he trusts anything but his own strength . . . the strength of his anger."

As she paused to wipe tears from her face, Ani sank beside her on the bench. Whether Mandisa knew it or not, she had revealed her heart. "So you love him."

"Against my better judgment," she said, a tinge of wonder in her voice. "I suppose I do."

"Are you certain? If it is marriage you seek, let me remind you that you were married once before. That husband did not bring you happiness."

"Idogbe bought me from my father and paraded me around like a possession, not a wife," she answered, her words cool and clear. She paused to wipe a fresh tear from her eye. "He was proud of me until he heard I would have a baby. Then he left without a word of warning."

"Perhaps—" Ani cast about for the right words— "you should thank the gods he stopped loving you. If the man made you so unhappy, his disappearance saved you much distress."

"He never loved me. And only after I saw true love did I fully understand. When Zaphenath-paneah gave me a place in this household, I saw what love truly is." She smiled to herself as she spoke. "As I watched him love Lady Asenath through the birth of two sons and the deaths of three others, I realized that honest love is persistent, it is gentle. Love protects, trusts, and hopes for the best. Love does not place the object of its affection on display. If you love someone, you will not abandon them."

"And they say I am the one who is wise," Ani answered, taking her hand. He squeezed it gently, another question on his reluctant tongue. "Daughter, you have answered your own questions, and you say you love this Canaanite. But does he love you?"

She closed her eyes and pressed her free hand over her heart. "That is what I must discover."

SHIM'ON TURNED ON HIS BED, agitated and unable to sleep. He had enough sense to realize Mandisa was furious when she left, and he didn't suppose he could blame her. After years of trying to block the bitter glances between his mother and his aunt Rahel, Shim'on knew about female jealousy. But he also knew that women somehow managed to deal with their grief and anger. His mother had, and life had continued despite the differences between Yaakov's wives.

But the woman in the courtyard today—her touch and her words had evoked feelings he thought long dead. In her eyes he was strong and free, a Canaanite warrior, a giant among men. In one glance she had restored the confidence and courage this captivity had inexorably drained from his spirit.

He, Shim'on the Destroyer, had begun to adjust to confinement. The realization stunned him, but which of his brothers would not have gone soft in such a place? The months had crawled by with agonizing slowness, the moments frozen in place, like the granite statues lining the streets of Thebes. He had asked Mandisa to bring him a shadow clock for telling time, and though she laughed at what must have seemed a foolish request, she had brought the clock and set it on a stand before his window. Every day he watched the shadow of the upright beam move over the calibrated horizontal arm. The only hours that passed with any swiftness were those he spent in Adom's or Mandisa's company.

Until today. How long had he stood before the woman who touched him? It might have been five minutes, but the span passed like a heartbeat, so quickly did she come and go. He would have to stretch that instant of pleasure into a week-long memory if he were to endure this enslavement much longer.

He turned again on his bed, unable to find a comfortable position. Sometimes he felt as if demonic hands clenched his heart, twisting the life from it. He had felt this guilty pressure many times before—at the slaughter of Shekhem, at Dotan when he would have killed Yosef—but lately the tension had intensified. He had to escape, to flee this misery, but he had no weapons, and no tools with which to form them, unless . . .

His eyes fell upon the shadow clock, useless in the night. The upright pole had been crafted of polished copper, a sliver as long as a man's hand. A dagger, in the right fist.

He rolled out of bed and gripped it. The horizontal piece broke off with one snap, leaving a jagged edge along the base of his new blade. The implement was not sharp, but if thrust with enough force, it would bite deep.

His mind curled lovingly around the thought of freedom, of his triumphant return to the camp of Yisrael. Already he could hear his brothers' cries of rejoicing, feel Dina's proud arms around his neck. And he would finally win his father's approval, for Shim'on's escape would cancel Binyamin's obligation to journey to Egypt. They would find grain somewhere else; if necessary, they would bribe their neighbors to buy food for them.

From out of nowhere, came a startling realization—he could escape only if he used this tool against Mandisa or Tarik, the only people who ever unbolted his door. One of them would have to be held hostage if this plan were to succeed. Killing the captain would not be problematic, even though Shim'on had come to respect the man, for a soldier expected such risks every day of his life. But he did not think he could hurt Mandisa, or even pretend that he might. She knew him too well; she would call his bluff.

The copper blade slipped from his hand and rang on the tile floor. Better to remain forgotten and alone than to risk failure and face humiliation again.

A scratching sound at the door interrupted his thoughts.

"SHIM'ON?" Tizara paused, waiting for the sounds of movement. Did he sleep? She dared not speak louder for fear of waking others.

"Who is there?"

She smiled, hearing the sounds of urgent breathing through the heavy wood. He was on the other side, awake and alert, as she had suspected he would be once he heard her voice.

"I am Tizara. Who else would come to you like this?" She couldn't restrain a ripple of laughter. "Would you like me to come in?"

She heard frantic scrambling sounds; in a moment he would be pounding on the door. "Hush, be still." She pressed her hands against the wood. "I have not come to pleasure you, but to help you return to freedom." She paused. "You and I together will escape from Mizraim. Would you like that?"

She felt a solid thud against the wood and knew he leaned against the door. "Why should I trust you?"

"Because I am a Canaanite, like you. Because I hate slavery as much as you hate captivity. And," she lightened her voice, "because I like your looks."

Flattery always worked. "Open the door."

"Shh, not now, my friend. First we must make plans. We will need provisions to survive the journey. I will procure a supply of food, cloaks, water pouches . . ."

"Why do *you* want to leave?"

His question caught her by surprise, and for an instant her facile tongue stilled. "B-because," she said, stammering. "Because doing anything as a free woman is better than doing nothing as a slave. I am not a nursemaid! I am tired of men telling me what to do."

She sank to the floor and leaned against the door. "When we return to Canaan, I will build my own house within the strong walls of Shekhem. I will own my own herds. I will do as I please, and never call anyone master again."

When he did not answer, she wondered if she should open the door so she could face him. No. This man was resolute in purpose and desire. She dared not trust him until she had no other choice.

"All right," he said, a bitter note in his voice. "While you are stealing, then, make sure you take enough of the vizier's silver to outfit this new house. Do not count on a marriage price from me."

She laughed. "Did I say I would marry you?"

"It matters not," came his slow and steady answer. "I will not marry again."

TIZARA'S VISIT seemed dreamlike in the reality of morning until Shim'on saw the broken shadow clock on the floor. So the harlot had visited him . . . and she wanted out, too. Why not let her help him? She had access to tools and provisions, and with her aid he could slip away without involving Mandisa. He would leave in the middle of a night, so Mandisa and Adom would know nothing of it until the next morning.

How long would it take the woman to prepare? The question buzzed in his brain all morning, unasked and unanswered, distracting him even when Mandisa brought him breakfast. She moved about the room, making casual and pleasant conversation, but she did not mention the possibility of his going into the courtyard or the garden. Neither did she refer to the events of the day before, but Shim'on knew her well enough to know the encounter with Tizara rested heavy on her mind.

When she turned to leave, he put out a hand to stop her. "Mandisa," he regarded her with a careful smile, "I suppose you are angry with me for what happened yesterday."

"Angry women make themselves beds of nettles," she replied, averting her eyes. "And I slept well last night, Shim'on."

"So you are not upset with me?" His index finger rose to her trembling chin. "I think you are lying. About your anger, and about how you slept."

She turned, hiding her face, and fumbled with the latch on the door. "I have to go."

"Don't." He caught her arm, and felt her muscles tense under his hand. Her back was to him, but if he would soon be gone, he wanted her to know he appreciated all she had done for him.

"Mandisa, I—"

"Stop," she interrupted, her head falling forward. He realized with sudden horror that she wept. "All right, I confess," she said, the words broken between her sobs. "I was angry. I'm trying to help you, but I can't . . . love you . . . until I know how you feel."

An unexpected warmth surged through him. By earth and heaven above, did she say *love*? Did something stronger than mere possessiveness lie behind her jealousy? His heart swelled with the knowledge that she *had* been jealous and she did desire him. She probably felt she couldn't compete with Tizara's explicit seductiveness, but she could easily find a place in his arms. If not for her soft presence, he would have lost his sanity here in the Black Land.

He turned her and pulled her close, cradling her head against his chest. "Mandisa, little bird," he whispered, caressing her wet cheek with his knuckle. Her moist, trembling mouth demanded comforting, so he bent and pressed his lips to hers. The kiss sent the pit of his stomach into a wild swirl, and he crushed her to him, enjoying the sensation of her warm willingness in his arms. He would demonstrate his gratitude in the best way he knew. Perhaps, if her gods smiled on her, she would bear a son to remember him in the days to come.

He raised his mouth from hers and met her eyes. "Shim'on—" she placed her hands on his chest—"I don't think you understand."

A fleeting doubt took shape in her eyes, but before she could utter it he shushed her. "If you want my love, let me give it," he murmured, moving his lips toward the base of her throat. "I owe you my life, Mandisa. Let me share my strength with you."

His lifted his lips to take hers again, but instead of a kiss he found himself moving toward empty air.

She twisted in his arms. "Let me go!"

"What?" A frustrated scream rattled at the back of his throat.

"This is wrong! Release me, now!"

"But it is love! If you want love—"

"*This* is not love! I can't do this!"

"You *can!*"

"You don't understand! You don't understand *anything!*"

In dazed exasperation, he released her. Spinning out of his arms, she bolted like a frightened animal for the door, then slammed it shut. He heard sobbing as she slid the bolt into place.

"Mandisa—" his pulse pounded as walked to the door and pressed against it— "you don't have be so skittish. You are neither a virgin nor a child."

"You don't understand," she cried again. But at least she lingered outside.

"What's wrong with you? I was *gentle!*" He gritted his teeth against the rising anger in his voice. "Woman, if I want to hurt you, I could have taken you at any time!"

He heard a renewed cry, then the sound of her footsteps running away.

CHAPTER TWENTY-FOUR

HE CURSED UNTIL HE COULD THINK OF NO MORE VILE WORDS TO SAY, THEN he paced from wall to wall until he thought he would go mad with frustration. The sun set, the sounds and activities of the vizier's house faded into the quiet lull of nighttime. Shim'on kept an eye on the door, sure that Mandisa would send Tarik to rebuke or punish him, but no one came to his chamber, no one moved in the hallway beyond.

When night had completely covered the villa, he stretched out on the too-short bed and closed his eyes. He slid into a thin doze, but the sound of the bolt sliding from its brackets brought him instantly awake.

His eyes flew open as anger and anxiety knotted inside him. Had Mandisa changed her mind? He wouldn't have her now, not for all the silver and gold in Pharaoh's treasure tomb. But Mandisa wouldn't come to him in the night; this had to be Tarik, ready to punish Shim'on for affronting one of the vizier's servants.

His hand closed around the makeshift dagger. In one agile move, he rolled from the bed and leapt to his feet. Despite his fears, he felt a hot and awful joy at the prospect of confronting his enemy and proving himself.

His chest felt as if it would burst as the door swung open. He held his breath, expecting to see the captain's compact, muscled figure in the torchlight, but a woman stood in the doorway, draped in concealing veils.

The voice was unmistakable. "Did you think I would not come so soon?" Tizara purred.

Shim'on cleared his throat as sanity and calm returned to his fevered brain. "I did not expect you tonight."

"After the madness of your afternoon, I expect you did not," she answered, her dark eyes shining from beneath a veil. She lifted it with two hands and gave him a frankly admiring glance. "And I thought, Shim'on, that you burned for me alone."

"Did the entire house hear?"

Even the smile in her eyes contained a sensuous flame. "None heard but me. I was lingering beneath your window in hope of forewarning you that I would come tonight. I heard everything, but Mandisa has said nothing to the others."

Shim'on nodded, mollified. At least he would not be leaving Mandisa to face the humiliation of public shame . . . not that he cared, in any case. But for Adom's sake, it would be better if the household did not hear what had happened between Shim'on and his mother.

Tizara tilted her head, and her smile took on a mischievous aspect. "That gossipy old steward tells me you have twice been married, Shim'on, so I marvel that you know so little of the softer sex. Did neither of your wives tell you that the joining of a man and woman has little to do with love?" One dark eyebrow slanted upward as she finished in a dry voice. "Trust me, I know about these things."

"Women," Shim'on clenched his jaw, "are foolish, and there is no pleasing them."

Her soft laughter warmed the room. "I would say the same thing about men, but we can argue on the journey. We should go while the house is quiet. All but a few guards are asleep. Are you ready?"

He looked around the room. He had no possessions, nothing to take but the makeshift dagger. He thrust it into the belt of his kilt, then caught the heavy cloak Tizara tossed him. "The guards will change their watch soon," she whispered, leading him out into the hallway. "We will slip by them now, while their eyes are heavy and they dream of finding their couches to sleep."

Shim'on nodded, his courage and determination like a rock inside him. "Let's be away."

TARIK SAT UP, breathless and cold on his bed as the real world made its way back into his consciousness. He pressed his lips together, listening to the house around him, and heard nothing but the pounding of his heart. Reassured, his swiped small sparkles of sweat off his upper lip. The nightmare had fled, leaving behind only a phantom of terror, a premonition of disaster.

When a shadow stirred in the darkness of his chamber, Tarik fumbled for the dagger beside his bed.

"Stop, Tarik! It is Ani!"

The old steward stepped into a small rectangle of moonlight near the center of the room. The pulsing knot within Tarik relaxed as he lowered his shining blade and swung his legs to the floor. "What are you doing here?"

"Do you not sense it?" The old man sniffed the air like a dog parsing a scent. "This afternoon when I poured oil into the master's divining bowl, the shape of Anubis came to me, then vanished. The raging fiend stalks our house tonight. I thought you might sense it, too."

"I had a nightmare," Tarik admitted. Rising from his bed, he slipped his dagger into his kilt and strapped on his sword belt. A moment later he had lit a lamp and led the way into the hall.

"Silently now, wake the master but not the other family members," he told the steward. "I will rouse extra guards and surround the outer walls of the villa. We will double the guard and keep watch all night if we must."

Ani nodded, a watchful fixity in his face.

TIZARA'S PREPARATION IMPRESSED SHIM'ON, but her lack of strategy distressed him. As they slipped through the quiet hallways she told him she had assembled food, extra garments, thick leather sandals, and several gourds for water. She had even managed to pull a donkey from the herd and tether him to the gate of the stableyard. She gave Shim'on a confident smile. "As soon as we gather the supplies I have hidden by the well—"

"But the stables and the well are on opposite sides of the villa!" Shim'on protested, halting in mid-stride to glare down at her.

Like all Egyptian villas, the innermost house was surrounded by a series of open courtyards that separated it from the noise, sights, and smells of the servants' quarters, granary, stable, kitchens, and garden. The stables and cattle yard were situated on the southwestern side of the villa so the prevailing winds could carry away the odors, but the well was located on the eastern side of the estate. In fact, Shim'on thought, recalling what he knew of the house, the well was near the vizier's quarters so his servants would not have to walk far to draw their master a bath. He and Tizara would have to walk within a few feet of the sleeping vizier.

"Foolishness, thy name is woman," he muttered, leaving the harlot in the shadows as he crept toward the well.

MANDISA WOKE to screams and shouting. Awareness hit her like a punch in the stomach, and one thought pierced through the fog of sleep: "They've killed him!" Then she heard Shim'on's angry bellow.

She dressed quickly, bent to check on her sleeping son, and then, as duty demanded, stepped into her mistress's chamber. Asenath had awakened and dressed, too, and seemed remarkably clear-headed as she picked up a burning lamp and inclined her head toward the hallway leading to the master's chamber. "They will bring him to my husband, and we shall hear a full accounting of it," she said simply, leading the way.

Mandisa followed, grateful that Asenath had not remarked upon Shim'on's foolishness. How had he managed to escape? And why had he risked his life? She had assured him time and again that his brothers would return before the famine's end. Zaphenath-paneah had promised it, and he had never been mistaken about a revelation from God.

The master was awake and dressed when the women entered, his bed covers unrumpled. If he had slept at all, he gave no indication of it as he greeted his wife with a kiss on the cheek. Asenath murmured a word in exchange, then sat in the carved chair by his bed.

Mandisa retreated to a corner of the room, but Zaphenath-paneah caught her eye. "Come, Mandisa, stand closer," he said, friendliness and concern in his tone. "Do not assume that I do not know what feelings you hold for the man who has been in your care." A half-smile crossed his face. "You love him, even as I do, and yet he continues to try our patience."

"Yes, my lord," she whispered, relief flooding her soul. She had barely managed to compose her face into stern, stiff lines when the double doors of the master's chamber burst open. A dozen erect guards, led by Tarik and followed by Ani, brought in two captives. Mandisa had expected to see Shim'on, but anguish almost overcame her control when she saw Tizara by his side.

Shim'on planted himself before the vizier with his feet spread apart, his head defiantly thrust back. His bold, black eyes raked the gathering, then trained upon Zaphenath-paneah. From where she stood Mandisa could feel the heat of his hatred.

Tizara, on the other hand, smiled shamelessly at the master, apparently not caring that his wife sat only a few feet away. She returned the master's scrutiny gaze-for-gaze, then a sudden tremor touched her lips. A blush colored her cheek as she lifted her gaze to the ceiling and crossed her arms in silence.

Zaphenath-paneah sat in his carved chair and took his wife's hand. "Why did you run from my house?" he asked, intending the question for both prisoners. He spoke in Egyptian and Mandisa translated.

When neither captive answered, the vizier turned to Tarik. "Were any of your men hurt?"

"One stable boy was cut with this," Tarik said, holding out a sliver of metal. Mandisa recognized the broken arm of a shadow clock and closed her eyes in despair. Shim'on had used her gift as a weapon. Against a youth.

"Will he live?"

Tarik nodded. "The royal physicians are attending to him now."

"For harming the boy—" the vizier's gaze flickered over his captives —"I could have both of you confined to Pharaoh's prison. But I am curious, and you have not yet answered me. Why did you run?"

This time Shim'on spoke. "If you knew what captivity does to a man," he spat the words in contempt, "you would not ask such a stupid question."

Mandisa managed a quick translation. Though the vizier had thus far shown mercy, his patience would not last forever. Every servant in this house and most savvy citizens of Thebes knew that her master had once a slave and a captive. Would Shim'on *ever* learn to restrain his temper? His anger was a wind that blew out the lamp of his mind.

"If I had been a captive, it is not likely I would have known the gracious treatment you have enjoyed," Zaphenath-paneah continued, not raising his voice. "Have you been whipped? Have you been chained so that your wrists bled? Have you been forced to lie in your own filth until maggots attacked your flesh? Have you been deprived of human companionship or kept from a kind word or a soft voice?"

Shim'on did not answer.

"I know what captivity does to a man," the vizier went on, pausing for Mandisa's translation. "Imprisonment can be the stone God uses to crush an impossible person who must rise to an impossible task. Will you be crushed, Shim'on, son of Yisrael? Or will you resist the work of God and harden your heart further?"

The vizier turned his attention to Tizara. "And you, young woman, have you been mistreated in this house? Has any man forced himself upon you? Has any woman cruelly mocked you? You stood in sore need of love and mercy when you first came to us. We have been generous with both, but have you accepted them?"

Mandisa felt the bitter gall of guilt burn the back of her throat as she listened. How many times had she avoided, scorned, and railed against Tizara? She had never said anything rude in the girl's presence, but she had made her thoughts known among the other women as they gossiped in the kitchen and worked at the well. Tizara was no fool; though the master had been loving and merciful, her servants had not fulfilled his expectations. And Mandisa had specifically promised to help the young woman feel at home.

Tizara did not speak, but lowered her gaze as he continued questioning her. When he had finished, she lifted her eyes.

"I am sorry, my lord," she said, her voice fainter than air. "You have treated me far better than I deserve."

Zaphenath-paneah offered a forgiving smile.

"Tarik, take his man back to his room and secure the door again. Do not whip or punish him. Tomorrow we shall continue waiting for his brothers."

"They will not come!" Shim'on argued, struggling against the cords around his arms.

"They *will* come," Zaphenath-paneah answered, and for an instant Mandisa wondered if her master spoke out of conviction or hope. Then the vizier lifted a hand and pointed toward the doorway. "Take him now."

When Tarik and the guards pulled Shim'on away, the brightness of a dozen torches left the chamber. When the men had gone, Zaphenath-paneah turned to Tizara. "You may go back to your room. You sleep in the chamber next to my sons, do you not?"

She nodded. Tears had tangled in her lashes and smeared the paint around her eyes.

"Resume your place, then. On the morrow we shall not mention this again." His voice was oddly comforting in the stillness, and Mandisa took hope from its gentle tone. If Tizara could be forgiven for running away, Mandisa would be forgiven for her less-than-loving attitude.

Tizara turned with stiff dignity and walked through the doorway. When she had gone, the master gave his wife a bright smile. "That wasn't so bad, was it? I was afraid one of them would be hurt."

Asenath looked at him in surprise. "Did you *know* they would try to escape?"

"I would have been surprised if they had not." Zaphenath-paneah sank back into his chair and stretched out his legs, gesturing to Ani. "My wise steward anticipated their moves and made their provisions readily accessible. I wanted them to prepare without trouble and be stopped without bloodshed."

"Both you and your steward are wise, my lord," Mandisa said, finding it impossible not to return the vizier's smile.

"Thank you, Mandisa. Ani, I must thank you for your attentiveness. Now that the excitement is finished, we should sleep well tonight."

Smiling out of an overflow of well-being, Mandisa looked to her mistress. But Lady Asenath was not happy; her face had emptied of expression and locked. "My lady," Mandisa whispered, "is something wrong?"

Zaphenath-paneah's smile faded. "My dear Asenath," the vizier repeated, "is something troubling you?"

"I am not troubled, my love," she said, speaking in a suffocated whisper. "We are going to have a baby."

CHAPTER TWENTY-FIVE

PACING IN HER CHAMBER, MANDISA PRESSED HER HANDS OVER HER MOUTH, stifling the cry that threatened to burst forth and wake Adom. In a thousand years, she could never have imagined a moment as horrible as the one in which Asenath told Zaphenath-paneah of the coming baby. Even Ani had been stunned by the news. The four of them, connected by the intimate ties of matrimony and servanthood, knew the vizier cared too much for his wife's life to have fathered the child. Unless the gods had assumed human form and visited Lady Asenath as they reportedly did during the conception of the pharaohs, the lady had been unfaithful to her husband—and he knew it.

Zaphenath-paneah's handsome face had not altered at the news, but he flinched as hurt and longing filled his gaze. Mandisa closed her eyes against the memory, unable to recall the pitiful sight of her sorrowing master without aching in regret. Her teeth chattered, her body trembled, so what tremors must her master be enduring?

Zaphenath-paneah had said nothing after his wife's announcement. He sat back and closed his eyes, his face utterly blank. Awkwardness hung in the room like a miasma so thick Mandisa could scarcely see her lady's face. Asenath murmured something about how the gods had answered her prayers to give the mighty Zaphenath-paneah another son, but no

169

one believed her. Mandisa gripped the back of Asenath's chair, her own emotions whirling like a piece of flotsam caught in the Nile.

The master had foreseen and planned for Tizara's and Shim'on's escape attempt, but how could he have prepared for treachery coming from one so close to his heart?

After a long, brutal interval, the vizier stood and extended his hand to his wife. Trembling, Asenath placed her hand on his, then closed her eyes as he bent to kiss her forehead. Without another word, he lifted his wife's hand to his cheek, then gave it to Mandisa. Through an icy chill that engulfed the group, the handmaid led her lady from the vizier's chamber.

In the hallway Mandisa tried to frame words of congratulation, but Asenath stopped them with an upraised hand. "I will talk no more tonight," she said, looking much older than her twenty-three years. She would not allow Mandisa to see her to bed, but dismissed her with a rapid shake of her hand.

The same hand the master had caressed.

Mandisa quivered at the memory and pressed her palms to her forehead. Only two days ago she had told Ani that the master and mistress demonstrated love in a way she'd never seen before . . . but apparently the master's love had not been enough for his lady.

So Zaphenath-paneah would cast her off.

And love was as insubstantial as a shadow.

CHAPTER TWENTY-SIX

THE SKY ABOVE HEBRON STRETCHED PURE BLUE FROM NORTH TO SOUTH, with no more than a little duskiness lingering in the west. Leaning hard on his staff, Yaakov moved stiffly toward the oak tree outside his family's settlement. The yellow day had opened peacefully enough, but soon the gaunt hills flanking Hebron would tremble in the heat haze.

Safe in the shade of the stalwart oak, Yaakov eased himself to the ground and tried to swallow the despair in his throat. He knew the inevitable confrontation would come today. They thought him old and blind, but last night when Dina remarked that the women had opened the last bag of grain, he had seen looks of concern pass between Re'uven, Yehuda, and Levi.

Their food was nearly gone. If he and his children were to survive the months ahead, another trip to Egypt would be necessary.

A tight pain squeezed his heart. For months he had dreaded this day. He had filled his prayers with petitions for Shim'on's escape, for rain, for some brilliant plan to find food from some source other than the formidable black land whose vizier now held Shim'on. *Surely the kings of the east have managed to store surplus grain,* he had reminded God Shaddai. *Or the kings of the Mitanni Empire . . .*

When God did not respond to Yaakov's hints, he took action for

171

himself. For months he had been sending servants to Togarmah in the north, Shinar in the east, even to Uz of the south, but the famine had struck those lands as viciously as Canaan. The people of those kingdoms sought grain in Egypt, too.

Yaakov shook his head, amazed that only one empire had exercised wisdom enough to prepare for disaster. Egypt's great power further complicated the matter, for an intricate network of unimpeachable governors, captains, and scribes connected Egyptian cities and nomarchs to its capitol at Thebes. Only the most skilled spies would be able to slip into a frontier outpost and buy grain without approval from the powerful vizier of all Egypt, and Yaakov's sons were not skilled spies. They had trouble enough playing the role of brothers.

A pair of vultures circled over a carcass in the distance, but Yaakov stared past the brown hills of Hebron into his own thoughts. How could God Shaddai allow universal famine? Never in the history of the world had every kingdom on earth been driven to another one for its survival. And despite Shim'on's detention in Egypt, Yaakov had to admit the vizier behaved generously. He fed those who came to him with outstretched hands though he could have forced the hungry nations into slavery and submission. Pharaoh would profit nicely for his vizier's largess, but the king's representative had not attempted to take unfair advantage of nations weakened by starvation and destitution.

So why had this wise and discerning vizier doubted his sons? Why had he insisted upon testing the truth of their words?

A familiar niggling suspicion reared its ugly head. Perhaps the man was astute enough to sense duplicity, even as Yaakov had once smelled treachery on his sons as strong as cheap perfume. . . but that horror took place more than twenty years ago. Since Yosef's disappearance he had negotiated an uneasy truce with suspicion, just as he had learned to share his tent with grief and loneliness.

He rubbed his chest, protecting the heart only Rahel and Yosef had been able to fully enter. They had slipped from his grasp like steam from a kettle, taking the better part of his life with them. Now dashed dreams and disillusionment raked at his soul. What remained of the covenant promise? Only a parched land and an assortment of bickering sons. El Shaddai had promised Canaan to Avraham, He had renewed his covenant with Yitzhak, He had wrestled with Yaakov and spoken his promise yet again. At Bethel, the *House of God*, the voice of God Shaddai had promised that all families of the earth would find blessing through Yaakov and his seed: *Here, I am with you,* God had said, *I will watch over you wherever you go. . .*

"Father."

Yaakov looked up, disturbed from his thoughts. Levi, Yehuda, Re'uven, and Dan stood before him, a delegation of the eldest sons. "We have no food, Father," Re'uven began. "We must return to Mizraim."

Yaakov nodded, stilling the last voices of resistance within him. "Go back, buy us a little food."

Re'uven lifted a brow and looked at Yehuda. He obviously hadn't expected that answer.

"But," Yehuda spread his hands in a gesture of helplessness, "the vizier solemnly warned us that we would not see him again unless our brother Binyamin is with us. If you will send Binyamin, we will go and buy whatever we need. But if you will not—"

Yaakov slapped his hands over his ears. "Why did you treat me so badly? Why did you tell this man you *had* another brother? If he had not known, he could not ask for Binyamin."

"The vizier asked specific and particular questions," Levi answered, frowning. "He asked if our father still lived, and if we had another brother. We answered truthfully, never dreaming that he would command us to bring our brother to him."

Yaakov lowered his hands and looked away.

"Father," Yehuda lowered himself to one knee, "send Binyamin in my care, and we will arise and go so we all may live. If we do not eat, you and the little ones will die. I myself will guarantee Binyamin's safety. If I do not bring him back and set him safe before you, then let me bear the blame forever."

"If you had allowed us to go when we first asked your blessing,"

Re'uven said, pressing Yehuda's point, "we could have gone and returned twice by now."

Yaakov turned and pinned Yehuda with a long, silent scrutiny. "I am an old man," he finally whispered, his voice breaking as he gazed past his sons toward distant memories of Yosef and Rahel. "In my youth I loved a woman and lost her; I loved a son and lost him. One son of Rahel's remains. If I lose Binyamin, all I shall have left are the raw sores of an aching heart."

He lifted his eyes to Re'uven's and strengthened his voice. "If you must go, take some of the best things we have as a present for the man: a little balm and honey, aromatic gum and myrrh, pistachio nuts and almonds. And take double the silver you did last time, so you can return the treasure you found in the mouths of your sacks. Someone certainly made a mistake by returning it to you."

His gaze lifted to the dun-colored, lifeless hills. Death was bearing down on them, and he could do nothing to stop it. He had no more choices, no way out . . . save one.

"Take your brother also," he said, a suffocating sensation tightening his throat, "and return to the vizier. And may El Shaddai grant you compassion in the sight of this man, that he may release to you Shim'on and Binyamin. And as for me—" he closed his eyes— "if I am bereaved of my children, I am bereaved."

CHAPTER TWENTY-SEVEN

MANDISA SIGHED AS SHE LIFTED THE BREAKFAST TRAY HER MISTRESS HAD not touched. The morning sky was a faultless curve of blue from one edge of the garden wall to the other while the air shimmered in honey-thick sunshine. Ordinarily Asenath would have rejoiced in a day like this, but today she lay silent and still on her chaise longue, one hand over her stomach, her pale face contorted by nausea.

"Dear wife—" Zaphenath-paneah reached to pat his wife's free hand— "I must know if you want to attend the party for Queen Tiy. Since Pharaoh's new bride is a commoner, he wants to invite as many of the nobility as possible. The guest list will be enormously complicated . . ."

His voice drifted away when Asenath did not respond. Two worry lines cut into his forehead as his gaze caught Mandisa's. She shook her head, silently warning him off, and the hopeful glint in his eyes faded.

Mandisa clicked her tongue in quiet pity. In the months since Asenath's shocking announcement, the master had behaved more nobly than she expected; indeed, he had done the complete opposite of what any other betrayed husband would do. Instead of casting his wife aside, he had said nothing of her obvious infidelity. With inconceivable patience he looked on her with tender pity even when Asenath battled the nausea and exhaustion of pregnancy.

The vizier was an endless surprise; his continued attention and affection toward his wife simultaneously baffled and thrilled Mandisa. Zaphenath-paneah remained at Asenath's side for longer periods of time than usual, took care that luxurious bouquets of blue lotus blossoms, her favorite flowers, filled her chambers, and asked Tizara to keep the boys quiet whenever Asenath was ill or resting.

The slaves, servants, and visitors who were not privy to the entire truth soon surmised that Asenath expected another child. Mandisa felt a curious, tingling shock the first time she saw Zaphenath-paneah accept a round of congratulations with his customary polished charm. Immediately afterward, however, she caught sight of her master in an unguarded moment, and her heart broke at the flash of grief that ripped through his eyes. The heartbreak she had experienced over Shim'on paled in comparison to the torrent of anguish her master endured.

Mandisa removed the tray from the stand near her lady's chair. She was about to murmur some foolish pleasantry to lighten the dismal atmosphere when Ani burst into the garden. Zaphenath-paneah looked up, and even Asenath managed to turn her head in the steward's direction.

"Life, health, and prosperity to my lord and mistress," Ani babbled. He bent at the waist, a token effort to lower himself to the ground, but obviously had no time for formalities.

"Remain upright, Ani, and tell me what brings your aged legs here in such a hurry," Zaphenath-paneah answered.

"The Canaanites from Hebron," the old man gasped, an expression of wonder creeping over his face. "They are standing outside the gates of your villa."

The master stared at his steward, tongue-tied and stunned, while Mandisa took a wincing little breath. Ani still had no idea of the brothers' connection to the vizier. "Shim'on's brothers?" she asked, finding her voice.

Ani's head bobbed like a cork on the river. "Yes, the loud one's bearded kin. Ten of them, my lord!"

All color drained from the vizier's face. "You say there are ten?"

Ani grinned like a well-fed fox. "Yes. The nine who came before, and another one, a younger man."

A muscle quivered in Zaphenath-paneah's jaw. "Tell the gatekeeper to hold them outside the villa. And send Tarik to my chambers at once. I will meet him there."

The vizier pressed his hand over Asenath's for a brief moment, then rose and left the women in the garden.

AFTER INSPECTING the positions of his guards, Tarik turned with a quick snap of his shoulders and nodded toward the vizier's gatekeeper. The double gates swung open and the ten Canaanites, wide-eyed and wary, progressed through the courtyard toward the portico.

Watching them, Tarik marveled. These shepherds, who had been indignant and insistent when they last stood before his master, had returned to submit to the vizier's demands. The strong-willed brothers who had rejected Zaphenath-paneah a lifetime before and argued with him a few months ago, had returned to humble themselves.

A few moments earlier, Zaphenath-paneah had given Tarik clear and concise directions: "Hold them at the portico so I may study them from the balcony of my chamber," he said, his voice simmering with barely checked agitation. "If they are desperate, or if our father is truly unwilling to release my younger brother, they may try to slip an impostor by us. But if the younger man truly is Binyamin . . ."

Tarik had bowed and left, understanding his orders. Now he stared at the visitors, knowing that his master also studied them from behind a screen of palms on his balcony.

"Halt!" Tarik commanded, hoping his scant knowledge of the Canaanite tongue would prove adequate. "Line up, so we may be certain you would not dare bring a sword into the vizier's house."

Obediently, the brothers stretched out in a line, shoulder to shoulder. Tarik's guards moved among them, patting their heavy garments with the flat edges of their swords in a calculated demonstration of diligence.

While his guards worked, Tarik found his eyes drawn to the younger man who stood in the center of the group, his hands hanging at his side. A blush burned the man's cheek. His black hair gleamed in the bright morning sun, growing upward and outward in great masses of curls. His clothing was simple, but rich; his head hung in the attitude of one who lives in a perpetual state of embarrassment. Dark eyes framed a handsome square face.

"By Seth's foul breath, those eyes!" Tarik muttered. "They are my master's!"

After a moment, Ani's thin, tremulous voice spiraled down from the balcony. "The master says bring them in," the steward called to Tarik. "I am to slay a lamb; the men will dine with Zaphenath-paneah at noon."

LEVI'S HEAD throbbed as he climbed the chiseled steps before the vizier's portico. Like the others, he worried that the Egyptian might wish to detain Binyamin as he had Shim'on. And what had happened to Shim'on? He had not been brought out to meet them.

"What if this vizier has sold our Shim'on to slave traders?" Asher whispered, hugging his arms as he walked. "Suppose the vizier realized he was not paid for our grain? What if he sold Shim'on to make up the difference?"

"What if he chooses to sell Binyamin, too?" Naftali asked. "Or all of us? It is not good that he has summoned us inside. If nothing were amiss, he would have taken our silver, given us Shim'on and our grain, and sent us on our way."

"The Egyptian is odd, there is no predicting him," Re'uven answered, leading the way into the reception room. "Yet we are at his mercy. Whatever his judgment, we shall deserve it."

Lethal calm filled his eyes when he looked at Levi. "In the past few months I have thought many times of Yosef, whom we sold into slavery. Can any of us say we do not deserve to suffer the fate we decreed for him?"

"Hush, Binyamin will hear you!" Yehuda hissed. Their collective gaze turned toward their younger brother. Aloof and distant as always, Binyamin wandered alone through the magnificent assembly hall, his hands behind his back, his eyes lifted to the bizarre paintings on the walls.

Dan nodded toward the other side of the room. "Look, now, what's this?"

A host of Egyptians, richly dressed in golden collars and white kilts, entered the room from another doorway. The latecomers stiffened when their painted eyes caught sight of the brothers. Levi cast them a withering stare in return.

"They look at us as if we are a bad smell," he muttered in a low voice. "I would like to wrestle that tall one with the earring. I'd show that self-important snob that we are not the stinking herders he thinks we are."

"Hush, Levi," Yehuda murmured, turning toward the entryway. "Someone else approaches."

A pair of sandaled feet shuffled through the doorway, then the bald, wiry man who had spoken from the balcony stood before them. "Greetings from my lord Zaphenath-paneah, Nourisher of Egypt and the World, Guardian of Pharaoh's Shadow," he said, speaking Canaanite in a clipped, careful accent. "You have been invited to eat the mid-day meal with my master."

Yehuda lifted a brow. "We have news for him, but we do not require much of his time."

"You shall eat with him," the little man answered. "My name is Ani; I am Zaphenath-paneah's steward." He glanced past them toward the portico and the courtyard, then rested his hands upon his scrawny, bird-like chest. "My master has instructed me to see that your donkeys are provided with fodder, and that your feet are washed." He lifted his hands and clapped; immediately a half dozen servants appeared with basins, towels, and pitchers.

The steward's lined face arranged itself into a careful smile. "Is there anything else you need?"

"Our brother." Levi stepped out of the circle. "What has become of Shim'on?"

The steward bowed his head. "He is preparing for you now. He will be restored to you soon."

"There is one other matter," Yehuda said, moving closer. "When we arrived home after our last journey to Thebes we found that our silver had been returned to our sacks. We didn't take it, and we want to pay for what we bought. So today we have returned the silver we owe, and we have brought more to buy what our families need."

"We have also brought gifts," Re'uven interrupted, "for your master."

The old man smiled again, an odd mingling of wariness and amusement in his eyes. "Be at ease, do not be afraid," he said, nodding. "Your God and the God of your father has given you treasure in your sacks; I had your silver. Now, if you will excuse me, here is your brother."

The steward turned and moved aside. A quartet of guards stepped smartly through the passageway and separated when they reached the reception hall. Levi half-expected to see the mighty vizier step out from behind them, but Shim'on stood there, as massive and self-confident as ever.

Levi put his worries aside with sudden good humor. "Shim'on!"

The Destroyer's eyes flashed with approval. "Brothers! How well you look!"

Ignoring the servants and the assembled Egyptians, the brothers surrounded Shim'on with much embracing and slapping on the back. He accepted their greetings with good nature, then slipped his burly arm around Binyamin. "My little brother," he said, his bushy brows rising in pleasure, "I have never been so pleased to see anyone in my entire life!"

"Did they treat you well?"

"Were you in the prison pits?"

"You look well-fed, Shim'on!"

"Not only well-fed—someone has been pampering our brother!"

They laughed, poked, and jabbed at one another in merry glee. After a few moments Levi pulled himself from the fray and stepped back to study his brother. He and Shim'on had been close; their mother said they were two of a kind, cut from the same cloth. He and Shim'on had always understood each other without a word of explanation . . .

But this was not the same Destroyer they left here months ago. Some quality in him had changed, an edge had softened, the warp and woof of the man had altered. The old Shim'on would have come charging out with threats of revenge and retribution, daring his hosts to take up arms.

Shim'on caught his eye and laughed. "Why, Levi, do you look at me like that?"

The others grew still and parted, their faces painted with surprise.

"I thought you'd be glad to see me," Shim'on went on, "but you're looking at me as if I had sprouted horns."

Levi felt the chasm between them like an open wound. Perhaps Shim'on had been tortured. Pain could account for the way his voice had softened, for his carefree humor and the solicitous way he inclined his head toward Binyamin. Though physically he bore no marks or scars, the Egyptians might have bewitched him or forced him to participate in their vile idol worship. Shim'on would have fought them, of course, but even the Destroyer's strength had limits.

But he would never admit them. And he would never confess that he'd been broken. But when they had returned to the tents of Hebron, Shim'on would heal and become his old self again.

"It is nothing," Levi murmured, his mind drifting away from the unsolvable mystery. He waved Shim'on's concerns away. "You look different, that's all," he said, shrugging. "You're wearing a kilt instead of a robe. And someone has cut your hair."

"Bah, it couldn't be helped, the Egyptians have foolish ideas about such things." Shim'on made a face as the others laughed. "At least I managed to keep my beard! But those things are done, my brother. I am ready to go home."

"Good," Levi answered, smiling thoughtfully.

MANDISA FOUND her place beside Tarik in the master's entourage and resisted the urge to cast a questioning glance at the captain. The vizier had already given them strict instructions. "My brothers must be tested," he had explained, his arms behind his back as he prowled his chamber. "They have brought Binyamin, which is good, but how can I know they will not cast him aside as they once did me? If their hearts are not loyal, I must be there to catch my younger brother when they cast him away. I would know the extent of their devotion. I must be sure their stony hearts have softened."

The master did not say exactly how he planned to prove his brothers, but Mandisa knew the elaborate stratagem would begin at dinner. She and Tarik were to enter the chamber ahead of the vizier's bodyguard, then she would take her place at Zaphenath-paneah's right hand while Tarik stood on his left, ever-ready to defend.

One of the young fan-bearers coughed softly as he moved into line behind her, and Mandisa glanced back. Zaphenath-paneah stood behind the fan-bearers, a stiff and regal expression on his face.

Mandisa's heart stirred with compassion as she looked at him. For an instant wistfulness stole into the vizier's expression as he met her eyes, then he smiled.

"He is ready," she whispered to Tarik.

A trumpet sounded. Like actors in a play they swept down the passageway and into the hall. The servants had already done their work, providing each guest with a chair, a footstool, and an empty dining tray on a stand. Behind each chair a servant waited with an amphora of scented water, a copper washbasin, and fresh linen for drying the hands.

Zaphenath-paneah had been quite explicit in his directions regarding the Canaanites: they were to be positioned far away from his Egyptian guests, and seated in a particular order. The oldest, Re'uven, was to be seated farthest from the vizier, and the youngest, Binyamin, at the vizier's right hand.

The guests, both Egyptian and Canaanite, rose from their chairs and prostrated themselves upon the polished floor as the retinue entered. As Mandisa moved to her position between the vizier and the youngest brother, Tarik barked the order giving permission for the guests to rise from the floor.

Shock ran through her when Mandisa's eyes met those of the young man next to her. This Binyamin looked remarkably like her master. If they would take the time to look, surely the others could see the resemblance!

Zaphenath-paneah took his seat in the gilded chair high upon the dais. Before the meal could begin, the oldest brother came forward and dropped a heavy pouch onto the floor before the vizier. "If it please you, my lord," he said, pulling several smaller sacks from the pouch, "our father bids you accept these gifts from the land of Canaan. We have brought you balm and honey, aromatic gum, pistachio nuts, almonds, and myrrh."

Mandisa hurried the translation, for tears were already rising in her master's eyes. He would have to be careful, or these men would know he understood them. She rushed through the list of gifts, stumbling over the elder brother's words, then folded her hands as her master indifferently summoned a servant to take the generous tribute away. Bounty from Canaan! Did Zaphenath-paneah's heart yearn to touch and smell and taste the things of home as strongly as she did?

The vizier sat forward and looked intently at the brother before him. "You spoke of your old father when you first stood before me—is he well?"

Mandisa translated the question and answer: "Yes, my lord."

"And this--" The master pointed toward the man next to Mandisa. "Is this the youngest brother, of whom you spoke to me?"

"It is, my lord."

Scarcely waiting for the translation, the master leaned forward to peer into the younger man's face. Binyamin turned a vivid scarlet. Mandisa lowered her gaze, her heart aching with empathy, as her master swallowed hard and blinked back tears. "May God be gracious to you, my son," Zaphenath-paneah whispered in a choked voice. Then the vizier of all Egypt leapt from his gilded chair and ran from the room.

Tarik followed without a moment's hesitation. After a moment of uncertainty in which the assembly stiffened in shock, Mandisa left, too. She found the master and his captain in the vizier's chambers where Zaphenath-paneah had once again fallen prey to his feelings. Deep sobs racked him for the space of a quarter-hour, then he lifted his head, wiped his streaked face with a square of linen, and asked Mandisa to reapply the painted lines of his eyes. He did not speak as she ministered to him, and Mandisa found herself silently asking the vizier's Almighty God to provide her master with the strength to confront yet another crisis.

When she assured him that he looked as dignified as before, he led the way as she and Tarik followed him back to the banquet hall.

Without a word of explanation, the vizier took his seat and commanded that the meal be served. The hungry Canaanites shifted in their chairs, unused to the Egyptian custom that often expanded dinner into a two- or three-hour ritual. Each tray or bowl had to be presented first to the master, who either kept it by his side or sampled it and sent it on its way to his other guests. Thus the hand of the vizier literally provided every dish.

While Zaphenath-paneah pretended to sample the feast of roasted duck, braised lamb, softened sweet breads, beans flavored with sweet oils, and honey-basted gazelle, Mandisa listened to snatches of Canaanite conversation around her. The brothers, who still rejoiced at Shim'on's reunion, remarked upon the bounty of the vizier's table and the striking fact that the Egyptian had unwittingly arranged them in birth order.

Afraid that her face might reveal too much, Mandisa kept her eyes from Shim'on, forcing herself to concentrate upon her master and his concerns. But Shim'on's booming voice, his wide gestures, and his resounding laugh seemed to fill the room, reinforcing her feelings of emptiness.

She had not visited his chamber in weeks, not since the night of his escape. Lady Asenath had needed her in the aftermath of that bizarre episode, and the master had requested that Mandisa remain with his wife. Tizara had been elected to feed Shim'on and listen to his complaints, so Mandisa was certain that the former harlot's image now filled his heart.

Amid the music of harpists and the twirling of dancing girls, the guests accepted food from the vizier's generous hand and filled their hungry stomachs. Mandisa shot Tarik a wry smile when she realized this was no ordinary banquet—Halima and the other kitchen slaves must have worked themselves into a frenzy to prepare so much on such short notice! And yet bowls continued to arrive from the kitchens: lumps of fat served with cumin and radish oil, bowls of brown beans, bright chick peas sprinkled with soft lotus seeds and flavored with marjoram. Slaves bore pitchers containing fresh grape juice flavored with pomegranates, figs, mint, and honey. After the round of meats and vegetables came the sweets: bowls of shining pomegranates, grapes, jujubes, honey cakes, heads of garlic, and delicately flavored sycamore figs.

Though tradition demanded that he at least pretend to sample every dish, the master ate little, but feasted instead of the sight of his brothers, particularly the youngest. Every other dish went to Binyamin, until an obvious crowd of serving women clustered around the young man's chair. The Egyptian guests whispered among themselves at this peculiar demonstration of favor, but Zaphenath-paneah seemed oblivious to everything but the handsome, shy man seated at his right hand.

Was he, Mandisa wondered, *trying* to incite the others to jealousy? Or was his heart overcome with longing for this long-lost shade of himself?

As she studied the faces of those eating and drinking in the reception hall, she realized that the twelve sons of Yaakov had been reunited for the first time in over twenty years.

But only one of them knew it.

CHAPTER TWENTY-EIGHT

BINYAMIN HELD UP A WARNING HAND AS YET ANOTHER DARK-EYED SLAVE approached with a platter from the vizier. "No, I couldn't eat another mouthful," he said, hoping the Egyptian girl would understand. He patted his stomach and smiled. "It is delicious, but I cannot eat any more."

The vizier's kind attention was embarrassing. He had, of course, been awarded such bounty because he sat closest to the vizier. The other Egyptians, stretching out to the vizier's left, had received comparatively little, but the vizier was obviously more interested in the men from Canaan. Did he still suspect they were spies? Or did he consider them unusual because they were eleven sons from one father? Re'uven had warned him of the great man's peculiarity, but Binyamin had seen nothing unpleasant in the man's aspect or behavior.

His eyes caught the dark gaze of the vizier's, and Binyamin turned away quickly, a blush burning his cheek. A moment later, the interpreter's soft voice cut into his thoughts. "My master says you have not eaten enough. Would you like more?"

Binyamin looked up and into the man's dark gaze. No trace of hostility dwelled there, only compassion and a certain overarching kindness. "Thank him, but I have eaten my fill."

The woman translated, and a strange, faintly eager look flashed in the

Egyptian's eyes. He spoke again and the woman repeated his words: "My master asks if you are well? What do you think of Egypt? How many children have you?"

Binyamin laughed, amazed that the great man would care for such trivial opinions and facts. "I am well, I am astounded by all I see, and I have nine sons," he said, feeling the man's sharp eyes upon him as he talked. "My wife is expecting another child soon."

"Nine sons?" The vizier's answer came through the woman. "Are you trying to fill the earth with Avraham's descendants completely by yourself?"

The teasing question caught Binyamin off guard. What had his brothers told the Egyptian at their first meeting? How did he know of Avraham? Yaakov's grandfather had sojourned in Mizraim for a time, but the people of the Black Land would not know of El Shaddai's promise to make Avraham's descendants as numerous as the sand of the sea.

"My lord," Binyamin asked, directly facing the vizier. "How do you know so many things? You have seated us according to our birth order, you know much about our father and our people. And yet you are a stranger to us."

The vizier watched Binyamin with an impassive expression as the woman translated.

"Who but God can reveal truth?" the vizier answered through the woman, caressing a graceful silver bowl as he spoke. The vessel had been engraved with the images of Egyptian gods, and Binyamin had seen similar bowls in the tents of many nomadic peoples. He recognized it as a divining bowl, used to foretell the future. A supplicant would fill the bowl with water, then pour oil on top of the water. The gods supposedly revealed truth in the swirls and designs of the floating oil.

"Perhaps God revealed these things to me," the vizier answered, lifting his gaze from the bowl. "And more which you shall know in time."

Binyamin could not think of a suitable answer, and after a moment, the vizier smiled and turned away. After lifting his hand and pronouncing a blessing of some sort in Egyptian, Zaphenath-paneah stood and left the room, his entourage trailing behind him.

"ANOTHER CHILD ON THE WAY? Binyamin, you spend too much time at home!" Shim'on teased, punching the young man in the arm. The brothers had been given bedding in a large chamber of the vizier's house and welcomed as guests for the night.

"At least I am not yet a grandfather!" Binyamin answered, returning Shim'on's playful jab. "Your oldest, Jemuel, is searching for a wife even now. You will have grandchildren piling on your knee before the next harvest."

"Jemuel is a fool." Shim'on rolled onto his stomach. "Marriage is for men who have no other options." He propped himself on his elbows, grateful that the servants had furnished them with blankets and furs instead of those sissified Egyptian beds. His brothers would tease him unmercifully if they knew he had lived in a dainty Egyptian chamber during his time of captivity.

Levi lifted a brow. "Are you sorry you married?"

"A man may marry if he needs sons, but I have six sons already," Shim'on answered, propping his head on his hand. "That's five legal heirs too many. I will never marry again."

"But men need women," Binyamin protested, sitting up. "Father says God Shaddai decreed it was not good for men to be alone."

"What men need there are women aplenty to give," Shim'on interrupted, snorting. "Right, Yehuda?"

A silence, thick as wool, wrapped itself around them. Shim'on stared at Yehuda, daring him to contradict his opinion, for they all knew that pious Yehuda had once unknowingly hired his own daughter-in-law as a prostitute.

"Indeed there are," Yehuda answered, his voice gruff, "but there are snakes in the desert, too, and I would not recommend that a man sleep with one."

Several of the brothers laughed, and the mood lightened. Shim'on glanced around the circle, grateful for each bearded, sunburned face. "So, tell me," he said, looking at Levi. "Father is well, but how is our sister?"

Yehuda groaned and buried his head in the furs beneath him while Levi's handsome face twisted in a smirk. "Dina is as Dina is," he said, shrugging. "She has not changed."

"Has she married?" Shim'on tried to keep his voice light.

Levi shook his head. "Nor will she. She sits in our mother's tent, alone most of the time except when the servants enter to help her. Sometimes she sews. Sometimes she makes baby clothes."

Shim'on said nothing, but stared at his hands, the same hands that locked Dina into the past by taking her baby and lowering it to the desert sands . . .

The remorse that pricked his soul was the mere tip of a long seam of guilt that snaked through the years back to Shekhem.

"Forget Dina." Levi's broad hand fell upon Shim'on's arm. "Tell me about the pretty woman who interprets for the vizier. When you were not aware of it, she studied you." His lips parted in a sly smile. "Or perhaps you were aware of it."

Re'uven's lower lip edged forward in a pout. "I thought she was watching me."

Yehuda lifted his head. "She was definitely watching our Shim'on, so explain the sudden color in your face, O Destroyer. You have been in this house a long time, so you must know the woman's name."

He knew much more than her name, but he forfeited everything the night he tried to escape. She would never look at him as she once did, she would never think of him in the same way . . .

"Her name—" Shim'on closed his hands— "is Mandisa. She is the Lady Asenath's handmaid."

Levi cracked an irreverent grin. "And why would a lady's maid care so much about you?"

"She was also my . . . attendant," Shim'on said, searching for a word to describe the relationship he had not completely analyzed himself. "She spoke Canaanite, so the guards asked her to tend me. We became—" he paused— "friends."

While the others wailed in laughter, Levi pretended to choke in disbelief. "You cannot be a woman's friend," he protested. "A woman can be your mother, your sister, your wife, or your lover. And since we know this Egyptian is not your mother or sister —"

"She is not wife or lover or Egyptian, either," Shim'on interrupted, looking at his hands again. "She is a Canaanite, and she is a friend. You may leave it at that."

Something in voice silenced them. Outside the chamber the wind groaned and a group of servants tumbled into laughter, but silence filled the room until Binyamin lifted his head. "Will she be upset when you leave tomorrow?" he asked, the light of concern in his dark eyes. "Perhaps you should say your farewells tonight, when you may have a private word with her."

"There is no need." Shim'on flipped onto his back and pillowed his head on his hands. "She is no more to me than the cook or the guard who watched my room. I am ready to go home, brothers, and I suggest we sleep."

The others mumbled in reply and settled on their beds. From far away Shim'on heard the familiar sounds of food being scraped from platters and the fountain splashing in the garden. Would he ever hear those sounds again? He knew he would never again enjoy the anticipation of Mandisa's gentle rap on his door. He might even miss the sharpness of her quick tongue.

He lay awake a long time.

SOMETHING MOVED in the darkness and Mandisa sat up, trying to see what had slashed her sleep like a dagger. "Who's there?" She drew the linen sheet to her chest, then reached out to wake Adom.

"Don't wake the boy."

Shim'on's voice spoke to her, but she could not see him in the darkness. A moment of sheer black fright swept through her—had he come to take revenge for his imprisonment?—then she stiffened at the challenge his presence presented.

"You should not be here," she said, steeling her voice with authority. "Come forward and show yourself, or I'll scream for the guards."

He stepped from the darkness at the rear of her room into a small square of light left by the waning moon. He looked tough and sinewy in the darkness, more powerful and determined than any man she had ever seen.

Heat stole into her face as she remembered their last private encounter. "I should probably scream anyway."

He moved a step closer. "I'm not here to hurt you."

"You have made a mistake. Didn't you mean to seek Tizara's chamber?" She cringed at the bitter tone of her voice. "I know what you want of a woman, and Tizara is better equipped and, I daresay, more willing to provide it than I."

His lips thinned in anger. "Woman, will you be quiet and listen?"

Adom stirred on his bed. Mandisa and Shim'on stared at each other across a sudden ringing silence, neither of them willing to wake the boy. When Adom turned and stretched out, still deep in sleep, Mandisa clenched her fist. "You have no more sense than a stone, coming to a woman's chamber at this hour. If you were a servant, Tarik would have you flogged for this."

"I am a prisoner here no longer," Shim'on answered, "and my intentions are honorable. I came to ask if you will leave with me tomorrow. Adom, too. There is room in my tent for both of you."

The concern in his expression amazed her even more than the proposal. "You want me to go with you? To Canaan?"

His expression stilled and grew serious. "It would not be right for me to leave you behind. I am now free. You should be, too."

Too stunned to answer, Mandisa said nothing as Shim'on knelt beside her bed, lifted her hand, and pressed it to his heart. With a sureness that made her breath leave her body, his eyes moved into hers. "Mandisa--" intensity marked his voice-- "I owe you so much. I am sorry if I have behaved wrongly toward you, but you must understand, I was not at my best in this place. But now I am free, so journey with us and leave this black land. Return to Canaan, the place of your birth."

She turned her hand to clasp his, not daring to trust her turbulent feelings. Was this a dream? No, his flesh was warm, his hand all too real. For a long moment, she looked at him. "Are you asking me to be your wife?"

"By heaven above, no." He dropped her hand as resolutely as he'd taken it. "I will never marry again. I've had two wives, and while they lived I made both of them miserable. Since I have a legal son, I have no further need of a wife."

Her mind reeled with confusion. "So you would have me live with you as what? A concubine?"

He lifted one shoulder in a shrug. "We will make whatever arrangement you like, but I won't marry you. You have told me about your first marriage and its misery, and I saw how my father tormented my mother. So you shall remain free and independent. I will protect and provide for you and Adom; that is the least I can do to show my gratitude. But since marriage makes men miserable, you will be free to go any time you please."

"And so will you." She pressed her lips together, trying not to lose her fragile control. He could walk away at any time, just as he had planned to escape and leave her behind forever. He would abandon her just as surely as Idogbe had.

"You are wrong, Shim'on," she answered, her cheeks burning as she stared at him. "Marriage doesn't make men miserable. Men make marriage miserable, and you have already brought me more misery than a hundred husbands."

His eyes gleamed with honest surprise, then a bemused smile crossed his face. "Consider my proposition carefully. I know you love me."

She pressed her hand to her forehead, unable to believe what she'd just heard. "How could I love a man so filled with anger and bitterness that he cannot see God's plain truth before him?"

"There is only one truth to consider here." His hand gripped her arm. "You love me, and you need someone to care for you and the boy."

"Adom and I were fine before you came, and we'll be fine after you leave."

"You are a *slave*, can't you get that truth through your lovely little head?"

"I am a free woman."

"No, you are bound to Zaphenath-paneah, his wife, his children, and his house, as surely as if you wore chains of iron around your dainty ankles. Your master says 'do this' and you jump, your lady says 'I want,' and you would fly to the moon to fetch whatever she desires. You weep over your master's sorrows and celebrate his joys when you ought to be creating your own."

"His sorrows are my sorrows, and my lady's joys are my joys because I love her, Shim'on. If you knew how to love, you would understand."

His eyes, black and dazzling, seemed to impale her. "You are a fool." He lifted his chin and released her arm. "I offer you the freedom to go where you want and do as you please, and you reject it. I offer you my gratitude, and you scorn me. So be it. As you labor for your mighty vizier and work yourself into an early grave, think of me."

"I will think of you," she answered, her flesh burning where he had touched her, "every time I hear one of the guards lose his temper and every time Tarik disciplines an unruly slave." The words poured from her like a river, impossible to stop. "You are a difficult man, impossible to endure! First you insult me by asking me to be a concubine, then you flatter yourself by saying that I love you. How could I? No woman could love a man like you because you have no idea what love is. You think love is only found within a woman's arms, but it is truly found by a woman's side, facing together the good and bad life brings. But you would weather a storm by storming the weather! You stomp through life, trampling the hearts of those who *would* love you if only you would let them."

"Love." The word fell from his lips like a curse. "Yaakov loved Rahel. That love condemned the rest of us."

"Even if your father did wrong, Shim'on, you cannot continue this way. Reach out to him, care for him."

He chuckled, a cold and bitter sound in the darkness. "How can I care for someone who does not care for me?"

"I've been asking myself the same question," she answered. "And I have realized one thing—you cannot offer love with a clenched fist. It must be given freely. I have tried to offer love to you, Shim'on. But you would not accept it."

"You don't know what you're talking about." He stood, defiance pouring from his dark eyes. "It is you, Mandisa, who will not be loved. You hide yourself behind the distinguished and noble Zaphenath-paneah. You refuse freedom in order to spend your life serving a man who will never consider you more than a slave."

She shook her head. "You are wrong."

"I am right." He bent forward until his face hovered only inches from hers. "When you think of me in the lonely years to come, remember that I behaved nobly toward you. In gratitude, I offered you a way out of the Black Land, and you refused it."

"I will remember this night until my dying day," she whispered, turning away. "But I will not be lonely without you, Shim'on."

She didn't know when he left, but a chill wind blew through the chamber, and she shivered, feeling more alone than she ever had in her life.

CHAPTER TWENTY-NINE

AN HOUR BEFORE THE BARK OF THE SUN GOD WAS TO BEGIN ITS JOURNEY across the dark sky, Tarik steadied the lamp in his hand and urged the flame to strengthen itself. When the coiled papyrus wick burned steadily, he held the lamp aloft and moved through the dark courtyard, checking to see that his master's orders had been carried out. Zaphenath-paneah had been quite explicit: each Canaanite's bag was to be filled to the brim with grain, then each man's silver was to be returned to the mouth of his sack. Tarik was to personally take the master's exquisite silver divining bowl and hide it inside the youngest brother's sack.

Moving steadily in the darkness, Tarik patted the sides of the restive donkeys and fumbled with each sack until he had checked all eleven. Then he slipped the silver bowl from a pouch under his cloak and buried it under the grain of the last donkey's load.

All was ready.

HALF AN HOUR later by the waterclock, Ani stood with Tarik on the wide porch as the eleven sons of Yaakov strode out of the villa and into the courtyard. The palm trees along the villa's walls stood black against the brightening sky as the brothers took the reins of their donkeys. Ani cleared his throat and stepped forward to bid the brothers a final farewell. Zaphenath-paneah, he told them, wished them a safe and prosperous journey. Speaking for the others, Re'uven thanked Ani for his master's hospitality and promised to give the vizier's greetings to their aged father.

The loud one, Shim'on, lingered a moment in the courtyard, looking around as if to imprint the villa upon his memory, then waved toward the portico where Ani and Tarik stood. "Farewell, Egyptians," Shim'on called, flashing a tight, grim smile. "Forgive me, but I hope we never meet again."

"I share your feelings," Tarik called, resting his hands atop his sword belt. Then, in a lower voice, the guard murmured puzzling words: "If only he knew."

Knew what? Ani lifted a questioning brow toward the captain of the guard, but Tarik kept his eyes fastened to the departing men and did not speak again.

As the last donkey disappeared through the gate, a soft sound broke the stillness of the early morning. Ani turned to see Mandisa weeping in the shadow of a papyrus-shaped pillar. Despite the Canaanite's brazen attempt to run away with Tizara, Mandisa apparently still harbored deep feelings for him.

"My dear child," he said, walking to the young woman's side. "If you loved him, why didn't you let him know?"

"I did," she answered, running the back of her hand along her wet cheek. "But he did not understand."

THE SHADED FINGER of the shadow clock seemed to be mired in the space between one black slash on the horizontal rod and the next, but finally the shadow moved. An hour had passed since his brothers' departure. Yosef's nerves tensed, half in anticipation and half in dread, as he turned to Tarik.

"It is time," Yosef said, his heart thumping as his gaze crossed the captain's. "Go after them."

Tarik gave a whirling salute and sprinted to join his men in the court-yard. After moving to his balcony, Yosef saw over twenty assembled battle chariots, each manned with a driver and an expert archer. The horses pawed the dust in eagerness, their heads straining forward, their tails arched.

Would this show of force intimidate his brothers into surrendering Binyamin? For an instant Yosef wondered if his plan was elementally unfair. Perhaps part of him *wanted* them to give Binyamin up—Yosef could keep his brother in Egypt where they could enjoy sweet fellowship and make up for twenty-two stolen years.

But if they surrendered Binyamin, their shame would prevent them from ever returning to face the vizier of Egypt. And Yisrael and his chil-dren would starve in the famine. Yosef could not believe that God Shaddai would allow such a thing to happen.

From the corner of his eye, Yosef saw Tarik jog across the sandy courtyard. The captain yelled out the command to mount up and leapt onto the back of his chariot. As the other drivers watched, Tarik lifted the vizier's standard with one hand and gripped a side rail with the other. At this signal, the villa's gates opened wide and cracking whips snapped the air. Amid the swirling dust, noise, and confusion, Tarik's chariot peeled away and the others followed in a parade of swift, efficient force.

SHIM'ON FELT a strange and tangible rumbling begin to move along the ground, like a storm coming out of the Sahara. Strong and unreasonable anxiety spurted through him. He stopped and lifted a hand to quiet his brothers, but they had already fallen silent. Their faces clouded with uneasiness as they turned to look back. Toward Egypt.

The earth trembled with the force of galloping horses, and the broth-ers' donkeys flapped their ears at the prospect of facing their regal cousins. Finally, rising from a valley of sand, the source of the sound appeared. The sun glinted off the bright opulence of a fleet of bejeweled chariots that stirred up the desert and pressed toward them in a V formation. The quiet morning echoed with the roaring shout of the approaching storm, and yet above the tumult Shim'on could hear his heart battering against his ears.

What evil was this? Were they never to be free from the power of the Black Land?

Before he could consult his brothers, the swift Egyptian guard had surrounded them completely. As the other sons of Yisrael stood in astonished silence, Shim'on widened his stance and put his hands on his hips, ready for a showdown. He had thrown aside the softness of Egypt like an uncomfortable garment; his blood now stirred with familiar energy and old passions. If the Egyptians wanted a fight, they had come to the right place. His home, the desert.

"Not now, Brother!" Yehuda called a warning. Shim'on held his stance, waiting.

The circle of Egyptians broke, and Tarik rode forward in a chariot that gleamed with gold. The captain's mouth had gone thin with displeasure.

Re'uven, Levi, and Yehuda looked to Shim'on. *You know him,* their glances seemed to say. *You handle him.*

"Life and health to you, Tarik." Shim'on dropped the reins of his donkey as he took a step forward. The two men exchanged careful, simultaneous smiles. "Why do we meet again so soon?"

Tarik grasped the frame of his chariot, shifting his weight to his arms. "My master Zaphenath-paneah has sent me to ask you one question."

"Which is?"

Tarik's cold, proud eyes raked over the brothers. "Why have you repaid good with evil? My master fed you, sheltered you, and provided for you, yet one of you has taken the silver bowl he uses for divination. You have committed a shameful wrong."

Shim'on stared at the captain in utter disbelief. "Why does your lord accuse us of such a thing? We would never steal from him. If we were thieves, my brothers would not have returned the silver they found in their sacks when they reached Canaan. Why would we want to steal from the vizier's house?"

Shim'on felt a hand upon his arm; Yehuda had come to stand beside him. "You may search us," Yehuda said, his voice steady and calm. "And if you find your master's bowl among us, the guilty one shall die and the rest of us will be your master's slaves. For I tell you the truth, the bowl is not here."

"I *will* search you," Tarik answered, his mouth twisting into a wry smile. He gestured to his guards, who dismounted from their chariots and tightened the circle around the brothers. "And the guilty one shall pay for his crime. The man with the cup shall be my master's slave, but the rest of you shall be held innocent of this offense."

Knowing that his bag did not contain the missing bowl, Shim'on stood motionless while his brothers scrambled to untie their sacks. The Egyptians watched the unloading with keen interest, and Tarik insisted upon personally searching each brother's load. He would begin with the eldest brother, the captain announced, and work his way through the line to the youngest, so no one would be overlooked.

In Re'uven's sack the Egyptian found the double amount of silver he had brought to Egypt.

"So you are not thieves?" Tarik asked, looking squarely at Shim'on. "Obviously, you are not the innocents you pretend to be."

At the sight of the silver, Shim'on wondered if they would all be imprisoned, but Tarik said nothing else and moved on to Shim'on's donkey. Apparently Zaphenath-paneah cared little for silver, but had sent his captain only after the divining bowl.

Shim'on had already reloaded his donkey by the time Tarik reached Binyamin. Confident that the vizier's captain had made an embarrassing blunder, Shim'on urged the others to load their donkeys as well. He had just stepped forward to help Levi with a stubborn strap when he heard Re'uven cry out.

Shim'on whirled around. From the sack on Binyamin's donkey, Tarik lifted the unmistakable silver bowl and held it aloft. Shim'on gazed at it in despair, the spark of hope in his breast completely extinguished.

Tarik lowered the bowl and tucked it under his arm. "Only this man needs to return with me," the captain said, studying the others with a curious intensity. "The rest of you are free to return to your father in Hebron."

"We will not leave him," Yehuda answered, his stentorian voice rumbling through the murmurs of sorrow. "I would rather die in Egypt than face my father without my brother."

"Almighty God, why?" Re'uven wailed, ripping his cloak in agony. "One was arrogant, the other a thief—why are the sons of Rahel a curse to us?"

"It matters not," Shim'on answered, resolutely swinging Levi's sack onto the donkey's back. He reached for the girth straps and secured the load. "We will go back to Thebes with Binyamin. I have spent a long time in the vizier's house, so perhaps he will listen to me and show mercy to our brother."

And if not, someone else in the villa might be persuaded to plead on their behalf . . . if he had not offended her too severely.

CHAPTER THIRTY

MANDISA HAD JUST FINISHED THINNING LADY ASENATH'S BROWS WITH A new pair of bronze tweezers when the master entered the lady's chamber. She paused, ready to bow or receive his instructions, but he moved impatiently through the room, his hands locked behind his back, his mind miles away. After waiting a moment, Asenath signaled Mandisa to continue her work.

As the tiny bronze hands of the tweezers moved deftly over the line of the lady's brow, the women continued their small talk and waited for the master. Occasionally Asenath asked Zaphenath-paneah about Pharaoh's wife or the upcoming party in honor of the Queen's birthday, but the master answered in incomplete, short sentences, clearly occupied with other thoughts.

Mandisa lowered the tweezers to the table and handed her mistress a looking brass. Why didn't her master speak? Did he no longer trust Asenath with the secrets of his heart? Or was he as sorrowful as she to see his brothers depart?

Asenath must have been thinking similar thoughts, for Mandisa could see tears rising in her eyes, like some slow fountain coming up.

She gave her mistress a smile. "Be at peace, my lady," she murmured, reaching for Asenath's favorite jeweled collar. "The master's mind is burdened with many thoughts."

She had just finished fastening the collar when the vizier halted his pacing and cocked his ear toward the window. Mandisa paused, straining to hear whatever had alerted him, and felt a shiver pass down her spine when she recognized the sound of hoofbeats.

Zaphenath-paneah's brows drew together. "Quickly, Mandisa, go to the window," he said, his voice edged with iron. "And tell me what you see there."

Was his expression of anxious hope mirrored in her own face? Not daring to question him, she grabbed a chair and dragged it to the high clerestory window. After hopping up onto the seat, she peered out. "I see riders, my lord," she called over her shoulder, barely able to keep the excitement from her voice.

"Tarik and his charioteers?"

"Yes." She exhaled a sigh of contentment. "And donkeys."

"How many men on donkeys? One—or eleven?"

A thoughtful smile curved her mouth as she turned. "There are eleven, my lord. All of your brothers have returned."

The arrested expression on his face broke into a look of pure relief and pleasure. He dropped his gaze as if to whisper a prayer of thanks to his God, then lifted bright eyes to Asenath.

"They came back together!" he said, the sound of tears in his voice. Eagerly he approached his wife, then bent and fingered a loose tendril of hair on her forehead. "Rejoice with me, beloved," he said, pressing a finger to her trembling lips, "for my brothers' hearts are changing."

He shifted his gaze to Mandisa. "If Tarik finds you, have him meet me in the central hall at once." He bent to place a quick kiss on his wife's forehead, then hurried from the room. In her excitement Mandisa nearly followed before she remembered that her duty lay in serving the wigless woman who still waited in her chair.

"I'm sorry, my lady." Mandisa moved toward Asenath's dressing table. "I'm sure you'll want to join them as soon as possible."

"Take your time," Asenath answered, her voice as flat as her eyes. "There is no hurry. He wants me rejoice with him, but I cannot."

Mandisa had been about to lift the heavy wig from its stand, but she paused, surprised by her mistress's words. "He has found his long-lost brothers," Mandisa answered, speaking in as reasonable a voice as she could manage. "And since he is your husband, they are your brothers, too. Surely you can be happy for him."

"I can't understand why anyone would be happy to find relatives in Canaan," Asenath grumbled, picking at her gown. "The captive we kept in the house caused altogether too much commotion. And herders stink; they smell like sheep when they fill a room. And yet my lord and husband wants me to rejoice with him, he wants me to welcome the same brothers who once wanted him dead. Well, I cannot see them with his eyes. I do not love them, and I don't think I can."

Mandisa took a quick breath of utter astonishment as hot, bitter tears slipped down her mistress's cheeks. Asenath had not given any sign that she would not accept the master's brothers. Mandisa had assumed she would be thrilled and delighted for her husband's sake.

"You are a loving woman." Mandisa left the wig on its stand and sank to her mistress's feet. "You charm all who meet you, my lady, and you are dear to my master's heart. But you have been ill, you are not yourself."

"You are right, I am not myself," Asenath repeated, closing her eyes. "And I have done something terrible." She took a breath as if she would speak again, then apparently thought the better of it. "My wig, please."

Mandisa stood and lifted the wig, fluffed it, and fitted it onto her lady's head. Asenath's countenance remained immobile, but the atmosphere of the chamber cooled as dramatically as if a rainy wind had blown through the house.

Mandisa pressed her hands to her knees and bowed. "If that is all, my lady, I will see if the master needs me."

"Wait." When Mandisa looked up, Asenath's bright eyes had clouded with hazy sadness. "Have you noticed, Mandisa, that the master is not . . . happy about the coming child?"

Torn by conflicting emotions, Mandisa hesitated. Did Lady Asenath really believe she could deceive those who knew her best? Against all human convention and reason, her husband had continued to support her. Was his love not enough? Did Asenath expect him to *exult* in the result of her infidelity?

But it was not a servant's place to rip away the veil. "The master adores you, my lady," she answered, taking her mistress's hand. "Because he loves you, he will love any child that comes from your womb. But I am certain he fears for your health."

Asenath managed a weak laugh of relief. "I have made arrangements for continual offerings to be made to Taweret, the goddess of prospective mothers. I know both the baby and I will be safe."

"I pray you are right, my lady." Mandisa bowed again, masking her inner turmoil. Asenath needed a comforting counselor, someone who would speak plainly, but Mandisa did not think that her mistress would listen to a handmaid.

And Shim'on and his brothers were waiting. Mandisa backed out of the room and left her mistress alone in her chamber.

CHAPTER THIRTY-ONE

Zaphenath-paneah, Tarik, and a host of guards and servants had assembled in the reception hall by the time Mandisa arrived. Ani and the brothers were not in sight, and Mandisa realized that again she was to play a part in an unfolding drama. Today, however, though the stage was set for business as usual, everyone in the room sensed that some momentous event was about to take place. The vizier's excitement was palpable; he exuded it like a scent.

Zaphenath-paneah smiled at Mandisa in gratitude as she took her place at his left hand, then Ani entered and bowed before the vizier. "They are in the vestibule, Master, and as anxious as hens with one chick," he said, lifting his bright eyes. "Shall I send the Canaanites in?"

The vizier crossed his legs at the ankle and gripped the arms of his chair. "Yes."

Ani scuttled away, and Mandisa turned to catch Tarik's eye. A gleam of mischief shone there, and she drew in her breath, curious about the drama they were about to enact. Who had devised the script? Tarik obviously knew his part, and perhaps Ani, but she had no idea what might happen in the next few moments. Might Shim'on be forced to remain behind again?

She closed her eyes, silencing the thought. *Don't wish it. Don't wish for him. He cares nothing for your heart, he does not love you. He has no idea what love is.*

The doors to the vestibule opened and the brothers rushed in, their former deference swallowed up by frantic worry. The youngest man, Binyamin, walked between two guards. His wrists were bound, albeit loosely, his legs hobbled by a sturdy papyrus rope. One of Tarik's lieutenants brought forward the vizier's silver bowl and placed it on a stand by Zaphenath-paneah's chair.

At the sight of the waiting vizier, all eleven of the brothers prostrated themselves on the floor.

"What is this you have done?" Zaphenath-paneah said through Mandisa, addressing the youngest brother, Binyamin. "Do you not know that God speaks to me? You could not have hoped to escape."

Binyamin lifted his head to speak, but one of the older brothers shushed him and rose to his knees. "What can we say to you, my lord?" he asked, opening his hands in entreaty. "I am Yehuda, and I have no words to offer in explanation. What can we say? How can we justify ourselves? God has discovered your servants' crime." He hung his head; the silver threads of his hair glowed in the diffused light of the chamber. "Here we are, servants to my lord, we and the one in whose hand the bowl was found."

Mandisa froze when Zaphenath-paneah did not wait for the translation. "Heaven forbid that I should do this to you," the vizier answered in fluent Canaanite. "The man in whose possession the cup has been found shall be my slave. But as for the rest of you, go in peace to your father."

Yehuda shook his bushy head. "Please, my lord," he said, apparently too worried to notice that the vizier now spoke his language, "may your servant please speak a word in your ears. And do not let your anger flare up against me, for you are equal to Pharaoh! We know this. We would not take advantage of you."

Mandisa looked at her master. He nodded in regal assent, and Yehuda advanced until he stood only two paces from the master's elevated chair. The two men stared at each other eye-to-eye.

"My lord asked his servants," Yehuda began, lowering his voice, 'Have you a father or another brother?' And we said to you, 'We have an old father and a young son of his old age, whose brother is dead, so he alone is left of his mother, and his father loves him.' Then you said to us, 'Bring him down to me, so I may set my eyes on him.' But we said to you, my lord, 'The lad cannot leave his father, for if he should leave, his father would die.' But you said to us, 'Unless your youngest brother comes down with you, you shall not see my face again.'"

"Why are you telling me what I already know?" Zaphenath-paneah interrupted, his brows slanting in a frown. "I am not a forgetful old man, that you need to remind me of anything."

"I beg your pardon." Yehuda hung his head. "But there is more to the tale, an episode you have not heard."

Zaphenath-paneah's jaw tensed. "Tell it."

Yehuda thrust his hands behind his back and stiffened his spine. "When we returned to your servant my father, we told him your words. And after a while our father said, 'Go back, buy us some food rations.' But we said, 'We cannot go down. If our youngest brother is with us, then we will go down; for we cannot see the Egyptian's face unless our youngest brother is with us.'"

Yehuda fell silent, trembling with the intensity of his memories. "Then your servant my father said to us, 'You know my true wife bore me two sons; and the one went away from me, and I said, "Surely he is torn, torn to pieces!" and I have not seen him since. And if you take this one also from me, and harm befalls him, you will bring my gray hair down to Sheol in sorrow.'"

The roar of absolute silence filled the chamber as Yehuda paused. Zaphenath-paneah sat still, his eyes narrow, his posture militant. Mandisa knew she watched a volcano on the verge of erupting.

"So now," Yehuda snatched a deep breath, "if I return to your servant, my father, and the lad is not with us—in whose life his own life is bound up—it will be, that when he sees the lad is no more, he will die. And we will bring the gray hair of our father down to the grave in sorrow. But since I pledged myself for the lad to my father, let me bear the blame for this deed before you and my father forever."

Yehuda dropped to his knees. "Now, therefore, please my lord, let me remain here instead of the lad. I will be a slave to you in whatever capacity you wish, but let the lad go up with his brothers."

"You would give yourself in his place?"

"Yes." Yehuda lifted his eyes and his hands in a gesture of supplication. "For how shall I return to my father if the lad is not with me? I cannot bear to see the evil that will overtake him. I cannot watch him die."

Silence loomed between them like a heavy mist. Yehuda seemed to melt in the tension, floundering before the brilliance of Zaphenath-paneah's gaze.

"Tarik," Zaphenath-paneah finally said, his granite eyes locked upon Yehuda's, "clear the room of everyone but these men."

Tarik's face folded in disappointment as he gave the terse command. The fan bearers, guards, servants, and incense bearers filed out of the chamber. Mandisa hesitated, not sure whether or not she should stay, but then she heard a soft message from her master's lips: "Mandisa, your mistress will need you now."

She slipped away from the chamber, following Tarik. The double doors had just closed behind her when the reception hall filled with the sound of the master's weeping.

"I TOLD YOU HE WAS A LUNATIC," Shim'on said, lifting his head as the vizier broke into loud, wrenching sobs. Such a noise! And why? Zaphenath-paneah ought to be angry. He should have thrown them all into prison, but the grand vizier of all Egypt had just thrown his arms around Yehuda and wept now as though his world had come to an end.

"What should we do?" Levi asked, warily rising from the floor. "Is he truly insane? What if he attacks us?"

"Be quiet, he understands you," Dan cautioned. "Did you not hear him speak Canaanite? He has deceived us, brothers."

"We are eleven against one." Shim'on rested his hands on his belt and gazed at the inexplicable sight before him. Locked in the vizier's embrace, Yehuda turned slightly and threw Shim'on a bewildered glance as he patted the vizier on the back, soothing him the way a woman comforts a hurting child.

"Do nothing yet," Re'uven cautioned, keeping his voice low. "He has done us no harm."

Pulling away from Yehuda, the vizier turned to face them. "Ah, my brothers, I do not blame you for thinking me deranged." He palmed tears from his cheeks, then opened his hands at his side. "Do you not see?" he asked, gazing at them with a look of mad happiness. "Can you not hear that I speak Canaanite as well as you do? Do you not know me?"

Shim'on looked at Levi, who frowned and wrinkled his brow.

"I suppose I cannot blame you, for I am much changed," the vizier went on, looking at them with no trace of his former animosity. "I am your brother."

Wave after wave of shock slapped at Shim'on. *Yosef.* That voice. The familiarity. He should have *known*, he should have *seen*. Who but a son of Yisrael would tell his servants about El Shaddai? But it was impossible!

Levi stumbled backward. "It is a trick."

Shim'on peered at the man who had held him captive, then stepped forward.

"Shim'on, do you not recognize me?" the vizier asked, swiping at the makeup on his face. "Look." He tore the alien wig from his head to reveal a close-cropped haircut, then lowered his hands in an almost humble posture. His voice, when he spoke again, was low and husky. "I am your brother Yosef, whom you sold into Egypt."

"It is! It is Yosef!" Binyamin shouted, running across the room. Laughing, the vizier threw his arms around the younger man and pressed him to his chest, one joyful heart pounding against another.

Levi watched through narrowed eyes. "Yosef was half-dead when we sold him to the slave traders. How can one rise from the grave to a throne?"

"By the power of God," Yehuda answered, his face lighting up like sunshine bursting out of the clouds. He ran forward to join the embrace.

The murmurs of the others rose like a fog around Shim'on.

"Can this be true?"

"Over twenty years ago."

"He was only a boy."

"And we nearly killed him." A thin thread of suspicion still laced Levi's voice.

Shim'on stepped closer to hear what the vizier was saying to Binyamin. "Do you recall how you always wanted to go with the older brothers, but Father made you stay with me?" Zaphenath-paneah asked, his eyes darkening with emotion. "We would tease Bilha and Zilpa until even Aunt Lea was ready to chase us out of the camp. And of the women, you must tell me—how is Dina, our sister?"

"By heaven above," Shim'on murmured, "he *is* Yosef." For though he had often mentioned the names of Yaakov's wives to Mandisa, he had never thought to tell her the names of the maidservants who became Yaakov's concubines. And how else could the vizier know that Yaakov set Lea's sons to work in the fields while Rahel's sons remained safe in the camp?

Shim'on's blood ran thick with guilt. Had he, in his innermost heart of hearts, known the truth? He had certainly hated Zaphenath-paneah with the same intensity he once hated Yosef. But now the Egyptian vizier who had held Shim'on's life in his hands reached out to welcome the brothers who had abandoned him to slavery, even to death.

"Do not be grieved or angry with yourselves because you sold me here," the vizier said, his deep-timbered voice so different and yet so like Yosef's, "for God sent me before you to preserve life. For the famine has been in the land these two years, and there are still five years in which there will be neither plowing nor harvesting. The Almighty God sent me before you to make you a remnant on earth, to keep you alive as a great body of survivors."

Yehuda shook his massive head. "But—we sold you."

"You did not send me here, but God," the vizier answered, his eyes glowing. "God Shaddai has made me Father to Pharaoh, lord of the royal household, and ruler over all the land of Egypt." The man's tear-stained face broke into a smile. "Hurry and return to my father, and tell him all that has happened to me. Tell him that God has made me lord of all Egypt, and tell him that I wait for him to come down here. You shall all live in the land of Goshen, where there is good land for grazing, and you shall be near me, you and your children, your children's children, and your flocks and herds and all that you have. There I will also provide for you through the five years of famine to come, lest all of you be impoverished."

"Can it be?" Levi whispered, his voice still heavy with doubt.

Yosef's paint-lengthened eyes met Levi's gray ones. "Here, your eyes see, and the eyes of my brother Binyamin see, that it is Yosef speaking to you. Now you must tell my father of all the weight I carry in Egypt, and all you have seen; and you must hurry and bring my father down here."

And while Shim'on watched, still wondering how such a thing could be true, Zaphenath-paneah, no, *Yosef*, flung himself upon Binyamin's neck and wept anew, and Binyamin wept upon his neck. And then Yehuda and Re'uven, Yissakhar, Zevulun, Gad, Asher, Dan, Naftali, and Levi went to him, one by one.

Shim'on was the last to greet his brother but, like the others, he kissed Yosef on both cheeks and mingled his tears with the vizier's.

CHAPTER THIRTY-TWO

ANI SQUINTED AT THE SHARD OF CLAY IN HIS HAND. HE HAD SCRIBBLED several items of concern upon the pottery, things to do before the master's brothers departed for Canaan.

Such a to-do, such a surprise! He never would have guessed that the noble Zaphenath-paneah could spring from the same stock as Canaanite herdsmen, but when the vizier mingled among them Ani could see a family resemblance. Of course the vizier was a bright star whose glory far outshone the others, but the youngest man, Binyamin, possessed a similar glow and good nature . . .

Ani clicked his teeth, urging himself back to the duties he had yet to fulfill. Two days of feasting and rejoicing had been hurriedly planned to welcome the vizier's brothers to Thebes. Even Pharaoh and his house had been informed so they, too, could celebrate this important event. The young Pharaoh had been most gracious, offering the vizier's family a place in the best land of Egypt as shelter against the famine. Pharaoh had also offered a fleet of wagons for the brothers to take with them to Canaan in order to bring their wives, children, and little ones to enjoy the Black Land's bounty.

The vizier had also been more than gracious. To each of his brothers he gave a luxurious set of garments, but to Binyamin he gave three hundred pieces of silver—far more rare and valuable than gold—and *five* sets of garments. To his father, Yaakov, he planned to send ten male donkeys loaded with frankincense, scented oils, and medicinal herbs, the best products of Egypt, and ten female donkeys bearing grain and bread, sustenance for the coming journey.

The vizier's household had been completely shaken by the incredible news. Ani had been a little offended to learn that Tarik and Mandisa knew of the vizier's relationship to the Canaanites long before the weighty revelation, but his hurt had been assuaged when Zaphenath-paneah clapped him on the shoulder and told him he knew a man of Ani's wisdom would enjoy the challenge of seeking the truth far more than being told outright.

"You were right, as always, my lord," Ani had answered. "And I *had* discerned something special about these men. My gods were not far from revealing your secret, I am certain."

In the glow of Zaphenath-paneah's happiness and Pharaoh's blessing, the entire house rejoiced. But, Ani noticed with some anxiety, there had been no signs of rejoicing from the mistress's chambers. After formally meeting and greeting her husband's brothers, Lady Asenath had withdrawn to her rooms, ostensibly to give her husband more time alone with his family.

Asenath was not the only woman to avoid the brothers' reunion. Tizara and Mandisa also took pains to remain out of sight. Tizara hid herself, Ani reasoned, because she wanted to remain on good terms with the master who had shown her mercy. Mandisa, on the other hand, probably wanted to avoid meeting Shim'on.

Ani worried about Mandisa. Under less hectic circumstances he would have sought her out and inquired after her feelings, but now he had no time for affairs of the heart. Donkeys waited to be packed, wagons needed to be oiled and inspected, a populace yearned for information about the vizier's great news. The women, Ani decided, would have to work through their own problems.

JUST BEFORE SUNRISE on the day the brothers were scheduled to depart, Mandisa paused in the darkened passageway that to the garden and the kitchens. Insects whirred in the tall grasses at the far edge of the garden pool and the leaves of acacia trees fluttered in light applause. Apart from the sounds of nature, this part of the house lay still and silent. After two days of nearly continual feasting and celebration, the vizier and his boisterous brothers slept.

She had come through the courtyard where a host of wagons and donkeys stood ready for the journey, freshly watered and harnessed. She had heard that the brothers had gone to sleep just after sundown so they might rise early and depart from Egypt in the cool of morning. She shuddered in a moment of deja vu. The household had experienced this scene of departure before, but Shim'on had not come to her chamber last night to ask her to travel with him. He had not, in fact, sought her at all in the last two days. Now that he had been proclaimed brother to the vizier, he probably intended to find a more attractive, more expensive-looking concubine.

The stars had begun to fade behind a sky of blue velvet as she slipped through the garden, and she knew she should hurry if she wanted to fetch food for herself and Adom before the brothers woke and demanded the servants' attention.

She had just left the garden and entered the passageway leading to the kitchens when a massive Canaanite form stepped in front of her, blocking her path. "Excuse me," she said, not looking up.

"Mandisa." Shim'on's voice was cool and faintly reproachful. "I wondered if I would see you before we left."

She steeled her heart and lifted her chin. "And so you have."

Despite her intention to remain aloof, he captured her eyes and gave her a smile that sent her pulses racing. Her emotions whirled and skidded at the sight of *something* in those eyes, and for a moment she hoped he would ask her to leave with him again.

His fingers curved under her chin. "My gentle jailer," he said, his thumb tenderly tracing the line of her cheekbone and jaw. "I have been thinking in the last two days."

"That is good. A change for you, is it not?"

"Hush, woman." The glitter in his half-closed eyes was both posses-sive and gently accusing. "I was never in any real danger here, was I? You must have known who I was, and you would not have let the vizier's brother starve. And Tarik would not have hurt me, not even in an escape attempt."

She shrugged, irritated at the thrilling current moving through her. "I would not have let you starve," she repeated, wanting to be away.

"So you *did* know the truth. You knew the vizier was my brother, and yet you said nothing."

"What does it matter?" Standing this close to him, knowing he was about to leave, both pained and aggravated her. "I was commanded not to reveal what I knew."

"And like a slave, you obeyed. And yet you and I shared something special; I had the feeling you could tell me anything." From out in the courtyard, one of the horses whickered, the only sound in the morning stillness. She tried to look away, but he held her eyes. "We shared secrets, you and I—so why did you not tell me about the vizier?"

"We did not share all our secrets, Shim'on." She forced herself to think; it was difficult to remain clear-headed when he stood so close to her. "And my kindness to you had nothing to do with your relationship to my master. I cared for you because you needed help."

"Is that the only reason? Halima took care of me, too, but she refused to come when my behavior became . . . intolerable."

"I can tolerate more than Halima."

"So you cared for me to test the mettle of your endurance?"

"I cared for you because I am a servant who chooses to obey her master. That is, was, always will be my reason. It's why I take care of Lady Asenath, why I tend to the little boys."

"You're lying, woman. You have told me yourself, you obey your master and mistress because you love them. Just as you love me."

Her blood pounded; her face flamed with humiliation. "You flatter yourself."

"You do love me. And yet you will not come with me. Why not?"

"I've told you. I will not be a concubine."

"What if I asked you to marry me?"

She bit her lip, caught off guard by the sudden vibrancy of his voice. Was he jesting? No, his dark, earnest eyes were probing hers, seeking an answer. His hand caught her arm and slipped to her wrist, his fingers closed about her hand.

Had the last two days changed him? No. More likely he fancied himself among the nobility and realized that a wife was more socially acceptable than a concubine. He wanted a wife by his side to share his glory as the vizier's brother, to oversee his home and his sons . . .

Better to tell him the truth. "I cannot marry you, Shim'on," she said, boldly meeting his gaze. "I cannot give myself to a man whose heart brims with anger and hate."

"But I was angry because I hated Zaphenath-paneah," he answered, shrugging. The steady tone of his voice gave her hope. "And now that I know he is my brother, I can no longer hate him. So all is forgiven, the past has been put behind us."

He stepped forward, penning her between his chest and the wall, radiating a vitality that drew her like the moon summons the sea. "Come with me, Mandisa." His hand tightened around hers. "The wagon is loaded, but there is room for you and Adom. Or say you'll wait for me, for we will return as soon as we have collected our father and our families."

She closed her eyes as her heart swam through a haze of feelings and desires. As much as she wanted to deny it, she did care for Shim'on, cared so deeply that life in the vizier's house would be as dull as a whetstone without his belligerent presence. And his hate of her master *had* dissipated since the vizier's startling revelation. But the hard layers of his heart could not be shed in two short days; the roots of his bitterness extended far deeper than hatred and jealousy for one younger brother.

He was not yet the man who could love her the way she needed to be loved. At the first provocation, his temper would flare up and he would strike out at whomever stood nearby. He had softened a little around the edges, but his stony heart had not changed.

And she knew just how to prove it to herself.

"I'll not go with you." She opened her eyes. "You were right, you know, when you came to me in the night. Adom and I do need a man, but we are not possessions, and I will never settle for less than a man who loves me as his equal. Since Zaphenath-paneah paid my debts and redeemed me from slavery, I will never think of myself as less than a free and independent woman. I must have a man of strength, someone who will remain with me no matter what."

He dropped her hand and flexed, knotting the muscles in his arm. "Do you think I am not strong? I am twice the size of that Egyptian guard you're so fond of. And as for loyalty, Levi and I once killed the men of an entire city for our sister's sake!"

She shivered under the hot light in his eyes. "A man who is quick to become angry with lesser men only proves his weakness," she answered, ready to duck if his temper lashed out in her direction. "And your anger strikes at everyone from the servants to the vizier himself." She tipped her head back and stared into his eyes. "Only a man of great strength can give the gentle kind of love Adom and I deserve. You might be capable of this love one day, Shim'on, but I would rather serve here under Zaphenath-paneah's protection than go with you now. Until you change, I cannot give my heart to you."

"A woman does not ask a man to change," he said, crossing his arms as his voice snapped. "Either she loves him as he is, or she does not love him at all."

She felt suddenly vulnerable in the face of his anger, and she hated feeling vulnerable. "Shim'on, I didn't mean—"

"Be silent." Cutting her off, he stepped backward, his eyes stony. "You have insulted my strength and my honor."

"This is why we can never marry," she whispered, her heart breaking. "You *are* strong, but your weakness lies in the inner man. You must be strong enough to control your anger instead of letting it control you. Forgive me for hurting you, but I did it to prove a point."

"Forgive you?" His bitter laugh raked her heart. "A man can only bear so much."

Without another word he turned on his heel and strode away. She wavered, torn between remaining silent and running after him to assure him that she did appreciate his many fine qualities.

But if he had loved her, he hated her now. Strength and loyalty were his two best attributes, and her biting tongue had just disparaged both.

Her experiment, however unwise, had proved her suspicions. Shim'on the Destroyer was still the roaring lion she had confronted nearly a year ago.

"BROTHERS, I BID YOU FAREWELL," Yosef called, his gaze lingering on each face as the caravan assembled in his courtyard. "Bid my father hurry and come down, and do not argue on the journey. The strength of Yisrael is in your union; your only danger is discord. Be at peace with each other from this time forth, and as brothers we can live together."

Binyamin left his donkey and ran forward for one last embrace. Yosef clung to him for a long moment, inhaling the scent of his strength.

"Hurry back," he called as Binyamin pulled away.

"I will." After one last look, Binyamin returned to his pack animal. Re'uven gave the command to move, and the caravan started forward. Yosef left the portico and retreated into his chamber, his heart too full for words.

CHAPTER THIRTY-THREE

"Mandisa, you seem anxious," Lady Asenath said, lazily waving her hand. "I should think you'd be relieved that the rabble of relatives has gone."

"I am relieved, my lady." Mandisa forced a smile and turned toward the couch where Asenath lay. "Though they have only been gone a short time, the house seems quite empty without them."

"I think silence is sublime," Asenath answered, lifting her head so Mandisa could slip another pillow beneath it. "And I do wish my husband would hurry back from the palace. Pharaoh is demanding too much of his time these days."

"Pharaoh has much on his mind," Mandisa answered, sinking into a chair by Asenath's side. The lady's belly had grown rapidly in the last few weeks, and she was increasingly uncomfortable in social situations. Her gowns, designed to be worn like a second skin, did not forgive the bulge of impending birth at her middle. Asenath preferred to sit at home in a loose-fitting robe rather than wear the pleated gowns that served as maternity wear in upper Theban circles.

"When Zaphenath-paneah comes in, send a runner to fetch him to me," Asenath said, closing her eyes. She sighed and clasped her hands over her belly. "This is the seventh month, Mandisa, do you realize? The babies I lost died in the fourth month. The gods will be good to me this time. Just as they performed the miracle at conception and allowed my husband's seed to grow within me out of season—"

"The master knows, my lady." Mandisa bit her lip, horrified that the words had fallen from her lips. She was too tired, that was the problem, she had felt listless all week. Her eyes burned from sleeplessness and an overwhelming numbness had weighed her down ever since the brothers departed . . .

"He knows what?" Asenath lifted her head. Her eyes were wide with false innocence, but her voice was thick and unsteady.

Mandisa sighed. She had spent every possible moment of the last month with her mistress, and she felt like a parent who has spent too much time with a hyperactive child. The lady's charade had drained her.

Gathering up her slippery courage, she leaned forward. "May I speak as an honest friend, Lady Asenath?"

Her mistress nodded.

"Your husband, my master, knows the child you carry is not his."

"You lie!" The lady's expression clouded. "The child *is* his, the gods have worked a miracle! And my husband believes in miracles, he is always talking about the wonders of his God—"

"This is not a miracle," Mandisa answered, sudden tears stinging her eyes. "And your husband knows it."

Asenath took a deep breath as if she would argue, but let her head fall back to the couch. After a long moment, she pressed her hand to her forehead and began to weep. "I have done a terrible thing," she whispered as tears found their way down her cheeks. "I went to visit a priest at the temple of Min."

Mandisa shook her head. "I do not know this god."

"He is the god of fertility, the bestower of potency. He is the god who brings rain to the parched earth, the one who quickens life within a woman's womb."

A sense of foreboding descended over Mandisa with a shiver. "You gave this god an offering?"

"An offering of silver . . . and of myself. The priest promised that I

would conceive, and he swore that only he and Min would know of it."
Raw hurt glittered in her dark eyes as she turned to her handmaid. "And
now you tell me that my husband knows! And if he does, why does he
treat me with such kindness?"

"Your husband," Mandisa answered, carefully choosing her words,
"loves you as he loves his own flesh. When you turned from him to
another, how could he not know it? But he treats you kindly because he
loves you."

Asenath shot Mandisa a quick, denying glance, then looked away. A
host of emotions—denial, anger, and fear—flickered across her face, then
she looked at Mandisa with something fragile in her eyes.

"Why? Why does he—how could he still love me?"

"Because," Mandisa admitted, her words dredged from a place far
beyond logic and common sense, "sometimes passion is unreasonable."
She strengthened her smile. "You need never fear, mistress, I know
Zaphenath-paneah. At first I thought he would cast you aside, but now I
know he will never abandon you. You are fortunate, my lady."

"Fortunate," Asenath echoed. The hand that had been stroking her
belly stilled. "Will my husband feel *fortunate* to provide for another
man's child?"

Mandisa squirmed beneath the touch of her mistress's gaze and the
look of pain behind her question. "Zaphenath-paneah loves all children,"
she finally said. "Do not be anxious, my lady, about his heart. But have
mercy on my master, and do not ask him to pretend."

WHEN ASENATH FINALLY SLEPT, Mandisa left her guilt-ridden mistress
in her chamber and walked to the garden to consider her own situation.
In good weather, if all went well, the journey from Thebes to Hebron
would take about two weeks. More than a month would pass before
Shim'on could return. But once they arrived in Hebron the brothers
would have stories to tell and plans to make, so perhaps they might
tarry as long as two months, even three. But before the season of

Shemu had passed, Shim'on and his family would return to Egypt. Though the people of Yisrael were to abide in Goshen, Shim'on might come to visit the house of Zaphenath-paneah. And he might press his case a third time; perhaps he would even try to prove he had changed. Or, because she had insulted him, he might visit with a Canaanite wife by his side.

In either case, she couldn't face him again, but what options did she have? Unless she could convince Lady Asenath to take an extended journey to Heliopolis, Mandisa had no place to go. But Lady Asenath had been complaining of discomfort for weeks, and was in no condition to travel.

A hoarse call from the balcony interrupted her musings. "Mandisa!" Tizara shrieked, her face ashen under the bright sunlight. "Come quickly! And bring Ani! The time of travail has begun!"

THE BABY WOULD NOT COME. Through hours of intense labor that wracked Asenath's frail body, the child refused to be born. Ani sent for priestesses of the goddess Taweret, but while they twirled and whirled daggers at invisible spirits, Asenath grew pale and weak upon her couch. A pool of sour, stinking blood covered the bed linens like a crimson mantle, and though Mandisa had tried to change the soiled cloths, Asenath screamed and wept whenever anyone attempted to move her.

Zaphenath-paneah, who had been summoned from Pharaoh's house as soon as it became apparent that his wife was in danger, insisted upon remaining at her side. He sat at the head of the narrow birthing cot, his hand grasping Asenath's, his lips at her ear.

As night fell, amid the shrieking and wailing of the priestesses, Mandisa heard the midwife exclaim, "Thank your gods, my lady, you have a son!" Zaphenath-paneah's face went white at the words, and only then did Mandisa understand the full import of the midwife's statement. If the baby had not yet come forth and the midwife could see the male part of the child, the birth was breech.

"My mother," Zaphenath-paneah said, turning to Mandisa, "died when Binyamin was born this backward way."

"Do not be anxious, my lord." Mandisa gave him a smile more confident than she felt. "Asenath is in God's hands."

"Is she?"

Asenath's labor continued into the night. By sunrise on the second day, the exhausted priestesses of Taweret abandoned the vizier's wife to her fate. The frustrated and tired midwife grew ruthless, attempting even to force her hand into the birth canal to turn the child. But the pressure and pain caused Asenath to faint, and the cord of life, visible through the birth opening, ceased to pulse.

When it became apparent that the baby had died, Zaphenath-paneah cradled his wife's head and shoulders in his arms and whispered words of comfort and encouragement.

By sunrise on the third day, everyone in the house knew the mistress stood on the threshold of the Otherworld. Weeping and silent, Tizara brought Efrayim and Menashe to say their farewells; they embraced their mother and kissed her on the cheek before Tizara led them away. Tarik, Halima, and a host of other servants paraded through the chamber and promised to do their best to prepare Asenath for her eternal life, but she had already closed her eyes and seemed not to hear their frantic assurances.

By mid-afternoon on the third day, both Mandisa and the master were exhausted, drained of will and thought. "Why don't you go to your chamber and sleep for a while?" the master asked, stepping away from Asenath's bedside. He turned toward the high window and seemed to study the shaft of sunlight that trapped slow convections of dust.

"If it please you, my lord, I will remain until the—until she no longer needs me," Mandisa answered.

For another hour the two of them waited without speaking. They traded places: Mandisa stood beneath the window, lost in her own thoughts, the master sat at the side of Asenath's bed, imprinting his memory with the image of his beloved wife, still carrying the unborn child.

Without warning, the lady opened her eyes. "My husband?" Her words were jagged and sharp, sounds torn by the blade of a knife.

"Here, beloved." Zaphenath-paneah lifted his head and took her pale hand in his.

"I have been foolish, my lord. I thought another child would make you happy."

"All I ever wanted was you, Asenath. Children are an added blessing from God."

She spoke in a weak and tremulous whisper. "I have played the harlot with another god—"

"Shh, Asenath, don't talk now." As the husband lowered his face to his wife's, Mandisa retreated into the shadows of the room, unwilling to intrude upon the private moment.

THE BURNING PAIN of her loins had faded to a distant memory, and Asenath's hands and legs had gone as cold as an empty bed. She felt surprisingly light and carefree; the heaviness that had pressed upon her stomach, back, and legs had completely vanished. The only burden upon her now was guilt, but Zaphenath-paneah sat by her side, his dark eyes inches from hers, his gaze probing her soul.

"I did something," she began, forcing the words from her stubborn tongue.

"I know all about you, beloved," Zaphenath-paneah said, his tone unfailingly patient and compassionate. "Your denial has kept us apart these last few months, but I was ready to listen any time you wanted to talk. Nothing you could ever do would make me turn you away."

"I was so selfish. When God Shaddai would not give me what I wanted, I left him for another."

His fingers fell across her mouth. "You don't have to talk."

She closed her eyes, too weak to resist him. "Please." His fingers lifted, and she ran her tongue over her parched lips, struggling to find the words. "I left your God, the Almighty one, because He seemed too distant and unaccommodating. Because he said no."

Zaphenath-paneah did not answer, and with an effort she opened her eyes to look at him. His usually lively gaze sparkled with weariness. She blinked in surprise when she saw that he held her hand pressed to his cheek; she hadn't felt the pressure of his skin against hers.

"Beloved wife," he said, "God honors a repentant heart." His voice, without rising at all, had taken on a subtle urgency.

"I know." Tonight there were no shadows across her heart, only a feeling of glorious happiness within it. "When you did not cast me aside, my love, I knew your God would not abandon me, either."

He drew her into his arms, and Asenath closed her eyes, glorying in the shared moment.

HER RAGGED BREATHING stuttered and died, and then there was nothing but silence and the pounding of Yosef's own aching heart.

"Beloved?"

Her mouth was as pale as her cheeks, her eyes closed in eternal sleep. Yosef sat up, still clutching her icy hands, his sense of loss beyond tears.

Why couldn't she trust his love? He had spent the last years of his life protecting her, trying to convince her that she was the most precious person in his world, and yet she would not believe him. He had seen the pain in her eyes when he denied her requests, but he had only refused her out of love.

"Oh, Asenath." He cradled her against his chest as he traced her cheek with his fingers. "How like a child you were! Could you not know I would give my own life rather than allow you to suffer like this?"

Somewhere outside the villa a pair of servants broke into a brawling argument, giving voice to the unuttered shouts and protests lodged in Yosef's own throat. He pressed Asenath to him, breathed in the scent of her skin and hair one last time, then released the keening wail of grief.

TARIK STOOD at attention by the gatekeeper's lodge, his eyes raking the face and figure of each guest. Hundreds had already filed through the villa to pay their respects to Zaphenath-paneah in the loss of his wife and unborn child.

The priests of Amun had come first to prepare Lady Asenath for mummification. Mandisa had helped them wash the body, excise the baby, and anoint the skin with oils and unguents. The tiny, perfectly-formed child was washed and wrapped in linen. The unnamed son would be placed in Asenath's arms, and together they would sleep in a coffin within a sarcophagus within a tomb.

Such great sadness after such great joy! Though Tarik stood like a warrior, stiff and proud, his spirit whirled in chaos. A war of emotions raged within him, a battle more vicious than any physical conflict he had ever experienced. Rumors within the household fueled his unrest. Some servants were saying that the mistress had tried to induce the labor of the child after discovering it would be the offspring of a Canaanite herdsman. Wiser, more practical voices proclaimed that the physicians had long said another pregnancy would result in Asenath's death. The incident had only proven the physicians right.

How could a man at the pinnacle of power be so vulnerable to pain? Tarik had never imagined that any earthly relationship could engender such feelings of loss and devastation, but he suffered with his master, and Zaphenath-paneah suffered greatly. The joy had gone out of the vizier's eyes, and despite the pleasure he found in making arrangements for his family's arrival in Goshen, sorrow had carved merciless lines on his strong face, muting his youth. Tarik wondered if the vizier would ever find a way to lift the shadows of pain from his countenance.

And yet Zaphenath-paneah persisted in his worship of the invisible and almighty God. If Wepwawet had led Tarik through such a torturous experience, the captain knew he would have cursed that god and followed another. But the vizier did not condemn his God or cry out. He continued in his silent and steadfast devotion, preferring solitude to the noisy Egyptian ceremonies designed to speed Asenath to the Otherworld.

There remained the traditional seventy days of mourning, the necessity of filling and preparing the lady's tomb, and the mummification of the body. It was a pity, Tarik decided, that Lady Asenath would not meet Yaakov, Zaphenath-paneah's noble father. Perhaps in the afterlife the Egyptian noblewoman and the Canaanite prince would be friends.

CHAPTER THIRTY-FOUR

"THEY ARE HOME!"

One of the grandchildren released the cry, and Yaakov lifted his head from his couch and pulled himself upright with an effort. His sons had been gone nearly forty days, more than enough time to make the trip to Mizraim and back, and with each passing day his heart had grown heavy with the nauseating sinking of despair.

Swallowing the grateful sob that rose in his throat, he stood up and hobbled to the opening of his tent. There on the curve of the hilly horizon he could see a caravan of loaded wagons and donkeys.

He frowned. The grandchildren were mistaken, for his sons had not left with the means to purchase such riches. This was another caravan, one bound for Aram or Uz. But perhaps they would have word of his sons and know if Binyamin was still among them.

Bracing himself for disappointment, he stepped out of his tent.

SHIM'ON SAW the old man before the others, recognized his father's distinctive lumbering gait, the way he rocked on his hips as if they were stiff. Re'uven had said they shouldn't expect to see him outside, but

Shim'on knew better. He'd been gone for nearly a year, so Yaakov would be waiting with the children and the curious servants, eager for news of his second-born son.

Satisfaction pursed Shim'on's mouth as he spied his father's white hair and flowing beard. Yaakov had come forward to greet him. Perhaps Mandisa was right, the old man did care.

His reserve and apprehension thawed in an instant. "Father!" he called, waving as his confidence spiraled upward. He slipped from the wagon where he rode with Levi and thundered over the hard ground, ready to forget the past and embrace the man with whom he'd had so many misunderstandings.

Yaakov's eyes lifted, he turned his head in search of the son who had called his name.

"Father!"

Another voice rang through the tumult of greetings, and Yaakov's face brightened in a sudden look of eagerness. "Binyamin!" he cried, lifting trembling arms. "Blessed be God Almighty, He has brought you back to me!"

Shim'on stopped abruptly and leaned forward, breathing hard, while Binyamin raced to his father's arms and was enveloped in an embrace. Women, children and servants surrounded the caravan, and after a moment Shim'on heard Levi's voice in his ear. "Give him time with the lad, Shim'on, he'll be glad enough to see you later. But now his attention is reserved for the young one."

Still catching his breath, Shim'on nodded. Like an old wound that ached on a rainy day, he climbed back into the wagon and reluctantly welcomed the familiar pain he had nearly forgotten.

YAAKOV DID EMBRACE HIM LATER, perfunctorily, when the brothers assembled to share their news. "Yosef is still alive," Yehuda repeated as they sat in their father's tent. Yaakov, his arm firmly entwined with Binyamin's, shook his head in disbelief.

"Indeed, he is ruler over all Egypt," Re'uven added, leaning forward in eagerness.

"Why would the idol-worshippers elevate a son of Avraham?" Yaakov said, patting Binyamin's arm as if to reassure himself that his youngest son had actually returned.

Yehuda gestured outside where the children and wives were gleefully plundering the pack animals. "How could we come to you with such fine wagons and the best goods of Egypt if they had not done so? Yosef said to tell you that the hand of El Shaddai brought him to that place. God Himself lifted Yosef from slavery and placed him on a throne equal to Pharaoh's so we might be preserved in this time of famine."

Yaakov shook his hoary head, still resisting the truth. Yehuda looked around the circle of brothers, silently pleading for help. He caught Shim'on's eye, but Shim'on only scratched his beard. *You are our spokesman, so speak for us*, he told Yehuda with a smile and a slight shake of his head.

They had been talking to Yaakov for more than an hour. In that time they had confessed what happened at Dotan and quickly followed the news of their treachery with the glorious report of Yosef's current condition. And Yaakov sat like a stone, with no reaction to either their shameful confession or the stunning summary of their latest venture into Egypt.

"We are to leave this place and go to Egypt," Yehuda said, "so we may prosper under Yosef's hand."

"How can we leave the land God promised to us?" Yaakov waved toward the sullen fields outside his tent. "How can we leave the cave where our fathers and mothers are buried?"

"How can we remain here, knowing we will die?" Levi demanded, his voice rising. "You talk of God, Father, and Yosef says God Shaddai has provided. If God can bring Yosef back to your life, can He not bring you back to Canaan when the earth is green again?"

Yaakov lowered his eyelids, and Shim'on couldn't tell whether the old man slept, prayed, or was simply considering their words.

"How like God Shaddai to do the opposite of what we expect," he finally murmured, lifting his gaze. His eyes had a burning, faraway look in them, and when he spoke again, his voice was strong and fervent. "It is enough; my son Yosef is still alive. I will go and see him before I die."

ALIVE. The shock of realization hit Yaakov again. Yosef, alive. Not dead, but living. In Egypt.

He had waited until his sons left his tent, then he grabbed his walking stick and moved with as much speed as his bones would allow toward the hill that looked toward the south. Now he stared toward Egypt, his heart stirring in a new and dangerous rhythm. A howling wind blew from the desert, and through the roaring din, Yaakov breathed one word: "Alive."

A great exultation filled his chest and brought tears to his eyes. "If a man dies, will he live again? All the days of my struggle I will wait. For there is hope for a tree, when it is cut down, that it will sprout again, and its shoots will not fail. At the scent of water it will flourish and put forth sprigs like a plant."

He closed his eyes, relishing the solitude of the hilltop. Because they had carried the guilty secret that Yosef lived, the other sons would never know the indescribable, unfathomable rapture rising from Yaakov's spirit, the ecstasy of resurrection.

The son he thought dead now reigned as a king.

A bottomless peace and satisfaction filled his soul; joy bubbled from his lips in laughter. Yaakov lifted his weak arms to the heavens as his shuffling feet moved over the sand. Through a blanket of clouds a single shaft of sun highlighted the hilltop where the happiness of Yaakov's heart spun him around and around in a delirious dance of delight.

AS THE OTHERS gathered their wives and children and made preparation for the journey, Shim'on wandered around the camp, refreshing the impressions and memories he had tucked into the dim recesses of his mind. The land of Canaan, once green with life, opened before him like an arid dustbowl. The few leaves that still dangled from trees were brown and stained with death. Nothing could live in this place much longer. If Yosef spoke the truth, none of the people in the neighboring towns would be alive in five years.

He strolled onward, blankly watching his sandals crunch into the dry and brittle sand. Before he ventured into Egypt he had considered his father a leader, but today Yaakov seemed a tired old man, one whose life revolved around a submissive son and patch of dusty earth that yielded neither food nor water.

Yaakov was the prince of a dead land. No wonder Mandisa had not wanted to return to Canaan. Who would want to live in this airless, desolate region after the splendor and abundance of Egypt? But Yaakov stayed because he believed he followed God's will.

A hot wind blew by him and Shim'on paused, remembering Yosef's words. *God sent me before you to preserve life.* Yosef was like Yaakov, he believed El Shaddai took a personal interest in the sons of Avraham. Did He? Shim'on knew that God Shaddai lived and was more powerful than the stone idols of Egypt. But could an Almighty God care about one man? Or was He concerned only with offerings and obedience?

Mandisa seemed to think her master's God could be known on a personal level. Avraham had experienced dreams and visions, and Yaakov wrestled with God in the night. But Shim'on had never heard His voice, and never expected to.

CHAPTER THIRTY-FIVE

Tizara's constant weeping grated on Mandisa's nerves. Zaphenath-paneah and the others bore their grief stoically, knowing that they would weep and mourn with abandon when Lady Asenath was interned in her tomb, but Tizara could not stanch the flow of tears that began every time she looked at Efrayim or Menashe. "Those little motherless boys!" she wailed, weeping into a linen handkerchief. "I was a motherless child, I know what they are feeling."

In the days immediately after Asenath's death Mandisa had gently pointed out that they still had a father and a maid to care for them. When that tactic failed to stop Tizara's tears, Mandisa tried adding extra work to the girl's assigned duties, but Tizara merely went about the house with a wadded scrap of linen pressed to her streaming eyes.

Now, her patience evaporated, Mandisa considered sharpening her tongue on the girl's grief. *Shim'on would love that,* she thought, standing as Tizara paced in the women's reception hall, her eyes bleary and red. *I tell him that whatever is begun in anger ends in shame, and here I stand ready to begin my own shameful trouble. And it wasn't so long ago that I felt guilty avoiding this girl. Now I cannot avoid her.*

"Tizara," she said, looking for an avenue of escape, "I think I will take Efrayim and Menashe to the garden to play with Adom. If you need me—"

She halted when Zaphenath-paneah entered the room. Duty forced her to stop and bow.

The vizier told the women to rise, then took a moment to greet his sons. After greeting them warmly, he sent the boys out to play. "I am glad to find both of you here," he said when his sons had gone. "I wanted to talk to you about the months ahead."

Tizara lifted her red-rimmed eyes toward the master. Mandisa sighed, half-expecting to see some frenzied distress in the woman's expression, but only trust and compassion shone from Tizara's gaze. In fact, the girl wore a wholesome and appealing look, a complete transformation from the manner in which she had formerly conducted herself.

When had this change occurred? And why had Mandisa not noticed it?

"You may rise, Tizara." Zaphenath-paneah's expression softened into one of fond reminiscence. "Today I give you your freedom. After all you have learned, I think you will now be able to manage it."

The girl's face locked with anxiety. "Must I leave this villa?"

The vizier sank into a chair. "I hope you will stay and care for my sons. They are fond of you, and now they need someone to watch over them more than ever."

A hint of fresh tears glistened in the wells of Tizara's eyes, but this time she did not lose control. Instead she smiled and bent low to kiss the master's foot. "I can never thank you enough," she said, clinging to his sandal. "I will serve you and your sons as long as I have breath in my body."

"I pray you will," the master answered, turning to Mandisa. A melancholy smile flitted across his features. "Your mistress is gone, and so is the man you tended. What, Mandisa, would you like to do now? You are a free woman. Perhaps you might like a position in Pharaoh's house."

She searched his eyes, searching for signs of disapproval, then relaxed when she found none. She clasped her hands. "I have been thinking . . ."

"Yes?"

How could she explain that she did not want to linger here for fear of seeing Shim'on again? It would not be proper to announce that her heart had been broken by the vizier's brother. Though her master had known of her affection for Shim'on, a reference to it now might be interpreted as a request for pity or even imply that Zaphenath-paneah owed her something. He did not. She owed him everything.

Better to leave the past behind.

"My lord," she asked, daring to look him in the eye, "may I ask what you believe about the afterlife? The other world?"

Zaphenath-paneah tilted his head; obviously, he had not expected that question. "Why do you ask?"

"I want to know, my lord, what will become of Lady Asenath if I do not remain here for the full seventy days. I am her handmaid, and if I am not here to see her safely into her tomb, will she suffer? I would not hurt her for the world, and yet part of me wants to leave this place, and soon."

If he guessed at her reasons, he did not speak of them. Instead, the vizier lowered his head into his hands and kneaded his forehead as though his head ached with memories. "I believe," he said, "that God Shaddai prepares a place for those who trust Him. I believe each individual is born with an immortal soul, similar to that part the Egyptians call the *ka*, that survives this life." He lowered his hands. "I do not believe we need all the goods and foods the Egyptians place in their tombs, for treasures have little to do with life or with God."

"So . . . my mistress?"

He eased into a weary smile. "If it sets your mind at ease, Mandisa, know that Asenath is already in the Otherworld, she has already passed from death to life. Before she died, she made her peace with God . . .and with me." He lowered his voice to a gentler tone. "If you wish to leave my house, your mistress will not suffer."

She sighed in relief. "Then I will leave you, Zaphenath-paneah. With gratitude, honor, and respect, I and my son will bid you farewell."

"HALIMA, I wanted to speak to you before I left."

The slave girl's eyes brimmed with tears as she clasped her floury hands. "Mandisa, you can't really go."

Mandisa lifted her head to look one final time at the vizier's well-stocked kitchen. Jars of honey, dates, and raisins lined the walls; the day's catch of fresh fish lay neatly arranged on the table, ready for filleting. She and Adom would eat their fill today, for who could say when they would have another opportunity to eat like this?

Halima forced a wavering smile to her lips. "Let me at least prepare you a basket, Mandisa. Sometimes I think you are the only friend who cares for me."

"Thank you, I'd be grateful," Mandisa answered, sinking to a low stool away from the fire. "But I need you to do something else for me, too."

The girl's eyes went round with curiosity. "What?"

"Be a friend to Tizara. Though at first I disliked her as much as anyone else, Zaphenath-paneah has shown me that I must serve her out of devotion to him, not because of anything she has done. I have tried to help her in the past few weeks, but I haven't done all I should. But she is much changed since the night she attempted to escape."

"Me, help *her*?" A note of alarm rang in Halima's tone. "I can't do that!"

"She is no longer what she once was."

"I don't care what she was, she is still beautiful. And look at me! I'm plain, I'm a lowly kitchen slave, and—" her flush deepened—"I'm fat! How could I even speak to her, and why would she listen to me?"

"You are a gentle and compassionate spirit," Mandisa said. "And you know something of heartbreak, for I've seen you look at Tarik when you think no one else sees."

Halima pressed her hand over her mouth.

"Please, Halima, succeed where I have failed. Serve our master by being a friend to Tizara, and God Shaddai will bless you for your efforts."

"God Shaddai?" Halima lifted a brow. "The vizier's invisible God? What could He possibly do for me?"

"More than you dream, Halima," Mandisa answered, rising. She paused to squeeze the girl's shoulders. "More than you can imagine."

CHAPTER THIRTY-SIX

As a scorching, arid wind blew across the drab valley of Hebron, Shim'on turned into the current, seeking its hot breath upon his face. He needed to be alone with his thoughts. For the first time in his life, the close quarters of the family compound made him feel as crowded as a hen in a cluster of chickens.

He walked to a slope outside the camp, glad to be away from the tumult as his brothers and their families worked to disassemble nearly three decades of their lives. A myriad of scents and sounds reached him: a meowing wail from one of the children, the ammoniac odor of the donkeys' pen, voices raised in argument.

Yosef had told them not to bring possessions, for whatever they needed could be found in Egypt, but still the women clung to sentimental objects. Re'uven's wife bickered with her husband, refusing to abandon the cradle in which she had laid her sons. At the edge of the clearing, Asher's and Dan's wives struggled to fit a bundle of sheepskins onto the back of an already-overflowing wagon.

Shim'on sighed and crossed his arms. He had no wife to argue with him, and no sentimental attachments to this place or any other. His father felt fondness for Hebron because he grew up here and Avraham had sojourned in this fertile valley. Here Yaakov had tricked Esav out of the eldest brother's rightful blessing, and from these pleasant pasturelands he had fled from Esav's fierce and angry hand.

Shim'on studied the distant horizon. How was his uncle Esav faring now? He and his people had moved south and westward beyond Mount Hor, and had little contact with Yaakov. Both brothers had departed from the land El Shaddai deeded to Yitzhak's descendants; only Yaakov had returned to claim it. But now Yaakov was preparing to leave his birthplace, knowing full well that he might never return. Shim'on supposed he understood why Yaakov would leave his beloved homeland in order to be with a more-beloved son, but when his eyes had filled with the glory of his long-lost favorite, how could they ever turn with approval upon the less-than-glorious sons he merely tolerated?

Mandisa was wrong. Shim'on lifted his gaze to the burning sun, welcoming its harsh heat on his face. *Mandisa said I should confront my father, that I would hear a reassurance that he loved me. But even as passionate as she is, she could never understand the depth of the love Yaakov bore Rahel or comprehend the breadth of the indifference he exhibited toward Lea. Mandisa is a loving mother, she could never conceive the constancy of the hatred and blame my father holds toward me. For I caused Rahel's death, and that he will never forget or forgive.*

A sensation of intense desolation swept over him and he rubbed his chest, massaging the stab of guilt that throbbed in his breast. A hunger for Mandisa's company gnawed at his heart, and he clenched his fist, fortifying himself against it. He was spending too much time alone; the solitude of his Egyptian captivity had affected him more than he realized.

He turned toward the camp. Though joyous activity buzzed throughout the compound, one tent stood silent in the desert heat. It had been Lea's tent while she lived, and Dina lived inside now.

Shim'on strode toward the tent, absorbing the sounds and smells of home: the scents of dung-fires and cooking food, the sharp clop of an ax, the sharp tang of wood shavings. He was overdue for a visit with Dina, he had not spent a moment alone with his sister since his return. Had she missed him at all during his time away?

Lea's tent was heavier and older than the others. Shim'on lifted the flap and frowned; the air inside smelled as if it had been breathed too many times. Squinting through the darkness, he saw Dina standing by a pile of furs, tall and formidable, with a shiny smile that was the softest thing about her.

"Shim'on," she said, her voice matter-of-fact.

She was a mature woman now, no longer a maiden. The dark hair that flew from her head in silky tangles had begun to gray at the temples. Her face was square and solid, the image of her mother's, but for the first time Shim'on noticed a soft sag beneath the chin.

"Dina," he made an effort to keep his greeting light, "how is my favorite sister today?"

"Your only sister," she said, her smile as wry as ever. The gold in her eyes flickered as he moved toward her. "You are heavier. Did you eat too much at the Egyptian banquets?"

"I am not heavy; the others are too thin." Shim'on dropped to a blanket. He waited until she sat across from him, then he spoke again: "I suppose you have heard that Yosef is alive and ruler of Egypt."

Her face creased in a sudden smile. "I have always known he still lived."

Shim'on stretched out on the blanket, determined to humor her. "How could you know? None of us knew what happened to him."

"You knew. Despite the story you told Father, I read the guilt in your eyes. And though I feared you had killed him, I knew God Shaddai would protect Yosef. He was too special to die so young."

He stroked his beard. "Why did you think we would kill him?"

"You killed my Shekhem," she replied, lifting one shoulder in a slight shrug. There was no rancor or blame in her voice, only the clear ring of truth. "And then you took my baby and left it in the wilderness. A heart hard enough to kill my husband and expose an innocent child would not hesitate to kill my brother."

Her words cut him, spreading an infection of remorse, but he glared at her and refused to consider them further. "The stink of this tent has softened your senses. That boy treated you like a prostitute! And the child was nothing, an illegitimate brat born of a cursed union."

"Shekhem made me an honorable proposal of marriage," Dina answered, speaking with quiet emphasis. "And the innocent child was as much a descendant of Avraham as you are, Shim'on. You were wrong to take it from me."

"Father did not stop me."

"Father." She repeated the word in a faintly contemptuous tone and waved her hand in a dismissive gesture. "Far too many times Father has done nothing while his sons committed evil. But I have prayed, Shim'on, I have agonized with the Spirit of God Shaddai. And for many years I have known that Yosef lives—just as I know my daughter lives, too."

His shock yielded quickly to fury. "Sister, you are a fool!" He crawled to her side and grasped her shoulders, resisting the urge to shake her into gasping acknowledgement of the truth. That child couldn't be alive; nothing could survive in the desert! Dina's baby had been born shortly after Rahel's death, and Yaakov had been so immersed in his grief that he had neither the time nor the willingness to consider his daughter's daughter. Zilpa, Rahel's maid, had been preoccupied with the care of newborn Binyamin, and Lea could not look at Dina or her child without weeping.

So Shim'on did what countless others have done throughout history. While Dina slept, he took the infant from her side, mounted a donkey, and rode away from the camp. When he was certain no one had followed him, he turned toward the family burial grounds: the cave in the field of Machpelah, before the city of Mamre. Once he reached the cave Avraham had purchased from Ephron the Hittite, he dismounted and placed the baby under the shade of a sprawling terebinth tree. There, at least, the child would experience a more merciful death than if he had left it on the sun-blasted rocks.

"Listen to me," he begged Dina now, a raw and primitive grief tearing in his soul, "You never had a child."

"As God lives, I did!"

"But it never should have been born. You must forget it; you have dwelt on the past too long. All day you sit here in this tent, never venturing forth unless the women insist you come out. You do nothing but make clothing for other peoples' little ones, but you should have married and had your own family by now."

"I *had* a family, Shim'on." She lowered her hands to her lap as her shoulders sagged. "I had a husband and a daughter. I belonged to a city. Then you and Levi came through with your bloody blades and put an end to my life. When I felt the movement of the baby within me I thought I still had a chance at happiness, but you stole that, too. Now I have nothing."

Her stare drilled into him. Shim'on released her shoulders and clenched his fists, furious at his vulnerability wherever she was concerned. "And you blame me for this?" He shouldn't care what she thought, for she was a woman, and a deranged one at that, but he couldn't banish her words from his mind. "If you must blame someone, blame our father. He was the one who cared nothing for you. I am guilty of many things, but the crime of not loving is his alone!"

"Really? Tell me, Shim'on—who have *you* loved?"

He stood, ignoring her challenge as he paced in reckless anger. "Our father didn't defend you when Shekhem and Hamor came calling. He didn't care a niggling whit for the babe when it was born. He has never cared about you, or me, or any of us, because we did not spring from Rahel."

"Our father may not have been perfect, Shim'on, but he never killed another man," Dina answered with easy defiance. "He may not have shown you the love you deserve, but he did not hate you. He grieved over your wrongs, he mourned when you chose to pursue the lusts of your heart instead of following El Shaddai."

"Can you forget," Shim'on boldly met her eyes, "how our mother wept into her pillow each night our father stayed with Rahel?"

"No," Dina admitted. "But can you not see what has happened since Rahel's death?"

"See what?" he yelled, choking on his own words. "I see an old man who adored Yosef and tethered Binyamin to his side like a dog."

"No, Shim'on." An almost imperceptible note of pleading filled Dina's face as she leaned forward, her gaze boring into him. "Open your eyes, Shim'on the Destroyer. Open your heart."

Shim'on found himself shrinking from the brightness of her watchful smile. Somehow she had gained the upper hand.

"Our mother named her firstborn Re'uven, 'God has seen my misery,'" Dina went on, her voice full of strength and confidence. "You she called Shim'on, 'the Lord hears that I am not loved.'"

"What are you prattling about?" Shim'on growled. "I know what my name means."

"Our mother called her third son Levi, 'my husband will now be attached to me,'" Dina continued. "And Yehuda means, 'I will praise the Lord.'"

"So?"

"Don't you see?" Dina tipped her head back and offered him a sudden, arresting smile. "Our mother came to accept who and what she was. When she stopped striving against our father and God, her grief and jealousy ceased. But by that time you and the others had grown up and moved out to the fields. And when Rahel died, our father came to depend upon Lea. He loved her too, not as passionately as he adored Rahel, but in a stronger, more practical way."

Dina's solid features softened. "When Mother died, Father mourned for her in private, then commanded that she be buried in the Cave of Machpelah with Avraham and Sarah, Yitzhak and Rebekah. In the tomb of our forefathers, she waits now for the husband who came to love her long after you left her tent. Our mother was honored, Shim'on. She was loved."

Shim'on looked away, his mind reeling with perplexing emotions. Had he spent a lifetime hating Yaakov for his mother's sake when Yaakov had come to love Lea after all? The loneliness and confusion of over forty years melded in one upsurge of devouring yearning—for what? For his mother? Or for the safety of his familiar bitterness? Out of regret, fear, and shame he had built a fortress to defend himself against his father, but now, in one moment, Dina had breached the wall.

"This is nothing but foolishness," Shim'on replied, more shaken than he wanted to admit. "Your good sense has left you, Dina, if you ever had any at all."

"I did not think you would understand," Dina whispered. "Don't you see? I don't hate you for what you did to my baby. I don't even hate you for killing Shekhem. God Shaddai, the Eternal One, has given me peace in knowing that He controls my ways."

"What kind of God would tell you to sit in your room and pout all day?"

She met his accusing eyes without flinching. "I am not pouting, I am praying. But until your stony heart changes, Shim'on, you will not understand the difference."

RESTLESS AND IRRITABLE, Shim'on stormed out of Dina's tent and walked toward the shed where his brothers had penned the donkeys. After fitting one of the creatures with a bridle, he mounted and kicked the miserable animal's bony sides, hurrying it toward the Cave of Machpelah and the terebinth tree.

Above him, a vulture scrolled the hot updrafts, searching for yet another victim of the famine. The gray bones of desiccated trees had begun to show; the dry and dusty world around him was as stark and bleak as a battlefield. Billows of brown powder drifted from what should have been oases, shadows of whisper-thin clouds moved like stalking gray cats over the lifeless countryside.

Above the horizon, the blurred and blood-red sun baked the earth and everything on it with merciless heat. How could a baby survive in the wilderness? Dina had always been a dreamer, she was like Yosef in that respect. Her conviction that Yosef still lived—if she had honestly held one —had been based on nothing more than wishful thinking. But her child could not have survived the desert's heat, the threat of jackals, or the nighttime cold.

Sweating and cursing the sun, Shim'on rode for a short time, then glanced around for a familiar landmark. The land to the north was as flat as stretched cloth, marred only by the hot sun and whining wind. There were no terebinth trees in sight, no recognizable trails, no wadis to mark Shim'on's progress into the countryside.

But at his right hand the land gathered itself into deep folds. Rocky cliffs rose above the barren landscape, and in the mountainous formation Shim'on thought he could see the vague outline of a cave.

He dismounted and pulled the brawling donkey with him toward the rocks. No trees remained to shade the place, only a few withered stumps marked the spot. Shim'on knelt at the base of the cut-off trunk nearest to the entrance of the cave. If the baby had died, wouldn't its bones be buried here beneath the sand? Or had the vultures and jackals scattered them?

He poked a finger into the dry sand and moved aside a handful of dirt. Nothing.

Using both hands, he scooped out a sizable hole and let the coarse powder trickle through his fingers.

Again nothing.

Crying aloud in frustration, he pushed his hands through the sand to his elbows, struggling against the weight of the earth as he thrust it upward. He pawed frantically, searching for even a tiny bone, some fragment he could show Dina to prove that her talk of dreams was as senseless as describing color to a blind man.

The claws of the wind raked at him, but still he dug, desperate for some shred of evidence. Dirt blew into his eyes and hair and between his teeth; he spat and cursed and continued flinging sand over his shoulders, scraping and burrowing around the base of the dead and withered tree. The heat, radiating from the sand, came at him like a mortal enemy, invading his mouth and nostrils as he gasped for breath. The hot sand beneath his hands and knees scalded and blistered his skin even through the fabric of his robe, but Shim'on did not care.

If he could find something here, even a shred of rotted fabric, he could assure Dina that this chapter of her life was done, forever finished. She had accused him of living in a past where Yaakov did not love Lea, but did she not live within a fantasy world of her own making? If she would accept that her child was dead, she could open her eyes to the real world. But she would have to see that God Shaddai did not work miracles, that the past could not be changed, that Shim'on was the monster who had murdered her child, so he *deserved* the burden of scorn he carried . . .

He clutched at a white shard in the sand and pulled it out, but it was the broken bone of an animal, probably a lion. Such a large bone would not fool Dina; she would insist upon believing in hope, forgiveness, even resurrection.

"God Shaddai!" He pressed his sandy, sweaty palms to his wet forehead. "If you are Almighty, why have you never helped me? My father says you guided him, Dina says you preserved Yosef, and yet you thwart me at every turn!"

The blindingly bright sand beneath him went dark. Shim'on looked up; the sky above him churned as a mass of dark, boiling clouds blew in from behind the horizon. As the atmosphere congealed around him, the donkey brayed and rolled its eyes toward the back of its head. A sudden, inexplicable burst of thunder sent the animal cantering over the trail of its own hoofprints.

Shim'on rose to run after the animal. "Stop!" The bawling winds snatched his voice away. No match for the terrified beast, after a moment he stopped running. Above him lightening cracked the skies apart, and yet Shim'on knew the storm would not bring rain. Yaakov's Almighty, illogical God had forsaken this land; He now loved Egypt, not Canaan. Just as Yaakov loved Rahel, not Lea, and Rahel's sons, not Lea's. Yaakov had even allowed his second son to be named *Shim'on, "The Lord knows I-am-not-loved"* . . .

Shim'on's brooding misery seemed to burgeon and spread until it mingled with the innumerable other sorrows borne by Lea, Re'uven, Levi, Yehuda, Yissakhar, Zevulun, Gad, Asher, Dan, Naftali, and Dina.

"Why, Father?" Shim'on sank to the sand and pressed his hands over his face, assailed by an overwhelming sense of bitterness and regret. "Why couldn't you love us?"

The wild wind hooted as if to mock him, but through the moving air a shaft of dull-gray light broke from the dark clouds and inched across the plain. Peering through his fingers, Shim'on watched it, tired and uncomprehending, until the searching light shone upon him.

A devouring heat singed his scalp and shoulders. He gasped, panting in terror, and looked up. A whirling ball of fire hovered in the sky above him, bright as a thousand suns. Shim'on felt sweat run from his forehead and under his arms, then a voice shattered the last vestige of his composure: *I love you.*

Beneath the damp hair of his head his scalp tingled, and panic welled in his throat. Was he losing his mind? He choked back a cry, more frightened than he had ever imagined he could be, and the gale around him increased from its first warning blasts to a great current of roaring air.

Curling to the ground, he closed his eyes and bowed his head, trying to maintain his fragile control. The sun had burned his eyes, the sandstorm had addled his wits; men often lost their reason in gales like this . . .

His muscles turned to water when the Voice spoke again: *I am El Shaddai, and I love all them who love me. The God of your fathers is a righteous God, a flame that will not be touched and must be approached with care. Bow your heart, Shim'on, son of Yisrael, and know that you are kneeling upon holy ground.*

Awe smote and held him, and he *knew.* No man could hear the voice of God unless he sought it, and Shim'on had been more willing in the last hour to hear from God than he had been in his entire forty-six years. He wasn't losing his mind. He had sought God and found His august presence, and now he could not turn his back on God Shaddai, the Invisible and Almighty One.

He squinted up toward the burning heavens, his knees rooted to the ground. "El Shaddai?" Never had Mandisa or his father prepared him for the dominant and imperious summons of a truly almighty being.

Be still and know that I am God.

The voice was unmistakable. Shim'on's heart turned to stone within his chest, weighting his body so he could not move.

Do not be afraid to go down to Egypt, for I will make your people a great nation there. But do not serve gods, the work of man's hands, wood and stone, which neither see nor hear nor eat nor smell. Seek the

Lord your God; you will find Him if you search for Him with all your heart and all your soul. When you are in distress, return to the Lord your God and listen to His voice. For the Lord your God is a compassionate God; He will not fail you nor destroy you nor forget the covenant that he swore to your fathers.

The voice swallowed up the wind. When it grew silent, Shim'on lifted his eyes. The flaming sphere had disappeared, the earth was soft and still, the air sweet with the scent of impending rain. Rocks danced in the steaming heat; from some distance away Shim'on thought he heard a bird singing.

Then, like tears from heaven, luscious, blessedly cool rain fell from a widening blue sky, mingling with Shim'on's tears and washing the dust of defeat from his face.

CHAPTER THIRTY-SEVEN

To Ani and a few others who devoutly followed the gods of Egypt, Zaphenath-paneah showed an appalling lack of concern for his dead wife's eternal welfare. "I cared for her while she lived, and know I will see her in the Otherworld," the vizier told Ani one afternoon. "But I do not believe physical objects will be of any use in the spirit world."

Horrified by the master's attitude and the prospect of what others would say, Ani finally convinced Zaphenath-paneah to allow him to fully prepare Asenath's tomb in accordance with Egyptian rites and traditions. Though Ani knew Asenath had placed her soul into the hands of her husband's invisible God, the citizens of Thebes would question both the vizier's love for his wife and his devotion to his God if he did not honor her with a proper burial. As a practical, sensible people, they believed in physical preparation and tangible gods.

And so to Ani fell the complete responsibility of preparing his mistress for the tomb. The lady's tomb lay on the west side of the Nile, past the dried-up, barren fields which should have been emerald with new crops, past the row of temples lining the Valley of the Dead. Like other members of the nobility, a mastaba had been ordered for her upon the date of her marriage, and the rectangular, flat-topped masonry building lay in a neat row with several others, just one "street" in the necropolis, a city designed for the dead.

The people of Thebes believed that at sunset every night the spirits of the dead rose from their vaults to linger in the doorways of their tomb chapels. Aided by magic formulas and amulets, they looked over the river to the living city, glowing like a lamp in the gentle dusk. They felt the breath of wind that moved over the river of life, smelled the sweetly damp scent of flowering crops and the aromas of mingled evening meals.

Burial was not an event to be taken lightly. Ani had to be certain that Asenath's chamber was adequately provisioned with food, furniture, and the lotus blossoms she loved. The temple of her tomb had to face the river; narrow passageways connected the temple with her burial chamber and a storeroom.

Asenath's tomb also had to be populated with servants. Because the Egyptians believed her soul would live and work in the Otherworld just as she lived and worked in her mortal life, servants were imperative. No civilized eighteenth-dynasty Egyptian would consider burying human servants with a master or mistress, so specially-engraved statues known as *ushabti figures*, were placed in the tomb. In the other world these figures would be magically animated to perform their mistress's bidding.

Since a host of slaves and servants had cared for Lady Asenath's mortal needs, Ani hired ten sculptors to create her ushabti figures: miniature cooks, litter-bearers, guards, corn-grinders, herdsmen, dancing girls, and maids.

The actual burial chamber lay beneath the surface of the ground, and a score of workers descended into its depths every morning to prepare the subterranean house for its eternal occupant. A team of skilled painters adorned the walls with hieroglyphic texts and pictures that described Asenath and depicted her most noteworthy worldly accomplishments. One set of pictures showed her sailing beside her husband, Zaphenath-paneah; another showed her with Efrayim and Menashe at her knee. The image of water was essential, for her soul would need water to drink, and the sail would encourage the breath of her *ka* to return.

Tomb paintings customarily showed the deceased standing with the god or goddess she had worshipped in life. When the artist came to Ani for instruction, he scratched his bald head. "My lady's god?" He knew the lady had recently worshipped at the temple of Min, the goddess of fertility, but some inner voice warned him that she would not want that goddess starting at her throughout all eternity.

"Paint the sign for Neter, the Invisible God," Ani finally told the artist.

The wall that would stand at the sarcophagus' feet was reserved for an elaborate inscription to eternally remind Lady Asenath of her glorious funeral procession. Spelled out in careful hieroglyphics, the message foretold what would happen within a few days:

A goodly burial arrives in peace, your seventy days having been completed in your place of embalming. Your mortal shell being placed upon the bier and sledge dragged by young bulls, the road opened with milk until you reach the door of your tomb. Your husband and children, united with one accord, weep with loving hearts. Your mouth is opened by the lector-priest and your purification is performed by the Sem-priest. Neter adjusts for you your mouth and opens for you your eyes and ears, your flesh and your bones being complete in all that appertains to you. Spells and glorifications are recited for you. There is made for you an Offering-which-the-King gives, your own heart being truly with you, your heart of your earthly existence, you having arrived in your former state, as on the day on which you were born. There is brought to you the Son-whom-you-love, the courtiers making obeisance. You enter into a land given by the king, into the sepulcher of the west.

DESPITE HIS HARD work and the success of his efforts, with every passing day Ani grew more nervous. The master's brothers might return at any time, and the seventy days of mourning for Lady Asenath had not yet been completed. What if the master's family came during the funereal? Would the Egyptian rites offend the Canaanites?

The mere thought of such a disaster shattered his composure. Enough troubles rose to vex him each morning; he did not need to invent new ones. Just that morning, as Ani stood on the deck of the felucca which ferried him across the Nile, one of the hired masons had approached with a basket.

"I have a question about this statue," he said, grimacing as he lowered the heavy basket to the deck.

Ani peered into the basket. Inside was an ushabti figure, a lovely statue of a kneeling woman. The base of the statue had been inscribed with Asenath's name and a magic formula through which the statue would be brought to life in the Otherworld.

Ani's dread melted into relief. "Why, it's perfect. What is the problem?"

"Who is it?" the man asked, lowering his callused hands onto the statue.

For the first time, Ani looked up into the man's face. The mason had a stony face that did not look capable of any pleasant emotion. His wide-shouldered, broad body was adorned only with a working-man's linen kilt.

"It is a maidservant," Ani said, speaking as if to a slow child.

The workman stared back with scorn in his eyes. "I know it's a servant. But who is it?"

"Lady Asenath's handmaid."

Unnerved by the big man's persistence, Ani turned away, but the man grabbed his arm. "Does this handmaid have a name?"

"My lady's handmaid is called Mandisa," Ani said. "Not that it should matter to a common laborer. Mandisa is a lady."

"A lady?" A flash of cynical humor crossed the man's granite-like face. "Yes, I am sure she is. I know her and her daughter."

Ani gave the man a triumphant smile. "You are mistaken. Mandisa has no daughter. She has only a son."

The amused look left the man's eyes. He stiffened, his square jaw tensing.

The felucca had reached the opposite shore. Ani stepped back from the railing, eager to be away from the man.

The sooner his lady was buried, the sooner their lives could return to normal.

STANDING at attention in the vizier's courtyard, Tarik dismissed his guards with a curt command and turned his attention to the list of concerns Ani had dictated for him. A season of adjustment had come to Zaphenath-paneah's household, and Tarik wondered if these changes were truly for the best. Since Lady Asenath's death, Tizara had taken complete and confident charge of the vizier's sons, and Mandisa and Adom had said their farewells and left the house. The steward, whom Tarik had always thought unflappable, seemed irritable and distracted without a mistress to consult for the daily running of the estate. And Zaphenath-paneah, his mind occupied with altogether too many things, spent much of his time in Goshen or at Pharaoh's palace. When he was home, the vizier walked around the villa with a distracted expression on his face. He was preoccupied with his wife's funeral and the arrival of his Canaanite family, but Tarik wondered how much of his master's silence was due to concentration and how much was a result of grief.

One of the slave boys from the gatekeeper's lodge skipped across the courtyard, a flushed smile on his face. "Hail, Tarik, captain of the guard! Anhur of the gatehouse salutes you!"

"What is it, boy?" Tarik answered, in no mood for diplomatic pleasantries.

"A stranger stands at the gate, seeking word of Mandisa."

"That lady no longer resides here. Send the man on his way."

"My master Anhur has said as much to the man, but he will not leave. He demands an audience with the vizier."

"The vizier cannot be bothered with petty trifles." Tarik made a shooing gesture as he climbed the steps to the portico. "Mandisa no longer lives here, and we do not know where she has gone."

The boy bobbed his head. "My master Anhur has said as much to the man, but he says he will remain until the vizier hears him. His name is Idogbe, and he says he will not leave until the vizier gives him his wife."

Tarik halted. "But Mandisa is a widow."

The boy's shaved head bobbed again. "My master Anhur has said as much to the man, but the stranger is no spirit, Captain. He is real, and has eaten nearly half the figs in my master's breakfast bowl."

Exasperated, Tarik leaned forward. "What has your master Anhur *not* said to the man?"

The boy blanched and took a step backward. "Why nothing, Captain."

"I thought as much," Tarik said, sighing. "All right. Tell your master to hold the man at the gate until I speak with Ani. Then we shall tell Anhur what to do."

"HE SAYS MANDISA IS HIS WIFE?" Ani's eyes widened in astonishment. "But she told us—"

"She thought he was dead," Tarik interrupted. He had found Ani in Zaphenath-paneah's chamber, finalizing arrangements for Asenath's internment. "But the man is alive, he is here, and he demands to see you, my lord."

He had expected the vizier to turn the man away with a polite word of regret, but Zaphenath-paneah looked up from his papyri with an undeniable gleam of interest in his eye.

"By all means, send him in," Zaphenath-paneah answered, a look of implacable determination settling onto his face. "I would like to talk to a man who buys a wife and abandons her when she finds herself with child."

IDOGBE SHUFFLED BEHIND THE GUARDS, trying not to gape at the luxurious surroundings of the grand vizier's house. Mandisa had lived *here*? Unthinkable that such a slip of a girl should rise to such an exalted position. So why on earth had she left this place?

The guards turned to face him, exposing the reception hall where a stately, remote figure sat upon an elevated dais. Remembering his manners, Idogbe walked forward and slapped himself onto the polished floor like a swimmer diving into the Nile. For Sebek's glory, he must not fail in this.

"Life, prosperity, and health to you, exalted Zaphenath-paneah!" he called.

"Who are you, and what is it you want?" The vizier's tone was coolly disapproving.

Idogbe lifted his eyes to the solitary, majestic figure in the gilded chair. "A woman, O glorious one. I have sought the Canaanite woman called Mandisa for many days, and Sebek, God of my strength, has led me to your noble house. If I had known she was serving you, I might have come sooner to offer myself. But not until I saw her figure among those destined for your wife's eternal resting place did I know that Mandisa resided here."

"You have not sought her in nine years," the vizier answered. The muscles in his back and shoulders rippled in a fluid motion as he leaned forward. "Mandisa told me her story before she entered my household. You abandoned her when she told you she would bear a child."

"How was I to know she would bear a son?" Idogbe asked, smiling with complete candor. He spread his hands in a helpless gesture. "A seer from the temple of Sebek assured me she would bear a girl."

"And so you left her?" The vizier's left eyebrow rose a fraction. "You took a woman away from her people and homeland; you planted a child within her, and then you departed." His handsome features sharpened into a glowering mask of rage. "I would not treat a dog as roughly as you have treated the woman you called your wife. The law says that if you abandon her, you divorce her. One-third of anything you own is now hers."

"But, O glorious one, I did not make her my wife." Idogbe turned his smile up a notch. He lowered his voice and edged forward, as though being closer would help the vizier understand. After all, Zaphenath-paneah was a man of the world, and a man of his position would have as many concubines and wives as Pharaoh, probably more, since Amen-hotep was still a child.

"Mandisa's true role was more like a concubine's," he said, hoping to disarm the solemn vizier with a let's-be-honest smile. "She was a pretty thing I bought for my pleasure. I never promised to love the girl, and the silver I gave her father was not a bride price. After all, she was a Canaanite—" he wrinkled his nose— "fresh from the fields."

"You didn't deserve her," the vizier snapped. "And you have no right to know where she is." He nodded at the guard who stood at his side. "This man is dismissed."

"But surely a man has a right to his son," Idogbe protested. "Even the son of a concubine belongs to the man who fathered the child."

Two impassive guards grabbed Idogbe's arms. "I haven't finished," he cried, pushing them aside. "By Sebek's destructive strength and in his name, the boy is mine; I have a legal right to him! By the life of Pharaoh, you should listen to me!"

But the vizier's attention was no longer listening and other guards swarmed forward, ready to eject Idogbe from the villa. A multitude of hands fell upon him, and though he could have beaten any single one of them easily, Idogbe allowed the guards to drag him from the hall.

Once they had deposited him on the sands of the courtyard, he stood, brushed a layer of grit from his knees, and fixed a steely eye on the bantam captain who had escorted him to the vizier. "The woman may not be my wife," he said, forcing his lips into a stiff smile, "but the boy is my son. And as certainly as Sebek is lord of the river, I will find him."

LOST in the heart of Thebes, Idogbe moved down a dark street, searching for a market where he could buy a hin of beer or even stronger drink. The confrontation at the vizier's house had lit a hot, clenched ball of anger at his center. Passersby scurried out of his way; he knew he made a frightening picture. Frustration always brought a hard frown and a glint of temper to his face.

He would not let himself be stopped by this powerful puppet of Pharaoh's. A man could own but a few eternal things in life: his name, his soul, and his sons. Neither the vizier nor Pharaoh himself had a right or a reason to keep Idogbe from his boy.

Turning toward the west, he moved with unhurried purpose toward the riverfront. From the birdlike steward he had learned that his wife had been Lady Asenath's handmaid, and he also knew *that* noble lady lay quiet in her chambers, still awaiting her tomb. So if Mandisa had truly left the vizier's house, she had not had time to go far.

And all things moved along the river. Even in its depleted state, the Nile was still the lifeblood of Egypt, carrying its people upon its verdigris back, watering the earth, bringing life and nourishment to an otherwise parched land. No one traveled without stopping for food in its merchant stalls. Wherever Mandisa had gone, she had followed the Nile. And since she would not go toward Canaan in the north, she had assuredly ventured south.

Humming a confident tune, Idogbe strode toward the river.

CHAPTER THIRTY-EIGHT

THE LONG TRAIN OF OX-DRAWN WAGONS SNAKED FROM ONE HORIZON TO the other as Yaakov, his sons, their wives, children, and flocks moved toward Mizraim. Behind them lay a trampled bit of dry earth with empty pens for sheep and goats, a desolate land that no longer held a chance for life or happiness.

With so many, Shim'on knew the seventeen-day-journey was certain to take twice its normal time. The women did not like to move quickly, and the children complained about the heat and the unusual routine. Many of the animals were weak from starvation and thirst, more than a few collapsed as the family moved forward. Re'uven commanded that the dead animals should be left where they lay and not skinned, an extravagant waste if Yosef had not promised to provide for all of them.

Shim'on made certain his sons handled his share of the family herds, then he fell into step beside his father's wagon. Dina rode in the back under a canopy, her face hidden by a thick veil intended to keep out dust. Shim'on wondered if she wore it to keep out the world.

"Dina?"

"Yes, Shim'on?"

He squinted toward the horizon, then shifted his gaze to the back of his father's head. Yaakov had not turned; he probably dozed in the heat.

"Before we left, I went to our family's burial cave."

She did not lift her veil, and he wondered if she had heard him. He could not see her eyes, only a slight movement of the veil as it fluttered with her breathing.

Finally, she answered. "What did you expect to find there?"

He let out a short laugh touched with embarrassment. He had hoped to find proof that her faith in God was useless. He had come home convinced that she spoke the truth.

"I didn't find what I expected," he answered, wiping sweat from his brow. "But I did find—something."

She shifted under the veil as the wagon creaked and jounced. "Will you tell me?"

His pulse began to pound at the memory of his encounter. "I felt like a man who has spent his entire life gazing upon the world and thinks he sees with the strongest and keenest sight a creature can possess. But then a voice summoned me, and just as a man's power of sight is dimmed and confused when he gazes at the sun's brilliance, I was compelled to admit my sight is nothing. And every idea, every belief I have ever held must be reevaluated in the light of this new brightness, in the knowledge that God Shaddai cares—even about me."

Dina did not answer, but Shim'on had not expected a reply. He walked in silence for several moments, knowing that she understood. Despair and grief had driven her to God Shaddai years ago.

"Were you frightened?" she asked, after a long silence.

"Yes, but yet not afraid. He told me . . . I was loved."

He saw the gleam of a smile beneath her veil. "Yes, that is how He is," she whispered, folding her hands at her waist. "To embrace Him is to know power, glory, agony, bewilderment, and fear—but never to be afraid. He is unutterable love, Shim'on. Though the world burns around you, He is love."

Shim'on did not understand everything she meant, but he nodded and slowed his pace until the wagon pulled ahead.

Of all his siblings, only Dina seemed to understand why his visit to the burial cave had left him shaken and unsteady. He had heard countless stories about how God spoke to Avraham and Yitzhak. Yaakov had often told the story of the night when he wrestled the angel of the Lord and earned the name Yisrael, or "he who strives with God." But until the Cave of Machpelah, Shim'on had never heard the voice of God, had never imagined that he might personally strive with such an exalted being.

The experience had humbled him and broken his furious spirit. After encountering the mind of God, he had seen his anger as a madness that would bring nothing but shame. Unchecked, it would bring death. But God was merciful, He would forgive.

On the long walk from the cave back to the camp, Shim'on realized what Mandisa meant when she told him he was not a man who could love. Shim'on would yet prove to her that he had changed. But first, there were wrongs to right.

He quickened his pace until he again walked abreast of his father's wagon. Yaakov sat at the front, his lined face turned toward the sun, his eyes closed.

Shim'on walked closer, matching the oxen's plodding gait. "Father?"

"Yes, my son?" Yaakov's eyes did not open, and Shim'on wondered if the old man even cared which son of Lea addressed him. For Binyamin those faded eyes would open, for Yosef they would even weep.

Enough. He had come to make peace, not to stir up old jealousies.

"Father, I have heard the voice of El Shaddai."

Yaakov's eyes did open then, and Yisrael turned toward him, astonishment lifting the lines on his face. "*You*, Shim'on?"

"Yes." Shim'on ignored the insult in the question.

"And what," Yisrael said, his tone filled with awe, "did God Almighty say to you?"

"The God of your fathers," Shim'on answered, staring at the dusty path beneath his feet, "told me we should not fear to go into Egypt. He warned that we should not worship gods made of stone or wood."

Yaakov turned his face back to the sun. "Anything else?"

Shim'on fingered his beard and stared forward. "The voice told me that El Shaddai would be found if I seek Him with all my heart and soul. 'When you are in distress,' He said, 'return to the Lord your God and listen to His voice. For the Lord your God is a compassionate God; He will not fail you nor destroy you."

Yaakov seemed preoccupied for a moment, then he rested his hands on his knees and gave Shim'on a rare smile. "El Shaddai spoke to me, too, last night at Beersheba. He told me that He would not forsake us in Egypt. We will go down to Mizraim, but in time God will bring us up to Canaan again. And then," his voice echoed with wonder, "El Shaddai promised that when I die, Yosef will close my eyes."

Sunshine broke across the old man's face at this last remark, and the twin adders of hate and jealousy rose in Shim'on's breast. In an effort to beat down the emotions that threatened to choke his voice, he punched the sand with his staff. He had come to this wagon to make peace.

"Father, you must forgive me."

"Forgive you, Shim'on?"

"For hating you." Shim'on heard a trace of venom in his voice, but he could not erase it. "I hated you for not loving my mother. I hated you for favoring Yosef, then Binyamin. I hated you for placing my mother and my brothers before Rahel when we advanced to meet Esav. I hated you for not rising to defend Dina when Shekhem accosted her." The bitterness and regret of a lifetime rose in his throat, shredding his voice. "And I hated you especially for not stopping me when I took Dina's child into the wilderness."

Shim'on waited for a response, and when none came, he dared to look up at his father. Yaakov sat motionless in the wagon, his chin set in a stubborn line, his expression pained.

"Father, will you forgive me?"

After a long, brittle silence, Yaakov spoke. "I am weary, Shim'on."

Had he not heard a word? Or was he choosing to ignore Shim'on's confession?

At that moment Shim'on understood the release that comes from asking forgiveness, and the sting of forgiveness withheld.

Is this how Mandisa had felt when he turned from her at the vizier's house? Even though in his heart he knew she had not meant to insult him, he had enjoyed denying her forgiveness. And so he had wounded her again. Just as Yaakov's silence hurt him now.

For a long interval Yaakov sat in the cart, staring mindlessly over the heads of the oxen. Finally he drew a deep breath. "I have lived a long life," he said, his voice dull and troubled. "I have done a few things to honor God, but many times, in my weakness and deception, I have dishonored His name. In a bit of trickery, I pretended to be my brother to steal his birthright. In a similar bit of trickery, Lea pretended to be Rahel to steal my love. God has not let me escape unscathed from my wanton deeds, and I fear I have paid the price for my mistakes with you, Shim'on."

"Father, I—"

Yaakov cut him off with a gesture. "I fell short as a son, and I have fallen short as a father. I am not a perfect man."

He turned, eyeing Shim'on with a calculating expression. "I had to keep peace between two wives, Shim'on, and you have none. I had to keep peace between twelve sons, and you have only six. Can you be a better father and husband than I with no wives and half as many sons?"

A muscle clenched along his jaw as he turned again to the horizon. "Judge your own house before you judge mine, Shim'on. Set your affairs in order. When you are a perfect man, come to me again."

CHAPTER THIRTY-NINE

MANDISA SWALLOWED HARD AND SQUARED HER SHOULDERS, WILLING herself to walk yet another fifty paces. At her right hand the river gleamed pale and gray beneath a silvery path of light cast by the moon. "Only a little farther, Adom," Mandisa said, her voice sounding worn in her own ears. Adom did not complain, though they had been walking all day. She felt as though she had been walking her entire life.

Two full weeks had passed since they left the vizier's house, and in the past twenty days they had wandered through Hierakonpolis, a city nearly as bustling and prosperous as Thebes, and half-a-dozen smaller villages. Any one of the towns would have been a good place to settle, but she had decided to take Adom to Elephantine, an island city near the river's first cataract. When El Shaddai again blessed the earth with floodwaters, Elephantine would be the first community to receive the benefits and blessings of the Nile's annual inundation.

Though an emerald strip of river grass still bordered the Nile, Mandisa yearned to see green when she lifted her eyes to the east and west. The emmer fields, from which the sun used to drink steam, now lay empty and barren. Even the skies had changed in the years of famine. The flocks of wild geese, pintail ducks, and widgeons that used to swarm over

Egypt had vanished as if they knew they could no longer nest in the bosom of the land.

Beside her, Adom yawned, and Mandisa felt a flash of sympathy for her son. The poor boy would have to adapt to life outside a luxurious palace, for there would be no garden or servants or maids in whatever household Mandisa could afford to furnish for him. Yet she was glad she had left the vizier's house while Adom was young. He was nearly old enough to choose a trade for himself, and a practical, ordinary outlook would be good for him. She would have to learn to make her own way in the world; Adom would, too.

As the sun sank toward the west and lengthened the shadows along the riverbank, Mandisa pointed toward a small huddle of trees. "There, Adom, is a sheltering place," she said, studying the riverbank to make certain no hippos or crocodiles had decided to beach themselves at the same spot. Since the drought had lowered the river's water level, the water creatures had become hungry and restive in their confinement. More than once Mandisa had been warned that dangerous animals lurked in the river grasses, waiting for a passerby to stumble and fall in the dark.

But the sparse stand of trees lay thirty paces from the river's edge on a high mound of gray earth. "Here, Adom." Exhausted, she found a sheltered spot under the branches of a still-green acacia. She cleared the ground with her sandal, checking to be sure no spiders or scorpions hid among the dry brush at her feet, then sat down with her back against the spindly tree trunk. Adom sat next to her, hugging his knees. She knew within a few moments the boy in him would overpower the emerging man. Funny how worry and weariness made children of men. Shim'on had behaved much the same way.

Adom's breathing slowed and deepened; his head fell upon her shoulder. Relieved that he slept so soon, she looked up at the sky above. Silver moonbeams laced the branches of the acacias; a quarter moon the color of dappled stone hung in the eastern sky. The dense papyrus beds along the edge of the river vibrated with insect life, beyond them, the silver water of the Nile shimmered against an endless sky. Mandisa closed her eyes and thanked God Almighty for another day of survival.

For it was El Shaddai who had brought her safely through the land, and no other god. None of Egypt's divinities had the power to predict the famine or provide the food she and Adom had eaten. They had found dates overlooked by harvesters, grapes growing wild on vines by the riverside. One merchant, about to toss the crocodiles his left over shat cakes, had changed his mind and given them to Mandisa and Adom instead.

No, none of Egypt's gods could provide like El Shaddai, but they were as plentiful as fleas on a dog. As she and Adom had traveled down the riverfront, Mandisa marveled at the many temples, statues, and shrines along the riverbank. Some of the elaborate shrines were made of stone and decorated with festive paintings; others were as simple as a small statue concealed within a hut of sticks and twigs.

She supposed her years in the vizier's house had dulled her memory of Egypt's pantheon of deities. Though Ani and a few of the household servants held special reverence for certain gods, Zaphenath-paneah had not allowed graven images in his private quarters or his temple.

Apparently the famine had invoked a national resurgence in personal piety. Every city, town, and village had erected a statue of its patron god or goddess at its gate in order to keep harm and want outside the city limits. In addition, each house had at least one replica of a favorite deity standing guard at the doorpost.

Mandisa flinched when a sudden splash cut into the silence. She scanned the river, her body rigid, until she spied the commotion in the water. Massive jaws churned the surface as a monster chewed its catch, and Mandisa released her breath. The beast floated by her, a dark shadow with golden eyes, a stone-like snout, and a wide body. His massive tail, as long as Mandisa was tall, whipped back and forth through the quicksilver river, propelling the creature forward.

Sebek. The crocodile god. Idogbe had been a devout follower of Sebek. A crocodile statue stood outside the door of their small house and once a year her husband had journeyed to Crocodilopolis, one of Sebek's sacred abodes, to worship the crocodile who supposedly emerged from the watery chaos at the moment the world began.

But Idogbe was no longer a part of her life, and Sebek was no god. Why couldn't anyone else see the futility of worshipping stone and carved wood?

Despite Zaphenath-paneah's allegiance to El Shaddai and his forthright insistence that the Almighty God preserved Egypt from ruin, the Egyptians had not hearkened to the voice of their vizier. Tuthmosis IV, the present Pharaoh's father, had listened to and respected Zaphenath-paneah's words, but though the new king honored his tutor-vizier, he did not possess the courage to shelve the ancient cults and the priests who also advised him. Plus, Mandisa mused, Pharaoh probably preferred to maintain the old religions because doing so insured that he would remain at the head of Egypt's pantheon of gods. According to the old beliefs, the king reigned over his people as the incarnation of the god Horus. As such he was divinity himself, and only he had the right to petition the gods in prayer.

"Not so," Mandisa murmured, her eyes growing heavy. "For I have seen the provision of the Almighty One. He has heard Zaphenath-paneah's voice, and He will hear mine."

Mandisa took a long, deep breath of the cool evening air. It was good to have one God, and logical that only one could be supreme. She had seen the hand of El Shaddai in the reunion of Zaphenath-paneah and his brothers, and He had bountifully provided for her and Adom in the past few days. So why couldn't she understand His will regarding her and Shim'on?

Surely she had been right to leave Thebes, for how could she face Shim'on when he returned? He refused to love her; he looked for every reason to avoid caring for her. And she could not love a man whose heart had been hardened and carved of hatred and jealousy.

"Almighty God, wherever you are—" she opened her eyes to the darkening sky above— "keep your hand on us as we journey to our new home. Comfort Zaphenath-paneah in his sorrow, and Efrayim and Menashe. But especially Shim'on, O God . . . heal the hurts of his heart."

Under the vast and endless plain of evening, Mandisa slept.

WATCHING from a small boat floating in the lazy river current, Idogbe recognized the woman who had been his wife. He had been haunting the river for days, moving from village to village, counting on Mandisa's instinct to flee in the opposite direction of Canaan. The wilderness was no place for a single woman and a young boy, and he knew she would not want to face her people with a son and no husband. With nothing but desert to the east and west, she could only have gone southward.

Paddling silently, without even a ripple in the windless calm, Idogbe urged his papyrus skiff closer to shore. The boy lay on the ground next to her, one arm resting idly in her lap. Idogbe's mouth puckered with annoyance. She ought to take better care of his son, especially a boy who had spent nine years in the house of a vizier. Undoubtedly the lad was bright; perhaps he had already picked up a rudimentary knowledge of writing. At scribe school the boy could learn more, and within a few years he would prove himself able enough to serve in the temple of Sebek at Crocodilopolis.

A man needed a son to provide for him, to see that he was properly supplied for the afterlife. Until the day he'd learned the boy existed, Idogbe had worried that he might die unknown and unmourned, that his immortal soul would vanish like a puff of steam. But he had a son, a bright boy who might be offered in service to the fierce and strong Sebek to insure bountiful rewards in this life and the world to come.

Igdogbe's gaze drifted from the sleeping boy to the mother. He smiled, thinking about the first time he had seen her. Always restless for fresh horizons, he had been a wanderer even then, one of many merchants on an expedition to the lands of Shinar. The caravan had stopped outside a compound of tent dwellers, and he saw Mandisa standing by the well. She wore a brightly patterned Assyrian garment, a stark contrast to the bleached linen garments of Egyptian women. Her dark hair, so different from the neat, tidy Egyptian wigs, had tumbled carelessly down her back. One escaping curl fell over her forehead, mesmerizing him.

He had never considered taking a woman for his own, but in that moment he knew he would have her.

He scarcely knew how he found the words, but an interpreter led him to her father's tent. Within the hour he had offered the herdsman ten deben weight of silver; before sunset that afternoon he had set the girl on one of his pack animals and turned toward Egypt.

Though the girl was beautiful, an aura of melancholy surrounded her even in bright sunlight. She wept frequently and her lustrous eyes widened with alarm every time he approached. Her tongue proved quick as she learned the Egyptian language. Within six months after Idogbe installed her in his house, Mandisa had become like other Egyptian women, complaining that he spent too much time away from home. So when she told him she expected a child, he paid a priest of Sebek a handsome amount to look into a divining bowl and predict the child's sex.

The priest lied. Perhaps Mandisa had bribed him, or perhaps the man had his own reasons for misleading Idogbe. But rather than father a girl and be responsible for two whining women, he had gathered his silver and left Thebes, preferring to let Mandisa think him dead than to return and let himself be nagged into an early grave.

Now he studied her in the moonlight and recalled that she was not often unpleasant. Her ivory shoulders, barely visible through the linen gown she wore, evoked memories he had long since buried. Her hair, shorter now but still curly, was still as black as a starless night. Even from this distance he could see the hollow of her neck, filled with moonlit shadows. How rewarding it would be to kiss them away . . .but he had not come all this way for her. And if he were to succeed in his intention, Mandisa could not know that Idogbe still lived. She must believe that her son had vanished without a trace.

He would have to plan carefully. He stroked the surface of the water and looked at the shore ahead. A small lagoon, used in more plentiful days to irrigate the fields of an entire village, lay off to the west. He rowed forward until the skiff lanced its way into the still waters of the waiting lagoon.

CHAPTER FORTY

"Look there, Father!" Zevulun, who drove the oxen pulling Yaakov's wagon, pointed toward the south. "Mizraim! The Black Land!"

Straining against the beating of his own heart, Yaakov pushed himself up from the pile of furs where he had been reclining. For several days they had been traveling through desert as gray and lifeless as a tomb, but now a ribbon of green appeared in the distance. A blush of pleasure burned his cheeks. How good of God to provide fertile fields and Yosef, too!

Re'uven, who rode beside the ox-cart on a donkey, lifted his head and pointed in the same direction. "What's that?" A line of Egyptian war chariots bordered the wide green plain, then one chariot pulled away from the others and came forward, churning up the dust of the desert as it raced toward Yisrael's caravan.

"Who rides at the front of our train?" Yaakov demanded, his stomach tightening. "Is it Binyamin?"

Re'uven strained to look ahead toward the beginning of the caravan. "Yehuda rides there. Have no fear, Father, I'll see that all is well."

With his legs pumping against the sides of his donkey, Re'uven set out. Yaakov sat up and folded his hands, his stomach churning with anxiety. Though El Shaddai had told him not to fear Egypt, the thought of entering a pagan land aroused old apprehensions and uncertainties. Avraham had nearly lost Sarah here and Yosef had disappeared into the bowels of this dark place for over twenty years. What if Yaakov and his people were totally absorbed, eaten alive? They might never emerge as a distinct and separate people again.

But God had told him not to fear. The Almighty had spoken even through Rahel, who had thought she was only being witty when she named her first-born *Yosef,* the word for "add" which sounded remarkably like the word for "remove." "God has removed, *asaf,* my reproach," she said as the midwife lifted the squalling child from her womb. "May Shaddai add, *yosef,* another son to me!"

"Ah, Rahel," Yaakov murmured, his eyes stinging at the memory of her life and love. "God removed our Yosef, and then added him again. As he will remove our people from Canaan, then bring us back. I will not fear."

"Father!" Re'uven called, trotting back from the front of the caravan. "Yosef has sent these chariots to intercept us. They will lead us to Goshen where he waits to welcome you."

Yaakov held up a hand, not trusting his voice to answer. As the oxen started forward again, he settled back into his furs, wrapped in a silken cocoon of euphoria.

FOUR HOURS LATER, a different company of Egyptian charioteers darted toward them, the horses' hooves drumming the dry desert like a herd of thundering elephants. Onward the Egyptians came, dizzyingly swift, resplendent in white kilts and gleaming chariots pulled by elaborately harnessed stallions.

Yaakov stirred uneasily. What would he see in Yosef's face? An idolatrous Egyptian or the son he had taught and loved? For so many years he had struggled to accept the fact that his beloved, handsome Yosef was dead. Now he struggled to imagine Yosef alive, forty years old, and an Egyptian ruler. Would this Zaphenath-paneah still possess the dear qualities that had made Yosef so special? Yaakov was not certain he could handle the disappointment if the mature man did not resemble the valiant, beautiful youth.

Three chariots pulled away from the oncoming company. They turned sharply in a V formation, then two followed as the leader moved and steadily down the line of Yisrael's caravan. Yaakov frowned, squinting into the bright glare of the sun. Two men rode in the first chariot, one held the reins while the other stood tall and straight, his hands upon the rim of the conveyance, his eyes intently studying the wagons. The tall, olive-skinned man wore a wig in the style of the Egyptians, a flowing crimson cloak, and a spotless white robe.

Abreast of Yaakov's wagon, the first chariot halted. As the tall Egyptian leapt out of his conveyance, Yaakov stared across the distance between them, his heart pounding.

The Egyptian leaned into the wagon, then his warm hands clasped Yaakov's. "Father," the man said, his voice husky with emotion. Before Yaakov could respond, the weeping Egyptian fell on his neck and kissed him.

Yaakov blinked with bafflement. "Yosef?" He pressed his hands to the Egyptian's shoulders. When the vizier of all Egypt lifted his face to within inches of Yaakov's, the father searched for signs of his missing son.

The paint-lengthened eyes, the wig, the oiled skin—none of these meshed with the Yosef of Yaakov's memory. The man's face shone with a sort of beauty beyond the reach of a seventeen-year-old boy. But there was something in his eyes . . .

A hot, exultant tear trickled down Yaakov's cheek as he pressed his trembling hand to the Egyptian's cheek. He felt his heart turn over the way it always did when Rahel looked at him with that same pleading, loving expression. "Rahel's eyes," he murmured, feeling the vizier's tears on his fingertips. "You have Rahel's eyes."

If a man dies, will he live again?

Yes! Praise be to God Shaddai.

"Father," the Egyptian exclaimed again, and this time Yaakov wrapped his arms around the son he had long thought dead.

"Now let me die, since I have seen your face," he whispered, relishing the feel of Yosef in his arms. "Now I can die, knowing you are alive."

Yosef's trembling limbs clung to his father; he had no desire to back out of that longed-for embrace. God was so good. His father still lived, a miracle in itself, and Yaakov's eyes had *known* him, had welcomed him as if they had been parted only a few hours instead of more than twenty years.

"You shall not die, Father," Yosef said, still holding tight. His tone was playful, but his meaning was not. "You shall live with me in Egypt. And God will give you many years here, so we may fellowship with one another. And you shall know my children, and understand why God Shaddai wrought all these things."

At last, reluctantly, they parted. Without shame, Yosef palmed tears from his face, but his eyes never left Yaakov's. "You were always in my heart," he told his father, so choked by emotion that he could barely lift his voice above a whisper. "I never forgot the things you taught me about God Shaddai."

"Praised be his name." Yaakov cried, his arms closing around Yosef again.

Tears of joy came in a rush so strong that Yosef sobbed in his father's arms, but Yaakov held him close, crooning the soft words that a father gives to a much-loved son.

Yaakov met Efrayim and Menashe that same day, then Yosef himself led the children of Yisrael into the land of Goshen, the place prepared for them. "I will go up and tell Pharaoh that you have arrived," Yosef told his family. "He knows you are shepherds."

"Will he expect us to mingle with his people?" Yaakov asked, still uneasy about living in a land of idol worshippers.

271

A smile nudging itself into a corner of Yosef's mouth. "The Egyptians detest herdsmen; those who keep livestock are an abomination to them."

"As they are to us!" Levi laughed. "Let them stay away, I have no urge to visit their sinful cities."

"We will remain here, in this well-watered land of Goshen," Yaakov answered, silencing his headstrong offspring with a stern look. He turned back to the magnificent man who was his son. "And as for you, my Yosef, am I to meet the mother of your sons?"

A look of tired sadness came over the vizier's face. "My lovely Asenath was laid in her tomb a few days ago, Father. You will have to wait and meet her in the Otherworld."

Yaakov nodded, appraising his son's silent pain. Yosef's despair seemed genuine; he had truly loved the Egyptian woman he mourned. Just as Yaakov had loved Rahel—and Lea.

"It is enough, my son."

Yosef gave his father a smile and placed his hand on Yaakov's shoulder. "It may be that Pharaoh will come to visit you, out of respect," he said, the warmth of his smile echoing in his voice. "If he comes and asks your occupation, tell him again that you are herdsmen. Thus he will leave you alone here, and you and your people will not be molested in any way. You will be free to live, work, and worship as you please."

"And what of you?" Yaakov asked, taking his son's hand. "Must you continue living in Thebes?"

The vizier's large, black eyes, so like Rahel's, seemed to fill with shifting stars. "God has set me in another place," he said, his voice gentle, but firm. "Though my heart is always with you, I must do the work Almighty God has called me to do."

As his heart sank with swift disappointment, Yaakov gave his beloved son a smile and an encouraging nod. "Then go with God," he said, holding Yosef's hand until the last possible instant.

CHAPTER FORTY-ONE

SHIM'ON WAS PLEASED TO DISCOVER THAT GOSHEN SUITED HIS FAMILY well. Bordered by the Mediterranean Sea, called the Wadj-ur or "the Great Green" by the Egyptians, the delta that supported the region of Goshen was part of Lower Egypt. The fertile land, well-watered by seven river branches of the Nile, was heavy with layers of effluvium and silt, perfect for fields, flocks, and herds. The vast area, inhabited by few Egyptians, was blessed by continued moisture, gentle winds, and solitude.

Yosef proved himself generous beyond all imagining. He provided the children of Yisrael with food, the tools with which to construct shelters like those they had known in Canaan, and additional livestock to replace the animals that had died on the journey. The vizier of all Egypt lived with them in a tent for the first week after their arrival, eager to make certain his father and family were content and settled in their new home. And though Yosef was welcomed with open arms, Shim'on sensed that he would always remain apart from them. In a way he was still Yosef, Yaakov and Rahel's son, but the aura of his glory kept them at arms length. Even Yisrael, who had once scoffed at young Yosef's dream that his parents and brothers would bow before him, prostrated himself at Zaphenath-paneah's feet and called him, "My lord."

Perhaps because he had been imprisoned so long in the vizier's house,

Shim'on was the least awed of all his brothers. Two weeks after settling his sons into their new home, Shim'on said farewell to his family, mounted a donkey, and rode upriver toward Thebes. Ostensibly he had undertaken the journey to bring a report from Yaakov to Yosef, but privately he yearned to know if Mandisa would grant him a chance to speak with her.

So much had happened since he had last seen her. He had heard the voice of El Shaddai, and the angry fires in his soul had been quenched by his confession to Yaakov. If only she would listen to him long enough to hear his heart . . .

At the vizier's house, Ani greeted him like an old friend, and even Tarik had a smile for his troublesome former captive. "So, Shim'on the mighty Destroyer of Furniture has returned," Ani said, stumbling over the unfamiliar Canaanite words. "What do you intend to break on this visit?"

"Nothing," Shim'on answered, happy to meet the smile and the welcoming hand Ani offered him. "And you can speak Egyptian. I have learned enough to manage in this country."

"After a year in this house, you should speak it as well as the master," Tarik joked, slapping him on the back. "But if you've come to see the vizier, you'll have to wait. He is with Pharaoh at the king's house, interviewing emissaries from Babylon. A king of that city wishes to marry his daughter to our divine Amenhotep."

Shim'on followed Tarik and Ani as they walked toward the kitchens. "Another royal queen."

Ani turned a somber face toward Shim'on. "I suppose you heard about Lady Asenath."

Shim'on nodded. "The vizier told us when he introduced his boys to my father. I was sorry to hear the news."

The steward's mouth curved in a mirthless smile. "Things are much changed now, of course. Tizara tends to the young masters when they are not with their father."

"I thought Mandisa would care for the boys," Shim'on remarked, looking around. "She has a fondness for the children."

Tarik halted on the pathway. "You haven't heard?"

Shim'on's stomach dropped like a hanged man. "What?"

The captain folded his arms. "Mandisa and Adom left about three weeks after the mistress died. A short time after that, an Egyptian called Idogbe came here, searching for her. The master dismissed him at once, but he seemed quite intent on finding Mandisa."

"Not that he wanted her, for the master ruled she was not his legal wife," Ani added. "The man wanted Adom. He said he left her because he thought Mandisa would bear a girl, but when he came back and discovered that she'd borne a son . . ."

Ani's voice trailed away, but he did not need to explain. Shim'on knew all too well that sons were valued far above daughters. Part of Yaakov's prestige in Canaan lay in the simple fact that he had produced twelve sons.

Shim'on took a deep breath. "Where did Mandisa go?"

"No one knows," Tarik answered. "But I don't think she wanted to remain in Thebes. She has no family here."

"For some reason, I think she was especially afraid of meeting you again," Ani said. His bright eyes narrowed into speculative slits. "Why would she fear you, Shim'on, son of Yaakov?"

Shim'on felt limp with weariness. "Why wouldn't she fear a Destroyer?"

ZAPHENATH-PANEAH INVITED Shim'on to dinner that evening, and the former prisoner was pleased to discover that the meal would be served in the vizier's chamber. He went speechless with surprise, however, when he heard Yosef tell Tarik to place a chair for Tizara between himself and Shim'on.

"You expect me to share my meat with a harlot?" Shim'on asked when Tarik had left the room. "Really, Yosef, has the girl's beauty addled your brain?"

"You once attempted to run away with Tizara," Yosef answered, regarding his older brother. "Why won't you eat with her? What has changed?"

Shim'on shrugged. "Things were different then. I was a captive and she a slave. And we were both allied against *you*."

Yosef smiled, but his expression held only a ghost of its former warmth. "Now you are brother to the vizier of all Egypt," he said, sinking into his chair. "And now you are too important to eat beside a woman with a troubled past."

"I'm not speaking of her past—I'm speaking of what she is! You can't be blind, Yosef, for all that you pretend to be."

"I see far more than you think I do, Shim'on. And in Tizara I see a young woman in need of friends and family."

"But she has played the harlot, and probably would not hesitate to do so again if given the chance."

"Is your own past so pure?"

Shim'on winced, surprised that the words stung. Sometimes he forgot that Yosef knew everything about Shekhem, about Dina's baby, and of course, about Dotan.

"Tizara will sit between us and you will not be unkind," the vizier continued, his voice regal. "You will be on your best behavior, whatever that may be. Do not forget that you are in my house, Shim'on. Though I am your brother, by the hand of God Almighty I am also lord of Egypt. I love you, but I will discipline you if you insult the others of my household."

Irked by Yosef's words and his aloof manner, Shim'on settled back in his chair, determined to endure the evening and retire as soon as possible. Yosef would always be a mystery, an enigma; sometimes he made no more sense than the mad, inexplicable images of dreams. Why was he so intent upon cultivating a relationship with the woman of shame? For a moment Shim'on considered the possibility that Yosef thought to marry the girl, but surely the noble Zaphenath-paneah would never take a tainted woman for his bride!

The doors swung open; two guards escorted Tizara and the boys into the room. Efrayim and Menashe fell on their faces before the vizier, then, at a word from their father, they leapt up and scampered to his side. After greeting each of his sons with an embrace and a quick kiss, Yosef welcomed their nursemaid.

Shim'on found himself staring as if he'd never seen a woman before. If such a thing were possible, he would have sworn some other soul had come to inhabit Tizara's body as she slept. For though the willowy form every man in the villa desired had not altered, the spirit within the woman had completely changed.

With her eyes demurely downcast, Tizara crossed to the empty chair between the two men and seated herself. The beauty that had once tempted Shim'on now fascinated him. An aura of untouchable glory surrounded her and drew him like honey draws a fly.

"Tizara?" he asked, scarcely able to believe *this* woman would know him.

"Shim'on!" Her eyes lit with the excitement of recognition when she looked up; her smile was sweet and serene. "It is good to see you again. Haven't the boys grown?"

"Yes, they have," he murmured, distracted by her nearness. "Many things have changed within this house."

She offered him another shy smile. "Indeed they have."

BY THE TIME the last dish had been taken away, Shim'on had convinced himself that Yosef intended *him* to marry Tizara. He waited until the former slave girl had taken the boys to bed, then he turned on his younger brother in indignation.

"I know what you are planning," he said. "Tizara is not good enough for *you*, but you would have no problem marrying her to me. She is from Shekhem, too, which makes things nice, doesn't it? Do you think you can relieve my guilt by bringing me a bride from that cursed place? You can fix some things, Yosef, but a Canaanite woman will not erase the wrongs of my past."

Yosef's mouth quirked with humor. "Why would I want to marry you to Tizara? Good nursemaids are difficult to find."

"Then why did you invite her to eat with us? Women do not eat with men, especially in Egyptian households."

"Who says families may not eat together?"

"Servants are not family members. You did not invite Tarik to eat with us, or Ani, and they are closer servants than your children's maid."

"Tizara is family."

Shim'on blinked. What had Yosef done? Adopted the girl? Betrothed her to one of his sons? The Egyptians were odd; he should not be surprised by anything Yosef might do as Zaphenath-paneah.

Yosef stood and moved toward the balcony stairs. "Come with me, Shim'on."

Shim'on followed, his brain whirling.

Yosef thrust his hands behind his back as he led Shim'on toward the section of balcony that overlooked the garden. "Do you believe El Shaddai keeps His hand on us always?"

Shim'on hesitated. Only a few weeks ago he would have answered no. But since that time the hand of God had moved through his life like a whirlwind, uprooting old hates and sorrows.

"I do."

"Then look there." Yosef pointed to the garden below. "And tell me what you see."

Shim'on could see nothing, then Tizara moved into a glow of torchlight at the edge of the reflecting pool. Slender, supple, and lissome, she swayed to the music of the night, dancing with shadows thrown by the moon. The hard and brittle brightness of her manner had completely fallen away; she looked like a playful young girl.

"I see," Shim'on muttered, a note of impatience in his voice, "a harlot who has been spoiled by her master."

"Admit the truth, you see a different woman," Yosef answered, leaning on the railing. He gave Shim'on an enigmatic smile. "Forgiveness and mercy change lives. A harlot entices men away from the love of God, and Tizara has enticed no one in this house. But we have other harlots in our lives, other gods we choose to serve."

Shim'on felt everything go silent within him.

"Your anger, Shim'on, was a harlot," Yosef went on, watching the girl. "And your guilt, and your rage. And though I can tell you have changed since you were held here—"

Shim'on tightened his grip on the stone railing. "I have."

"Even still, anger and guilt have risen within you because Mandisa is gone."

Shim'on flinched, resenting Yosef's intuition. How could a man know so much without being told?

Yosef read the question in Shim'on's eyes. "I can see, Shim'on," he said, without even a hint of boastfulness. "I know that you love Mandisa. And she loved you so much that she left this place rather than face you again."

Shim'on caught his breath as a deep, unexpected pain smote his breast.

"Go after her," Yosef urged, his dark eyes piercing the distance between them. "Go quickly, before it is too late."

Something—humility?—kept Shim'on from arguing. "I'll go now," he said, turning from the rail.

"Wait. There is one more thing. Do you remember what Dina looked like when we were young?"

Shim'on turned and nodded, his throat too clotted with emotion to risk speaking. He did not want to think about Dina now. Though she had forgiven him, thinking of what he'd done to her still filled him with a deep sense of shame.

But at the mention of her name, memories ruffled through his mind like wind on water: Dina dancing by the oasis at Hebron, Dina giggling as he chased her through the camp, just as Tizara laughed in the sheer beauty of a warm and lovely night . . .

His heart went into sudden shock. The dancing girl in the garden was the image of Dina, not as she looked now, but as she had looked twenty years ago. Tizara's features were more refined, as if an artist's hand had smoothed out imperfections, but he could not deny the resemblance.

He heard his voice, stifled and unnatural: "Remarkable. Tizara looks much like Dina."

His words seemed to hang in the evening air. Yosef turned toward him, smiling as if Shim'on were a small child.

"Yes." Yosef spoke in an odd, yet gentle tone. "She ought to look like our sister . . . because Tizara is Dina's daughter."

Shim'on staggered toward the balustrade in hypnotized horror. "It can't be true." He stared again at the girl, his heart racing and his fingers fluttering with fear. "The baby died. I left it alone. No one lived within miles of that burial cave."

"God sent someone," Yosef answered, "just as He sent someone to sustain Hagar in the wilderness. Who are we to question His ways?"

The girl continued to dance beneath the moon, completely unaware of the men watching from above. "How do you know this?" Shim'on whispered, still reeling in disbelief.

"I suspected something when the Spirit of God spoke to my heart and urged me to buy her," Yosef said, leaning his elbows on the balcony railing. "And she looked so much like the young Dina I remembered. Even so, I would never have been sure, but I heard Mandisa tell Halima that Tizara had an unusual birthmark on her scalp. Apparently she discovered it while washing Tizara's hair."

Shim'on shook his head. "The baby had no birthmark."

"It did. But you never looked at the child, Shim'on. I was playing in Dina's tent the day you took it away, I saw you leave with the baby held close to your breast." His voice trembled slightly in the darkness. "I don't think you were able to look."

Shim'on tore his gaze from the girl and turned to hide the tight place of anxiety in his heart. "Why did you not tell me sooner?"

A faint note of sadness tinged Yosef's voice. "I wasn't certain you—and the others—were ready to hear."

We weren't. Like a drowning man, Shim'on held it tight to the balustrade as a tumble of confused thoughts and feelings assaulted his spirit. He wasn't sure how long he stood there, clinging to the balcony railing like a frightened cat, but after a while he heard the soft sounds of

Yosef's footsteps on the stairs and eventually Tizara's graceful form melted into the veiling darkness.

The child had not died.

He stared into the moonlit garden, his heart pounding as the memory of his own words mocked him: *A Canaanite woman will not erase the wrongs of my past.*

But a Canaanite woman had done just that. The baby lived; by the grace of God his sin had been obliterated.

His skin burned with the memory of the hot sand on his hands at the family tomb, the emptiness of the awful moments when he had frantically searched for proof of his unspeakable crime. His frenetic digging had produced no bones, no trace of a human body, because the baby who had seared his soul with guilt lived and breathed and danced . . .

Shim'on thumbed an unmanly tear from his eye. Dina had believed. She had known Yosef and Tizara still lived. Though she couldn't see or touch the objects of her faith, she believed. She knew.

He lifted his eyes to the night where the stars blazed like gems upon a velvet sky.

You can restore that which was lost.

The intensity of the inner voice lifted the hairs on Shim'on's arms.

You took the child away; you can take her back to her mother.

A cry of mingled relief and surprise broke from his lips. Yosef had been restored to Yaakov, Tizara would be returned to Dina. How gracious, how good, was God Shaddai.

As soon as he found Mandisa and Adom, he would take Tizara home.

CHAPTER FORTY-TWO

SHIM'ON SCARCELY KNEW WHAT DROVE HIM, BUT YOSEF'S REVELATION LIT a fire in his soul, a fevered energy that would not be quenched until he had found Mandisa and pressed his suit with her one final time. He hurried from the balcony and stalked purposefully toward the stableyard. Tarik would give him a horse, perhaps even a chariot.

"Tarik!" Shim'on pounded on the door of the captain's quarters. In an instant the door swung open and Tarik spilled out of the chamber. "What is it?" he barked, his hands busy tying his swordbelt at his waist.

Apparently Shim'on had roused him from slumber, for the guard's eyes were heavy and he had not taken the time to don his wig. "Be at peace, Tarik," Shim'on said, trying to keep the impatience from his voice. "But I need a horse. Your master will give permission, you have but to ask him."

Tarik frowned. "By the crud in Sebek's teeth, Shim'on, whatever do you want with a horse?"

"I'm going to find Mandisa."

"Tonight?"

"Yes. So please, allow one of the stableboys to saddle a horse for me."

Tarik rolled his eyes, but moved toward the stable. "You'll need a chariot; no self-respecting Egyptian rides astride. My best chariot drivers have been dismissed for the day, but perhaps I can find someone willing to go with you."

"I'll go alone."

The captain gave Shim'on a look of frustrated disbelief. "You are a madman, and you're not accustomed to handling a chariot. You'll overturn it on the first corner."

"Then forget the cursed chariot and give me a horse! I'm not an Egyptian, and I don't care what people say when they see me astride one of the beasts!"

"Well." Tarik's face closed in a prim and forbidding expression as he crossed his arms. "I suppose the vizier's brother must know best. Tell Chuma the stable boy to put a bridle on the black stallion."

"Good." Shim'on took two steps before second thought restrained him. "Thank you, Tarik," he said, turning. "And may I give you one bit of advice?"

Tarik leaned against the wall. "I suppose you will whether or not I want to hear it."

"You're right." Shim'on lifted a warning finger. "The kitchen slave Halima loves you, everyone can see it. Marry her, my friend, before her hope is gone. Or you will wake up one day a lonelier man than I."

As Tarik sputtered in confusion, Shim'on turned and jogged toward the stable.

IDOGBE SLEPT FITFULLY, unwilling to lose himself in deep sleep lest he miss the opportunity to intercept Mandisa. A half hour before sunrise, as the eastern sky began to glow, he crept from his hiding place and peered through the brush. The woman and the boy still slept, curled together like a mother lion and her cub.

Idogbe peered at his son's face and felt pleasant surprise. The boy's single lock of hair emphasized the pale clarity of his complexion, and in his clear-cut features Idogbe could see the beginnings of genuine masculine beauty. Undoubtedly the lad would prove to be a cut above the ordinary runny-nosed brats who dwelt like river rats along the Nile. Yes, this child would be a fine oblation to Sebek. The Prince of Destroyer Gods, the One-Who-Conquers-Life-and-Death would bestow many favors upon Idogbe for surrendering his son to the priests.

"O Sebek, the Crocodile, hail to thee, thou Crocodile of the Land of the West and the sweet river!" he chanted under his breath, his gaze fastened to the boy. "I am thy kinsman, Sebek! As the sun shall rise, as the disk shall shine, as the services shall be performed in thy temple, so shall this child be better than he was, born of the woman Mandisa, born of Idogbe, the Egyptian! Aid my cause, Sebek, for if thou will not hear my words, I will crush a nest full of thy eggs in the Forecourt of Crocodilopolis! Then indeed shall thou come forth from the temple to aid me, to gather thy son, born of the woman Mandisa, born to thee, O mighty Sebek, god of my strength!"

As if he had sensed his father's prayer, the child stirred and lifted his head. Idogbe ducked behind a stand of papyrus, his heart beating thickly. The time was near. When the child left his mother's side, Idogbe would approach and ask for directions to the nearest temple, a friendly question that would not arouse suspicion. Perhaps he would ask the boy to lead him for a short distance, and as soon as they were beyond the range of Mandisa's hearing, Idogbe would restrain the boy's arms and force him into the waiting skiff. Once the child understood the great honor Idogbe intended for him, he would happily accept it.

Dawn crested the horizon at that moment, sending light up and over the earth. Mandisa stirred, brushing sand and dirt from her hair and shoulders. Her mouth curved with tenderness as she spoke to the boy, then he helped his mother rise and they walked together to the riverfront.

From his hiding place, Idogbe cursed his ill luck. Even an attentive and devoted mother could not stay beside the boy forever. Like the hovering spirit of Horus the Falcon, Idogbe would remain nearby. And the moment the mother and son parted, he would make his move.

THE SUN, a dazzling white blur, stood fixed in the wide sky, packing a punch only a lizard could love. Achy and exhausted, Mandisa forced herself to put continue putting one foot in front of the other and wondered if she would faint from the heat. She had never realized how cool and sheltered the vizier's house had been; she had taken the fans, the cool tile, and high, breeze-catching windows for granted. Here the proud sun reigned in the white-blue sky, and only the faintest scribbles of clouds deigned to shelter mortals on the land.

As they walked, she considered the jobs she might have to undertake to support herself and Adom. Women in Egypt generally chose one of four professions: they entered the priesthood, trained as midwives, or studied to become professional mourners or dancers. Mandisa knew she was long past the agile age of professional dancers, and the priesthood was not a suitable profession for a woman with a child, for she would have to leave Adom for extended periods of time.

Why would she do that for a god she would not serve? She reached out to run her hand over the dark fuzz that had begun to cover Adom's shaved head. She might have considered joining a priestly order to serve El Shaddai, but He had no temples and no cults in Egypt.

Before Asenath's death she might have considered midwifery, for she had delighted in assisting at the Efrayim's and Menashe's births. But with her mind still heavy with the memory of Asenath's travail, Mandisa did not think she could bear to watch another pregnant woman endure labor. The grievous memories of her beloved mistress were still too fresh.

There remained the profession of mourning. Professional mourners were well paid for their roles in the burials of esteemed men and women, and the work was simple enough—one had merely to weep, wail, and tear one's robe at the appropriate moments. And—a wry frown twisted her face—of late she had experienced enough grief to give a convincing performance. Perhaps God Shaddai had allowed her heart to break so she might be of comfort and service to others in similar situations.

She lifted her head, relieved to have found a workable solution for her situation. Twining tendrils of hope broke through the surface of her despair, and she knew El Shaddai would provide. If she had to beg for a position to grind corn, she would, but no matter what happened, she would remain free. She would not consider selling herself into slavery, nor would she marry because she had no other options. She would never again allow herself to become a man's possession.

MANDISA LET out a long exhalation of relief when she and Adom reached Elephantine shortly after mid-day. After begging a bit of bread from a compassionate merchant, they slipped aboard a ferry which carried them to the island city. Adom was wide-eyed with wonder as they walked around the bustling settlement, but Mandisa quickly realized that she would not find a place to live within the walled city. The common people lived on the river's eastern shore and rowed themselves to work for the noble island families. Shortly after dark each night, they returned to their hovels at the river's edge.

A grizzled fisherman gave them a ride back from the island. When Mandisa and Adom stepped out into the ankle-deep mud, the man gave Mandisa a valuable bit of information. "My sister had a hut about a hundred paces from here," he said, pointing to the riverbank. "But last month she died of the fever. You and your boy should take the place. No one will bother you."

Mandisa felt a warm glow flow through her. "Truly?"

"You'll find the house right on the river," the old man said, his round face melting into a smile. "There's a statue of Sebek by the door. My sister believed the strength of the crocodile god would guard the house."

Yet apparently the god was not strong enough to guard the woman within. Mandisa thanked the man again and took Adom's arm as they trudged toward the shoreline.

She found the hut exactly where the man had said it would be, one hundred paces from the boat landing and only ten paces from the dike that would restrain the river during the inundation. The small house, built of sun-baked bricks, stood like a welcoming beacon. The door hung aslant from its supports, but Mandisa pulled it open and stepped inside.

Since darkness was approaching, she did not look around, but found a quiet corner in which she and Adom could lie down.

As she watched her weary son sleep in the moonlight, Mandisa lifted her gaze to the sky beyond the window and thanked El Shaddai for his provision. In a pouch around her neck she still had a few pieces of fine jewelry, gifts from Lady Asenath. Surely some noble woman of Elephantine would pay dearly to wear earrings or a bracelet once worn by the vizier's wife.

"We will prosper here," she whispered, tenderly stroking her son's bare back. "We will make this house a home, and I will find work in the city beyond. And you will grow strong. There will be nothing here to remind us of hard times, no one to remind us of the past."

Tears sprang to her eyes but she held them in check, determined not to mourn for what could not be helped. El Shaddai had led her to this place, so she would not look back.

Outside the house, Idogbe chewed the loaf of bread he'd bought from a merchant and grunted, watching the scene before him with ever-increasing delight. Though Mandisa had led him on an irritating journey out to Elephantine and back again, she had made his task easy by taking the empty hut. She would grow confident here, she would send Adom outside to fetch something . . . and Idogbe would claim his son.

He took another bite, pleased with himself and the world.

"Mother, do I have to stay inside and work? There are boys my age by the river."

Sighing, Mandisa put down her borrowed broom and walked to the window. Despite the many warnings she'd heard about hungry animals in the river, an army of boys prowled the dike and the riverbanks beyond. They laughed, scampered over the sand, and occasionally dipped into the river to splash the heat from their bronzed backs. Her poor son, who'd had only little boys and older men for playmates, desperately wanted to join them.

"All right. But you must not turn your back on the water. Stay with the other boys, find a friend, and do not wander far from this hut."

"Thank you, Mother!"

Adom raced through the doorway and Mandisa bit down hard on her lower lip. He had lived his entire life in the safe shelter of the vizier's villa; he did not know about rivers, crocodiles, or village boys. But, she supposed, watching him scamper toward the other boys, if they were going to live on the Nile, he had to learn.

"Be careful," she called again.

She stood at the window, watching as he walked up to a circle of boys. As curious and natural as fish, they circled Adom. Mandisa held her breath, fighting momentary panic, but then Adom said something, and within a moment they were all chattering like magpies. She smiled, dismissed her worries, and returned to the business of cleaning the house.

IDOGBE'S HEART lurched when he saw the boy run out of the house . . . alone. The lad ran to a cluster of river urchins and began talking, a sure sign of a born leader.

Grinning to himself, Idogbe settled down by a tree, in plain view of the boys, but behind the house. He didn't care if the children saw him. If his son felt at ease, the snatching would be easier . . . when the time was right.

MANDISA WORKED HARD, humming contentedly to herself. Occasionally she walked over to the neighboring houses to borrow tools and supplies, always promising to repay. Her neighbors, all of whom were farming families hard-hit by the famine, were cheerful and polite, but expressed no interest in where she had come from or what she intended to do.

Mandisa surmised that many people had been uprooted by the famine. They probably assumed that she would come, remain a while, and then move on like so many others.

The modest house would be quite comfortable. Poor families did not have furniture, for wood was scarce and valuable, but two low mud-brick platforms had been built next to the walls to serve as beds. A few dusty baskets had been left in the house, and in one of them Mandisa found a fire drill and a few pieces of tender she could use to light a lamp. A small brick dome, open at the top, had been built into the front of the house to serve as an oven. Mandisa smiled when she looked at it. She had not cooked in over five years, so Adom might have to suffer through a few experiments before she produced something edible. But for tonight, this first evening in their new home, she had reserved a loaf of lotus bread, provided by Halima's generous hand.

She looked out the window. Her son stood outside, waving to one lone playmate who was heading home. "Adom, wash your hands in the bucket by the side of the house. It is time to eat."

"Yes, mother," he called, reluctantly dragging his feet through the sand.

Mandisa's smile broadened. A boy ought to play so hard that he resisted coming in.

One of the neighbors had lent Mandisa a lamp, a sloping, oil-filled bowl filled with twisted rags soaked in tallow. Mandisa lit the rags with a spark from the twirling fire drill, then lifted the bowl to the window sill. Kneeling on the hard floor of packed earth, she unwrapped the lotus loaf and broke the bread into two generous hunks. Her stomach tightened at the sight and scent of the food, and she mentally thanked Halima and God Shaddai for providing it.

She paused, her hands in her lap, waiting for Adom to open the door. When he did not come, she stood and moved to the window, searching the gathering gloom for a sign of her son. She did not see Adom.

She lifted the lamp and moved to the doorway to peer out at the landscape. The children had all gone home for dinner; the aromas of baking bread and boiling stews filled the air. "Adom!" she called, rising on tiptoe. "Adom! Come home!"

No one answered. Holding the lamp in an unsteady hand, she stepped out into the night, trying not to tremble as fearful images rose in her mind.

AN HOUR later she sat alone by a bonfire on the riverbank, still clutching the glowing lamp. Her frantic screams had brought a score of people from their homes. After hearing her few words of explanation, the men lifted their lamps and moved away, the night filling with the soft sound of bare feet moving toward the Nile.

"Crocodile," one woman said.

"Drowned," said another.

Mandisa closed her eyes and shivered with fear and fatigue. *El Shaddai, where are You now?*

The night became a world unto itself. The dark moments passed, one after the other, indistinguishable. Someone built a fire of dry rushes on the riverbank in hope that Adom would see the blaze and find his way home. The flames leapt up and threw the darkness back, but still Adom did not appear. Mandisa stalked the fire in an endless circle until someone forced her to stop.

Now she sat in the fire-tinted darkness, the flames at her left hand, the river at her right. Regrets and questions buzzed in her brain. Why had she let Adom go outside? Why hadn't she checked on him five minutes earlier? What devilish spirit had possessed her when she decided to leave the safety of Zaphenath-paneah's house? And where was the vizier's Almighty God when she needed Him most?

Someone threw a pile of dung fuel into the firepit and she cringed as a volcano of sparks erupted into the night sky. Fire shadows danced on the silvery waters of the treacherous river. She clenched her fist, hardening her frightened heart behind a barrier of anger.

What had the cursed river done now? By refusing to flood the valley it had attempted to kill the people of Egypt. Since they still lived, had it settled instead for killing one young boy? Why did it choose her innocent son?

Her nails cut into her palm as something stirred in the darkness at her right hand. Even through the fog of apprehension she heard the steady tramp of a horse's hooves, a muffled greeting, belligerent voices. She did not turn until a dark, powerful figure strode into the circle of firelight and called her name.

She felt a sudden darkness behind her eyes and a chilly dew on her skin. She had to be dreaming, for Shim'on could not be nearby any more than Adom could be gone.

She lowered her head, confused.

"Mandisa, I've just heard," Shim'on said, kneeling beside her. He was real, his flesh-and-blood hand was holding hers. His eyes, when she looked into them, were filled with compassion. "How long as Adom been gone?"

Mandisa tried to find the words. "I-I looked outside, and he was there. I turned, I lit the lamp and called again, and he didn't answer."

"At sunset, then." The line of his mouth tightened a fraction more. "Not so long ago. He can't have gone far, Mandisa. We'll find him."

"He's gone to the Otherworld." She pulled her head to her knees and fought against despair. "Adom is dead."

"No." Shim'on's voice broke with huskiness. "I've been riding for two days to find and warn you. Idogbe, your husband, knows about the boy. Tarik himself told me that the man appeared at the vizier's villa. Zaphenath-paneah decreed your marriage was not valid, but Idogbe the Egyptian left swearing that he would find and take his son."

His words didn't register in her confused mind. "Idogbe?"

"He has been following you," Shim'on repeated, grasping her arms. "At every village where I inquired about you and the boy, those who had seen you repeated that another man sought you, too. Don't you understand? Adom is not dead. Idogbe has taken him."

She pressed her hand to her mouth, absorbing his words and their meaning. Idogbe—*alive?* And wanting her son?

Rage swooped in to replace her desperation. "I will find him." Alarm rippled along her spine as she grasped Shim'on's hand and pulled herself to her feet. Her breath came raggedly as she struggled to curb her wrath. "How dare he take my son! Adom is mine, Shim'on."

He released her and stepped back, studying her thoughtfully. "I am here to help, and I have a horse. I can search faster than you."

She moved toward the animal before he could protest. "I'm going with you."

"Wait." He caught her arm and whirled her around. "I didn't come only to warn you. I came for another reason as well."

"Whatever it is, it can wait," she answered, wrenching free of him. She hurried toward the horse, knowing he would have no choice but to follow.

CHAPTER FORTY-THREE

THEY RODE THROUGH THE NIGHT, TRYING NOT TO MAKE UNDUE NOISE LEST they disturb Idogbe sleeping somewhere along the river. The lush grass at the riverfront made a wet slicking sound against the stallion's legs, a sound almost muffled by the insect hum that vibrated from the water's edge. Mandisa strained to sort through the river sounds for any noise that might belong to a struggling twelve-year-old boy.

Shim'on had given her his cloak to cover herself, for the narrow Egyptian shift she wore was not suitable for riding astride a horse. Without arguing, she donned the cloak, then ripped out the side seams of her tunic. She had never ridden anything but a Canaanite donkey, and felt insecure atop the great moving mountain of horseflesh. But her arms were about Shim'on's waist, and he seemed as immovable as the pyramids. Mandisa was unspeakably grateful for his presence.

Occasionally they stopped to let the horse drink from the moonlit river. "Do you think Idogbe travels on foot or by boat?" Mandisa asked during one stop, noticing the great number of skiffs moored up and down the shoreline.

"He followed you by boat," Shim'on answered. "But now that he has the boy, I think he will travel by foot. It would not be wise to take a twelve-year-old, particularly an unhappy one, in a skiff. The boats are too easily upset, and too many dangers lurk in the water. He would not want to risk overturning."

Mandisa nodded, grateful that at least one of them was able to think clearly. She was not sure how or why Shim'on had come, but she knew El Shaddai had sent him. Clinging to his waist, she felt a strange numbed comfort, almost as if she were clinging to the Almighty God Himself.

As the night passed into day, they cut a wide zigzag swath among the riverfront, venturing inland and then returning to the water's edge. Shim'on stopped every man with a child, and paused to study more than a few women. At first Mandisa didn't understand, then she shook her head. "Idogbe would never disguise himself in a woman's cloak," she said. "Never. I am sure he is not disguised at all, for he must think I assumed Adom is dead."

"You may be right," Shim'on admitted, urging the horse forward with a gentle kick. "But I would never forgive myself if we let this skunk of a man slip by us."

She clung more tightly to him, closing her eyes against the emotion that swelled hot and heavy in her chest.

For three days they made their way downriver, stopping only to eat, feed and water the horse, and steal quick naps in the shade. Shim'on insisted that they travel through the night, for Idogbe was likely to stop at sunset and rest in the darkness. But in village after village, city after city, Shim'on and Mandisa found no sign of him or Adom.

While they rode, Mandisa tried to guess why Idogbe would take the child. "He wanted a boy, I am certain of that," she explained, her words falling into the rhythm of the horse's brisk steps. "He often spoke of the value of sons as a key to immortality. All Egyptian husbands want a house full of sons."

"But why would he want the boy now?" Shim'on tossed the question over his shoulder. "He does not seem the type to prepare a home for children. When you knew him, how did he make his living?"

"Any way he could," she answered. "When I met him, he had just returned from the east with a group of traders. When we lived in Thebes, he would buy grain and lentils from our neighbors and travel up river to sell them at an inflated price." She sighed, remembering. "He was not often successful."

"Did he ever speak of other aspirations? Some occupation he might like to have tried? Something he might want a son to do?"

She frowned, unwilling to open the door to a host of memories she'd tried to lock away. "I don't know . . . perhaps. For a time he worked with the masons who make statuary. Once he tried to be a lay priest, but his ideas were too bizarre even for the priests of Sebek. He always admired the scribes. He said they held the power of the law in their hands."

"Could he write?"

She shook her head. "He had a keen mind for numbers, but he had never been taught the hieroglyphics." Suddenly, her mind blew open. "The temple schools! He could leave Adom with the priests so he won't have to worry about caring for him. Then when Adom is of age, a portion of everything he earns as a scribe will go to Idogbe."

Shim'on pulled back on the reins. While the stallion bent to browse the new grass at the water's edge, he turned in the saddle to look at her. "Which temple school?" he asked, his voice gentle. "Mandisa, there are scores of schools, for Egypt has more temples than—"

"Not for Idogbe," she answered, her eyes watering. "Idogbe worshipped Sebek. Idogbe would take Adom to the Temple of Sebek at Crocodilopolis."

"And where is this city?"

She closed her eyes and struggled to remember. "It is in the region called Land of the Lakes. A three-day journey north of Thebes."

"Almost to Goshen, then," Shim'on said. "I think I know the place. I rode through it on my journey from Goshen to Thebes." She thought he would look away, but he kept his eyes on her.

"Well?" she asked, feeling her flesh color. "Are we going or not?"

"Yes, my lady." Tightening the reins, he urged the stallion forward.

SINCE NEARLY ALL of Egypt's citizens had moved toward the life-giving river in the time of drought, Shim'on planned to follow the winding course as far as Herakleopolis. If he hadn't found Idogbe by then, he assured Mandisa, they would follow the tributary which broke off to the west and fed the area known as *Ta-she*, or Land of the Lakes. If they hadn't found Adom by the time they reached Crocodilopolis, they would go straightway to the Temple of Sebek and inquire after him. If the boy happened to be there, Mandisa could take her case to the vizier, who would certainly command the priests to release her son.

"I don't care what happens to Idogbe," Mandisa said, agreeing with Shim'on's plan. "He never loved me or his son, or he would have made me his wife. And he has been gone from my life for such a long time, I am content to leave his fate to the vizier. But I cannot rest until I find Adom."

Fed by a tributary of the Nile, the Land of the Lakes was the most bountiful region of all Egypt. Past pharaohs had begun a series of hydraulic systems to evenly distribute the flow of water throughout the land. Though drought had reduced all but the narrowest sliver of land along the Nile to barren desert, here Shim'on and Mandisa beheld papyrus plants, palms, and olives growing in great abundance. A series of dikes, retaining walls, sluices, and canals regulated the flow of the tributary and the lakes into which the water ran.

A few hours south of Crocodilopolis, Shim'on stopped just after sunset. "I will leave you for a little while," he said, offering her his hand as she dismounted. "There's a small settlement over there that might have oats for the horse. I'd hate to return the vizier's beast overtired and undernourished."

Mandisa slipped from the stallion and walked to the river's edge. As Shim'on hobbled the horse and led him to water, she wrapped herself in his cloak and knelt to splash her dusty face. As the tepid water washed away her weariness, she dried her skin with the edge of the cloak and smiled. The garment smelled like Shim'on—robust, earthy, and full of life.

The beauty of the crushed diamond water soothed her anxious spirit. The moon shone full almost directly in front of her, backlighting a few far-flung clouds along the eastern horizon. A dozen campfires dotted the darkness of the riverbank. Mandisa knew most of them belonged to families in search of food and trade, trying their best to survive in the time of famine.

Someone moved farther down the riverbank, and Mandisa's eyes focused there. A young woman held her young daughter by the hand, attempting to bathe the child. Mandisa heard the little girl gasp at the first shock of coolness upon her legs. The mother laughed, a tender, lilting sound, and the child squealed and tried to scramble into her mother's arms.

Mandisa turned away from the sight. As long as her arms remained empty, she would never be able to look at a mother and child without weeping.

From somewhere in the distance another child cried, a man screamed, someone else yelled. Mandisa pulled the hood of Shim'on's cloak over her head, distressed by the sounds.

"Mandisa! Catch him!"

The cry came from nowhere, borne on a gust of river wind. The voice was Shim'on's, but who was she supposed to catch? The horse? A thief?

"Mother!"

She froze, a spasm of panic trilling across her body. "Adom!" Frantically she scrambled up a mounded dike, and then she saw him. Adom was fifty paces away, running in her direction, on the opposite bank of a wide irrigation ditch. Behind the boy she saw his pursuer, a hulking brute who raced in a crouch, his arms pumping.

Her breath caught in her throat as she recognized him. Idogbe.

"Adom!" Mandisa cried, waving her hands above her head. "This way! I'm here!"

A mud levee bordered the canal, and Mandisa plunged over it, struggling as the wet mud sucked at her sandals and feet. The silt was thick here, and each step felt like the earth's attempt to wrench her ankles from their sockets. She felt the thin straps of her sandals give way, then the mud pulled her down, covering her shins.

Adom stood now at the water's edge, his eyes wide. "Mother!" He paused, eying the ribbon of water between them.

Where was Shim'on?

"Adom!" She fought for the energy to keep moving toward him. She pulled one leg free and staggered forward, then stopped to wrest her other foot from the greedy muck.

Behind Adom, Idogbe raced forward, as sure-footed as a goat and as strong as the wind. Adom glanced back at the shrinking distance between them, then plunged into the canal.

"No, Adom!" Mandisa cried. Though her son had often splashed in the garden pool of the vizier's house, she did not think he could swim. She thrust her arms toward him and slipped, falling upon her hands. The mire pulled her downward, muck squirted between her fingers as ooze slapped the side of her face.

"Mother!" The scream was louder now, shriller. With an effort, Mandisa lifted her head. Adom stood in waist-deep water, his eyes wide in a paroxysm of fear, his gaze fastened to something that moved in the canal. A rise of panic threatened to choke her as Mandisa followed his eyes.

In the distance, a crocodile was moving up from the river, his powerful tail sweeping in wide arcs as he swam toward the shrieking boy. She struggled to scream Shim'on's name, but the scream died in her raw throat.

SHIM'ON PRESSED his hands to his forehead, struggling to clear his brain. He had seen Adom and called to Mandisa, then an unexpected blow had come from behind, knocking him senseless. He could feel a sticky wetness on his forehead and warmth on his face, but the fiend who had struck him disappeared. Had he gone after the boy?

Shim'on pushed himself up from the ground, consciously commanding his legs to bear his weight. Colors exploded in his brain as he stood, and his chest tightened as a sense of inadequacy swept over him. What if he couldn't reach Adom in time? If Mandisa put herself between the boy and this madman . . .

He bit his lip to stifle the pain and staggered toward the canal he had crossed earlier. Through a burst of blinding white agony he saw a powerful, well-muscled man in the distance. Then the man disappeared, and Shim'on blinked, afraid his eyes had betrayed him.

No. His ears rang with Mandisa's screams. The man had gone down into the ditch, probably still chasing the boy.

Shim'on pushed himself, urging his body forward through pain and blood and darkness. His sandals kicked up dirt as he ran toward the sound of Mandisa's cries, then he stood at the edge of the irrigation canal and took in the scene with one glance.

Mandisa scrambled helplessly on the opposite shore, impeded by the thick mud, her hands outstretched for her son. Idogbe stood on the downward slope of the dike, a bloody battle-ax in his hand, a look of awe and reverence upon his face. And in the water, Adam floundered in terror as the golden eyes of a crocodile advanced from the river.

"Leave the boy where he is!" Idogbe called, his voice like an echo from an empty tomb. "See there! My lord Sebek comes to take his sacrifice, he has rewarded my faithfulness! He will increase my strength a hundred times and grant me authority in the life to come!"

"Adom!" Mandisa threw her head back and screamed a guttural cry of terror.

The boy's answering shriek chilled Shim'on to the marrow.

"Behold the god of my strength, the Destroyer!" Idogbe chanted, lurching like some demented monster on the muddy bank. "Behold Sebek, great of slaughter, great of fear! He washes in your blood, he bathes in the gore of sacrifice!"

Shim'on's blood slid through his veins like cold needles as he considered the hellish scene before him. The crocodile was advancing steadily. If Shim'on attacked the madman, the boy would not have a chance. But if Shim'on strode into the water, the maniac Idogbe would find Shim'on's head and shoulders an easy target for his battle ax.

El Shaddai, give me wisdom.

Shim'on stepped down, carefully negotiating the slick mud of the dike. With every step, his jaw became firmer, his muscles tighter, his heart more eager. If he had been born only for this moment, his soul would still praise the Almighty God. For Shim'on the Destroyer was ready to surrender his life. Better that innocent Adom should live than one who had killed so many.

His feet found firm footing on level ground near the water, and Shim'on plunged past Idogbe into the stream, scooping Adom up with one arm. When his ears rang with a frustrated scream, he knew the lunatic had charged, battle-ax swinging. A blow nearly knocked Shim'on from his feet, but he managed to remain standing long enough to thrust the boy to the safety of the opposite shore. Then he turned in the water to face the mad Egyptian.

The ex-priest seemed to swell as regarded his adversary. "What interest have you in this, Canaanite?" He crouched in the water, the ax slicing the air in front of him. He circled, keeping his eyes fixed upon Shim'on's. "Why have you interfered with my son's appointment with his destiny? Sebek chose this time and place. He-Who-Destroys was ready to accept my sacrifice."

"A man should sacrifice what belongs to him, and not to another," Shim'on answered, circling step-for-step with his adversary. "And your son will chose his own god. Leave him alone, Idogbe."

The Egyptian threw back his head and laughed. "You know my name! That is good, for a man should know the name of the one who is about to kill him."

"Then you should know that I am Shim'on, Son of Yisrael," Shim'on answered, striding through the waist-deep water. He stole a quick look at the glassy surface around him, but the crocodile had disappeared.

The ax whistled as it approached. Shim'on thrust up a hand to block it and succeeded, though the handle cracked against his arm with such force the bone went numb.

Idogbe screamed in frustration as the ax slipped from his grasp and dropped beneath the muddy water.

Shim'on stepped toward the spot where it had disappeared, blocking Idogbe from the weapon. And then the Egyptian was upon him, his fists striking like the mouths of snakes. In a dance of death they pirouetted, splashing in the water, smashing onto the bank of the levee. Shim'on spread his feet for balance and struck out with his good hand as often as he could, but then a sharp bite cut through the leather of his sandal and into his foot, startling him.

The ax.

Blood . . . and a crocodile in the water.

And then Idogbe's hands were around Shim'on's throat. As the night filled with a ripping mayhem of screams that made the stars above vibrate, Shim'on felt himself being pushed toward the water. He struggled to breathe, to resist, to fight, and then his eyes saw nothing but murk as the waters swept over his head, filling his nose, ears, mouth . . .

Almighty God, forgive me. Though I showed no mercy and deserve none, if you would look upon me now . . .

The anger that had been welling in Shim'on's soul vanished like a swift shadow. Hot emotions never resulted in cool judgment, and Shim'on needed wisdom now, for the man who faced him was superior in height, weight, and strength.

With every ounce of energy he possessed, Shim'on kicked upward. His foot found a vulnerable spot; Idogbe groaned and weakened his grasp long enough for Shim'on to launch himself toward the sky and fill his lungs with air.

The muscled Egyptian came at him again, as relentless as guilt.

So be it.

As the Egyptian's arms closed around his throat, Shim'on stopped resisting and went limp, allowing his weight to pull Idogbe beneath the surface.

All earthly noises but the pounding of Shim'on's heart disappeared in the dark, bubbling sounds of the riverworld. He rolled in the water, shifting the Egyptian to his side, then with a powerful effort Shim'on turned, pinning his enemy beneath him.

Placing his foot on the man's throat, Shim'on thrust himself up, gulped for air, then went under the water again until the man's scrambling stilled.

Praise be Your name, God Shaddai! For Shim'on the Destroyer is no more, I could not have accomplished this but by Your Hand.

When he was certain the fight had gone out of the aggressor, he pulled the Egyptian to the opposite bank, checked to be sure the man still breathed, then stumbled back through the water to Mandisa.

"Shim'on!" Her hands reached out to him as he collapsed on the bank beside Adom. He shivered as the fire of battle left his veins and a strange peace filled his heart when Mandisa's cool hand fell upon his cheek. "Are you all right?" she asked, her lovely face hovering over him like a concerned angel's. "You're bleeding."

"It matters not," he said, attempting to smile. "How's the boy?"

"Fine." Mandisa nodded to her son, whose teeth chattered as he squatted in the mud.

With a trembling hand Shim'on pointed toward Idogbe, who still lay unconscious on the far shore. "And what shall we do about him?"

"We will leave him to his god," Mandisa answered, patting her son.

Adom turned to face Shim'on. "I thought I'd never see you again. And I didn't like that man, but he said he was my father."

"A father is someone who loves you," Mandisa answered, slipping out of Shim'on's cloak. She draped it across her son's shoulders and Shim'on's chest, warming them together.

"Then . . . can you be my father?"

Shim'on lifted his hand to Adom's head. "If your mother approves," he said, his voice tentative as his eyes searched her face.

She didn't answer, but her eyes blazed with an inner fire, brighter than the light from the torches that had begun to appear on the banks around them. Shim'on felt an inexplicable smile sweep over his own face, and a delicious shudder heated his body when she pressed her hand to his forehead. "You are hurt," she said, concern in her voice as she examined the wound. "We should find a physician for that cut on your head. I don't know how you were able to stand and fight."

"It is nothing," he said, his heart pounding in an erratic rhythm.

She lowered her gaze to his. "Shim'on, son of Yaakov," she

murmured, her hand holding his face with a tender touch. "I owe you everything."

"It is nothing," he repeated, his common sense skittering into the shadows of the night.

"It is everything, you are everything," she answered, her breath softly fanning his face. "The first day I saw you, I knew you were capable of mighty deeds. Shim'on, son of Yaakov, once called I-am-not-loved, I saw your true heart. You had only to discover it for yourself."

He felt her lips touch his like a whisper, and then in her black eyes he found all he'd been searching for.

IDOGBE STAGGERED AWAY from the muddy bank, shoving past the concerned hands that reached out to give him aid. One glance at the far side of the canal assured him that he had failed, for a knot of people surrounded the man, woman, and child who had destroyed his plans for greatness and immortality.

He left the canal and moved toward the river, determined to confront the god who had failed him. "Come out, Sebek!" he cried, lifting his hands as he neared the rushes at the riverbank. "Come out and face your Chosen One! You could have taken them both, the boy and the man, and yet you left me to face humiliation!"

No answer came from the river, nothing moved in the silvery water. A pair of men who had bedded down on the rise of the bank stood as Idogbe approached, then retreated as if frightened by his bold intensity.

Let them be frightened. No one should interfere with a man who plans to confront his god.

"Are you there, Sebek?" Idogbe cried, splashing into the water. He shouldered his way through the tall reeds and felt the sharp-edged stems bite into the flesh of his shoulders. "I am here for you! Take my miserable life, since you have no other use for it!"

The water inched up his legs, covering his shins, his thighs, his waist. Still he continued to roar and shout, thrashing as the water crept closer to his chin. At once the muddy river bottom fell away, and the waters closed over his head. Idogbe tried to scramble back to place of firm footing, but in all his travels, he had neglected to learn how to swim. He bobbed up, once, twice, but could not move toward either shore.

But he knew Sebek was watching and waiting . . . somewhere.

CHAPTER FORTY-FOUR

SHIM'ON SLEPT FOR HOURS, PERHAPS DAYS. A FEVER BURNED THROUGH HIS body, but soft whispers and gentle caresses surrounded him as someone poured cooling water over his head, neck, and shoulders. He was aware of being moved, then he lay still for a long time, lost in the twilight world between wakefulness and sleep, between life and death.

He awoke in his prison chamber within Zaphenath-paneah's house. A tray sat by the door, the food untouched. The same chair filled the corner; he lay on the same uncomfortable, too-short bed. He even wore a linen kilt like the one Tarik had given him.

He stretched, feeling stiffness in his arms, and his head pounded when he tried to sit up. His mind spun with bewilderment. Had he managed to escape his confinement only through starkly realistic dreams? No, everything had changed. Though his surroundings belonged to his old life, he saw them through new eyes.

"I've been sick," he muttered, annoyed with his weakness. "A fever has played tricks upon my mind."

The usual sounds of activity flitted in from the windows. He heard the laughter of boys, the quiet whisper of slaves about their duties. From far away he heard the excited whinny of a horse and the lowing of cattle.

And then, with startling clarity, Mandisa's familiar knock sounded upon the door.

"Come in," he grumbled, sourness filling the pit of his stomach.

The latch clicked and she entered, her glowing face wreathed in a smile. "I thought you would be better today," she said, hurrying to his side. "Your fever broke last night."

He turned and lowered his legs to the floor. "I feel like I've slept a year. Look at that! I'm as weak as a kitten." He lifted his arm, which trembled as he struggled to hold it straight. He lowered it, braced himself against the bed frame, and was about to stand when he caught sight of her face.

There was something pleased, proud, and vaguely possessive in the way Mandisa looked at him. Shim'on paused to focus his confused memories.

"Mandisa," he began, closing his eyes, "I have been ill, so my thoughts are not as definite as I would like them to be."

"Perhaps I can help." Laughter echoed in her voice.

When he opened his eyes, he found her studying him with a gaze as soft as a caress. "I have dreamed—no, not a dream. Tell me, Zaphenath-paneah is my brother, is he not?"

"Whatever gave you that idea?" she said, her tone light and mocking. But her right hand fell upon his shoulder, and he wondered if she could feel the quickening pulse of his blood.

"And Idogbe took Adom, and you and I found the boy."

Her hand moved from Shim'on's shoulder to his jawline. "Adom is safe here in Zaphenath-paneah's house, where he belongs."

"And I fought with Idogbe, and afterward you said—"

"I told you I loved you, but you weren't awake to hear it," she whispered, her fingers teasing his hair. "You fainted, for you were bleeding badly. Some men on the riverbank tended to your wounds, but then you took a fever. When Zaphenath-paneah heard of it, he sent a wagon and brought you here."

Sighing in relief, Shim'on caught her hands. "So we are back where we began."

A dancing light twinkled in the depths of her black eyes. "Do you think so?"

"No." He breathed the word, and pulled her into his arms. "We are miles from that day. Shim'on the Destroyer is no more, he is gone for good. Shim'on the father, the husband, is now your captive."

"And what shall I do with this prisoner?" she asked, looking down into his eyes. A thread of uncertainty ran through her voice. "Shall I release him so he can join his people in Goshen?"

"Never release him." He stood and pressed her to him, bolstering his weakness with her strength. "You were right to refuse him before, but now he has broken his bonds. He is finally free to love you as you deserve to be loved. Let him remain by your side always, let his people be your people."

"As my God has become his God," she answered, her hand sweeping to the back of his neck. "For only God Shaddai could have broken through the stony stronghold of your heart." She tilted her head back to look into his eyes. "You did not tell me, Shim'on, what happened in Canaan."

Shim'on looked away, trying to gather his thoughts. He had been broken, bruised, exposed, humbled, uplifted, forgiven, scorned, and loved, all at the behest of the Almighty, and all within a short time. Only one force on earth could both destroy and comfort, simultaneously give light and pain.

"I saw God as a fire," he said, looking her straight in the eye. "A holy fire that cannot be contained or tamed. And yet in Him we can find safety, love, and life."

"How unlike the gods of Egypt," Mandisa whispered, slipping under his arm. "Though the people threaten and intimidate them, they remain silent. People believe their gods provide what they want, but idols cannot deliver what people need."

"I need you, Mandisa, as I have needed you since the day I first came here," Shim'on answered. "I will always thank God Shaddai for a mercy severe and loving enough to send you into my prison chamber."

"Even with my acid tongue?" She nestled against him. "You were not fond of it in the early days."

"I did not know what was good for me." He locked his arms behind her back. "It took an acid tongue to cut through the hardness of my anger."

Smiling, she lifted her face, and when Shim'on bent to kiss her, he felt the slow and steady, reassuring beat of his heart in his chest . . . no longer a stone, but a new and living creation.

𓅃

As Yosef watched in approval, Shim'on took Mandisa for his wife and Adom for his son. Tizara wept freely at the wedding, knowing that Shim'on would soon take her to meet her mother and a host of relatives to which she had never dreamed of belonging. "There is such a feeling of happiness inside me," she said, looking at Yosef with bright tears in her eyes. "Only your Almighty God, my lord, could show such mercy and love to one like me."

After many warm farewells and heart-felt embraces, the quartet prepared to move northward to the well-watered plains of Goshen. Zaphenath-paneah's entire household—slaves, servants, guards, and stockmen—gathered at the gate of the villa to watch them go. Tarik and Halima, their hands gently intertwined, watched from the shadow of one of the portico's pillars, away from prying eyes.

As Yosef stood on his balcony, his hand shading his eyes from the sun, he looked down upon his household and felt his heart stir with compassion. His people were so dear to him. He led them as wisely as he could, and yet they continued to persist in blindness. Though God Shaddai had demonstrated His foreknowledge and power to save, Ani still worshipped the knowledge of Thoth. Though God had bountifully provided for them in times of direst want, Halima still ran to the kitchen and knelt before the food bins, desperately trying to eat her way out of anxiety. And though God Shaddai had demonstrated the most tender, protective love imaginable, Asenath had refused His guardianship, choosing instead to follow an adulterous and destructive path.

But Asenath had returned, at the end. Shim'on had shattered his heart's temple of hate and anger, and Mandisa had learned that El Shaddai was more than just another god. Those three had left the ranks of deceived thousands who preferred the illusion of a safe and manageable deity, a god fashioned into a congenial, serviceable likeness.

"The others do not know, nor do they understand," Yosef murmured, his heart aching as he watched the scene in the courtyard. "They feed on ashes, their deceived hearts have turned them aside. And they cannot deliver themselves, nor realize that the gods they hold in their hands are a lie."

Oh, how he wished they would seek the truth! He had seen too much in his life, witnessed too much pain. God had called him to lead, but on some days he would willingly cast the mantle of leadership aside to relive an hour of service in Potiphar's house. In those carefree days his only concerns had been of pleasing his easy-going master and capturing a sweet smile from Tuya, the love of his youth.

Memories closed around him and filled him with a longing to turn back, but an inner voice, hauntingly familiar, nudged him out of his musings: *Why are you in despair? And why have you become disturbed? Hope in God, for you shall yet praise me.*

A sense of strength came to him, and Yosef lifted his head. The four travelers passed through the gates; the assembled company broke up as each man and woman went back to their duties. Yosef stepped back into the coolness of his chamber, grateful for a moment of reflection. The villa felt strangely quiet without Shim'on, Mandisa, Adom, Tizara, and Asenath. In the days ahead he would undoubtedly feel the hollow sting of loneliness.

But Pharaoh was a young man, and beginning to show real potential. The king's first wife, Queen Tiy, was a commoner, and in dire need of a proper education. And beyond the palace lay Egypt, the bold, black land to which God had called Yosef years ago.

Hope in God, for you shall yet praise me.

Yosef would not allow himself to be distracted. He had not finished his work.

EPILOGUE

YAAKOV WAS ONE HUNDRED THIRTY YEARS OLD WHEN THE CHILDREN OF Yisrael came into Egypt. There they prospered during the remaining five years of famine, and continued to live in Goshen under Pharaoh's benevolence.

After seventeen years in Egypt, at the age of one hundred forty-seven, Yaakov called his sons together. From Yosef he extracted a promise that he would not be buried in Egypt, but that his sons would carry his remains back to the cave of Machpelah, the burial site of Avraham and Sarah, Yitzhak and Rebekah. . . and Lea.

Yaakov called for his sons, and blessed them, including the two sons of Yosef, Efrayim and Menashe. And because he understood that God had willed that Yosef be sold into slavery, he did not fault the sons of Lea for their betrayal. But in his final blessing he did not forget other sins of his sons' younger days:

Re'uven lost the inheritance of the first-born because he once slept with his father's concubine.

Shim'on and Levi were passed over because they had killed men and cruelly maimed bulls.

A special blessing went to Yehuda, and from his descendants arose King David, and from David, a savior, Yeshua the Christ.

The first-born's double inheritance went to Yosef's sons, Efrayim and Menashe.

Mandisa stood with the other women as Yisrael pronounced his final blessing. For an instant, as Yaakov harshly decried the past sins of Shim'on and Levi, the old unloved look shadowed her husband's countenance.

But then Yaakov motioned toward his sons, and passed his hands of blessing over each of their heads, bestowing favor and forgiveness in one gesture. As Shim'on stood, his eye caught Mandisa's, and his face lifted in a weary smile. The anger had disappeared from his eyes; forgiveness from a holy fountain had washed it away.

After Yaakov's death, Yosef instructed the physicians of Egypt to embalm his father, and the people of the Black Land mourned seventy days. When the days of mourning had been fulfilled, Yosef, his brothers and their children, and a company of Pharaoh's servants went up to Canaan to bury Yaakov. When the Canaanites saw the great company, they remarked upon it and named the place where they mourned Abel-Mizraim, or "the mourning of Egypt."

When the burial was done, Yosef, his family, and the Egyptians returned to Mizraim, the black and fertile land of the South.

AFTERWORD

I must begin by giving credit to the works of Thomas Mann, specifically the novels comprising the **Yosef and His Brothers** series. Though my books are nothing like his, Mann opened my eyes to several ideas and possibilities that would not otherwise have occurred to me. For this novel, I am also indebted to Donald W. McCullough and his book, **The Trivialization of God.** Without McCullough's insights I would never have realized how prevalent idol worship still is—only the names have changed. Instead of Horus, we worship success. Instead of Min, we devote ourselves to prosperity.

Reginald Heber, author of the hymn, "Holy, Holy, Holy," once wrote, "The heathen in his blindness bows down to wood and stone."

In Romans 1:21-25, the Bible amplifies his comment:

For since the creation of the world God's invisible qualities—his eternal power and divine nature—have been clearly seen, being understood from what has been made, so that men are without excuse. For although they knew God, they neither glorified him as God nor gave thanks to him, but their thinking became futile and their foolish hearts were darkened. Although they claimed to be wise, they became fools and exchanged the glory of the immortal God for images made to look like mortal man and birds and animals and reptiles . . . . They exchanged the truth of God for a lie, and worshipped and served created things rather than the Creator— who is forever praised. Amen.

As I researched ancient Egyptian religion, I was struck by the similarities between their beliefs and Christian theology. In the earliest dynasties, the Egyptians were monotheistic, believing in one all-powerful and invisible God who created the world out of water. (Egypt was settled, after all, by descendants of Ham, one of Noah's sons.) They were devout believers in an after life. They believed that their Pharaoh, a physical incarnation of a god, could give his life in intercession for his people and "resurrect" in the afterlife to take his throne.

Though in the beginning they must have understood the Truth, in a relatively short time they forgot about the invisible, eternal God and worshipped gods they made themselves. They exchanged the Truth for a devious perversion.

But we must not feel superior to them. Men still replace God with idols of their own making, many of which can appear even in the lives of Christians. To the human eye, the idols of this generation have little in common with the wooden and stone figures of ancient Egypt, but to a discerning heart they represent the same substitutes for our devotion.

At various times during my years of following God Almighty, whom I know through the fellowship of His Son, I have allowed His place to be usurped by idols of my own making: my search for knowledge, my desire for personal comfort and happiness, a quest for the earthly definition of success, even the beloved faces of my husband and much-longed-for children. It is far too human a tendency to take our eyes off God and fasten our gaze to substitutes that, though they may be lovely and precious, were never intended to satisfy the soul's yearning for God.

But God Shaddai is faithful and forgiving beyond my capacity to understand. His mercy, a patient waterfall upon my stony heart, has hollowed out a place that can be filled with nothing but Him.

—Angela Hunt

DISCUSSION QUESTIONS FOR BOOK CLUBS

Discussion Questions

1. Did you read the first book of this series, *Dreamers*? Joseph, or Yosef, is not the protagonist of this story, but he still plays an important part. How is Yosef different in *Brothers*? What has changed him?

2. Reread the epigraph by Thomas Wolfe. How do you think it applies to this story?

3. If Yaakov's (Jacob's) family lived in contemporary times, we'd probably label it dysfunctional. How did Yaakov's children reflect Yaakov's flaws and deficiencies? How did Yaakov's grandchildren suffer for the mistakes of the previous generations?

4. Why do you think Shim'on and Levi took such violent action against the city of Shekhem? What motivated their response? If you'd been their parent, would you have condoned their actions?

5. Even if you had not read the story of Dina and Shim'on in this book, how could Shim'on assault on the city of Shekhem have affected his relationship with his sister?

6. What sort of woman was Mandisa? What do you think drew her to Shim'on?

7. Have you ever wondered why Yosef resorted to such manipulation of his brothers when they first appeared in Egypt? (Demanding they

bring Binyamin, hiding the silver bowl, returning the silver, accusing them of being spies . . .) Did his thoughts and motivations become clearer after reading this fictional treatment of the story?

8. What sort of attitude did the Egyptians hold toward their gods? Do you think contemporary people ever consider their gods (if they claim to worship any god at all) in the same way?

9. Can you imagine any reason why God might have wanted to move the children of Yisrael into Egypt for many years? (Hint: Read Genesis 15:14-16).

10. If you were a lay counselor and Yaakov and his sons came into your office, how would you advise them to begin settling their family problems?

11. Are modern people really that much different from ancient Egyptians? In what ways are they different? In what ways are they similar?

12. Which character in the story could you most relate to? Why?

13. Idolatry is one of the story's themes. What sorts of idols did the characters of this story worship? How did the author illustrate this theme?

PREVIEW OF JOURNEY, BOOK 3

THE GILDED BARGE TRAVELED AS SWIFTLY AS AN ARROW DOWN THE ancient river that was the heart and soul of the Black Land. Common folk from the settlements at Herakelopolis paused along the banks to admire the golden vessel; fishermen on their small papyrus skiffs raised their hands in salute as Zaphenath-paneah, the Father to Pharaoh and the Bread of Egypt, passed by.

Sitting beneath the barge's brightly emblazoned canopy, Yosef's thoughts whirred above the pounding of the drummer who urged the oarsmen to unity. The message from Re'uven in Goshen had implored Yosef to hurry. Their father Yaakov, now called Yisrael, lay near death. He waited only for Yosef and his sons to arrive before he would pronounce his final blessing and depart for Paradise.

The barge passed the entrance to a lagoon, black and heavy with the flood's fertile silt. On the mounded bank a pair of young boys waved and shouted as the barge flew by like a giant dragonfly, its oars shining wings in the sun.

Yosef marveled at the ordinariness of life. A bright light was preparing to leave the earth, yet the sun still hovered overhead like a steady, unblinking eye.

The background noise provided by the chanting oarsmen could not penetrate the heavy silence enveloping the barge's passengers. Menashe and Efrayim sat beside Yosef under the canopy, their eyes fixed to the muddy banks sliding by, their thoughts far away. Whatever they were thinking, Yosef knew their thoughts were nothing like his.

He signed as his gaze returned to the flooded riverbanks. The seasons of desperate drought and famine had passed. For the last twelve years God Shaddai had allowed the Nile to bless the kingdom. The Black Land had blossomed from Goshen to the southern reaches of Nubia and beyond. God had brought Yosef's family to his door for preservation in the time of hunger, and they had remained near him, protected and secluded in Goshen, for the past seventeen years.

His eleven brothers seemed content to remain in the fertile pasture-lands of the Delta where they herded flocks of sheep and goats and raised cattle. In his inner heart, Yosef wondered if they remained because they enjoyed living in the area or if guilt compelled them to linger so Yisrael could spend his remaining years in fellowship with the son they had sold into slavery.

But their motivations did not matter. God Shaddai had led the sons of Yisrael to the Black Land and Yosef, vizier of Egypt, had been their salvation in the time of famine. They owed their lives to him, though Yosef suspected many of them would rather die than admit it. Most of his brothers despised Egypt as devoutly as they had once despised Yosef, for it was a hedonistic kingdom, given to idolatry and wine and the pursuit of happiness.

Happiness had never come easily to the sons of Yisrael, but they had been quick to accept help from Egypt's bountiful fields and generous granaries. And, after begging forgiveness for their harsh treatment of Yosef so long ago, they had accepted their brother and his place in the royal society.

Yosef's mind curled around fond memories of Pharaoh Amenhotep III and the Royal Wife, Queen Tiy. He had been the current Pharaoh's tutor, guardian, and counselor for nearly thirty years; he had nurtured Amenhotep through the death of his father, numerous rivalries and crises at court, and the threat of war. He had even advised the young king to marry for love when it became apparent that Amenhotep's heart had fixed itself on Tiy, a commoner.

One of Yosef's many honorary titles was "Father to Pharaoh," but God Shaddai had wrought it in word and deed. Perhaps—Yosef's gaze strayed to the strong profiles of his own sons—he was more a father to Pharaoh than he was to the two young men who rode beside him now.

But God Shaddai had placed him in Pharaoh's life, and had seen fit to keep him in the royal throne room. He had lived fifty-seven years in the shadow of El Shaddai's guiding hand; he had seen the best and worst life could offer. And because he was as certain of his calling as he was of the sunrise to come, Yosef's heart brimmed with peace.

But what feelings stirred in his sons' hearts, he could only imagine.

THE SUN WAS NOT SHINING over the Delta.

Bilious black clouds, blown from the Great Sea, hung so low over Goshen they seemed to compress the earth. Yaakov's sons and grandsons huddled outside the patriarch's tent, their heads lowered as if they sought to escape the rain to come. As Yosef and his party approached on the trail from the river, Re'uven lifted his hoary head and nodded in a grim greeting.

"He waits for you and your sons," he said, striding toward Yosef in stiff dignity. "He will not rest until he has spoken to you."

Yosef forced a smile and nodded before lifting the flap of his father's tent. Dinah and Tizara stood inside, and their faces broke into relieved smiles as Yosef entered. Dinah moved away toward the brazier where glowing coals held back death's chill, but Tizara bowed herself to the ground.

"Rise, Tizara," Yosef said, momentarily annoyed by his niece's obeisance. His eyes flitted over the still form on the fur-lined bed. "Are we too late?"

"Of course not, my lord." Tizara lifted her head. "He has tremendous strength, and he waits for you. I will wake him."

Moving as softly as a shadow, she placed a gentle hand on the old man's bare shoulder. Yaakov's cheekbones jutted forth like tent poles under canvas and the fullness of his lips had shrunken to thin lines of gray. Yet an inherent strength remained in his face, and when the heavy eyelids lifted, the faded eyes were still compelling.

"Grandfather Yisrael," Tizara whispered, "your son Yosef has come."

With visible effort, Yisrael sat up and peered in Yosef's direction. "My son?"

"Yes, Father." Leaving the dignity of his own authority behind, Yosef stepped forward, once again a dutiful son waiting to hear his loving father's wishes.

"I am glad you have come." Yisrael's words came slowly, as if drawn from a deep well. "Listen to what I will tell you, for I am old, and will soon join my father and his father."

"I am listening," Yosef answered, his voice thick.

A look of tired sadness passed over Yaakov's features. "God Shaddai was seen by me in Luz, in the land of Canaan; he blessed me and he said to me: 'Here, I will make you bear fruit and will make you many, and will make you into a host of peoples. I will give this land to your seed after you, as a holding for the ages.'"

He paused, gathering strength. "So now, your two sons who were born before I came to you in Egypt, they are mine. Efrayim and Menashe, like Re'uven and Shim'on, let them be called mine! But any sons you beget after them, let them be yours, by their brothers' names let them be called, respecting their inheritance."

Yosef nodded silently. By his words Yaakov had indicated Menashe and Efrayim would share Yaakov's inheritance equally with the other eleven sons—in effect giving Yosef the double blessing due the firstborn, and immediately passing it on to Yosef's children. Re'uven was Yaakov's eldest son, but Yosef was the firstborn of Rahel, whom Yaakov had always considered his true wife. Even though after Rahel's death Yaakov had come to love Lea, his second wife, he never forgot he had intended for Rahel and Yosef to hold the favored legal position of the first wife and first-born son.

The patriarch squinted past Yosef. "Who is with you?"

"The sons God gave me here, in the land of Mizraim."

The point of the old man's tongue slowly moistened his underlip. "Pray bring them over to me, so I may give them my final blessing."

Immobilized by the shock of grief, Yosef could not turn, but Menashe and Efrayim had heard and were already moving toward their grandfather's bed.

Yisrael lifted trembling arms and searched for the strong shoulders of his grandsons. When his fingers had firmly grasped each young man, he pulled them close, kissed their cheeks, and embraced them.

"Oh, my son Yosef—" his voice rang with awe as his arms encircled Yosef's sons— "I never expected to see your face again, but God has let me see your children as well!"

Yosef stumbled forward to kneel at his father's side, and Menashe drew back to make room. In respect for Yisrael's age and position, the young men bowed their heads while Yosef clasped his father's hand and wept. The flash of joy that ignited at their reunion had not dimmed in seventeen years; too soon he would again endure the wretched suffering of parting.

"Now," Yisrael said, his voice fragile and shaking, "bring your sons to me, so I may bless them."

Yosef stood and motioned to his sons. Efrayim had been about to approach Yaakov on the left side of the bed, near Yaakov's right hand, but Yosef made a sharp gesture, indicating that the young men should switch places. Menashe, as the eldest, should receive the greater blessing, traditionally bestowed with the right hand.

Yosef's heart swelled as his handsome sons fell to their knees to receive the blessing. Yisrael closed his eyes, lifted his hands toward heaven, and spoke in a voice that rang with command: "The God in whose presence my fathers walked, Avraham and Yitzhak, the God who has tended me from the day I was born until this day, the messenger who has redeemed me from all ill-fortune, may He bless the lads!" Yisrael then crossed his arms. The right hand, which should have fallen on Menashe's head, fell instead on Efrayim's. Apparently unaware of his mistake, the old man continued: "May my name and the name of my fathers, Avraham and Yitzhak, continue to be called through them! May they teem like fish to become many in the midst of the land!"

"Wait, Father," Yosef interrupted. A thin blade of foreboding sliced into his heart as he watched history repeat itself. Yaakov stole Esav's rightful blessing, Lea usurped Rahel's rightful place. Second-born Efrayim should not be favored above Menashe . . .

"Not so, Father." Yosef took hold of Yaakov's right hand, intending to lift it from Efrayim's head and place it on Menashe's. "Indeed, this one at your right side is the firstborn, place your right hand on his head."

"No, Son." Yaakov lifted his pale eyes, the light of intent shining in them. "I know what you are thinking. The firstborn will be a people, he too will be great, yet his younger brother will be greater than he, and his seed will become a full-measure of nations." He lowered his gaze to his grandsons. "By you shall the children of Yisrael give blessings to one another, saying: 'May God make you like Efrayim and Menashe!'"

As his spidery hands fell from the boys' heads, Yaakov leaned back in exhaustion, but contentment shone on his face. "I am dying." He looked up at Yosef. "But God will be with you, He will return you to the land of your fathers. And I give you one portion over and above your brothers." He paused, his chest heaving. "Call the others, for I must speak with them before I depart on my final journey."

Stunned by the sound of weakness in his father's voice, Yosef darted to the tent doorway and hoarsely summoned his brothers.

MENASHE STOOD SILENTLY in the shadows with the women as his grandfather pronounced his final blessing on his sons: Re'uven, Shim'on, Levi, Yehuda, Zevulun, Yissakhar, Dan, Gad, Asher, Naftali, Yosef, and Binyamin. Many of the uncles wore puzzled looks, Menashe noticed, as blessings and warnings poured from Yaakov's tongue; Shim'on and Levi seemed to wilt beneath their father's harsh words. But the blessings Yisrael bestowed had little to do with the men as Menashe knew them, and he wondered if the old man's words were meant to be taken literally. Would God Shaddai bring Yisrael's predictions to pass? And what had Yaakov intended when he gave Efrayim the blessing of the right hand, the blessing that rightfully belonged to the first-born?

Perhaps he shouldn't allow the gesture to bother him. After all, what was a blessing? A dying man's words, a heartfelt wish for prosperity. Ordinarily the first-born would receive double the inheritance of any other children, but he and Efrayim would share Yaakov's estate evenly with their eleven uncles. So the blessing wasn't a matter of property or inheritance. Yaakov had said that Efrayim would have more descendants, but in the space of a man's lifetime, what did that matter?

Yet his younger brother will be greater than he. The memory of those words burned in Menashe's brain. He and Efrayim had always engaged in the typical battles and contests of sibling rivalry. Until recently Menashe had been two years smarter, two years stronger, two years taller than his brother. But now that he was twenty-five and Efrayim twenty-three, maturity had evened the ground from which they competed. In time he would be two years slower, two years weaker, two years nearer the tomb . . .

Why should a blessing bother him? Looking around, Menashe noticed that none of his uncles seemed terribly upset by their father's predictions. Shim'on and Levi, for instance, whom Yaakov had practically cursed for their fierce anger, stood in the back of the room, composed and quietly awaiting their father's passage to Sheol.

From his couch, Yaakov rallied his strength again; the women helped him sit up. "I am about to gathered to my kinspeople." His breath rattled in his throat and his eyes closed as if he did not have the energy even to look around the room. "Bury me by my fathers, in the cave that is in the field of Makhpela, that faces Mamre in the land of Canaan. There they buried Avraham and Sara his wife, there they buried Yitzhak and Rivka his wife, there I buried Lea."

He murmured a few other comments in a voice too low for Menashe to hear, then Yaakov lay back, curled on the bed, and breathed his last.

A pain squeezed Menashe's heart as his weeping father threw himself on the patriarch's body and kissed Yisrael's sunken cheeks.

JOKIM, son of Shela, son of Yehuda, sat outside by the fire, joining a circle of weeping men. Though none of them were so foolish to think that a man one hundred forty-seven years old could live forever, Yaakov had always been among them, the one constant in a sea of change and trouble. Yaakov was the one who decreed that they should always live in tents so they could move when and wherever God Shaddai commanded; Yaakov heard the voice of God Almighty in the night. Yosef would be the patriarch now; he had inherited the blessing of the firstborn, but Yosef seemed as distant as a mountain on the horizon. He kept himself in the city of Thebes, and he would forever be drawn away by his duty to Pharaoh.

Jokim looked over at his father and grandfather. Pain had carved merciless lines on Yehuda's face and tears streaked his heavy white beard. Jokim's father, Shela, drew his lips in and stared at the fire as though the mysteries of Yaakov's life flickered there. Silence, thick as wool, wrapped itself around the mourners as each man strove to imagine the days to come without Yaakov's pervading influence.

Uneasy in the somber heaviness, Jokim slipped away from the old men and wandered among the tents. The women had no time to mourn, their hands were busy preparing food and making beds for the guests who would soon descend on them. The Canaanites traditionally mourned for thirty days: three days of tears followed by seven days of lamentation, followed by twenty days of receiving those who came to pay their respects and offer condolences. Yaakov of Hebron had been well-known and respected in the land of Canaan. Kings and princes from the entire civilized world would soon begin to wend their way to Goshen in order to acknowledge the great man who had begotten an even greater son.

Jokim stopped at the sight of Menashe and Efrayim near the animal pens. The two brothers, both of whom were about his age, were strikingly handsome even though they dressed and painted themselves in the manner of the Egyptians. They wore fine Egyptian wigs, neatly trimmed and anointed with oil, and the white of their kilts dazzled against the somber hues of Yaakov's tents and the Hebrew's dyed tunics. Menashe, the eldest, had a lean and narrow face. His smooth olive skin stretched over high cheekbones, and his carbon-black eyes seemed to pierce whomever they studied. A healthy beard had begun to shadow his chin and upper lip, and Jokim supposed that the Egyptians had not had time to shave before boarding the barge that brought them to Goshen.

Now Menashe's brow was furrowed, his hands tight on the rail of a pen that confined a group of lambs too young to swim through the encroaching floods.

"Hello, cousins," Jokim said, approaching cautiously. He did not know his Egyptian relatives well, for Yosef and his sons spent very little time in Goshen. Menashe and Efrayim rarely accompanied the vizier on the infrequent occasions when he did visit, and Jokim could not recall speaking to his kinsmen more than once or twice in his lifetime. But here they were, of the same age, and apparently caught up in the same flood of confusing emotions.

Menashe inclined his head in a formal gesture, but Efrayim flashed Jokim a heartfelt smile. "Greetings. Jokim, isn't it? You are Shela's son?"

"Yes." Jokim tried not to let his relief show in his face. Yosef's sons were nearly Egyptian royalty, he had heard they often dined with Pharaoh's children. Yosef's wife, their mother, had been a beautiful Egyptian noblewoman, so Efrayim and Menashe had inherited attractiveness and position from both parents.

Efrayim, Jokim decided, must have received his mother's looks. His face was not as narrow as Menashe's, his eyes not as direct or piercing. At his neck, a dark curl escaped from under the straight tresses of the Egyptian wig, and his smile was wide and quick, immediately putting Jokim at ease.

"Shall we sit?" Efrayim pointed to the rail fence. "We would like to hear what has happened in the last few days. Unfortunately, in Thebes we do not often hear reports from the Delta."

Jokim smiled, realizing that Efrayim was being tactful. Most people in Thebes cared nothing about what happened to the Hebrews at Goshen.

He shrugged and perched on the top rail of the pen. "The weakness came on Yisrael gradually. He grew weaker and more feeble, and last night he told the women to send for Yosef. My grandfather Yehuda saw it coming—for the past week he has said the end was drawing near."

Jokim tilted his head and studied Efrayim's expressive face. "Can you tell me what went on inside Yisrael's tent? My mother said I should not go in."

Efrayim shot a quick glance at his older brother, who muttered something in the Egyptian tongue and walked away.

"Yisrael gave his blessings." Efrayim's left brow rose a fraction. "He included me and Menashe among his sons. We did not expect that, of course, but the most unusual thing—" He paused.

Jokim leaned closer. "What unusual thing happened?"

"It probably won't mean much to you," Efrayim said, moistening his well-formed lips, "but he placed his right hand on my head even though I knelt at his left side. My father sought to correct Yisrael's mistake, but Grandfather insisted that he meant to do it." A hint of boastfulness crept into his voice: "Yisrael said I will be mightier than my brother."

Jokim leaned backward, astonished by the news and Efrayim's casual delivery of it.

Efrayim lifted both brows as his face split into a wide grin. "Oh, the drubbing I can give Menashe now! He always held it up to me—his being the eldest, of course. But he'll never say anything again, because I can answer him with Yisrael's own words. I am to be a mightier man, and from me will come a tremendous nation!"

Jokim stared in amused surprise. The boast would have sounded impertinent coming from anyone else, but Efrayim uttered it with such bold nonchalance that it did not seem untoward or tactless. "What do you think Yisrael meant?"

"I don't know," Efrayim answered, slipping from his perch on the rail. "But I will have a merry time with Grandfather's words while I can. It is not every day that I manage to defeat my elder brother."

ALSO BY ANGELA HUNT

Roanoke

Jamestown

Hartford

Rehoboth

Charles Towne

Magdalene

The Novelist

Uncharted

The Awakening

The Debt

The Elevator

The Face

Let Darkness Come

Unspoken

The Justice

The Note

The Immortal

The Truth Teller

The Silver Sword

The Golden Cross

The Velvet Shadow

The Emerald Isle

Dreamers

Brothers

Journey

For a full list, visit www.angelahuntbooks.com

BIBLIOGRAPHY

Bianchi, Dr. Robert S. Splendors of Ancient Egypt. London: Booth-Clibborn Editions, 1996.

Brier, Bob, Ph.D. The Murder of Tutankhamen. New York: G.P. Putnam's Sons, 1998.

Budge, Sir Wallis. Egyptian Religion. New York: Barnes & Noble Books, 1994.

Budge, E.A. Wallis. The Mummy: A History of the Extraordinary Practices of Ancient Egypt. New York: Wings Books, 1989.

Bunson, Margaret. The Encyclopedia of Ancient Egypt. New York: Facts on File, 1991.

Cahill, Thomas. The Gifts of the Jews. New York: Doubleday, 1998.

Coleman, William. Today's Handbook of Bible Times and Customs. Minneapolis, MN: Bethany House Publishers, 1984.

Comay, Joan. Who's Who in the Old Testament. Nashville, TN: Abingdon Press, 1971.

Coogan, Michael D., ed. The Oxford History of the Biblical World. New York: Oxford University Press, 1998.

David, Rosalie and Rick Archbold. Conversations with Mummies. New York: William Morrow, 2000.

Davis, J.D. Illustrated Davis Dictionary of the Bible. Nashville, TN: Royal Publishers, Inc., 1973.

Editors of Time-Life Books. The Age of God-Kings. Alexandria, VA: Time-Life Books, 1987.

—. Egypt: Land of the Pharaohs. Alexandria, VA: Time-Life Books, 1992.

—. What Life Was Like on the Banks of the Nile. Alexandria, VA: Time-Life Books, 1997.

Fox, Everett. The Five Books of Moses. New York: Schocken Books, 1995.

Grower, Ralph. The New Manners and Customs of Bible Times. Chicago: Moody Press, 1987.

Halley, Henry. Halley's Bible Handbook. Grand Rapids, MI: Zondervan Publishing House, 1927.

Hart, George. Ancient Egypt. New York: Alfred A. Knopf, 1990.

James, T.G.H. Ancient Egypt: The Land and Its Legacy. Austin, TX: University of Texas Press, 1988.

Jenkins, Simon. Nelson's 3-D Bible Mapbook. Nashville, TN: Thomas Nelson Publishers, 1995.

Kaiser, Walter C., Peter H. Davids, F.F. Bruce, and Manfred T. Brauch. Hard Sayings of the Bible. Downers Grove, IL: InterVarsity Press, 1996.

Kaster, Joseph. The Wisdom of Ancient Egypt. New York: Barnes & Noble, 1993.

Manniche, Lise. An Ancient Egyptian Herbal. Austin, TX: University of Texas Press, 1989.

—. Music and Musicians in Ancient Egypt. London: British Museum Press, 1991.

Metzger, Bruce M., and Michael D. Coogan, eds. The Oxford Companion to the Bible. New York: Oxford University Press, 1993.

Montet, Pierre. Everyday Life in Egypt in the Days of Ramesses the Great. Philadelphia: University of Pennsylvania Press, 1981.

Murray, Margaret. The Splendour That Was Egypt. London: Sidgwick and Jackson, 1949.

Osman, Ahmed. Stranger in the Valley of the Kings. San Francisco, Harper & Row, 1987.

Potok, Chaim. Wanderings: Chaim Potok's History of the Jews. New York: Fawcett Crest, 1978.

Pritchard, James, ed. HarperCollins Atlas of the Bible. London: HarperCollins Publishers, 1997.

Romer, John. Valley of the Kings. New York: Henry Holt and Company, 1981.

Schaff, Philip. Through Bible Lands. New York: Arno Press, 1977.

Schulz, Regine and Matthias Seidel, eds. Egypt: The World of the Pharaohs. Cologne, Germany: Konemann, 1998.

Smith, Wilbur. River God. New York: St. Martins Press, 1993.

Spencer, A. J. Death in Ancient Egypt. New York: Penguin Books, 1991.

Steindorff, George, and Keith C. Seele. When Egypt Ruled the East. Chicago: University of Chicago Press, 1957.

Stern, David H. Complete Jewish Bible: An English Version of the Tanakh (Old Testament) and B'rit Hadashah (New Testament). Clarksville, MD: Jewish New Testament Publications, Inc., 1998.

Unstead, F. J., editor. See Inside an Egyptian Town. London: Barnes and Noble, 1986.

Vercoutter, Jean. The Search for Ancient Egypt. New York: Harry N. Abrams, 1992.

Wilkinson, Richard H. Reading Egyptian Art. London: Thames and Hudson, 1992.

Willmington, Harold L. Willmington's Bible Handbook. Wheaton, IL: Tyndale House Publishers, 1999.

Made in the USA
Middletown, DE
15 August 2020